Mapton on Sea

Sam Maxfield

Published by On the Wing Press
'Mapton On Sea' copyright © 2015.Samantha Maxfield

This novel was previously published under the title The Last Resort

Samantha Maxfield asserts the right to be identified as the author of this work in accordance with the Copyright Designs and Patents Act 1988. All rights reserved.

This book is a work of fiction. Any references to historical events, real people, or real locales are used fictitiously. Other names, characters, places and incidents are products of the author's imagination, and any resemblance to actual events or locales or persons, living or dead, is entirely coincidental.

To Steve, for all our holidays in 'Mapton'

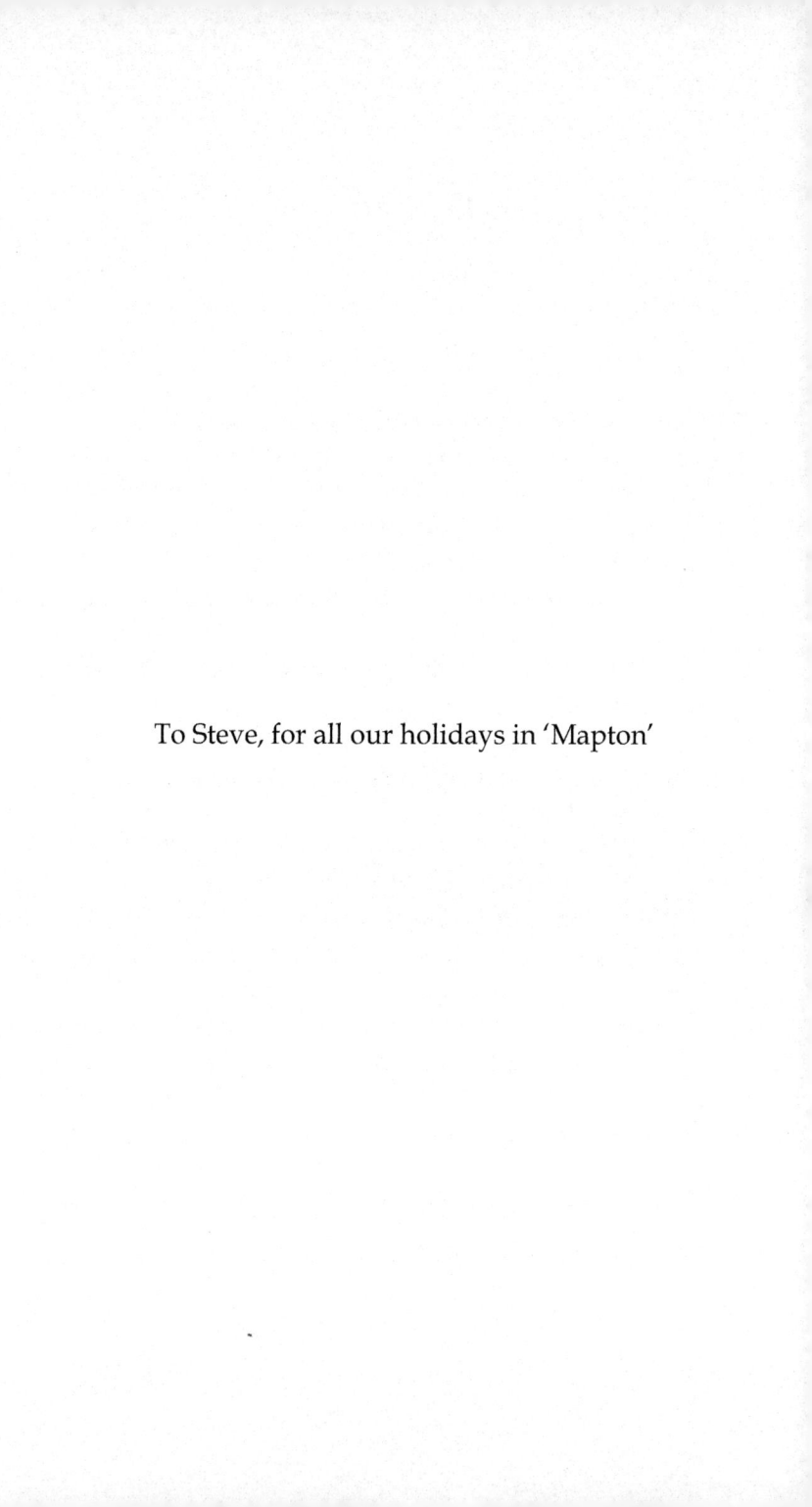

Stella Gets the Call

The call came in the dead of night, the way those calls nearly always do.

Stella fumbled for the phone. ''lo?' she mumbled.

'Is this Stella Distry?' a woman asked.

Stella sat up, finally clearing sleep. She pushed her curls out of her face, heart pumping. 'Yes,' she said. 'Who's this? What's wrong?'

'It's about your grandmother, Gina Pontin. She's had an accident. I'm calling from Lincoln hospital. Now don't panic – it was just a tumble. She's broken her right arm, bruised a couple of ribs, and sprained her ankle. We can't send her home alone but she's being very difficult. Abusive actually. You're down as her emergency contact number.'

Stella squeezed her eyes shut. 'You want me to come and get her?'

'Yes,' the woman sighed. 'Yes, we do.' Even over the phone her relief was palpable.

'It'll be morning before I can get there,' Stella said.

'That's fine,' the woman said. 'Just as long as I can tell her you're on your way.' She sounded positively gleeful.

'You can,' Stella said. 'But it won't make her happy.'

She perched on the edge of the bed, stomach in knots. She supposed she'd have to stay with Gina until she could find a carer for her. A few days at the very most. Fewer if she could help it.

Then there was her cat, Henry. Who would feed him? Her neighbour was away and none of her friends lived near enough. She'd have to take him with her which meant somehow stuffing him into his cat carrier which he normally resisted tooth and claw. That done, he'd howl non-stop in the car then punish her for days by showing her his back.

She sighed. Between him and Gina there were good times ahead.

Following the death of her parents when she was twelve, Stella had barely survived the years she'd lived with her maternal grandmother. Still, at least Gina didn't live in Nottingham anymore. Stella couldn't face returning to the old house on Bobbin Street. Gina had uprooted, five years ago, to the seaside town of Mapton-on-Sea. From what Stella gathered, it was a shabby little neglected resort, long past its glory days, reachable only by narrow back roads that wound and zigzagged through rural Lincolnshire.

Not that she'd ever visited Gina there.

Stella girded herself and set about gathering vital supplies, carefully selecting a couple of sketch books, watercolour pencils and a packet of multi-coloured Sharpies for doodling. She added her iPad, Kindle and iPod nano. All things to help her survive a few days with Gina. Almost as an afterthought she stuffed a carryall with random clothes and toiletries.

Henry was still snuggled down under the duvet, one tabby ear poking out. Stella eyed him ruefully. She'd leave the trauma of getting him into the carrier till the last minute. If he stayed asleep she might be able to just scoop him up and stow him before he knew what was happening.

Nothing else about the day ahead would be that easy.

#

Stella heard Gina before she saw her.

'And you can sod off too,' Gina's voice reverberated around the ward.

Stella paused; maybe she could just turn around and leave. No one had spotted her yet.

'We need this bed,' a man's voice, deep and mellifluous, said. 'We're going to sit you in the day lounge, okay? Just till your granddaughter comes for you.'

'I've a right to this bed,' Gina replied. 'I've paid my taxes all my life. I pay your wages.'

'There's TV in the lounge,' a woman said. 'C'mon now. We're going to help you into this wheelchair.'

Don't you put your hands on me,' Gina spluttered, slapping at the nurse.

Gina was in the bed nearest to her, flanked by a tall, thirtyish male orderly and a female nurse.

The nurse admonished. 'We have a policy on abusive behaviour, Mrs Pontin. It's entirely unacceptable.'

'I weren't abusive' Gina said.

'You struck out at me,' the nurse responded.

'I didn't!' Gina protested. 'I never laid a finger on yer. What's your name? I want to put in a complaint. You can't go around accusing people of something they ain't done.'

Stella could tell by the lift of her chin that Gina was enjoying herself.

'Gina,' she said sharply, walking up to the bed. 'Stop it.'

For a second Gina's face lit up, then she pouted. 'Took you long enough,' she said. 'Thought you weren't coming.'

Stella ignored her, speaking to the nurse. 'I'm sorry,' she said. 'I heard what she said. Don't take it personally. It's how she is.'

'Don't bleedin' apologise for me,' Gina cried.

This time the nurse ignored her, responding to Stella. 'It's all right; she's insulted everyone on the ward. Are you her granddaughter?'

Stella nodded. 'I've come to take her home.' She could almost see the words 'Thank God' flashing above the nurse's head but the woman remained professional, simply saying: 'Come to reception with me. There're some forms you need to sign.'

Leaving the orderly to get Gina into the wheelchair, she led Stella to the desk around the corner, produced the appropriate paperwork, and gave her a bottle of prescription painkillers to administer to Gina.

'Good luck,' she said sincerely.

Stella thanked her and returned to the ward in time to hear Gina say. 'And watch where you're putting your hands, young man.'

#

Henry was definitely not happy. He had started crying the moment the door was latched on his cage. His cry was pitiful, set on a frequency designed to cause maximum pain to human ears. He kept it up for an astounding three hours in the car to Lincoln, rested his vocal chords during a brief nap while Stella had been in the hospital, then resumed it for the drive to Mapton-on-Sea.

Gina wasn't having it.

'Why d'yer bring that little sod?' she snapped.

'My neighbour's away,' Stella said. 'There was no one to feed him.'

'Cat's manage,' Gina said. 'They know how to look after 'emsen. If he doesn't shut up I'll go off me 'ead.' She started to yowl, mimicking Henry.

Henry stopped, startled, and then yowled louder. Gina cranked up an octave. It was a yowl off. Neither of them was willing to yield. They carried on for five minutes until Stella pulled off the road, braking so hard it pitched them all forward until the seatbelts snapped them back.

Gina screamed in pain. 'What d'yer do that for? Oh, me ribs. Quick, where's me painkillers?'

'The nurse said no more for another two hours. They're prescription. Strong.'

'Not bloody strong enough,' Gina said. 'Not if you're going to treat me like that.'

Henry, who had fallen silent after the jolt, resumed his mewling.

The women groaned.

'Right,' Gina said. 'If this doesn't work, he's out.' Suddenly, she roared. A huge lion-like roar that shook the car.

Henry abruptly shut up, cowering into the recess of his cage.

They waited.

He stayed quiet.

Finally, Stella restarted the car, indicated and rolled back onto to the road. It was seven thirty in the morning and already her head was pounding.

After a mile or so, Henry tentatively tried an experimental whine. Gina roared again. He stopped, remaining silent for the rest of the journey, even when they pulled in at a garage so Gina could pee.

'Can't you hold on?' Stella sighed. 'We're nearly there.'

'I'm desperate,' Gina said. 'I can't hold it in no more. It's me age, and I ain't got me Tena pants on.'

It was a tiny station with one pump and an unfamiliar brand of petrol. A mechanic's garage loomed beyond it, with two rusting, beat-up old cars parked out front. Stella was glad she'd filled up earlier because the price on the pump was astronomically high. She supposed, as the only petrol around for miles, the owner could afford to charge what he liked.

'Stay here,' she told Gina. 'I'll see if they've got a toilet.'

'Hurry up,' Gina said. 'The dam's about to burst.'

Stella slammed the car door and ran for the garage. A man in oil stained blue overalls stepped out to meet her.

'Please,' she said. 'Have you got a toilet my gran can use? She's in a wheelchair and she's desperate to go.'

The man regarded her solemnly. He looked over at

the car; Gina had pressed her face against the window and was nodding frantically.

'There's one round back,' he mumbled. He returned to the garage without another word.

Stella dithered, wondering whether to ask for his help hoisting Gina into her wheelchair but decided against it.

Getting Gina out of the car into the wheelchair that had been folded in the boot (loaned from the hospital, not entirely regulation, but they were so eager to get rid of Gina, they let Stella take it) was awkward, and, for Gina, painful. Both parties swore extensively.

Stella trundled Gina round to the back of the garage, aware that the mechanic had probably watched the entire show without offering to help. It gave her the creeps.

'Go faster,' Gina groaned. 'I'm gonna wet me bleedin' sen.'

Stella spotted an ugly concrete extension on the back of the garage. The door was wooden, with a large gap at the bottom and top. She ran around Gina, unlatched the door, and peered into the cramped space. It stank, spider webs gathered thickly in the corners and the seat was broken off, so that a person could stand over, or perch on, cold urine-spattered ceramic. Stella didn't peer into the bowl.

'I'm not going in there,' Gina said.

'You are,' Stella answered. She manoeuvred the wheel chair to the entrance. 'You're going to have to lean on me,' she said, trying to find a way to haul Gina up without hurting her.'

'Ow,' Gina cried. 'Ooowww.'

Somehow, Stella managed to grapple Gina into

position over the toilet.

'I'm not sitting on it,' Gina said.

'Okay,' Stella panted. 'Can you manage your knickers while I hold you up?'

'Close the door,' Gina said. 'I'm not showing the world me short and curlies.'

'No one's going to see you,' Stella, said. 'I'm blocking the view.'

'Close it,' Gina demanded.

'Fine,' Stella snapped. She lowered Gina onto the bowl, ignoring her outraged protest, turned, and shut the door. There was no lock, she noticed. Suddenly she was grateful for the large gaps at the top and bottom. They provided the only source of light.

'It's coming,' Gina squealed.

With a last heroic effort Stella pulled Gina up, grasping her under her undamaged left armpit.

She was just in time. Gina let go, the urine spilling out of her in a rushing, hissing stream. It took a full minute to run its course.

Stella's arms were beginning to shake when a knock sounded on the door.

Disbelievingly, Stella asked. 'Yes?' She craned her neck to see behind her.

'Ahem,' a man's voice said. 'I just remembered we're out of toilet roll. I've got some newspaper here.'

A hand thrust over the top of the door, clutching a few scraps of torn newspaper.

'Bog off,' Gina shouted.

The hand disappeared. Stella listened to the mechanic's footsteps retreating. 'Lean forward onto me,' she grunted. Gina did. 'C'mon,' Stella said, hobbling Gina backwards out of the toilet. As she did she had a sudden image of her artist's studio flooding with morning light. She should be there right now, sitting down at her easel to paint, not hauling Gina out of a spidery, stinking toilet.

When Gina was back in her chair, huffing with pain, she said. 'You haven't flushed.'

Stella lost it. 'Fuck the flush,' she said.

Gina pursed her lips. Not much was taboo to Gina, language-wise, but she hated the F word. 'I didn't raise yer to use language like that,' she tutted.

'All right,' said Stella. 'Sod the flush, bugger the flush, screw the flush. Better? More refined for you?'

'I taught yer to flush,' Gina sniffed. 'And to wash yer hands.'

'Gina,' Stella said. 'Do you see a sink? Because I don't. I have some hand gel in the car. We'll use that.'

'Pleeease flush,' Gina wheedled. 'I can't abide an unflushed loo.'

Stella blew air down her nostrils like an angry bull. She clenched her fists. 'Fine,' she said and stamped back into the toilet to yank the chain.

Back in the car Stella dug the gel out of the glove compartment and handed it to Gina. Stella locked the doors. She felt like she was in Deliverance country but the mechanic had made himself scarce.

Relieved of the pressure on her bladder, Gina dozed fitfully. Stella should have relished the quiet as she drove but instead she beat herself up about her behaviour back at the garage. Gina brought out the worst in her. Just two hours in her company had undone years of building a new self-image. A rather more refined self.

A few years ago Stella had begun to make enough

money from her illustrations and paintings to support herself without teaching. Recently, her paintings had become much sought after, their value soaring. She'd acquired her lovely (but exorbitantly expensive) studio loft, which she'd decorated with Farrow and Ball White Tie paint to set off her flea market finds: 30s vases filled with fresh flowers, original art and crocheted throws. Her kitchen was complete with labelled spice jars, a fruit bowl on the table, bulbs of garlic to hand and hummus in the fridge. Homes and Antiques Magazine did a photo-spread of her at work in her studio home. They wrote 'the calming purity of the white walls are set off by the pop of colour in Stella's paintings and vintage throws.'

Her best friend, Lysie, called Stella's style 'magazine casual'. She always laughed when she said it – a good natured laugh but one that disturbed Stella, although not enough for her to probe deeper into what 'magazine casual' meant to Lysie. She only knew that Gina, in the unlikely event that she ever saw her loft studio, would hate it.

The one thing missing was a garden, but then her flat looked out over a green park square, so it was hardly a problem, and Henry was a house cat. Besides, Stella had issues with gardens.

It was, after all, Gina's front garden that had started the Bobbin Street War.

Stella glanced over at Gina, snoozing with her mouth open. She frowned at the offensively unnatural shade of her grandmother's dyed red hair and wondered why she continued to keep it that colour. At least she wasn't taking Gina back to Bobbin Street. Just the thought of returning there made her stomach lurch. Shuddering, she firmly pushed unwanted memories back into their box and concentrated on the road. They were nearly at Mapton-on-Sea.

Make it Mapton

Stella's first sight of Mapton was a grim one. Grey clouds hung low and oppressive over the fields of East Lincolnshire, leaching the scenery of colour. The caravan parks came first. Grids of magnolia static caravans sprung up like strange rectangular fungi. Each park had a sign for a clubhouse advertising karaoke, tribute acts, and bingo. The closer to the town the parks were, the shabbier they appeared to be. Finally, as Stella drove around the bend of Seaview Road, the last park loomed on the left.

'That's the kinky one,' Gina informed her. She'd perked up as the familiar sights of home loomed.

'Kinky?' Stella asked. 'How?'

'Oh, the caravans are all right,' Gina said. 'But in another bit they got these chalets – from the seventies – and they have showers in the middle of the living room and huge windows you can see right in. They're for swingers you know. They get all sorts in them. It's disgusting.'

'You seem to know a lot about them,' Stella said, smiling.

'Everyone knows about it,' Gina said.

They drove past the clubhouse, a squat block clad in orange uPVC. Completing the look, white plastic letters spelled The Paradise Holiday Park. The second 'a' of 'Paradise' had dropped off and the 'e' hung at a precarious angle.

'Mind you they do a two course Sunday lunch for £4.95,' Gina said. 'You can't say fairer than that.'

Stella shuddered at the thought of a Sunday lunch that cost under £2.50 a course. What kind of meat was it? Horse, she thought. Or donkey.

She looked for the sea on Seaview Road and saw only a stone wall and a high grassy bank to her left. Beach huts squatted on top of the bank. It should have been a pretty sight but the huts had clearly fallen into disrepair and were mostly boarded up, their eaves peeling paint beneath corrugated iron peaked roofs. To the right low, stuccoed houses faced the stone wall.

'Not much of a sea view for them.' Stella nodded to the houses. She noted that every garden seemed to have an array of gaudy garden ornaments, each a little more flamboyant than the previous house.

'They did when they were built,' Gina said. 'But after the flood of '53 they needed better flood defences so they built the wall and the bank. Still, they get a nice view of the beach huts.'

Stella glanced sideways to see if Gina was joking. She wasn't.

'Turn right at the end, Fisherman's Lane,' Gina said. 'I live next to the park.'

'That sounds nice,' Stella said. Maybe only the outskirts of Mapton were grim.

'It's beautiful,' Gina replied. 'Absolutely beautiful.' She puffed up with pride.

Stella took the next right and found herself on a narrow lane. Original fishermen's cottages whitewashed and pretty, surrounded by June flowers edged the rough road.

'Oh, this is lovely,' Stella breathed. 'You live down here?'

'I said so dint I?'

'You said you lived next to the park.'

'I do. It's at the end of the lane.'

Soon the cottages fell behind them and new bungalows appeared; orange brick, flat-faced rectangles with white PVC doors and window frames, net curtains and gravelled fronts. Many shared the taste for garden ornaments Stella had previously noted. Plastic gnomes, lots of fairies – some brightly coloured, some cast in resin to look like stone – windmills, wishing-wells, flowerpot men and miniature scarecrows.

Gina's house was the last on the left. The lane was a dead-end with a circle to turn in. Beyond it was the park.

Stella didn't immediately recognise it as a park. What she saw was a set of ugly grey railings, rising upwards of six feet like the spiked boundaries of an internment camp. Behind them stood a grubby, yellow inflatable castle and a motley collection of children's rides.

She couldn't see a single tree or patch of grass.

She stopped the car and stared at it. 'That's the park?' she asked.

Gina followed her eyes 'It's part of it.'

'That fence goes all round it?' Stella asked. 'It's like Colditz. Do people try to tunnel out?'

'Oh, gi' over,' Gina said. 'Anyway, wait till yer see the lake. It's idyllic.'

Getting Gina out of the car and into her wheelchair was almost as fun as before. Stella wheeled her up the path to Gina's front door.

'Got your keys?' Stella asked.

As Gina was rooting about in her handbag two things happened. A ferocious yapping began from behind the door, and an old man drove up on a mobility scooter.

'It's just me, Bing,' Gina shouted. 'It's just yer ode mam.'

The yapping changed from warning to joyous frenzy.

The old man stopped the scooter on the path. He stepped nimbly off it and performed a slight bow to Gina and Stella.

'Mrs Pontin,' he said. 'I'm so relieved to see you home. Are you all right?'

'Do I look bloody all right?' Gina barked. 'What yer doing on my scooter?'

'Returning it.' The old gent smiled as though Gina hadn't just shouted at him. 'I heard about your tumble and went to pick it up for you.' He flashed a generous set of false teeth, turning to Stella. 'I'm Gina's neighbour,' he said. 'George Wentworth.'

Stella smiled. 'I'm Gina's granddaughter, Stella,' she said, offering her hand.

George held it and said, 'I thought as much. You have your grandmother's good looks.'

'Oh bugger off,' Gina said.

Stella smiled apologetically. 'She's tired,' she said. 'Still in shock. Thanks for bringing the scooter back. It's very kind of you.'

'Kind my arse,' Gina snorted. 'He wants intercourse as payment.'

'Gina!' Stella said.

'I keep telling him he won't be getting any, but like most men he don't listen,' Gina said. 'Now get that door open or Bing's gonna hurt him sen.'

Bing was throwing himself alarmingly hard against the door.

George gave up gracefully, smiled goodbye at Stella, and ambled back up the path.

'That was rude,' Stella said to Gina.

'I know,' Gina said. 'Bloody cheek. I tode him enough times.'

'Not him, you!' Stella growled.

Gina ignored her, finally producing the keys. 'I'm coming Bing,' she called. 'I'm coming, ducky'.'

#

Two hours later Stella gazed at Mapton's 'lake' – a concrete boating pond, water dark under the glowering sky, green and scuzzy at the edges, silted up with goose guano and feathers. A brick bridge crossed its centre and a couple were rowing under it as though they were in Venice, snuggling beneath a ponti.

Huge white pedalo swans floated near the hire hut.

The grass around the pond was frazzled and littered with droppings by the resident Canada geese.

The park had no trees.

Stella stared gloomily into the water.

Back in the bungalow Gina was sleeping, dosed up with her prescription painkillers and exhausted. Bing Crosby, a wiry Jack Russell, wouldn't let Stella go near Gina. He was curled up on the sofa beside her, fur the colour of a sweat stain on the collar of a white shirt, fangs bared, muzzle matted with dog food or worse. He growled whenever Stella moved too close.

Henry was still in his carrier, and although safely locked in Gina's spare bedroom – now Stella's bedroom – he refused to leave the basket, even ignoring the temptation of food.

Stella had smuggled him in when Bing was being

fed and the door to the kitchen had been firmly shut. It was only so long before Bing discovered him or vice versa.

The thought made her shudder.

Ostensibly, she was on her way to buy provisions. Really she just had to get out of the house but staring at the concrete lake was making her feel worse. To the right of the lake was a large car park. If she went through it, Gina had explained, she'd come onto the street that led in to the town centre and thus to the Co-op, the "big' store in the town until Lidl had arrived two years ago. But the Lidl was further to walk to and best visited by mobility scooter or car.

Stella turned her back to the lake. She could see Wonderland, and hear the interminable motor of the inflatable castle. Behind that was a crazy-golf course and a kiddies' paddling pool with water jets and beyond that the seawall, with steps leading up to it. It all looked very dreary under the threatening clouds.

Maybe if anything could make her feel better at the moment it was the sight of the sea. She didn't hold out much hope for the beach based on what she'd seen so far but the sea was the sea.

When she reached the stop of the steps the wind hit her hard. It was sharp and cold. The sort of wind that found its way through any gaps in clothing, that pinged nipples, whipped away caps and whistled down collars. But it also smelled like the ocean, the bracing salt tang of far off adventure that stripped the nostrils and cranked open the chest so that lungs could fill like sails.

Stella filled her lungs. Her hair flew around her face. The beach, she saw, even under the grey sky, was wide and flat and inviting. The sand was fine, dark gold and stretched either way for miles. The tide was out, but the sea was near enough to reach easily, not so far away that going for a paddle was a major expedition.

Stella knew from experience that her Converse would let the sand in despite being hi-tops. It was the little holes – sweat holes, Lysie called them – punched into the sides that did it, but Stella didn't care.

She needed to be on that beach even if it was bloody freezing for June.

She walked along the concrete promenade until she found a ramp down to the beach. The first contact with her feet on sand, through rubber souls nonetheless, felt like a balm. What was it, she wondered, about the sink and spring of sand that was so satisfying? It changed the rhythm of your walk, absorbed the shock normally taken by the knees, forced you to work harder but slowed your pace until, gradually, your heartbeat slowed with it.

Stella headed towards the sea but got distracted by the shells and pebbles strewn along a strip of the beach that marked the tide-line where the retreating sea had deposited its detritus. Instead of reaching the sea, she turned left and followed the trail of carelessly scattered treasure and tat, raking through it with her eyes and occasionally her fingers. She didn't know much about the sea, only recognising the most obvious – razor shells, severed crab claws, or the husks of crab shells. She found a complete crab, and nudged it with her toe. Sure it was dead she picked up the tiny crustacean to examine it. She was both entranced and revolted by its spider-like, segmented limbs, one claw bigger than the other, the softer underbelly, and green-greyish armoured shell. To her land-locked eyes this was an alien creature.

It was so perfect she felt compelled to draw it. Setting it back on the sand, she searched her bag for a tissue to wrap it in but came up empty.

Stella cursed herself for coming out with her handbag instead of the rucksack she carried on her walks around the city. She always travelled with plastic bags in her backpack, for just this sort of thing. Trawling for 'treasures' was one of her favourite pastimes. It was one of the few things she shared with Gina – although their idea of 'treasure' was nearly always diametrically opposite – and it was Gina who had taught her how to go out 'tatting.'

She looked towards the promenade. A café perched on the seafront, painted in bold yellow and aqua stripes. Further along the concrete promenade other cafes and shops clustered closer together, marking the beginning of the main holiday strip. Beyond them rose the back of the fairground.

Stella decided to head for the nearest café – the yellow and aqua one. Delicately, she retrieved the crab and carried it gingerly up the beach to the ramp and onto the promenade. As she moved closer she could read the café's sign: "Rick's Café Americaine'. It surprised her, the reference to Casablanca, here in this run-down little seaside town on the east coast of England.

She peered through the door. Inside the décor was that of a cramped American diner, three bar stools along the counter, and four booths along the wall in sparkling chrome and red leatherette.

A man was wiping down the counter. He looked up as she entered and said: 'Morning, ma'am. What can I get ya?'

His voice was deep and gravelly, his accent American or as good an imitation of one as she'd ever heard.

'Erm,' Stella said, non-plussed by this unexpected greeting. She held out her hand, palm-up, displaying the crab. 'You wouldn't have anything I could put this in, would you?'

The man looked at the crab and then at her. His face was handsome in a creased, weatherworn sort of way.

'Please,' Stella added.

'It's dead, right?' he said.

Stella nodded. 'Oh, yes.'

'And when you say 'something to put it in', you don't mean that in a between two slices of bread sort of way?'

Stella smiled. 'No,' she said. 'I mean have you got a plastic bag or a serviette or something.'

He held her eyes a moment longer, his the blue of worn-in denim and amused. 'Sure,' he shrugged. 'Why not.' He reached under the counter and pulled out a paper bag. 'Will this do?'

'Perfect,' Stella said. 'Thanks.' Carefully she placed the crab in the bag and then folded the paper securely around it, until it resembled a small parcel.

She glanced at the board above the man's head. The words 'filter coffee' jumped out at her. She'd had a mug of Gina's instant Nescafe and a Styrofoam cup of liquid masquerading as coffee at the hospital. Real, hot, fresh coffee.

Suddenly life was looking brighter.

'I'll buy a coffee please,' Stella said, spotting the pot. 'Black.'

'Okay,' the diner-man said. 'But on one condition.'

Stella frowned. 'Huh?'

'You go wash your hands,' the man said, nodding towards a door, marked toilet, at the back of the café. 'You've just been messing with a dead crab and I maintain high hygiene standards in this joint.'

'Oh,' Stella said. Suddenly she felt shamefully dirty. 'Good idea.'

She used the toilet while she was there and came back to find a large mug of coffee steaming on the countertop.

'If you want it to take away, I'll pour it into a paper cup with a lid,' the diner-man said.

'This is fine,' Stella said, perching on a stool. The coffee was hot but she had asbestos lips so she took a sip and sighed.

It was great coffee.

She was about to say so when a loud honk interrupted her. Stella jumped.

'Hey,' the diner-man grinned over towards the door. 'I told you before, Sue, no honkin' on a Monday.'

A fat woman sat astride a mobility-scooter in the doorway. A Yorkshire terrier peered from the basket strapped to the front of the scooter. Ribbons trailed from the handlebars and the basket itself was entirely covered in badges. Next to that was a bulbous black horn – the kind you squeezed.

'That weren't a honk, Rick,' the woman said. 'That were a little parp-parp to wake yer up after a weekend's hard drinkin'.' Her laugh was the wheezy bark of a life-long smoker.

'Told you before, Sue. Never touch the stuff,' Rick said. He turned to the hot water dispenser behind him, dropped a teabag into a paper cup and filled it up. He set the cup on the counter to let the tea brew.

Sue laughed again. 'You hear about Gina Pontin?' she asked.

Rick shook his head. 'She heckle the karaoke again at The Paradise?'

'No,' Sue wheezed. 'They banned her on karaoke nights. No, she took a bad tumble from her scooter. Got rushed to hospital in Lincoln last night'

'That's too bad,' Rick said. 'She okay?'

'Broke her arm,' Sue said, 'and came home in a wheelchair according to George Wentworth. Serves her right. Lucky she didn't fracture her skull the way she speeds. She's a tough nut, though, that Gina. Take more than a tumble to crack her thick head open.'

Rick grinned and took the teabag out of the water. He topped it up with milk and two generous sugars, stirred, stuck on a lid slid from under the counter and carried it over to Sue.

The Yorkshire terrier yipped.

'How you doing, Scampi?' Rick said, ruffling the dog's fur.

Sue handed Rick the money, placed the tea in a convenient holder she'd screwed to the handlebars of the scooter – one of many useful attachments – and continued. 'You know that granddaughter Gina's always boasting about?'

'The one no-one's ever seen?' Rick said. 'Ahuh.'

'Well she's real!' Sue said this as though she'd

pronounced dodos had been found alive and well, living in a garden in town.

'No kidding,' Rick said, sauntering back behind the counter. 'Who says?'

'George,' Sue said breathlessly. 'He met her this morning. She brought Gina home.'

'Well who knew?' Rick said, throwing up his hands. 'Gina wasn't lying.'

Stella watched him. He seemed to be joking, his expression wry, tone mild but it didn't comfort her. The moment she'd heard Gina's name she braced herself. How many times had she heard gossip about Gina. None of it good. Sometimes it was like this – overheard and unintentional on the part of the gossips. Too many times it was maliciously aimed at her, slyly disguised as sympathy, beginning with an 'is it true…?'

Is it true your grandmother caught five-year-old Freddie Tart peeing against her back gate so she tied him to a washing line post for three hours?

Is it true your grandmother stood up and badmouthed old man Dickson at his own funeral and made Mrs Dickson faint?

Is it true Gina Pontin caused Margaret Jenkins to… Stella abruptly cut off that thought.

A chorus of horns – a discord, Stella might have called it another time – interrupted Sue's reply.

'Better get goin',' Rick said. 'The gang's ready to ride.'

Sue reversed out of the doorway. 'She's supposed to be pretty,' she shouted. 'But you know George…'

'Yeah, yeah,' Rick said, flicking his cloth in a shooing gesture. 'It's all 'intercourse' with George.'

Sue barked her sea-lion laugh.

Stella caught a glimpse of her 'gang' – a flotilla of pensioners on festooned mobility scooters. They moved off with an electric hum.

Rick watched them go. 'That's them,' he said to Stella. 'Mapton's Hell's Angels. Vicious criminals, all of 'em.'

Stella smiled weakly. Her eyes still stung from Gina's name.

Rick regarded her. He took in her clothes, her wind-blasted hair. 'You a day-tripper?' he asked.

Stella shook her head. 'No, I'm here for a few days.'

'Holiday? Weather's bad today but it's supposed to brighten up tomorrow. We were lucky last week – half-term – had a few warm days to kick off the season.'

'I'm not on holiday,' Stella said. She took a swallow of coffee. It really was good. She looked directly at him. 'I'm here to look after my grandmother. I'm Gina Pontins'' granddaughter.

There was a beat of silence. Rick grimaced. 'Well, don't I feel like a jackass,' he said.

Stella waved it away. 'I'm used to it,' she said. 'Gina's never won any popularity contests.'

'Aw, she's okay,' Rick said. 'Small-town folks just like to gossip. I'm sorry you had to hear us. It'll teach me a lesson. Listen, coffee's on the house.'

Stella protested but Rick refused her money. 'Tell you what,' he said. 'Come back tomorrow. Then you have to pay.'

Stella smiled. 'All right,' she said. 'Deal.' She swallowed the last mouthful and stood up to go.

'Which way's quickest into town from here,' she asked.

'Turn left and carry on up the prom until you reach the fairground,' Rick said. 'Fairground won't open till noon but the gates'll be open and you can cut through to the town centre.'

'Thanks,' Stella said. She headed for the door.

'See you tomorrow, Crazy Crab Lady,' Rick called after her.

She turned, grinning. 'See you tomorrow, Bogart,' she said.

#

An hour later Stella returned to Gina's to discover that the worst had happened. Bing had sniffed out Henry.

Pandemonium reigned.

Bing was scrabbling at Stella's bedroom door, snarling and yapping, flecks of foam flying rabidly from his muzzle.

Gina was yelling at him to stop. Henry was yowling from the bedroom – a high-pitched screech that was driving Bing Crosby into an ever more frenzied state. He began trying to dig up the carpet in an attempt to tunnel under the door.

Stella dropped her shopping and swooped down on Bing, grabbing his collar and yanking him back from Henry's door.

'Bad dog!' she said. Bing snapped at her but couldn't twist round until she released his collar. Stella had no intention of doing that. She dragged him to Gina's bedroom, flung him in, and slammed the door just as he catapulted himself at it. He hit it, yelped, and bounced back into Gina's room.

Stella felt a moment's guilt, hoping he hadn't hurt

himself, but then he resumed his attack – this time on Gina's door – and she gritted her teeth and strode into the lounge.

Gina was frantic. 'You better not have hurt him!' she shrieked. 'You need to get yer stupid cat outta here.'

'If Henry goes I go,' Stella said. 'I told you, I had no one to feed him and I had to come get you. That's a vicious little dog you've got, Gina.'

'He's just protecting his own,' Gina protested. 'It's not right to bring a cat into his territory. Poor thing – once he smelled it he went insane. I hate cats, yer know that. Always have. Sly, nasty things. Only reason yer have one is cos I hate em.'

Stella snorted. 'I'll go back to London in the morning, then, shall I? Take Henry with me. Bing can look after you.'

Gina glared. 'I can't even get me sen off the sofa,' she said. 'But I suppose you don't care. All I did fo' you, taking yer in and raising yer. Well, you go on, leave me like this. That's all the gratitude I can expect, ain't it?'

Gina began to sniffle.

Stella gritted her teeth.

Soon Gina was sobbing and Stella had moved onto grinding her teeth. She hadn't ground her teeth like this for years.

'Stop it, Gina,' Stella sighed. 'I promise I won't go until I've found someone to look after you.'

'You shouldn't want to get someone else,' Gina sobbed. 'You should do it yourself. I'm yer gran and yer only kin.'

'I've got a life, Gina,' Stella said. 'I've got

commissions and deadlines to meet.'

'I'll tell yer about deadlines,' Gina said. 'I'm livin' on one. I won't be around much longer, yer know. And then where will you be? Eh? No sign of a husband nor any kiddies. You'll be all alone, and then you'll know how it feels.'

'I know how it'll feel,' Stella retorted. 'Bloody great, that's how it'll feel.'

'You little cow,' Gina yelled. 'No bleedin' gratitude. I should never have taken yer in. I was always too soft for me own good.'

'Soft in the head,' Stella retorted. She headed for her bedroom, opened the door and thanked herself for having had the sense not to unpack yet. All she had to do was find Henry (who wasn't in his basket), grab her bags, and get out. What had she been thinking? There was no possibility on Earth that she and Gina could rub along, even for a few days.

'You come back here when I'm talking to you,' Gina screamed.

Stella got down on her knees to peer under the bed. Two terrified round eyes stared back. Henry had wedged himself under the bed between the back and side walls of the room. He had found the exact spot beyond her reach.

'Great,' Stella muttered.

'You get back in here right now!' Gina demanded.

Stella ignored her. She lay on her stomach, stretching her hand out towards Henry. 'C'mon baby, it's all right. I won't let the nasty dog hurt you.'

The nasty dog was still yapping away, scratching at Gina's door.

'C'mon Henry,' Stella cooed.

Henry suddenly darted forward and with a hiss, swiped her hand with his claws. Stella snatched her hand back, cursing. Henry retreated to his unreachable spot, staring at her balefully.

Gina yelled from the lounge: 'I suppose this is still about Margaret Jenkins. She wouldn't have taken you in you know. It wasn't her who fed and clothed you and put a roof over your ungrateful little head.'

Stella saw red. She hauled herself to her feet, marching into the lounge only to see Gina, who'd managed to hoist herself off the sofa, topple into the coffee table and crash to the floor. Gina let out an agonised yowl, one of pure pain. She'd landed on her broken arm.

Stella leapt to help her up but Gina resisted, like a wounded animal caught in a trap. She was close to hysteria. They struggled before Stella finally managed to wrestle her back onto the sofa. She gave Gina another painkiller with some water and waited for her to calm, then she knelt before her and forced Gina to look at her.

'I am going into town to try to find someone to look after you,' she said. 'Don't you dare mention Mrs Jenkins to me ever again.'

Gina looked down. The pain or the shock had her temporarily whipped.

'Right,' said Stella, standing. 'I will leave Henry locked in my room and Bing in yours and I'll be back as soon as I can. I suggest you try to get some more sleep while I'm gone.'

Retrieving her bag and her keys, Stella left. She didn't hear, or chose not to hear, Gina's plaintive voice calling out to her: 'But I need to go for a wee again.'

#

Stella's head pounded. How dare Gina speak the name of Margaret Jenkins? She stared unseeingly at Wonderland through the railings, forcing herself to breathe deeply. She had no idea where to go for help in Mapton - where any of the services were, who could give her advice. She felt lost and helpless, wound up by Gina to a degree she hadn't experienced since escaping to university so many years ago

'Don't cry,' she muttered. 'Don't let her make you cry.'

She looked at her car, considered getting into it and realised she couldn't drive. Not right now. She'd be liable to crash, or worse, knock someone down. She couldn't feel responsible for another death. She couldn't.

Hearing the waves lapping the beach she turned towards the sound, remembering Rick. It would be embarrassing to return to his café so soon but she didn't have anywhere else to go. He could show her a map of the town, tell her where to find a doctor's surgery, or recommend a carer. She needed a friendly face, even if that face was almost a stranger's.

It was lunchtime; two of the booths were taken and all of the stools. Three tables had been set out on the beachfront despite the grey sky and they were taken by folk hardier than Stella, two of them on mobility scooters. Stella hardly noticed them.

Rick looked up and smiled as she walked in but his expression morphed into concern as she drew near.

'Hey,' he said, coming round the counter. 'You look like you've had a shock. C'mon.' He led her to the free back booth, sliding in opposite to her.

Stella saw that her hands were trembling. Ah, the old Gina effect. She clasped them on her lap but Rick hadn't missed it.

'Coffee?' Stella squeaked hopefully.

'Uh uh,' Rick shook his head. 'Camomile tea for you with honey. You don't need caffeine.'

Stella protested weakly. 'Who drinks camomile tea in a diner?'

'I do,' Rick said, standing up. 'And I'm the boss.'

He moved away, disappearing behind the counter and into the kitchen. A moment later a woman emerged from the kitchen, peering curiously at Stella, until a customer came in from outside and took up her attention.

A couple of minutes later Rick returned with a steaming mug of camomile tea and slid back into the booth.

'So,' he said. 'What's up?'

Stella shook her head, suddenly embarrassed. She laughed shakily. 'Oh, nothing really. I've just been... Gina'd.'

Rick grinned. 'Most folks in Mapton have been Gina'd at some time or other,' he said. 'But they don't usually look as shaken up as you.'

'It's been so long since I saw her that I'd forgotten what it was like,' Stella sighed. 'I got the call from the hospital this morning. I didn't have time to prepare myself. I had to bring my cat – Henry – I didn't have anyone to feed him...'

She trailed off.

'Gina hates cats,' Rick said.

Stella was surprised. 'How did you know?'

'She threw Pam Stimpson's cat in the boating lake last summer after she caught it in her garden with a bird in its mouth.'

'Oh,' Stella gasped. 'She didn't drown it?'

'Nah,' Rick said. 'Most animals can swim if they have to. It was a mighty pissed off moggy though. And Pam was beside herself. Gina shouted her to come watch her drown her cat and Pam chased her down to the lakeside wearing only a pair of baby doll pyjamas and her curlers. It was early, so not many people saw her but those that did can't forget it. If you get to meet Pam you'll understand why.'

Stella briefly lowered her forehead to the table. 'I'm sorry,' she whispered.

'Why?' Rick asked. 'You didn't do it. Pam called the RSPCA out and threatened Gina they'd take Bing away but the poor RSPCA man got so scared, caught as he was between Gina and Pam that he just got back in his van and scarpered.' Rick tapped her lightly on her knuckles. 'Tell you what,' he said. 'I'll take your cat for a couple of days while you sort out this mess and get someone to care for Gina.'

Stella blinked. 'You'll… Henry won't like it… Have you got a cat?'

Rick shook his head. 'I've got no pets,' he said. 'But I grew up around cats. My mom loves 'em.'

Stella hesitated. 'I don't really know you…'

Rick nodded. 'You're right. I could be the Cruella De Vil of cats. I have a whole closet full of cat-fur coats. Damn, I thought I'd beaten this compulsion.'

Stella laughed. 'You know what I mean. I can't impose on you like that, and I'm not sure I can hand my cat over to a stranger.'

'Okay,' Rick said. 'But the offer's still good. Tell me what happened.'

Stella told him about Bing and Henry, about her row with Gina and even about the car journey and the toilet stop at the garage. By the end Rick was laughing.

'Gina and I don't have a good relationship,' Stella ended. 'We never have.'

'So,' Rick said, cocking his head to the side. 'As I see it your choices are this: You pack up and leave your grandma to cope by herself…'

'But she can't even get up off the sofa,' Stella protested.

Rick nodded. '… leaving your immobile, helpless grandma to cope by herself, or you stay, while Bing Crosby tries to kill your cat (and that little devil-dog won't give up, believe me) and you end up killing your grandma and her dog – which won't look good for you at the trial – or you let me take your cat for a couple of days while you look after your grandma and find a carer, thus allowing you to leave knowing she's being taken care of.'

Stella narrowed her eyes at him. 'The way you say 'Grandma' makes her sound like a sweet old lady.'

'I know,' Rick grinned. 'Words are slippery things.'

Stella sat back, sipping her tea. 'All right,' she sighed. 'Henry's yours, although I'll warn you now, he won't like you.'

'Cats are territorial,' Rick said. 'He won't like anything until he's back home but at least he'll be safe from Bing, fed, warm and not quaking with fear under the bed – at least I hope he won't be.'

'Thank you,' Stella said gratefully. 'Now, I've just

got to coax him into his basket.'

'Tuna,' Rick said. 'Never met a cat who could resist tuna. I'll give you a little bit to take with you.'

Stella glanced over to the counter. The dark-haired woman serving glared over at them. 'I think your colleague needs help,' Stella said.

Rick craned round. 'Okay, Ang,' he called. 'I'm comin'.' He turned to Stella. 'Finish your tea. I'll bring some tuna over and the address of the health centre in town – maybe they'll be able to help you. You can drop Henry off here later.'

Now she was feeling calmer Stella remembered that the nurse at the hospital had given her the name of Gina's GP. She dug into her bag and pulled out the paper. It matched the address Rick had given her. Armed with her small Tupperware container of tuna, Stella waved goodbye to Rick and turned towards town.

She felt guilty, remembering Gina hadn't had any lunch yet, but she couldn't face returning, not without having sorted something out first.

The health centre was on Maldives Road. The name made Stella laugh. She'd noticed Malta Avenue and Seychelles Close on her walk, as though Mapton-on-Sea hoped that by naming its streets after exotic holiday destinations the glamour of azure seas and white sands would rub off on Mapton itself.

Stella had been to Malta and couldn't recall counting five mobility scooter shops in one small town. Or even one. Mapton surely held the record.

There were four mobility scooters parked outside the health centre, neatly lined up side-by-side, making Stella think of horses tethered to the hitching post outside of a saloon.

The waiting room was busy. Stella asked the receptionist if she could see Dr Graves. The receptionist, a middle-aged woman with flint-coloured hair and eyes, looked askance. Appointments were made in advance only, she said. Would she like to make an appointment for next week? Stella shook her head. 'It's urgent,' she said. She leaned towards the receptionist, feeling as though almost everyone in the room was listening behind her. 'It's not for me. It's about my grandmother. She had a nasty fall and was released from Lincoln this morning, but I need to get some help for her.'

The receptionist regarded her coldly. 'Hmm,' she said. 'Well, you will have to sit and wait until the doctor's ready. That could be over an hour, you know.'

Stella hesitated. 'All right,' she conceded. 'I'll wait.'

The receptionist nodded curtly. 'What's your name?' she asked.

'Stella Distry,' Stella said. 'My grandmother is Gina Pontin.'

Stella was sure she heard a gasp from the waiting room. The muted conversations died abruptly. The receptionist's head shot up. Her cold, stony face had turned fearful. Her hand hovered over the appointment book.

'I'll see what Dr Graves says,' she murmured, and disappeared from the window hatch.

A minute later she was back. 'Dr Graves will see you now,' she said. 'She was having her lunch but she's cut it short for you. Go through the door to your right. Dr Graves's office is three doors down the corridor on the left.'

Stella half-expected her to slam the window hatch shut but instead the receptionist shouted past her. 'Mr Pimms, Dr Smith will see you now.'

Stella turned round. All eyes were on her. She hurried past them to the door and scurried into the corridor, relieved as the door swung shut behind her.

Small towns, she thought. Strange places indeed.

Dr Graves was a petite blonde in her thirties. She was brushing crumbs from her skirt when Stella knocked and entered.

'Mrs Distry?' she asked, smiling tentatively.

'Ms,' Stella said. 'But Stella's fine. Thank you for seeing me on such short notice.'

'You're welcome,' Dr Graves said, gesturing to the patient's chair adjacent to her desk. 'Before we start I must tell you that your grandmother, Gina, rang about half an hour ago. She was very distressed.'

'Ah,' Stella said, heart sinking.

'She seems to think you are trying to force her into a home…'

'What!' Stella said. 'I'm doing no such thing.'

'She was very upset.'

'Yes, well,' Stella spluttered. 'That makes two of us.' She took a deep breath. 'Let me explain the situation,' she said and proceeded to tell Dr Graves about the phone call from the hospital and about Gina's immobility.

Dr Graves listened sympathetically. 'I understand,' she said. 'I've actually already talked to the hospital, and you're right, in her condition and at her age, Gina can't be left to fend for herself. She needs someone to look after her, at least for a couple of weeks until she can walk again. But with her broken arm she can't use crutches to get around. She's lucky she didn't break a hip.'

Stella relaxed. 'So you can arrange for someone to do that?'

Dr Graves grimaced. 'Er, actually, no I can't. Gina won't allow it.'

Stella stared at her. 'What do you mean?'

The doctor sighed. 'She wants you to do it.'

Stella swallowed. 'I can't,' she said. 'I have a career and a home in London and… and I'm very likely to kill her if I have to stay.'

Dr Graves smiled faintly. 'It's up to the patient. They have to agree to have a home assessment before a carer can come in. It's clear from my conversation with Gina that she won't agree to that, and as I know Gina very well I know why she won't agree to it.'

'Because…?' Stella prompted frantically.

'Because she wants it to be you,' Dr Graves said. 'Look, er, Stella. Gina comes into my surgery at least once a week…'

'Once a week! Whatever for?' Stella asked.

'For whatever she thinks she has on any given week,' Dr Graves said. 'Some of her claims are perfectly true – high blood pressure, for example – but many are imagined – excuses to see me – although she would never admit that. But really she's just lonely. She wants to talk, and what she often talks about is you.'

'Me,' Stella exclaimed. 'Why on earth does she want to talk about me?'

'She's proud of you,' Dr Graves said. 'Which is amazing because she hates everyone else.'

Stella snorted. 'She hates me too.'

Dr Graves shook her head. 'No, I don't think so. What she wants most is to see you.'

'All we ever do when we do see each other is fight,' Stella said.

Dr Graves shrugged. 'That's Gina.' Her tone gave it all away. Stella looked at her. 'Is she rude to you?' she asked.

'Frequently,' Dr Graves said. 'But I put her in her place. I banned her for an entire month once; she's been better since then.'

'I'm sorry,' Stella said. 'It can't have been easy to keep her out.'

Dr Graves nodded. 'So you see, without Gina's consent I can't really help you. But you could try a private agency, although, again, if Gina refuses to let them in I'm not sure what you can do. Of course, you can leave, go back to London. Gina will be helpless but I'm sure she'll make enough noise to bring the emergency services running. We might be able to get the social workers in then, but it's not easy and it's a slow process.'

Stella considered it. 'I don't think I can do that,' she said. 'Although God knows I'd like to.'

Dr Graves smiled warmly. 'Tell you what,' she said. 'I'll give you the name of an agency I think is really good. So many of them aren't, you know.' She tore off some headed notepaper and scribbled a name and number down. She stood, handing it to Stella and guided her to the door. 'Good luck,' she said.

#

Stella got back to Gina's to find her snoring on the sofa. Bing had resumed his yapping the moment he heard the key in the lock. On the coffee table next to the sofa a coffee mug brimmed with a suspiciously yellow liquid.

Stella gently prodded Gina, who woke grumbling. She squinted resentfully at Stella.

Stella pointed to the mug. 'Is that what I think it is?' she asked.

'Lucky it was there,' Gina said. 'I'd a peed mesen otherwise. Not that you'd care.'

'I'd care,' Stella said. 'It'd be me cleaning you up.'

A flicker of something flashed across Gina's face – hope maybe. 'You not running out on me then?' she asked casually.

'Not today,' Stella said.

'Tomorrow then?'

Stella sighed. 'Let's just get through the rest of today and tonight,' she said. 'We'll deal with tomorrow when it comes.'

She was surprised when Gina just nodded. Looking more closely at her grandmother Stella noted how pale and drawn she looked. She was thinner than she'd ever been in Stella's memory, not frail but wiry.

'When did you lose weight?' Stella asked.

'Since I was seventy I can't keep it on,' Gina said. 'Dunno why.'

Stella nodded. Gingerly, she picked up the brimming mug of urine. 'I'll get rid of this. D'you want a cuppa? Something to eat?'

Gina brightened. 'D'you know what I fancy? Eggs Yolka Polka.'

Stella paused, the mug dangerously tilting. She righted it. 'Eggs Yolka Polka?' she repeated. It was a phrase she hadn't heard in years. She smiled. 'All right, but I'm not dancing when I make it.'

'The dancing's the best bit,' Gina said. 'Just don't make my tea in that mug.'

Eggs Yolka Polka

Eggs Yolka Polka was simply eggs mashed with butter and pepper. By the time Stella turned eleven she'd discovered that many, many people ate mashed eggs – some with butter, others with mayonnaise, sometimes on toast, more often in sandwiches. This discovery disappointed her. Until then she'd thought mashed eggs was the invention of her grandmother.

Stella loved her grandmother Gina. Unlike other children she never called Gina by a title – not Gran or Nana or Grandma - only Gina, because Gina accepted nothing other than that. Secretly this thrilled Stella. Adults were always addressed differently. Mum and Dad, rather than Ivy and John. At the newsagent she was served by Mrs Tilton; she had no idea what Mrs Tilton's first name actually was. Mr Ericson was her maths teacher, Mr Snow, the milkman and Miss Blake, her form teacher. In fact all adults were to be addressed politely and formally. Yet all adults were allowed to call her Stella. Mr Ericson frequently called her Estella which greatly annoyed her, but her attempts to correct him had been swatted away, as though her name was merely a rough peg on which to hang a question – perhaps on fractions or multiplication – rather than in any way representative of herself as an individual with an identity.

Adults lived by rather rigid rules it appeared to Stella, except for one.

Gina.

Gina who didn't like to be called Grandma and insisted on being called Gina, although it drove Stella's mother mad.

'I'm trying to teach her some manners,' Ivy grumbled.

'It's bad manners to call someone something they don't want to be called,' Gina said. 'Remember how Jimmy Turner used to call you Poison Ivy. You didn't like that did you?'

'It's hardly the same,' Ivy said. 'Being called Gran is not an insult.'

'It is to me,' Gina said. 'I'm in my prime. Gran makes me sound like an ode hag. I won't answer to it.'

'If you don't want to be a grandmother I won't bring Stella round,' Ivy sniffed. 'You weren't much of a mum either.'

'How can you say that?' Gina said. 'I beat that Turner boy black and blue for you.'

Gina won because she always did, but also because Stella's parents loved to go dancing on a Saturday night, so Stella often came for the evening and slept over at Gina's.

At six (when she first started to stay overnight) Stella knew just how Dorothy felt landing in Oz, the exact moment when the world transformed from black, white and greys to the stupendous colours of Munchkinland. It all seemed to be recreated in Gina's tiny house. Even Toto was there (although Gina called him Fred Astaire not Toto, and he was old and a bit grumpy).

Gina's house was stuffed with knick-knacks, glittering and glorious to Stella's young eyes. Spanish dancer dolls, ceramic ballerinas and milkmaids; a glass cocktail cabinet filled with tiny glasses etched with gold, Babycham glasses and a plastic Babycham deer; cutlery with fake mother of pearl handles in pink, blue and yellow. A green cut glass trifle bowl adorned the Formica table in the kitchen. Framed pictures of musical stars, carefully cut out of magazines, smiled from the walls.

But even better than all of this was Gina's food.

It was generally agreed on Bobbin Street that Ivy had done well to marry above her, given who her mother was and her dubious illegitimate start. Her husband was a lecturer at the new polytechnic, while Ivy herself was the secretary to the dean of the college. The young couple believed in growing their own food, baking bread, and feeding their daughter a nutritious, well-balanced diet.

Stella didn't encounter the joys of sliced white bread until Gina introduced her to it. Mother's Pride or Sunblest were the best for squidging up into tight little balls before popping into the mouth. Her mother's bread was heavy, usually brown and didn't have the qualities or the pleasure associated with Play-Doh. You couldn't do much with it other than eat it.

Trifle was a dessert she approached with fear since her mother had become enraged the previous Christmas when the 'bloody custard' had gone lumpy and she'd 'over-whipped' the cream. Forced to try a mouthful Stella had almost spat out the congealed phlegmy mass. Her mother insisted she'd like the underneath layer which was jelly, but to her horror it had soggy, grainy stuff clumped in it. These, according to her mum were sponge fingers. Stella didn't want to eat anything with fingers in ever again.

So, when Gina suggested one afternoon that they make trifle, Stella shuddered with dread. Then a miracle happened. Gina pulled a bright packet out of the cupboard – a Bird's Strawberry Trifle – with a picture on the packet so beguiling that Stella couldn't equate the promise of such a creation with the one her mum had produced.

They made it; all that needed adding to the powders were milk and water and time to set. Gina discarded the sponge fingers at Stella's request and then, for the finale she allowed Stella to shower the creamy topping with pink and yellow sugar sprinkles. The trifle was a triumph, both artistically with its unnaturally coloured layers offset beautifully by the green glass bowl, and in terms of taste and texture. The whole thing was as smooth on the palate as a Mr Whippy. The pink and yellow layers tasted as sweet as a child imagines such colours should and matched the spoon handles perfectly.

Stella also learnt that potatoes could come out of tins not just the ground. The first time she saw tinned potatoes she thought they were small boiled eggs. Peas also came out of tins. In fact almost everything Gina ate magically sprang out of cans, packets or bags. It was so much more convenient than the muddy carrots her mother dug up and then had to scrub, or the peas that needed podding (although Stella liked doing that) or the loose leaf tea that clogged the spout of the teapot. Gina used teabags – PG Tips because she liked the chimps on the ads.

One of the few foods that Gina ate, unpackaged, or processed, was eggs. As she pointed out to Stella, eggs came in their own neat packaging. Stella believed her until she dropped one raw egg on the floor. After that she considered the 'packaging' to be a pretty weak design.

Still, despite this flaw, Eggs Yolka Polka was a treat to be treasured. First came the boiling, counted down by Gina's Mrs Clucky chicken timer, a hen roosting atop a nest clicked round and round until the precise moment of hard-boiled perfection was reached; then it let out a volley of shrieking clucks. Anticipating the cacophony was nail-bitingly exciting. Gina would whisk the eggs off the gas and plunge them into a bowl of iced water to stop black rings forming around the yolks. Then she and Stella would settle down to watch the Saturday matinee film on BBC2. Next came the peeling, out would come the butter, white pepper and salt. Gina would divide the eggs, butter and seasonings into two bowls, hand a fork and one of the bowls to Stella. 'Wait for it,' she'd say before crossing over to the little Dancette record player and placing the needle on the record already primed to go. Then Brian Hyland's Itsy Bitsy Teeny Weeny Yellow Polka Dot Bikini would blare out and they would each begin mashing their eggs whilst dancing around the kitchen, twirling round each other, laughing, as Fred Astaire gambolled around their feet, snapping up the flecks of egg mixture that flew out of the bowls. It was the liveliest Fred Astaire ever got.

Finally, they would spread the egg mixture between two soft slices of Sunblest, add cress, garnish with Golden Wonder crisps, pour out two glasses of orangeade, and collapse at the table to relish their creations.

Eggs Yolka Polka.

Henry gets the Heave-Ho

An hour later Stella had left Gina propped up in front of the TV with her egg sandwiches and was coaxing Henry into his carrier with Rick's tuna. By the smell in the room Henry must have made some kind of dirty protest under the bed – a nice present for Stella to clear up later. Her priority right now was to get Henry to Rick's Café and Bing Crosby out of Gina's bedroom. She was getting worried that the dog had dehydrated but at least she knew he was still alive; his snarling as she passed his door was proof of that.

Henry, bless him, chose to fall for the old tuna trick. Stella let out a huge sigh of relief as she closed the door on his basket and latched it. Henry gave a faint mew of protest but it was half-hearted. He looked and sounded despondent.

'I'm sorry,' Stella said. 'But I'm going to get you out of here, Henry, and find you a nice place to stay without any dogs or other cats. It's only going to be for a few days, until I can sort something out for Gina.'

Henry refused to look at her.

Stella carried him out to the car and stowed him safely on the passenger seat, looping the seat belt over the carrier. 'Be back in a second,' she said.

'I'm letting Bing out,' she called to Gina, as Bing snarled on the other side of the door.

'About bloody time,' Gina said. 'My poor baby. Bing! Bingo! Come to mamma.'

Stella grasped the handle, exhaled, and pushed it open. Bing Crosby shot past her, ignoring Gina's calls and hurled himself into the room Henry had left only minutes before. He was a dog possessed. Henry's smell drove him wild. He dived under the bed, sounding rabid; he re-emerged covered in Henry's excrement but strangely calmer.

His ears pricked at Gina's voice. 'Bing Crosby, you get here now!'

Ignoring Stella, Bing dashed out of the room, joyously yapping. A moment later Gina screamed.

'He's covered in shit! Get down Bing, get off me.'

For a moment Stella considered walking out and quietly closing the front door behind her. She squeezed her eyes shut. One, two three...

'STELLA!'

Stella opened her eyes, scanned the room, and spotted an old tatty looking blanket folded on the chair by the window. Grabbing it, she ran for the lounge. Bing was writhing his shitty little body against Gina in ecstasy, trying to lick her face while she struggled to push him away with her one working arm.

Stella threw the blanket over Bing and scooped him up, carried him, wriggling and struggling, to the bathroom. She slammed the bathroom door behind her so he couldn't escape, turned on the showerhead over the bath, and deposited Bing Crosby in the bathtub, whipping the blanket off and hosing him down before he understood what was going on. Stella grabbed his collar as he made a leap for freedom and washed him as thoroughly as she could. Then she stretched for a towel and did her best to rub him dry without losing her fingers.

Stella was a dirty mess but with Bing relatively clean she went to deal with Gina, which proved to be a much harder task.

When she finally rolled up to Rick's she found him stacking the outside table and chairs neatly inside the diner.

He stared at her with undisguised amazement. 'Every time you turn up you look worse than before,' he said.

Stella was grim-lipped. 'Thanks,' she said. 'That makes me feel so much better.'

Rick smiled. 'I didn't mean that the way it sounded. Wanna talk about it?'

'No,' Stella said shortly. 'Are you still okay to take Henry?' She held up his basket.

'Sure am,' Rick said. He peered in at Henry. 'Hey fella. Had a bad day?'

Henry peered balefully back at him and meowed pitifully.

'Yeah?' Rick nodded. 'Well how d'you like to come stay with me? No dogs, no cats, no crazy women. Sound good?'

Henry meowed again.

'Thought so,' Rick said. He straightened. 'It's a ten minute walk. Can I carry Henry for you?'

'If you hold him steady,' she said. 'He doesn't like being jostled.'

'Who does?' Rick said, as he took Henry's carrier from her. 'Hey fella, I'll be real careful with ya.'

They walked slowly. Occasionally Henry emitted a pathetic meow but no panic. Stella thought he was probably too worn out to complain with his usual gusto.

The clouds had blown away to reveal a late afternoon sky of clean blue, setting off the sea and golden sand to pleasing effect.

'It's a lovely beach,' Stella said. 'For such a butt-ugly little town.' It had slipped out before she even knew she was going to say it. God, thought Stella, it's the Gina effect.

Rick glanced at her. 'I see you've inherited your grandma's tact.' He sounded amused.

Stella grimaced. 'Sorry,' she said. 'It's been a hard day.'

Rick nodded. He guided her to the left and led her down some concrete steps that led away from the promenade and the seafront onto a street of assorted houses, with an occasional B&B mixed in.

Rick said: 'Mapton is the sort of place where you have to look for the beauty wearing different lenses. You can't apply the same laws of aesthetics here as most other places.'

'What do you mean?' Stella asked, intrigued.

Rick shook his head. 'It's hard to explain. Imagine you're wearing glasses and the focus of the lenses has been created through your education, your class, what you've been taught is beautiful and what isn't. To see Mapton properly you have to take them off.'

Stella considered this. It wasn't a new idea to her. She was an artist and used to seeing things in ways others didn't. Still, there were limits.

'I understand,' she said. 'But I'm never going to find shell suits, or dog poo, or... that!' She gestured to a grotesque giant resin robin atop a faux stone wishing well in a nearby garden. 'I'm never going to find them beautiful, or even acceptable.'

Rick looked directly at her. 'Well, I guess you don't like my house then,' he said, pointing to the front gate of the offending garden. 'Or even acceptable.'

Stella felt her blush start from her toes. She began to stutter out another apology. Then Rick grinned. 'I'm being mean,' he said. 'This isn't my place. But now I've seen it I'm thinking of getting me one of those plastic robins.'

Stella gave him a stony look.

The net curtains of the lower right window of the house twitched. Rick waved cheerily. 'C'mon,' he said. 'Mrs Teller will ring the police soon. She knows a potential robin stealer when she sees one.'

'And they say Americans have no sense of humour,' Stella said.

'I think that's a sense of irony,' Rick corrected. He led her round another corner and there, set back in a large lushly green garden, was a castle.

Stella gaped.

It was a very small castle, red brick, rather than ancient stone, but it did have four stumpy towers topped by crenelated parapets.

'Who owns that?' Stella said.

'Me,' Rick said happily. 'It's mine. So, you see American's do have a sense of irony. They say 'an English man's home is his castle''. Well, I ain't English but I'm the one living in a castle on the East Lincolnshire coast.'

Stella stared at it. 'It's got to be Victorian,' she said. 'Only a nouveau riche Victorian would build something like that.'

Rick turned to her in surprise. 'You're right,' he said. 'A guy named Mortimer Vaughn built it. He made his money bringing the railway to Mapton and opening it up as a resort. He was a big shot round these parts. He commissioned this house because he loved Tattershall Castle and wanted a sort of miniature version.'

'And to show off,' Stella said.

'Of course,' Rick nodded. 'Victorian entrepreneurs and Americans share the same vulgar need to 'show off'.'

Stella squirmed. She seemed unable to stop unintentionally insulting his taste. 'That's not what I meant to imply,' she said. 'Actually, I love this kind of architecture. I chose to study William Morris for my degree thesis at Art school.'

'The wallpaper guy?' Rick asked.

Stella nodded. 'That's what he's known for now but he did far more than just wallpaper patterns. He was a genuine polymath in the arts.'

Rick cocked his head, interested. He was about to ask a question when Henry emitted such a plaintive meow that both Rick and Stella were ashamed to realise they had almost completely forgotten the reason they were here. Henry needed a home.

A temporary home, Stella corrected herself.

'Sorry, fella,' Rick said. 'Let's get you inside.' He unlatched the low, double wrought iron gate and led them up a gravel drive to the house. A huge arched doorway framed a solid oak door.

'What no portcullis?' Stella remarked wryly.

'Nah,' Rick said. 'No point without a moat or drawbridge.' He fished in his pocket for his keys, handing Henry's basket over to Stella. 'Opening this door is a two hand job,' he explained. 'The oak's a bit warped and sometimes sticks.' He jiggled the key in the lock, pulling the door towards him simultaneously, before seeming to change his mind and pushing against it. After a few seconds the lock tumbled and Rick pushed the heavy door inwards.

It suddenly struck Stella that she was about to enter the house of a man she didn't know, and that nobody she knew, other than sofa-bound Gina, had any idea that she was here.

Suddenly she felt very stupid and a little bit afraid. She stood, frozen on the threshold. Idiot, she told herself. You idiot.

Gina's warning flashed into her head. 'He'll want intercourse! Why would he offer to look after your cat? It's another kind of pussy he's interested in.'

Of course Gina thought every man was only ever after intercourse, but she had a point. Why would a man who wasn't a friend offer to look after her cat? Because it was the perfect excuse to lure a woman to his (quite secluded) house. A house that looked like a castle. No one with a house that looked like a castle could be normal, could they? What if it was some kinky kind of sex-den inside?

It was Gina's fault. Only a brush with Gina would have scrambled her brain enough to accept such an offer. Usually, Stella was very cautious about men.

'Hello?' Rick broke into her thoughts. 'Earth to Stella? Are you coming in?'

Stella blinked. She clutched Henry's carrier and remained glued to the spot.

Rick peered at her, puzzled. Then his eyebrows shot up. 'Ah,' he said. 'I getcha. Hmm. Yeah. I can see why it might seem...' He trailed off. 'Awkward.'

They regarded each other. 'Would it help you to know I'm gay?' Rick brightened.

Stella processed this. She discovered she felt oddly disappointed. 'Oh,' she said. 'Well, yes, I suppose it would.'

'Only I'm not,' Rick said, frowning.

'Then why…?'

'Because I thought it might help,' Rick shrugged, looking lost.

'Then you should've stuck to the lie,' Stella said and laughed. Rick laughed with her and Stella found she could move.

'Look,' Rick said. 'I'm a simple guy. You seemed like you needed some help and I saw a way to do it. I'm gonna take your cat for a coupla days while you sort yourself out, but there's no strings attached. I'm not expecting 'intercourse' as some sort of payment if that's what Gina's told you.'

Stella started. 'How…?'

'Aw, c'mon. Gina thinks all any man wants from a woman is 'intercourse.' It's become a kinda catchphrase round here. What's more Gina thinks that every man round town wants it with her.'

Stella felt the familiar embarrassment that had plagued her life with Gina. 'I'm sorry,' she whispered.

'Don't be,' Rick said. 'Gina makes life around here more interesting. And as a woman you have every right to be suspicious of me, but I'm asking you for Henry's sake, if you can take a chance, just spend half an hour getting him settled in so he knows you've been here and will come back for him.'

'Okay,' Stella nodded. She reminded herself she had pretty good instincts about people and from their first meeting Rick had felt okay. Still, she thought as she stepped into the dim interior, I know some killer karate moves if I'm wrong and I'll be taking my cat with me.

Bing Bites Back

By the time Stella got back to Gina's she felt much better. The only thing Rick had pressed her into was accepting a chicken salad sandwich on rye, which had the added bonus of working like tuna on Henry. Rick set down a small bowl of shredded chicken for the cat and their friendship was sealed. They'd eaten in the garden room, a brick and glass walled extension at the back of the house, with a hardwood floor where Rick said Henry would be staying.

'I don't 'do' pets in the kitchen,' Rick explained. 'I like furry things but in my kitchen I regard them as dirty little critters who consider cleanliness to be achieved by licking their own asses.'

After he'd eaten, Henry had prowled around the room, sniffing skirting boards, peering under and over furniture. Satisfied there were no dogs or rival cats around, he sprang onto a Lloyd Loom chair, circled a few times, before settling onto the cushion.

Stella looked anxiously at Rick. 'Do you mind?'

'It's fine,' said Rick. 'He's my guest. I popped out earlier and picked up a litter tray and some food. I hope Whiskas will do?'

'Oh God,' Stella groaned, slapping her forehead. 'I completely forgot. Here,' she said scrambling for her purse. 'Let me reimburse you.'

Rick shook his head. 'We'll sort it out tomorrow. I've got the receipt.'

'Okay,' Stella sighed. She glanced at her watch. 'I'd better get back to Gina before anything disastrous happens.'

Rick smiled. 'Good luck with that. Do you need a

lift back?'

'No,' Stella said. 'I remember the way and I like walking.'

She gave Henry a scratch but he hardly lifted his head. 'You be good,' she said to him.

The moment she put her key in the lock Bing started to yap. Warily entering in case he nipped at her ankles, Stella called out 'Hello?'

'Oh my God,' Gina screeched from the lounge. 'You've been gone so long I was about to call the police.'

Bing stood in the doorway to the lounge. Once he recognised her he put his ears flat and his tail between his legs and slunk back inside.

'Did he attack you?' Gina screeched again. 'Come here, let me look at you. If he laid a finger on you…'

Stella presented herself. 'He didn't attack me,' she said. 'He made me a chicken sandwich.'

'Oh,' Gina huffed, pouting. 'And what did he want for that?'

'Nothing,' Stella said. 'He was just being nice, that's all. Sometimes people are nice, Gina.' She looked more closely at her grandmother's face. 'Have you been crying?'

'I thought you were dead,' Gina wailed.

Stella perched on the edge of the sofa. 'Don't be ridiculous,' she said softly. 'I've only been gone an hour.'

'It's more than that,' Gina said.

'Two hours at the most,' Stella said. 'No, not even that.' She reached for the kitchen towel she'd left on the coffee table and tore a piece off.' Gently she dabbed at Gina's face.

Gina's sobs calmed to sniffles. 'I thought you'd left me,' she whispered.

Stella said nothing for a minute. 'You are a silly,' she said.

They watched TV until nine, when Stella felt she couldn't keep her eyelids open. She'd been woken in the early hours yesterday and after that... well, it had been non-stop.

'I'm going to have to turn in soon,' she said. 'I'll help you to the bathroom and get you ready for bed if that's okay? It's time for your pain meds as well.'

Stella wheeled Gina into the bathroom and helped her onto the toilet. She waited outside while Gina did her business. Bing stood in the doorway to the lounge again, still with his hangdog pose, yet Stella felt nervous of him. She wasn't convinced he was beaten. There was a certain glint in his eye.

'Come in,' Gina called. Stella obeyed.

'I feel filthy,' Gina said. 'Get me some Femfresh wipes. They're in the cabinet there.'

Femfresh. Stella stopped. She hadn't thought about Femfresh in years. It was another Gina obsession – feminine hygiene – and the belief that the vaginal odour is a dangerous, intoxicating odour that men can sniff out from metres away. Therefore a young woman should always have a supply of Femfresh wipes to hand, popped into her handbag along with her lipstick and keys.

The day that Stella pulled her pencil case out of her schoolbag in English 3B, only to witness, to her horror (and in slow-motion) a pink packet of Femfresh wipes fly into the air (placed in there by Gina so that Stella could avoid the terrible shame of unwanted odour) was a day that changed her school life, which until then had been a refuge from home. That was the day she was christened with two new names: Fanny Fresh or Kipper Knickers, depending on the whim of the utterer.

'The top cabinet,' Gina said.

Stella reached for the door. She stared into the cabinet but she couldn't see the wipes. 'They're not there,' she said.

'Yes, they are,' Gina insisted. 'I can see them. That white packet.'

Stella blinked. She'd been searching for the exact shade of pink she associated with public humiliation.

She plucked them off the shelf and deposited them into Gina's hand. 'I'm not wiping you,' she said brusquely. 'You'll have to manage yourself.'

'I wouldn't bleedin' let yer,' Gina snorted. 'Just pull some out for me and bog off.'

Stella pulled a clump of damp tissues from the pack and placed them on Gina's knee. 'I'm going to look for something better than a mug for you to pee in if you need to during the night,' she said.

Stella rummaged around in the small kitchen trying to find something suitable, aware that Bing was skulking just out of sight but trying to ignore him. She found a little enamel tin jug, larger than a mug but small enough to slip underneath Gina. It had folk-art flowers painted on a black background. 'You,' she muttered to it, 'have just been demoted to a piss-pot.'

Once Gina was in bed, propped against her pillows, with the tin jug on her bedside table, she said. 'I always have an Ovaltine in bed. It helps me sleep.'

Ovaltine. Another Gina memory, but a better one

than the Femfresh. 'I'll make us both one,' Stella said. 'I'll take mine to bed too.'

'Let Bing out in the back garden,' Gina said. 'He needs to do his business. He's not been out all day.'

Stella shuffled exhaustedly to the kitchen and opened the back door. 'Bing?' she called. He slunk out from under the kitchen table, edged past her warily, then shot out of the back door.

Stella switched the kettle on, rifled through the cupboard for the Ovaltine, and swiped two clean mugs. She'd placed Gina's contaminated mug on the doormat to remind her to get rid of it. She didn't think even boiling it in bleach would make it usable again. Besides, it had a picture of Ken Dodd on it, which in Stella's eyes rendered it hideous and typically Gina.

She glanced toward the door. The Ovaltine was steaming in the mugs but Bing still hadn't returned. She decided to give him a couple more minutes. She'd take Gina her drink, and deposit hers by her own bed, then come back to round up Bing and lock up.

Stella was half way through the lounge, carefully balancing the brimming mugs, when she heard the growling. Cautiously she swung round. Bing Crosby was standing in the threshold between the kitchen and the lounge, hackles bristling, little doggy eyes fixed on hers and sparking hate. In that split second she could see what he was thinking – that she had no hands free; that she was carrying a precarious cargo that didn't allow for defensive action – but it was too late. Bing launched himself with deadly accuracy at her right ankle, jaws snapping shut like a spring trap. She felt the agonising sink of sharp teeth into tendon, screamed and dropped the mugs, hot liquid spilling down her legs. The spray hit Bing but he didn't let go. He worked his teeth in further, trying to shake her ankle to death, the way he would a rabbit, except that her ankle was attached to her leg and Bing's force was such that he almost bodily lifted himself off the carpet instead.

Stella staggered, flailed for the nearest object she could reach, found a mug and whacked it as hard as she could against Bing. Bing hardly noticed. Stella grabbed for his collar and began to choke him, until finally, unable to breathe, he let go to gasp for air.

Stella collapsed to her knees. She stared at Bing. He stared at her. His tongue lolled out as though he was laughing. It was like a challenge. Stella lunged for him but Bing saw it coming and he shot away, back through the kitchen and out into the night.

Stella lurched after him, ignoring the pain in her ankle and slammed the door shut, locking and latching it after him. Leaning against the door she began to cry. The tears kept coming, the sobs painful waves of pain breaking in her chest.

It was the perfect ending to a perfect day.

In her bed, Gina had already forgotten she wanted Ovaltine. She was asleep, snoring lightly, knocked out by painkillers.

In the garden Bing Crosby was busy tunnelling. He was on his way to a life of crime that would become legendary in years to come.

Stella Gets her Wheels

By the following morning Stella's ankle had swollen black and blue and she could hardly put her weight on it. She had suffered a terrible night of broken sleep, plagued by the agony of her ballooning ankle and the stench of cat faeces. Too exhausted to get up and stagger to the lounge sofa, she had stuffed a pillow over her face to block out the noxious smell.

Stella pushed the pillow away to see the sun infiltrating the curtains. Her ankle throbbed. She groaned. Before she could clean under the bed, see to Gina, or think about Henry, she knew she had to see a doctor and get a tetanus shot. She'd cleaned the wound as best she could and slathered it in Savlon last night but it needed medical attention. This was proven when she swung her legs out of bed and gingerly tried to put her weight on her right ankle. It barely held.

'Shit,' she muttered. 'Shit, shit, shit.'

It became increasingly apparent that her ankle was out of service. Even driving to the doctor's looked unlikely. Stella didn't trust herself to be able to control her acceleration, never mind brake in time. She was grateful that she had packed a dress as her ankle was too swollen to squeeze into her skinny jeans.

Her problem now was to work out how to get to the doctor's surgery. She briefly considered calling Rick, but her pride stopped her. How much could she ask one man to do for her? She'd only met him yesterday and it was already getting embarrassing.

An idea struck her. Gina's mobility scooter.

Stella was relieved to find Gina still asleep when

she hopped into her room. She scribbled Gina a note: 'Bing bit me. Gone to doctor's for tetanus shot. Back soon. Taken your scooter.' She found the scooter's ignition key on the hall table and armed with one of Gina's crutches tentatively cracked open the front door.

There was no sign of Bing Crosby. Still, Bing was a cunning beast, so she inched the door wide enough open to stick her head out and swept the perimeter before hopping onto the doorstep.

Still no Bing, but George was across the lane planting a meticulous row of petunias in his border. He waved, clambered to his feet, and began making his way towards her. Despite his gardening chores, he was as dapperly dressed as he had been yesterday.

'Good morning,' he called. 'Beautiful day. How's the patient?'

'Still asleep,' Stella said, trying to return his cheerful smile. 'Unfortunately I'm the one in need of some medical care today. Bing bit me.' She pointed to her ankle. She'd re-bandaged the wound but it was still visibly swollen and discoloured above and below the actual bite.

George's expression turned to dismay. 'Oh dear,' he said. 'How awful! That dog...' He bit off his words.

'I need to take Gina's scooter,' Stella said. 'Would you show me how to work it?' She was half hoping he'd say he had a car and offer to drive her but if he did drive there was no car parked outside his house.

'What? Oh, of course. Or I could call an ambulance for you? Or a taxi... although we only have one taxi in Mapton – Jeff's – and he'll be asleep right now. My car's at the garage.'

'The scooter will be fine,' Stella said. 'I just need to know how to stop and start and steer.' She held out the ignition key. 'Will you show me?'

George took the key and pulled the weather protective cover off the scooter, then hopping on he slid the key in the ignition. He waved at the dashboard. 'Set the speed dial first then use the throttle to start,' he said. 'When you want to stop just let go.' He gave her a demonstration and then made her climb on and practise until he was satisfied she'd mastered the scooter, including the reverse throttle.

'Keep it on 4mph,' George said. 'This one goes up to 8mph but you're not ready for that. Best to keep it slow and safe.'

Stella nodded. 'Will do,' she said. She smiled at the symbols on the dial – it went from tortoise to hare speed.

'Do you want to me to stay with Gina while you're gone?' George asked. The idea seemed to perk him up. 'I've got a mobile,' he said, pulling a basic Nokia out of his trouser pocket. Give me your number and I can call you if needs be.'

Stella must have looked surprised because George laughed. 'Don't expect an old dodderer like me to keep up with technology do you? I use this to text with my granddaughters.'

They exchanged numbers and Stella was ready to glide away on her scooter.

At first she felt ridiculous. Old people used mobility scooters, or the infirm, disabled, or, Stella, thought darkly, people like Gina. People, she suspected, who didn't really need them but were too bloody lazy to walk.

Because it was early the streets were quite clear. If it wasn't for her throbbing ankle she might admit to starting to enjoy herself, the scooter humming efficiently beneath her, eating up the pavement. On the opposite side of the street a man trundled past on his own scooter and waved. Stella waved back.

She parked outside the medical centre in an area seemingly designed for mobility scooters. Two were already docked – one a sturdy, sensible grey and black, the other festooned with teddy bears, as though they'd been caught in the headwind of the scooter and splattered across it like flies on a windscreen.

Inside, the receptionist was the same flinty woman as yesterday; she immediately recognised Stella. All Stella had to say was 'Gina's dog bit me. I need to see Dr Graves,' and she was ushered through, the receptionist even lending her an arm to lean on as she hopped to Dr Graves's office.

Stella wondered if this was how the children of dangerous gangsters felt – always treated deferentially due to the ferocious reputations of their parents.

Dr Graves stared disbelievingly at Stella's ankle. 'This is a bad bite,' she said. 'Seriously bad.' She pressed the Achilles tendon with her fingers, making Stella flinch. 'It happened last night? Did you clean it?'

Stella nodded. 'And I applied Savlon.'

Dr Graves examined the puncture wounds. 'We need to clean it out again with a saline solution and give you a tetanus shot, unless…' she looked up at Stella.' I don't suppose you've had one recently?'

Stella shook her head. 'No.'

'I'm concerned about the tendon,' Dr Graves said. 'But I can't tell whether it's damaged without an X-Ray. Luckily, we're an outreach clinic for the area so we're better equipped than most surgeries and we have a consultant from Grimsby who comes in every Thursday. I can get you x-rayed and booked in again for then. In the meantime you need to keep off that ankle.' She turned to her prescription pad and began to scribble. 'I'm also going to give you some antibiotics. Dog bites carry all sorts of nasty surprises. Best to be on the safe side.'

Stella listened to all this in dismay. All she'd expected was a tetanus shot.

'If I can't be on my feet,' she said. 'Who's going to look after Gina?'

Dr Graves looked up from her pad. 'Hmm. You're right.' She pointed to Stella's ankle. 'Even Gina can't argue with that. She'll have to accept getting someone in. Did you ring the agency I gave you?'

'No,' Stella sighed. 'It didn't seem worth the fight.'

'Well, it is now,' Dr Graves said. 'Are you still willing to pay for a private carer? Maybe a live in one?'

'Gina will never agree,' Stella said. 'Although if she did I could go home,' she added as a wistful afterthought.

Dr Graves laughed, rather cruelly Stella felt. 'Gina will only agree if you stick around,' she said. 'It took a lot to get you here.'

It took Stella a moment to pick up on the implications of this. 'You think she had the accident on purpose?' she asked. The thought was too awful and utterly Gina.

'I doubt it,' Dr Graves said. 'It would be quite hard to do, I think, but Gina's not one to waste an opportunity. She wants you in Mapton.'

Stella felt a little sick. It was as though she was trapped in the old sixties series The Prisoner. She envisioned a giant balloon blocking all exits from Mapton.

'If we can get in a live-in carer where would I stay?' Stella said. 'And how much is this all going to cost me? I'm doing well but I'm not rich.'

'Why don't you move into Gina's static?' Dr Graves suggested.

'Her static?' Stella was bewildered.

'She has a static caravan in her garden,' Dr Graves said. 'She calls it her 'studio'. It's where she does her painting.'

Stella looked at her blankly. 'Painting?'

'Oh dear,' Dr Graves said. 'You really don't know your grandmother, do you? Let me give the agency a ring for you.'

#

Of course Gina was hysterical when Stella returned. She demanded to know where Bing was, to which Stella had no reply. She insisted that Stella must have goaded Bing into attacking her and refused to look at Stella's ankle.

'It's your fault for bringing that bloody cat into the house. Bing's as good as gold normally. He's never bitten anyone in his life.'

Stella snorted.

'You'll have to stay in bed until the carer arrives,' she said. 'Dr Graves said I must stay off my ankle and I certainly shouldn't try to support you.'

Gina froze. 'Carer! No sodding carer's coming into my house,' she spat.

Stella shrugged. 'Well I can't look after you,' she said. 'Your dog's left me lame. I need to use one of your crutches to hobble around.' She rustled round in her handbag. 'Look,' she said, pulling a grease-stained paper bag out. 'I bought you a pasty from the bakery. Cheese and potato. That'll keep you going till she gets here. I got one myself.' She dropped down clumsily on the bed next to Gina. 'Let's watch telly till she arrives.' Stella picked up the remote off the bed and switched on Gina's bedroom TV. Shifting a pillow behind her she stretched out.

Gina glared at her. 'Are you gone out?' she said.

'I think it's the drugs,' Stella explained cheerily. 'Dr Graves gave me something for the pain. I feel quite lightheaded.'

'Well lucky you,' Gina snapped. 'Mine don't do that.' She unwrapped the pasty and sniffed it. 'I won't have a stranger in my house.'

'Uhuh,' Stella mumbled. 'See about that.' Her words trailed off as she dropped off to sleep.

Gina poked her. 'Oy!'

Stella mumbled something else, shifting slightly, and snuggled further into the pillow.

Gina sighed and bit into her pasty. She clicked through the channels until she found Jeremy Kyle and prepared to be outraged.

At eleven-thirty Stella jerked awake to the synthesised notes of God Save the Queen. 'What's that?' she asked.

'Doorbell,' Gina said. 'Don't answer it.'

'It'll be the carer,' Stella said eagerly. 'I'd better get

it.' She wobbled off the bed, grabbed a crutch, and hopped into the hallway. A small, wiry woman stood on the doorstep. She looked to be about forty.

'I am carer,' she said. 'From Blue Sky agency. You are Gina Pontin?' She looked pointedly at Stella's ankle.

'Oh no,' Stella said. 'I'm her granddaughter. Gina's inside. Please come in.'

The woman picked up the wheeled suitcase she'd brought with her and followed Stella in.

'Nice doorbell,' the woman commented.

Stella looked back at her, not sure how to answer.

'Your grandmother have national pride, yes?'

Stella shrugged. 'She likes novelty things,' she said. 'Things that make her laugh.'

The woman nodded, face betraying nothing.

Stella took her into the lounge. 'Look,' she explained, closing the door. 'I just wanted to give you some warning. Gina doesn't want a carer although she needs one. As you can see I won't be able to get about very easily for a few days but I will be around to support you. Gina can be...' she hesitated. 'Very difficult. Even rude. You mustn't take it personally; she's like that with everyone.'

The woman nodded. 'Okay,' she said. 'I can handle. I deal with rude people all of the time.'

Stella smiled. 'All right,' she said. 'My name's Stella by the way. Stella Distry.'

'I am Grazja Bobienski,' the woman replied. 'You show me where I sleep before I meet client.'

It struck Stella that she hadn't cleaned the spare room. The stinking, gross spare-room.

'Oh no,' she said. 'I have to clean it first. I'm really

sorry. My cat did a poop under the bed and I haven't been able to get to it yet.'

She looked so stricken that Grazja said. 'No problem. I clean. You not able to do it at moment.'

Gina's voice interrupted them. 'Stella,' she said. 'Is that the carer? You tell her she's not needed.'

Grazja looked at Stella with steady grey eyes. 'Let's meet her,' she said. 'I tell her I am needed.'

Stella felt herself quail but she nodded and ushered Grazja through to Gina's room.

For some reason, in the few short minutes Stella had been gone Gina had grabbed a lipstick from her handbag – a bright pink – and liberally applied it. Gina always wore lipstick outside of the house. She wouldn't face the world without it.

She looked a little clownish wearing it now, sitting straight up in bed with her yellow nightie and dyed red hair sticking up in clumps.

'Gina,' Stella said. 'This is Grazja. She's going to help me look after you.'

'Hello Gina.' Grazja smiled for the first time since she'd arrived. 'It's good to meet you.'

Gina bristled. 'You're foreign,' she said. 'I won't let a foreigner touch me.'

Grazja continued to smile. 'This is right, Gina. I am Polish. You are very quick to hear my accent. Is that a pot of urine I see, Gina? I will empty that for you.'

Gina grabbed the enamelled jug of her precious effluence and cradled it against her bosom, managing to slop some on her duvet in the process. 'Don't you touch it,' she spat. 'I don't want you in my house. If I wanted a carer – which I don't – it would be an English woman. Not some dirty foreigner, coming here to steal honest people's jobs. And don't think you can steal anything – you'll not be getting the chance to rob me.'

Stella opened her mouth to protest but Grazja's voice cut through the room. 'Don't worry, Gina. I only steal from people with good taste. I will leave you to hold your own pee for now and come back when you are ready to behave. Stella, please show me my room. I must clean it.'

'Your room!' Gina roared. 'SteLLLLA!'

Stella shut the door on Gina. 'I'm so sorry,' she said to Grazja. 'I'll understand if you go.'

'No go,' Grazja said. 'I like challenge.'

A crash came from Gina's room, followed by a scream of rage and pain. 'She has fallen over,' Grazja remarked.

Stella hopped towards the door but Grazja stopped her. 'No, no. I go.' She opened the door, while Stella peered over her shoulder. Gina lay on the floor, flaming-cheeked. The enamel jug had gone over with her and pee soaked the carpet and Gina.

Grazja went to help her up but Gina squealed and struck out at her. Grazja danced back lightly. She put her hands on her hips and scrutinised Gina. 'You want to lie in your own piss, Gina?'

Gina growled.

Stella started for her but Grazja held her back with a warning hand.

'Gina,' she said. 'I would very much like to help you clean up your mess and get you better.'

'Stella can help me,' Gina said, dissolving into frustrated tears. 'Help me Stella.'

Grazja turned to Stella giving her a look that froze

her into place. 'Stella cannot help you, Gina, because Stella is hurt. Stella pay me money to look after you, Gina. You think Stella pay money if she don't care. No. This is how you pay Stella back, like naughty child.'

Gina howled and beat her one good fist against the carpet. Grazja waited her out, then, deeming the time right, moved forward to help Gina up. This time Gina tolerated it.

Stella hopped to the chest of drawers and pulled a fresh nightie out of the top one. This one had bold pink roses on a green background.

Grazja was strong. Gina was hung limply but Grazja had no problem helping her onto the bed. Gina groaned.

'Your ribs bruised, yes?' Grazja said. 'I look at your hospital record soon. First we need to clean you up and then carpet. I get stuff out of my car to give you sponge bath. We fix you up.'

Grazja whisked out. Stella heard the front door click.

'Are you all right?' she asked Gina.

Gina's lipstick had smeared across her chin and cheeks. 'I hate you.'

Stella nodded. Fair enough.

'I'm not letting her wash me,' Gina said. 'She could be one of them lesbians,' she said. 'Like that Martina Navratilova.'

Stella smiled faintly. She looked out of the window into the back garden. Dr Graves was right. A whopping great rectangular static caravan filled half the space.

'Why have you got a caravan in your garden?'

Stella asked.

'What?' Gina sniffled. 'Oh. It's where I paint my pots and whatnot.'

'Pots?'

'Yeah,' Gina said. 'I sell em to tourists.'

Stella nodded, as though she understood. But she didn't really. Since when had Gina been creative?

They heard the front door open. Gina stiffened. Grazja bustled back in with a washing-up tub and various items.

'I think I'll have a look at it,' Stella said, hurriedly.

'Don't you bloody dare leave me,' Gina shouted.

'She's trained,' Stella said. 'A professional. Aren't you?' she said to Grazja.

'Yes,' Grazja said. 'I am trained nurse, not just carer. You not need worry.'

#

Stella found the keys to the static hanging on a hook near the back door. She peered warily through the glass, on the lookout for Bing. She'd last seen him disappear out of this door. He could be hiding behind or beneath the caravan. Then she spotted the tunnel dug out under the back fence and knew why they hadn't heard or seen him since last night. He'd escaped.

Still, he might be skulking nearby, so it was with trepidation and readiness to wield the crutch that Stella stepped out. The back garden was gravelled, although by the lack of weeds, Stella assumed it had a proper lining laid beneath the pebbles. Painted pots were scattered lacksidasically around, planted, as was Gina's way, with plastic daffodils and tulips. By June these were a little out of season but that was the beauty of plastic, Stella thought – a material for all seasons. A memory of Bobbin Street, planting bulbs with Mrs Jenkins and waiting for them to bloom, flashed into her mind. She pushed it away. Stella didn't like to think of Mrs Jenkins.

A suspicious brown 'twig' poked out of the gravel. Stella didn't want to investigate further. She'd had enough of faecal matter, thank you very much. No doubt the 'twig' was deposited by Bing. Instead she kept to the concrete slabs that bordered the gravel and hobbled her way to the caravan steps.

Inside was unexpectedly delightful.

The static had been customized into a studio. The seating had been stripped out and replaced with long workbenches that ran along two walls. Pots of paint, jam jars filled with paintbrushes, artists' mixing palettes, tubes of acrylic... many of the materials Stella had in her own studio at home covered the benches. A shelf under the bench held terracotta and enamel tin pots, some decorated and others waiting to be adorned. In the middle of the floor space an easel had been set up with a high stool to perch on. Stella examined the half-finished canvas – a vase of chrysanthemums, painted in zinging shades of orange and yellow. The style was naive but undoubtedly charming.

Stella felt dizzy. Was this Gina's? When had Gina taken up painting?

An unfamiliar emotion poked her. It took a moment to recognise it – jealousy. Art was her thing. Her talent had set her apart from Gina. It had got her a place at art school and taken her far away from Bobbin Street.

Now here was art colluding with the enemy.

Stella stared at the canvas. No, she concluded, drawing a deep, shaky breath. This wasn't art, this was merely amateurish dabbling, a hobby for an old woman. Dismissing it as such, Stella hopped further into the caravan. There was a tiny kitchenette and beyond that a short hall. A door on the right led into a tiny bathroom and at the end of the hall was a bedroom with a small double bed with a bare mattress.

Stella hobbled back to the main room. She spotted a fan heater plugged into a socket and switched it on. Warm air began to blast into the room. She flicked it off, satisfied to find electricity.

She could manage with this, she thought. She could manage quite happily. She just needed to get bedding and maybe move an easy chair in, and she could make a little nest.

Finally something was going her way.

Bing's Spree Begins

Bing's descent into criminal life might never have happened if Angela Jones, Rick's short order cook and second in command, hadn't left the back door to the kitchen open and the kitchen unattended. Rick didn't like the back door to be open because of flies, but Ang had only popped out to the bins for a minute and with two large bags of rubbish in hand it had seemed too much trouble to put one down to pull the door closed behind her.

Bing had been making his way home, driven by hunger, when he'd smelled the only thing in the world he loved more than Gina. Sausages.

It was a smell to drive a dog mad. He hunted the source of it with his quivering nose and arrived at the back of the café just in time to see a woman emerge, hoisting heavy bags.

She left the door open.

Bing was drooling. He was a dog used to being fed regularly – not just his mealtime bowls, but treats and titbits throughout the day. He hadn't been fed for over eighteen hours and the enticement was just too much.

He shot into the kitchen. The sausages he'd smelled had been cooked but they had already been served. Waiting on a plate was a link of uncooked sausages and their aroma was almost as strong to his sensitive nose, however they were perched above him on a counter top and he was too small to jump that high. Instead he sprang onto the stainless steel pedal bin at the end of the counter and launched himself from there. He hit the worktop, skidding into the plate which slid onto the floor and smashed. Bing had snagged a sausage, dropped back to the bin and was halfway to the door, a snake of sausage links slithering behind him by the time Ang returned. Bing shot between her legs and was away, fleeing with his booty before she could even begin to scream blue murder.

A second later she did, causing Rick to run in from the diner to see what was wrong, but it was too late. Bing had made his escape.

He dragged his treasure underneath a shrub in a nearby car park. The sausages were coated in dirt but Bing was undeterred. This was a dog that would sneakily eat other dogs' poo when Gina wasn't looking. It was the one thing that could enrage his mistress – although Bing didn't understand why – and could earn him a shouting at and an occasional slap.

The sausages were even better than poo. Bing had just sunk his teeth into one when a long nose thrust under the shrub and a mouth snapped at a sausage.

Bing went berserk. He bit the nose and shot out from under the bush to confront the intruder. The other dog – a larger, ill-put-together mongrel - yelped, pulled back and found itself faced with a snarling yapping dervish that darted and danced around him, nipping at ankles, toes, and tail with astounding speed.

The smaller dog had sharp teeth and crazy eyes and the mongrel recognised it as an alpha immediately. He had the choice to run or submit. The lure of the sausages made the choice for him. He submitted in the desperate hope that the alpha might cast him some scraps.

The mongrel cowered, belly to the ground, indicating to Bing his submission. Bing snapped and snarled and showed his hackles for another minute until he was sure the other dog was truly cowed. Then he crawled back under the shrub to eat his breakfast while the mongrel lay nearby watching, occasionally edging very slowly forward on his belly, whimpering.

Bing finished all but two of the sausage links. These he nudged out to the mongrel who pounced on them, tail wagging joyously.

Then they did some bum sniffing, a little play fighting, and finally wandered off together, Bing leading the way.

Bing didn't know it but he had started to form the pack that would become Mapton's most infamous criminal gang.

Stella Shakes a Paw

It was late afternoon when Rick took in the astounding sight of Stella on a mobility scooter. He had started to think she wasn't coming today- even that she'd done a runner, dumping her cat on him. He'd understand if she did; Gina Pontin could do that. Being related to her had to be hard.

Still, he was relieved when he saw her. Pleased too, in a way he hadn't been pleased to see anybody in a long while. There was something about Stella – with her God-awful surname that sounded like dysentery - that he liked. Sure, she was a little snobbish but then she was a city girl and an educated one at that. And Mapton was unappealing on a first viewing. On quite a few viewings, if he was honest but he had grown up in an ugly little town in the Mid-West that squatted in the midst of endless prairie like a pimple on a pretty face. Mapton was a beauty spot in comparison.

Some folk might think it strange that Rick felt so settled on the east coast of England, but the flat farmlands and big washed-blue sky of east Lincolnshire reminded him of being back home. That and he had wanted to get lost. Who would come looking for him here?

Stella looked good too. He liked the way her brown hair fell in natural curls around her shoulders. Too many women fussed and coiffed their hair. They ironed the life out of it and then tried to put it back in with chemicals. Stella's face was fresh and natural. She might wear make-up but if so it was the kind that enhanced rather than smothered. When he'd first seen her, her cheeks and the tip of her nose had been flushed pink from the chill wind. Cute.

Cuter was the request she'd made for something to stow her precious beach find in. The crab. She didn't say it but Rick could see she'd been so damned excited by that crab. Her face had shone with the wonder of it. Because it was wonderful. Yet Rick hadn't met many full-grown women – he corrected himself – many people who would think so. A crab was a crab. A pebble a pebble. So what?

And she appreciated real coffee.

All in all, the crazy crab woman had piqued his interest. That hadn't happened in a very long time.

He straightened up from wiping down an outside table and watched her pull up on the scooter.

'Hey,' he said. 'I didn't figure you for a scooter pooter. What's going on?'

Stella ruefully pointed to her bandaged right ankle. 'I got bitten,' she said.

Rick squatted down to peer at it. 'Looks bad,' he frowned. 'Gina bite ya?'

Stella laughed. 'Almost,' she said. 'It was Bing. He waited until my hands were full and then went in for the kill.'

Rick frowned up at her. 'Sounds nasty,' he said. 'Must've shook you up.'

Stella nodded. 'I saw the doctor this morning. She gave me a tetanus shot and antibiotics. She wants me to see some consultant on Thursday – make sure the ligament's not damaged.'

'Wow,' Rick whistled. 'That must've been some bite. Bing's a snappy little dog but I didn't figure him as vicious. What did Gina say?'

'She says it's my fault for bringing Henry into the

house.'

Rick raised his eyebrows. 'Well, I guess that would upset him but even so...' He looked sympathetically at her ankle.

'How's Henry?' Stella asked.

'Great,' Rick said, standing up. Jesus, he didn't like the way his knees popped when he did that. He hoped Stella hadn't heard the creaking. 'We had a chat this morning and he did his business in the litter tray. Seemed happy. Chowed down on his Whiskas.'

'Good.' Stella seemed relieved.

'What's happening about Bing?' Rick said. 'You can't have him around if he's gonna bite you.'

'He ran away,' Stella said. 'He was in the garden but he tunnelled out. He'll come back – dogs do, don't they? He's very loyal to Gina.'

'Yeah. But when he does...?'

Stella sighed. 'I'm not sure what to do but the good thing to come out of this is I've managed to get a carer for Gina. Live-in! I've moved out to the caravan; it's in the garden. I didn't even notice it yesterday but it's a one bedroomed static. Gina uses it as a studio. She paints, you know?'

This all came out in such a rush that Rick had a hard time keeping up. 'You've got a carer for Gina? How'd that happen so fast?'

So Stella told him about her trip to the doctor's and Grazja's arrival. He laughed at her description of the ensuing battle. 'This Grazja sounds like a match for Gina.'

'Oh, she is,' Stella nodded happily. 'She was completely unfazed.'

'So she's got Gina whipped?'

'Noooo,' Stella laughed. 'Grazja won the first battle. Gina's regrouping. I know the signs. She seems to be going along with it but she's just conserving energy and weighing up the enemy.'

'You seem remarkably chipper about it,' Rick said.

Stella looked at her ankle. 'The funny thing is I'm almost grateful to Bing. He's given me a 'get out of jail' pass. I've got the static to retreat to and I know Gina's being looked after. It's clear even to her that I can't lift her out of bed or wait on her, at least not for a few days. I'd never have got a carer past the door otherwise.'

'You didn't think about going home?' Rick asked.

'How?' Stella said. 'I can't drive. Anyway, strange as it sounds I actually want to make sure Gina's all right. She is my grandmother.'

Rick was pleased. But he didn't show it. 'You think Grazja will stick it out? Sounds like you expect more trouble.'

Stella nodded. 'I've warned her but she just shrugged. She's small but she seems strong and tough. She asked me what happened to my ankle. When I told her about Bing she pulled her face and said 'Dog bite me, I bite dog.'

Rick laughed. 'Talking of dogs,' he said. 'Ang got a shock this morning...' He stopped abruptly. 'Oh no,' he groaned. 'I bet it was Bing.'

Stella looked alarmed. 'Bing bit Ang?'

'No,' Rick said. He told her about the sausage incident.

Stella tried not to laugh but failed. 'I'm sorry,' she spluttered.

Rick grinned but he was worried. The summer

season was just about to kick in. The last thing Mapton needed was a biting dog going feral. Once a tourist – worse, a kid – was bitten it was all over. Mapton wasn't Skegness – it needed the numbers. The wet summer last year hadn't helped.

Besides, who wanted to see a kid bitten anyway, irrespective of profit? That was the sort of thing that shouldn't happen on vacation.

'Have you reported Bing to dog control?' he asked Stella.

Stella stopped smiling. She looked perplexed. 'I didn't even think about it,' she said. 'It's not the first time I've been bitten by one of Gina's dogs.'

Rick cocked his head. 'You say it like it's normal. Most dogs don't bite.'

Stella shrugged. 'Gina's do. Not bad – not like this – but little nips. At least with me.'

'Do other dogs bite you?' Rick asked.

'No. Never. My friend Lysie has a Husky. He loves me.'

'Is Gina cruel to her dogs? I mean, why do they bite?'

Stella looked defensive. 'No! She's not cruel to them. She loves them – spoils them if anything. All her dogs adored her. The problem is that she hates other people so they do too.'

'Does that mean Gina hates you?' Rick asked softly.

Stella stiffened. He regretted the question as soon as he asked it but he was intrigued.

'She must do,' Stella said icily, 'as all her dogs have bitten me.' She was upset.

'Hey,' Rick said. 'I'm sorry. That was real insensitive of me. My mom always said I needed a stick shift to drive my mouth cos when I put it in automatic I say the dumbest things'

Stella smiled weakly.

'You know what I reckon,' Rick said. 'Those dogs all bit you cos they were jealous. They know Gina loves you.'

Stella looked towards the sea. When she looked back her face had closed. 'What do I owe you for the Whiskas?' she asked.

'Don't worry about it,' Rick began to say but stopped when he saw her expression. 'Er, a fiver will cover it.'

Stella nodded. She reached for the bag in the front basket of the scooter, found her purse and pulled out a note.

Rick took it. 'Thanks,' he said. 'Can I get you a coffee?'

He could see her about to refuse and kicked himself again. She was English and kinda middle-class. Look at her offended sensibilities.

Then she surprised him, almost visibly dusting the chip off her shoulder, smiled and said. 'As long as it's filter.'

'Freshly ground beans,' he saluted and went inside.

#

Before Stella could ponder why Rick's question had upset her – after all assuming Gina hated her was nothing new – she noticed the flotilla of mobility scooters approaching along the promenade. Sue, the woman she'd seen yesterday at Rick's, led the formation, ribbons streaming colourfully back from her handlebars. She drew up beside Stella, scrutinising Stella's scooter.

'A Rascal Vision,' Sue said huskily. She gave a low, admiring whistle. Her gang fanned out around her, so Stella was soon surrounded by pensioners on scooters. She half-wondered if they were armed with flick knives.

'Sorry?' Stella said.

Sue looked at her as though she'd only just noticed the scooter had a rider. 'You've got a Rascal Vision,' she said. 'You're riding the Rolls Royce of scooters.'

'Not a Rolls Royce,' an old man with a sweep-over said. 'More like a Mercedes.'

Sue gave him a dirty look before turning back to Stella.

'Oh,' Stella said. 'I see. I wouldn't know. I'm just borrowing this one for a few days.'

'You hire it?' the old man called.

Sue rounded on him. 'Where would she hire a Rascal Vision around here?' she spat. 'Use your noddle, Frank.'

Frank went so red that Stella was tempted to lie just to back him up. Instead she just said. 'It belongs to my grandmother.'

Another woman, frail, with blue rinsed hair so fine that it rose like a nimbus of Love in the Mist around her head, nudged her scooter forward. 'You can't just ride a disability scooter,' she said. 'It's not right for an able bodied personto ride them. Besides, what if your poor grandmother needs it. A girl your age should walk.'

Stella pointed to her bandaged leg. 'It's only till my ankle heals,' she defended herself. 'And my grandmother can't use it at the moment.' She only just stopped herself adding 'Honest!' like a chagrined child.

'Hmm,' the old woman said. 'I suppose it's all right then.' She didn't sound entirely convinced.

Stella was relieved to see Rick emerge from the café.

'Hey, you guys' he called, threading his way through the scooters. 'Are you scaring my customer?'

The atmosphere changed suddenly. Everyone brightened at the sight of Rick. Stella thought that if it had been dark she would have seen each face glow.

Rick handed Stella a large coffee – in a mug, she noted, not a lidded disposable cup which she could whisk away. If she wanted this coffee she had to stay put. Rick leaned down and whispered in her ear: 'Mind if I introduce you? Get it over with?'

Stella noticed two things at once. One was Rick's smell – a hint of sweat and deodorant and soap. A heady, pleasant, masculine scent. Number two was the nudge Blue-Rinse gave Sue when Rick leaned in close to Stella and the raised eyebrows they exchanged with each other.

Stella was also suddenly aware of Rick's light stubble next to her ear and the crazy idea that if she wanted to she could reach out and rub it.

'Okay,' she whispered back.

Rick straightened. 'Stella,' he said easily. 'Let me introduce you to the Marauders, Mapton's answer to the Hell's Angels.'

This caused guffaws and cackles of laughter from the pensioners. 'Oh Rick,' someone called. 'You are a one.'

'And Marauders, this is Stella Distry. She's Gina Pontin's granddaughter.'

There was a terrible moment of silence – or it was it just Stella's imagination? – and then everyone began welcoming her to Mapton, shaking hands, saying they'd heard about Gina's accident and wishing her well. Soon Stella felt bombarded by questions, but Rick expertly dispersed the pensioners, herding them into twos and threes and placing them around tables and taking orders until Stella was left only with Sue.

Sue was clearly the head of this gang.

'So this is Gina's Rascal,' Sue said. 'Must be new. She was still riding her Comet last time I saw her. Still, that were a few weeks back after she…' She stopped whatever she was going to say, some terrible thing Gina had done, no doubt. 'Anyway, it were a while back. I had a rotten cold that got on me chest and I couldn't go out much.' She leaned forward conspiratorially and lowered her voice. 'That's when Frank started thinking he could take me place – lead the gang. Started to organise little outings without me. Thought I wouldn't know but Mildred let me know. I started the Marauders. Just cos we named the club after his caravan don't mean it's his.'

She glanced sideways. Stella followed her look to where Frank was sitting chatting with a couple of ladies. He looked up and for a moment he and Sue eyeballed each other. Then Frank broke, averting his eyes. He let out a nervous cough.

Sue smiled triumphantly.

Stella was amused. 'Frank's got a caravan called Marauder?' she asked.

Sue nodded. 'Yeah. You know how they come with little names on the side. 'Spirit', 'Explore' 'Crusader'. Frank's is a Marauder.'

'Bit aggressive isn't it for a caravan?' Stella said. 'Why not "pillager' or 'berserker' – you know like the Vikings. They were marauders.'

Sue grinned. 'That what's Rick said when he saw the name on Frank's caravan. It was him who suggested we name our scooter club after it. Tickled him to think of a bunch of pensioners marauding around Mapton.' She paused. 'Not that I'm a pensioner. But the rest are.'

Stella nodded. She judged Sue to be in her fifties. She wore a red cap. Hair, so black and dead it had to be dyed, tendrilled around her face and was pulled into a thin ponytail through the hole at the back of the cap. Her face was large and ruddy, sparse eyebrows filled in with black kohl. Her breasts ballooned beneath a sweatshirt and her bum spilled over the side of her seat.

Sue looked Stella straight in the eye. 'Some people think I ride my scooter cos I'm too fat and lazy to walk. Actually tell it to me face or shout it in the street. But I can't walk – not far anyway. Arthritis you see - the arches in me feet 'ave collapsed. I'm fat cos I can't get no exercise…' She grinned. 'And I like chips too much.'

Stella laughed with her. 'There are a lot more mobility scooters here than anywhere else I've been,' Stella said tentatively. 'Why is that?'

Sue thumped the table. 'Because Mapton's bloody paradise for scooter pooters,' she said. 'It's completely flat – not a hillock in the whole town – the promenade is wide and runs for two miles along to Siltby. Half the houses are bungalows. Loads of pensioners retire here you know. Considering this is a seaside town, property is bloody cheap, and look what you get...' Sue threw her arms wide to indicate the vista. 'Sea views and sea air. Bingo every day, company... it don't come better than Mapton.'

Stella nodded. 'Makes sense,' she said, and then was startled as a furry head popped out of the basket on Sue's scooter.

'Oh, so you're awake,' Sue said. 'Lazybones.'

She gave Stella the sappy smile that dog-owners always give when they expect the other person to be as entranced with their pet as they are.

Stella eyed the Yorkshire terrier warily. She learnt all too recently that small dog's bites could be worse than their barks.

'Say hello, Scampi,' Sue cooed. 'Say hello to the nice lady.'

Scampi cocked her head, regarding Stella with sparkling black eyes, pink tongue lolling. She gave a little yip and offered a paw.

Stella hesitated.

'Go on,' Sue said. 'She loves to shake hands.'

Stella still held back. Scampi waggled her paw, seemingly puzzled by her refusal to take it.

'I was recently bitten,' she said.

'Oh, Scampi don't bite,' Sue snorted. 'She ain't got no teeth. Look...' She gently pulled back Scampi's lips. Scampi bore this with patience. She was obviously used to Sue displaying her mouth. Her pink gums gleamed in the sunshine, unimpeded by teeth. 'It were my fault. I used to share my sweeties with her. The vet went mad with me when he found out and poor Scampi had to have her teeth out.'

Stella had never seen a toothless dog. 'How does

she eat?' she asked.

'Oh, I mush it up for her,' Sue said. 'Doesn't mind a bit. In fact she seems happier without them. I think they gave her pain – well, they would do wun't they?'

Stella leaned toward Scampi and slowly offered her hand. She barked joyously and immediately gave her a paw to shake.

'Pleased to meet you, Scampi,' Stella said.

Sue beamed. 'Ah, look at that. She likes you. Course she likes most people.' She took a sip of her coffee. 'So, what happened to your leg? Wasn't like that when you got here, was it?'

Stella briefly considered lying but she knew it was only a matter of time when word got out that Bing had bitten her. 'Gina's dog bit me,' she said, shrugging.

Sue whistled. 'That little bugger,' she said. 'Bing Crosby is the bane of Scampi's life. He worries at her, snapping and growling. That's when he's not trying to mount her. He gets her all upset and trembling. Gina thinks it's funny. She...' She stopped, remembering who Stella was.

'It's all right,' Stella reassured her. 'I know what she's like.'

Sue snorted. 'I'll bet yer do! You know, we thought you didn't really exist – Gina talks about you that much but you never come to visit. I were surprised when George Wentworth told me you'd come.'

'Well,' Stella smiled weakly. 'Here I am.'

Sue nodded. She looked Stella up and down. 'And Gina's dog's gone and done that to you. Shame on her. How you supposed to look after her now?'

'Oh,' Stella said. 'I've got a carer in.'

Sue reared back as though slapped. 'How have you managed that so soon?' she demanded. 'Carers are like parrot's teeth round here. There's such a high demand, what with all us disabled and old folk. Took me two years to get mine and she only comes in twice a week.'

'Er, it's a private agency,' Stella explained. 'I'm paying for it.'

'Ooh,' Sue sniffed. 'Lucky for some. Should get Gina to pay. If she can afford a Rascal Vision, not to mention that caravan she bought last year she must be rolling in it.'

'Just how much do these things cost?' Stella asked, patting her scooter.

'A Rascal Vision? About 5K,' Sue said.

'5K!' Stella was astounded. 'You can get a good second hand car for that.'

Sue nodded. 'It's brand new,' she said admiringly. 'Gina hasn't even had time to customise it yet. Her last one looked like a carnival float it had that much stuff on.'

She saw Stella looking at the ribbons and badges festooning her own scooter and added defensively. 'I mean all o'er it. Not just a bit of decoration.'

That sounded like Gina, Stella thought. She loved her gaudy colours.

Stella's ankle began to throb, reminding her it was time to get back. She was supposed to be resting up.

'I'd better be getting back to Gina,' she said. 'It was nice to meet you, Sue, and you too Scampi,' she said patting the dog's head. For a dog without teeth Scampi appeared to grin. She wagged her tail.

'She likes to stick her tongue out,' Stella noted.

'Can't help it,' Sue said. 'Got no teeth to keep it behind.'

#

Stella returned to find Grazja sitting with her feet up on the pouffe watching Alan Titchmarsh on TV, while Gina lay on the sofa, grumbling.

'You lazy Polack,' she said. 'You're supposed to be looking after me.'

'I take break, Gina,' Grazja said calmly. 'I work hard most of day and soon I cook meal but first I take break. Am legally entitled to it."

'It's an entitlement culture we live in,' Gina said. 'Entitled to this, entitled to that. Most of you don't know what a day's work really is.'

Grazja ignored her.

'Titchmarsh looks like a gargoyle,' Gina prodded. 'It's that glass eye.'

'Alan is very handsome older man, I think,' Grazja replied. 'He has green hands.'

'Fingers,' Gina crowed. 'Speak bleedin' English.'

She noticed Stella standing in the doorway. 'Oh, look who the cat dragged in. Can you see what you're paying for?' Gina said, pointing at Grazja.

The lounge had been hoovered, every surface sparkled, and Gina had a plate of Hobnobs and a mug of tea to hand. On the way through the hall Stella had popped her head into the spare bedroom. The awful smell of Henry's faeces had gone, the window was open to air the room, and the bedding had been changed.

Stella thought Grazja was amazing.

'It looks great in here,' she said.

'Thank you,' Grazja said. She peered at Stella. 'You

look tired and should be resting that foot. I put bedding in caravan. I start to cook evening meal in a bit. You lie down – put foot up on pillow – and sleep before we eat.'

She said this is in a way that brooked no argument.

Gina looked outraged. 'You can't tell her what to do.' She turned to Stella. 'I ain't seen you all day. And where's Bing? I'm goin' outta my mind wi' worry about 'im.'

'Er, he's around,' Stella said. 'He, erm, got some food at Rick's diner.'

Gina's eyebrows shot up. 'Why didn't Rick bring him home?'

'He didn't actually see him,' Stella said. She hesitated and then decided to tell them about the sausage theft.

Gina cried with laughter. 'Oh that's my Bing,' she said. 'That's my little scallywag. Bless 'im. He'll be home when he's had his fun. Oh God, laughing hurts me ribs.'

Stella Makes a Deal

Stella was up at six the next morning. She limped from the caravan to the kitchen. She'd just fitted her key to the lock when Grazja opened the door from within.

'Good morning,' she said. 'You early riser like me?'

Stella nodded. 'I'm going over to Rick's for breakfast. He's looking after my cat, Henry.'

'The cat that pooped in bedroom?'

'Yes,' Stella said. 'Sorry about that again. Bing scared him so he hid under the bed.'

'Why you bring cat?' Grazja asked. 'Cats and dogs no like each other.'

Stella explained. 'I didn't have time to get anyone to feed him while I was away. I got the call about Gina in the middle of the night.'

'You know Rick already?' Grazja asked.

It was six in the morning, a time when Stella was usually drifting around in semi-wakefulness, alone in her loft, not being bombarded by questions.

'He seems nice enough,' she said vaguely.

'No, I mean you already know him from times you come see Gina?' Grazja said.

Stella squirmed. 'Er, this is the first time I've seen Gina in a while,' she said. 'Since she moved to Mapton.'

Grazja scrutinised her. 'Hmm,' was all she offered. Then: 'You want coffee and toast?'

Stella shook her head. 'No thanks,' she said. 'I'll eat at Rick's. I just want to grab a shower and get going.'

Grazja glanced down at her bandaged ankle. 'I redo bandage for you after shower.'

Stella had forgotten about getting the bandage wet. 'It's okay,' she said. 'I can manage.'

'No,' Grazja said. 'I nurse. No problem for me. Won't take minute.'

Stella took her shower after peeking in on Gina who was, thankfully, still asleep, her leg elevated on two pillows. She snored softly.

Grazja expertly unwound the wet bandage and inspected Stella's ankle. She swore softly in Polish when she saw the puncture wounds and the bruising, wiped the skin dry, applied some antiseptic salve, and neatly re-bandaged her leg.

Stella thanked her profusely but Grazja waved her away. 'My job,' she said.

'It's your job to look after Gina,' Stella said. 'Not me as well.''

'You both need looking after,' Grazja replied. 'Besides, I charge you double.'

She said this so matter of factly that Stella believed her and gulped.

'Ha!' Grazja barked. 'Your face. Only joke.' She laughed. It was the first time Stella had seen her laugh. 'Go away now before monster wakes up.'

This time Stella laughed. 'I won't be too long,' she said.

'Good,' Grazja said. 'I need to go out for few things – food and stuff. You need to be with Gina when I'm out. She get lonely otherwise.'

'Okay,' Stella said. 'I'll be back before nine.'

The morning was beautiful, the sky cloudless. Even the artificial faun in next door's garden sparkled. Stella stripped the cover off the scooter and climbed on. She glanced over at George's house, half-expecting him to pop up from behind his azaleas, but the curtains remained closed in his bungalow.

She re-traced the route she'd taken two nights ago, taking a wrong turning once, but finding her way quickly enough until she saw his castle looming among other perfectly normal houses. Well, she amended, normal by Mapton standards. The house next door to Rick's seemed to be under attack from two giant butterflies clinging to the pebbledash.

Rick had left the iron gates open for her and she parked on the gravel path leading up to his arched oak door.

Rick opened the door, dressed in his usual jeans and T-shirt, head damp from his morning shower. He smelled good.

'Hey,' he said. 'Come in. Coffee's on and Henry's just had his Whiskas.'

Henry performed the standard snubbed cat reaction by pointedly ignoring her. Having just eaten he had some serious grooming to do; he turned his back on her to do it.

'He's embarrassed you've caught him before he's combed his hair,' Rick said. 'Let's leave him to it while I cook breakfast. We'll bring our coffee back in when he's ready.'

She hopped after him into the kitchen and perched on a stool at the breakfast bar while he cooked.

'You like pancakes?' he asked. 'I mean American ones, not those Shrove Tuesday crepes you English like to toss about.'

'With syrup?' Stella said.

'You bet. Blueberries and strawberries, syrup and crème freche.'

'No bacon?' Stella teased.

'Can't do it,' Rick said. He looked almost pained. 'Not with soggy English bacon. It's fine in a bacon butty but no good with pancakes. American bacon is crispier – thinner. In fact it's a different cut – belly mostly, not loin.'

'Wow,' Stella said. 'You know your bacon.'

Rick smiled. He began to pull ingredients from cupboards and an enormous fridge-freezer.

'For a man who lives on his own that's a big fridge,' Stella commented.

Rick shrugged. 'I'm American,' he said. 'It's in my nature.'

He deftly threw together his ingredients into a glass jug that slotted into a state of the art mixer - a glossy red KitchenAid that Stella had often slavered over in John Lewis but never bought, deciding her lack of culinary skills did not warrant that kind of spending. She made do with her perfectly functional Kenwood basic model. All she ever used it for was blending soups and chopping nuts and seeds to make a mix for her morning porridge.

'So,' Stella said. 'I've been meaning to ask – are you on the run from the law?'

'Eh?' Rick said bemused. 'Do I look like a criminal type?'

Stella shook her curls. 'No,' she smiled. 'But I can't see any other reason for a nice American like you ending up in a town like this. Mapton's the last place they'd look for you, right?'

Rick laughed. He heated up a skillet. 'It has a kind of edge of the world feel to it, I guess.'

'It has its own time-zone,' Stella said. 'Not just an

hour's lag but whole decades.'

'Three to be exact,' Rick said. 'It's still the eighties here.'

'Yes!' Stella exclaimed. 'Why d'you do that?'

'Do what?' Rick said, dropping batter onto the skillet.

'Only play eighties music in the diner?'

Rick gave her an amused look. 'It's the local radio station,' he said. 'To be fair they sometimes venture into the nineties.'

'But why?' Stella asked.

Rick shrugged, flipping a pancake. The aroma was making Stella's stomach growl.

'It must be something to do with all the wind turbines around here,' Rick said. 'They're, like, driving the airwaves backwards so we can only pick up radio from the past.'

Stella laughed. 'Of course,' she said. 'I'm too creative to think scientifically. I wouldn't have thought of that.'

'Yep,' Rick nodded emphatically. 'Plus, you're a woman. Guys, we know our science-shit.'

'Right,' Stella agreed. 'All I ever think about is handbags, kittens, and butterflies.'

'Well don't worry, babe,' Rick said, swaggering over with a plate of pancakes. 'You got me to explain the hard stuff.'

'Thank you,' Stella piped breathlessly. 'It's been such a struggle till now.'

Rick snorted. He laid out the fruit, crème freche, and maple syrup, handing her a plate. 'Dig in,' he said.

Stella did. The pancakes were perfect. Light, fluffy

stacks of heaven with a hint of vanilla.

'These are amazing,' she said.

Rick smiled. 'My mom's recipe,' he said.

'Did she teach you to cook?' Stella asked.

'She's the reason I got started.'

'When I was a child I used to cook with Gina,' Stella said, her eyes taking on a far-away look. 'Well, I'm not sure it was real cooking as most of it came out of packets but I used to like it.'

'What did you make?' Rick prompted.

Stella glanced at him. 'Bird's trifle.' She sniggered, as though trying to dismiss the subject.

'Trifle's good,' Rick encouraged her. 'What else?'

Stella darted him another quick glance like a nervous finch checking it was safe to feed. 'Well, there was one thing – just egg mayo really, but we used to call it Eggs Yolka Polka and it became a sort of ritual.' She smiled shyly.

'Tell me,' Rick said warmly, leaning his elbows on the breakfast bar.

So Stella described the ritual – Mrs Clucky the egg timer, watching the Saturday matinee, the song, the dance – the whole rigmarole.

Rick laughed out loud at the image of them mashing and dancing.

'That's great,' Rick said. 'I always knew Gina couldn't be all bad.'

Stella's smile disappeared. 'She can,' she said. 'I didn't know it back then. It was only later after my parents died...' She stopped. Shook her head as though clearing it.

'Anyway,' she said, forcing a smile. 'You still haven't told me how you ended up in Mapton.'

Rick shifted, standing to clear the dishes. 'It's a long story,' he said. 'One I'm not quite ready to share.'

'Oh c'mon,' Stella protested. 'After I just told you about Eggs Yolka Polka?'

'Tell you what crab lady,' Rick said. 'If you're still in Mapton by Sunday I'll tell you my story.'

'But that's.'

'Five days away,' Rick finished for her. 'And based on your luck so far I'm not convinced you'll last.'

Stella was outraged. 'You think I'm a quitter?'

Rick smiled wryly. 'You never wanted to be here. Two days ago you were looking for an out. Now you've got a carer for Gina. Sure, you can't drive home, but I'll bet there'd be someone willing to fetch you if you hollered loud enough. Boyfriend?' He asked this casually.

'No.'

'Friends then. A best friend right?'

Stella nodded. 'Yes.'

'Okay, so I know you say you want to stay for Gina, but let's face it, so far you've been bitten by her dog, endured her special kind of orneriness, had to lend your cat out, and ended up riding a mobility scooter in a town you think is the butt-hole of nowhere...' He held up his hand to fend off her protest. 'Which, I admit Mapton kind of is - which makes me crazy cos I've chosen to live in a butt-hole and I like it – but the point is you've got five days till Sunday to put up with Gina and Mapton, not just one without the other, but both. You're a cosmopolitan, creative, artistic woman from the city. Two days from now you're going be begging that best friend of yours to come get you and Henry.'

Stella opened her mouth to speak. Closed it. Glared at Rick. 'Okay,' she finally said. 'I think I can make it till then but what if I leave on Sunday? Do I still get to hear your story?'

Rick considered it. 'Nope,' he decided. 'Because if you last the next five days then on Sunday I'm gonna cook you dinner and it will be the best meal you've ever tasted in your life.'

'That's a bold claim,' Stella said.

'Yes ma'am,' Rick nodded.

'And you'll tell me your story?' Stella confirmed.

'Yes, I will.'

'Well then,' Stella said, extending her hand. 'It's a deal.'

They shook on it.

'Five days with Gina,' Rick whistled low.

'It'd better be the best meal ever,' Stella said.

'I guarantee it,' Rick said. 'Let's see if Henry's still ignoring you.' He refilled their coffee mugs and carried them through to the garden room. Stella hobbled after him. Her stomach fluttered. Had she just agreed to a date next Sunday? If so it was the first date she'd said yes to in a very, very long time.

The Kyle Connection

'It's begun,' Grazja said, as Stella entered the house.

'What has?' Stella asked.

'Gina's resistance,' Grazja replied. 'She wet bed on purpose this morning.'

'Oh no,' Stella groaned. 'Are you sure? Perhaps she just got desperate and couldn't help it.'

'She help it,' Grazja said. 'She did it when I was helping her up. She testing me is all. I expect something.'

'I can hear you, you know,' Gina shouted from the lounge.

Stella ignored her. 'What did you do?' she asked Grazja.

Grazja shrugged. 'I cleaned up. Mattress is drying, bedclothes are in wash. I go out, see if I can buy plastic mattress sheet. You make list with me?'

Stella nodded. She followed her through into the lounge where Gina was lying on the sofa.

'Where the bloody hell have you been?' she snapped at Stella.

Stella instantly reacted like a sulky teenager. 'Nowhere,' she said. 'Just out.'

'Out where?' Gina demanded.

'Just around,' Stella said. 'Getting some air.'

Gina snorted. 'Ha! I bet you went to see your new boyfriend,' she jeered. 'Have you been out all night, you little Jezebel?'

Stella rolled her eyes. 'I slept in the caravan,' she said. 'Remember?'

'So you say,' Gina said. 'You should be in the house with me. What's the point of you being here otherwise?'

'What is the point?' Stella said. 'I can go home if you'd prefer?''

'Oh, you'd like that, wouldn't you?' Gina hissed. 'Leave me in the hands of this thieving Polack. She could murder me and you wouldn't care.'

'I wish she would,' Stella spat.

'Enough!' Grazja's voice whiplashed through their spat. 'You bad as each other. Behave.'

Stella felt immediately ashamed. 'Sorry,' she whispered.

Gina was petulant. 'It's family business,' she grumbled. 'None of yours.'

'Whatever,' Grazja said, palm held out. 'Stella, you come into kitchen with me and make list of food we need. I go shop. You keep grandmother company.'

Stella obeyed.

'Don't give her any money,' Gina called after them. 'She'll run off with it.'

Grazja gave her a cold stare. 'Agency pay me for things I buy for clients. I keep receipts. They charge you at end. I no need money from Stella or you.'

'We won't pay the agency,' Gina said.

'That their problem, not mine,' Grazja said. 'They take you to court, not me.'

She firmly closed the kitchen door behind her.

'Right,' she said to Stella. 'Let's see what we need for next few days.'

Stella helped her check the fridge and cupboards and told her what Gina liked to eat. Grazja tutted. 'She recover quicker if she eats healthy.'

Stella smiled. She was still feeling sheepish over her childish reaction to Gina. 'She won't eat it,' she said. 'I know Gina. She'll just spit it out.'

Grazja nodded thoughtfully. 'I surprised at you,' she said quietly. 'You should be more respectful to Gina.'

Stella spluttered. 'But she…'

'Yes, yes. She no nice but she is your grandmother and she is lonely.'

'Why does everyone keep saying that?' Stella threw up her hands. 'She's lonely because she's horrible to everyone.'

'True,' Grazja said. 'This make me sad for her.'

'Sad? Why?'

'She is like person with skin condition. It itch so she scratch but that make it itch worse, so she scratch more. She could cool skin off with balm but she keep scratching. Eventually skin is so sore she can't bear anything or anyone to touch it and she is alone.'

Stella looked at her. 'I'm not sure that makes sense.'

'It does,' Grazja said. 'You just don't want to see it.'

'Er, okay,' Stella said.

'Anyway,' Grazja continued. 'You be good girl to your grandmother while I'm out, yes?'

'Yes,' Stella sighed. 'All right.'

'Good girl,' Grazja beamed. 'You like chocolate. Yes? I bring you some as reward.'

Stella smiled feebly. Between her inability to exercise, Rick's pancakes, and Grazja's bribe she thought she'd soon be able to add weight-gain to her list of woes.

Grazja wisely left by the back door, factoring out having to go another round with Gina, leaving Stella to face the dragon alone.

'Five days,' she muttered to herself. 'For the best meal of my life.'

Gina was flicking through the channels. She settled for Jeremy Kyle. Today's show was titled 'My Best Friend Stole my Boyfriend.''

'How's the pain today?' Stella asked, settling into an armchair.

Gina pulled her face. 'Surprised you care,' she said, keeping her eyes on the screen.

Stella tried another tack. 'I think my ankle's a bit better,' she said. 'Maybe the ligaments aren't torn.'

'Course they're not,' Gina sneered. 'Bing would've only gi'en you a nip. You're just pretending so you could get that bitch in to do yer work.'

Stella sighed. She picked up TV Week and flicked through it but soon the girls yelling at each other on screen distracted her. One lunged at the other, grabbing her extensions.

Gina hooted. 'Look at em go,' she said. 'Gals nowadays don't know how to behave like ladies.'

That's rich, coming from you, Stella thought but she was gripped. She'd never seen the Jeremy Kyle show before. She knew about it but never watched daytime TV. It was horrifying yet utterly compelling.

The audience hooted and shouted out; Gina hooted along with them. Two burly men in black tee shirts broke the girls apart. Kyle went up to each of them and stuck his face aggressively into theirs.

'Go on Jeremy,' Gina shouted. 'You tell em.'

One of the girls burst into tears and ran off the set. Kyle and the cameras followed her into the corridor backstage.

'He tells it like it is,' Gina says. 'Like me.'

Kyle was being pretty brutal.

Stella looked over at Gina. 'Maybe that's why you don't have friends,' she said.

'That's nice,' Gina said, looking hurt.

'Just telling it like it is,' Stella said.

Gina shot her a dirty look. 'Besides, I do have friends. I go to bingo and karaoke and the like.'

'Who with?' Stella pushed, unable to stop herself.

'I see people there,' Gina said. 'Like George and such.'

'You don't like George,' Stella said.

'He's alright,' Gina said. 'But he's a man. They all want the same thing.'

'Intercourse,' Stella nodded. 'I know. But what about female friends?'

'Women are catty,' Gina said. 'They can't be trusted. They can turn on yer very quick.'

'Not all of them,' Stella said. 'Haven't you ever had a best friend?'

Gina considered this. Her expression was unreadable. Finally she said quietly: 'Maggie Bone. We were thick as thieves since we were ten, even left school at the same time and got a job in the lace market together. Did each other's makeup, shared clothes, everything.'

'What happened to her?' Stella asked. 'You've never mentioned her before.'

Gina's eyes hardened. 'She betrayed me. She stole my fiancé.' She looked at Stella triumphantly. 'That's what friends do.'

'Oh,' Stella gasped. 'I didn't know. I'm sorry, Gina.'

'You don't know the half of it, missy,' Gina said.

'Yer think you do but you don't.'

'Tell me then,' Stella said, leaning towards her. 'I'd like to hear.''

Gina appeared taken aback. 'Not now,' she said. 'I'm tired. I need a nap.' She nestled back against the cushions and closed her eyes.

Stella waited but Gina kept her eyes resolutely shut. Stella was sure she was awake. The Jeremy Kyle show still blared on the TV. Stella couldn't take any more of it and switched it off. Sighing, she flicked through TV Week but her thoughts kept returning to Maggie. Could this woman be the key to understanding Gina? The reason why Gina was so angry at the world? Had she been betrayed by the two people she trusted most?

The idea excited Stella. It had never occurred to her that there might be a cause for Gina's dysfunctional behaviour. If there was a cause was there also a cure?

#

Grazja returned laden with bags. She was flushed with pleasure.

'This place bargain centre of world,' she said. 'It's got two indoor boot markets and many shops.'

'Boot markets?' Stella queried. 'You got some boots?'

'No,' Grazja said. 'It got stalls – you know – how do I say? Second hand?'

'She means like a carboot sale,' Gina said. 'Learn some bloody English!'

'Oh, you mean vintage,' Stella said.

Gina guffawed. 'I keep hearing that on the telly,' she said. 'It's a fancy southern word for second hand tat that should go in the bin. Anyway, Miz Polack here's wrong. There's only one indoor flea market in Mapton – the other one's all brand new stuff. Good stuff too.'

'Yes, very good, very cheap,' Grazja said, ignoring Gina's insults. 'I got us treat for tonight, Gina.' She pulled out a DVD. 'Meet in St Louis'. I see Judy Garland picture in bedroom. You no got this DVD,' she said, pointing to the glass cabinet where Gina's old films lined one shelf.

'You nosey cow,' Gina said. 'Looking through all my stuff. Besides 'Meet me in St Louis' is a Christmas film. I won't watch it in summer.'

'Never mind,' Grazja said. 'Stella and me watch it without you then.'

'Not in bloody here, you won't.'

Grazja shrugged, her happy glow undimmed. 'We see,' she said. 'Stella, you help me unpack?'

After lunch Grazja insisted that Gina needed some air. Gina initially resisted but it was merely from habit and her perverse need to resist. Stella could tell that she was eager to get out of the house after being cooped up for almost three days. She allowed Grazja to tuck a blanket around her (although the June weather had warmed up) and wheel her out for a trip along the seafront.

Stella gave a deep sigh of relief when they'd gone. She needed a nap – her ankle was aching – but she was loath to waste this quiet time alone. Instead she retrieved the beach crab from the fridge, now housed in an airtight container away from any food on the insistence of Grazja who had tried to throw it out, and took it out to the caravan. She arranged the delicate crustacean on a piece of tissue paper, took up her drawing pad and watercolour pencils, and began to draw. Soon she was in flow; there was nothing in her mind beyond the crab and the need to capture it on paper. Gina, Grazja, Mapton, Rick, her commitments at home – all these faded into nothing as she strove to capture the subtle colour changes and markings on the carapace, the precise segments of legs and claws, the exact position and shape of the eye-stalks.

For the first time since the phone had rung in the early hours of Monday morning Stella was completely at ease.

It didn't last.

It took her a moment to register the knocking on the caravan door.

'Who is it?' she called.

'Grazja.' The carer opened the door and popped her head in. 'May I come in?'

'Of course.'

Grazja closed the door behind her. 'There trouble,' she said. 'Gina assaulted dog catcher.'

Stella stared at her blankly. 'What?'

'It's true,' Grazja said, as though Stella didn't believe her. 'She saw dog catcher try to catch Bing Crosby and she threw handbag at him. Hit him in eye. Cut his face with...' She mimed opening a clutch bag.

'The clasp?' Stella suggested. 'She cut his face with the clasp?' She said this slowly, trying to digest it. Then repeated. 'She cut his face with the clasp when she threw her bag at him?'

'Yes,' Grazja said. 'The dog catcher.'

Stella was speechless. Finally she asked. 'Where is she?'

'Gina in house,' Grazja said. 'With police. They talk

to her. They not arrest her yet.'

'Is the dog-catcher pressing charges?' Stella asked, suddenly taking it all in.

Grazja grimaced. 'I not know meaning of 'pressing charges'.

Stella spoke loudly and slowly. 'Is the dog catcher going to take Gina to court for assaulting him?'

Grazja grinned, mimicking her tone and volume. 'I do not know,' she said. 'He seem very upset.'

Stella missed the joke. She was too absorbed by this new catastrophe. 'Just when I thought things were settling down,' she sighed. 'This is typical Gina.'

Grazja laughed. 'Yes,' she agreed. 'But it was very funny.'

Stella glared at her. 'It's not funny,' she said. 'This is serious.'

'Yes,' Grazja agreed. 'But you not there. It was very, very funny. How you say – farce?' She began to laugh in earnest, tears springing into her eyes. 'Sorry,' she gasped. 'You better go in house. I stay here and calm myself.'

Stella clomped out, slamming the door behind her. She could still hear Grazja chortling as she reached the back door.

She heard a weary male voice say. 'Please be reasonable, Mrs Pontin.' And Gina's indignant: 'I'm being bloody reasonable. Why don't you arrest the man who was trying to steal my dog?'

A woman's voice chipped in. 'We've been through this, Mrs Pontin. Mr Joules is our local animal warden. He'd had a report that your dog ran away and has been stealing food from local businesses. He was just doing his job, Mrs Pontin. He wasn't going to hurt Bing.'

'They put them down, though, don't they?' Gina cried. 'It's murder.'

'Only dangerous dogs get put down, Mrs Pontin,' the young woman replied. 'Is Bing dangerous?'

'No!' Gina said.

The man spoke. 'Only we heard that he bit your granddaughter? Is that right?'

It was at this unfortunate point that Stella limped into the lounge.

Gina rounded on her. 'I can't believe you told,' she spat. 'My own granddaughter a fink.'

'I didn't,' Stella protested. 'Don't blame me.'

The female officer, blonde and petite, introduced herself and her lanky red-haired partner as PC Dougherty and PC Johnston respectively. They both looked at her ankle.

'Is that the result of a bite?' PC Johnston asked.

'It was just a nip,' Stella laughed nervously. 'I brought my cat with me and Bing was upset. That's all.'

'That's serious bandaging for a nip,' PC Dougherty noted. 'You obviously can't walk on it.'

'Just some swelling,' Stella said. 'I'll be fine in a couple of days.'

The officers exchanged glances. They seemed to reach some sort of silent agreement as both rose. 'We'll be in touch if Mr Joules decides to press charges,' PC Dougherty said. 'And we'll let you know when Bing is caught. Whatever happens we'll be in contact.'

'We'll let ourselves out,' PC Johnston said.

Gina managed to wait until they'd got out of the

door. Then she exploded.

The Call of the Wild

Paul Ferguson first noticed his miniature Collie, Tammy, was missing at seven pm on Wednesday evening. He and his wife, Pam, sometimes regretted choosing that particular breed. They'd wanted a small dog that wouldn't need much walking, and Tammy had been so cute as a puppy - a tiny Lassie. She was still quite cute but she craved exercise the way Pam craved Mars Bars, and she was a small bundle of inexhaustible energy. Paul and Pam enjoyed ambling along the promenade on a fine evening - it wasn't that they didn't do any exercise - and Paul had tried taking Tammy along to the pub and the bookie's - both a stroll away - but this had revealed another unexpected downside to the breed. Miniature Collies or Shetland Sheepdogs to give them their correct title, (something Paul had only recently discovered) were often shy of new people.

Tammy, being a pretty dog, drew attention but she hated it. She squirmed away from probing hands, cringing whenever some child or well-intentioned stranger tried to stroke her. Occasionally she growled, wrinkling her nose to expose her wicked canines, causing hands to be snapped back sharpish. Luckily she never nipped and she was lovely at home, snuggled between them on the sofa, tail on one lap and head on the other.

But she needed to run, so Paul left her in the garden most days, where she careered around at intervals, circling, slinking on her belly, shooting back and forth, collapsing to pant for a few minutes before resuming. It was only when Paul decided to research her breed that he realised that her behaviour wasn't mad but genetic; she was rounding up imaginary sheep.

It was ironic, then, that on the day Tammy ran away, Paul had come to a decision. He was fast sliding into slothful middle age, his belly, which had been creeping over the waistband of his jeans for some years now, was beginning to block the view to his feet. Pam had joined a slimming club in January (although she'd somehow worked Mars Bars into her daily calorie allowance) and Paul had caught Freddie Wilkins trying to give her the eye at the club on Saturday night. It was time he took control but he'd be buggered if he'd join a gym. The answer, clearly, was tearing around his garden. He would start taking Tammy for long, brisk walks, maybe even work up to running with her. So, on Wednesday evening he went into the back garden, jingling her lead, only to be met with silence and a freshly dug hole under the six-foot fence.

Paul stared at the tunnel, puzzled. In the four years they'd owned Tammy she'd never before shown an inclination for digging. It was one of the reasons he hadn't wanted a terrier. Jack Russells, especially, were renowned for it.

#

Denise Robertson had a particularly ditsy Dalmatian named Prince. Prince was a beautiful dog and a friendly one. He adored anyone who adored him and Denise loved to show him off, parading him along Mapton's streets in her matching black and white outfits. Locals called her Cruella de Vil, although this wasn't a fair comparison. Denise never had the urge to wear Prince, merely to coordinate with him. Nor was he an accessory; it was more the opposite way round - Denise accessorised herself to match him.

So Prince lived up to his name. Worshipped by his owner and admired by all, he also shared one other trait common to royalty - enforced limitation in the pure-breed gene pool. Prince was deaf in one ear and remarkably stupid. It is a common belief that most Dalmatians are stupid and many are deaf. It is true of the latter but not so true of the former (although Dalmatian brains are under-developed in comparison to many other breeds). Prince, however, was just plain stupid, whether or not it was down to breeding or simply genetic chance.

For example, Denise could never let him off the lead. Not because he was unruly or attacked other dogs but because he wandered off. For a dog he had an astonishing lack of homing instinct or direction. Also he couldn't recognise his own name or register a familiar voice, including Denise's. This may have been partially due to his poor hearing but even on his right side he wouldn't respond to his name. His wandering off was lackadaisical, indicating no genuine inclination to explore, but once he was off then calling him back was impossible and if he was chased he would run just out of instinct.

For this reason Denise always kept him on the leash when they were out and about and made sure to properly latch the front gate when they were at home. In hot weather Prince liked to lie on the lawn and watch passers-by, hoping they'd stop to fuss him through the gate bars. They often did.

He was soaking up the early sun on Thursday

morning when three dogs approached the gate. It was clear who the leader was - the Jack Russell in front was small but smelled like power. He was flanked by a large mongrel who smelled friendly and a female miniature Collie who smelled nervous. The leader turned slightly, showing Prince his left side. His followers mimicked him. Prince rose and did the same, copying their actions instinctively. They were showing him they weren't aggressive - at least not right now. That done, it was time for some mutual anus sniffing with the leader. Prince was excited. This dog exuded alpha hormones. He shuffled on his belly, flipping over to show willing submission, wagging his tail in delight.

Then the mongrel did an astonishing thing. He rose on his hind legs against the metal gate, firkled around with his paw and lifted the latch.

It was a move he'd perfected over three months of living feral, gaining access to gardens and bins all over Mapton.

Prince was free. Without a single vague thought of Denise he wandered out, yet for the first time he had an aim. That was to follow this charismatic leader and join a pack.

At first he tried to jostle into the female's position but she snipped and snarled, so he fell back, placidly following. After a while she lifted her tail so he could sniff her delicious nether regions.

Prince was a happy dog. He had found his place.

#

Bing Crosby was in his element. Freedom suited him.

He'd had a confusing moment the previous day when he'd smelt his old mistress and lost his head.

Dozing in the crawl space beneath a beach hut with his beta, Mitch, a familiar scent had crept into his sensitive nostrils. Immediately he'd been overwhelmed with an uncontrollable yearning and sprang forward. Mitch had dared nip his heel to remind him to stay hidden - a routine they'd begun to develop during the bustling daytime hours - but the impulse to see Gina was too strong and Bing had emerged blinking into the afternoon sun. Then he saw her. She was being pushed along the promenade in a wheeled chair by a stranger.

Bing yipped excitedly and started forward but before he could reach her a loop descended over his snout. Bing jerked back, the loop snagging his nose before he pulled free. Snarling, he danced aside, turning to face his attacker. A man dressed in khaki loomed a few feet away, wielding a long stick with the loop on the end. He made the usual stupid reassuring noises humans make when they're trying to catch dogs and moved slowly towards Bing. Bing growled, hackles rising.

Mitch wriggled his bigger body out from under the hut and joined Bing, snarling too.

Other humans were beginning to gather, voices shrill and painful in Bing's ears, panicking him further. Then he heard her voice - Gina! She was calling him. For a second he took his eyes off the man, seeking her, and that's when the loop came down again, this time slipping over his entire head down to his neck. Instinctively Bing pulled back. The noose began to tighten, the stick going taut as the man held tight to it. And then the tension collapsed suddenly. The man went down, clutching his face. Bing managed to yank his head free of the noose. The air was exploding with sound; human panic and Mitch barking. Through it all, Bing could still hear Gina. Desperately he shot round looking for her. He spotted her gesticulating wildly at him, flapping her hands away from her chest. He heard her words. 'Run, Bing, run.' He understood, not from the words themselves but from her tone. He had permission. He ran and Mitch ran with him.

In his vague doggy way Bing felt that Gina had given him her blessing to live free.

That night he and Mitch had gone out with a purpose beyond just scavenging for food. They'd gone out to find their pack. Tammy had smelled desperate and unhappy. It wasn't hard to persuade her to join them and it was very exciting to find a bitch. The next morning Prince was as easy to pick up as a burr sticking to fur. He was submissive, eager, and stupidly enthusiastic.

Mitch knew all the best places for easy scavenging but Bing had bigger plans. His first adventure with the stolen sausages had given him a taste for the fine life. And a taste for crime.

Invitation to Rumble

Stella was back at the Mapton Medical Centre to see the consultant. Dr Graves popped her head into the waiting room. 'Come and see me afterwards,' she said. 'I'm not actually in surgery today. I've just come in to catch up on some paperwork.'

The consultant, Dr Youseff, peered at the X-rays and prodded Stella's ankle. He appeared disappointed.

'You've been very lucky,' he sighed. 'Very, very lucky.'

He poked the puffy bruised tissue. 'It looks worse than it is,' he said gloomily. 'Without examining the X-rays I would have said this certainly promised tendon, muscle, or nerve damage. Perhaps all three.' He sighed again and turned to the X-rays, picking up a pencil to use as pointer. 'Look here,' he said. 'You see how close it came to the Achilles tendon and here to the Peroneal Retinacula. It's miraculous really.'

Stella thought he might cry.

'You could've had years of corrective surgery ahead of you.' He said it in a way that a game show host might remind a contestant what prize they'd just narrowly lost.

'So I'm fine?' Stella asked.

Dr Youseff nodded. 'Yes. Once the bruising recedes and the puncture wounds heal you will be absolutely fine.' He perked up. 'Unless there is a secondary infection. But I suppose you're on antibiotics, had the tetanus shot, etcetera?'

'Yes,' Stella said.

He deflated again. 'You're fortunate not to have

rabies in this country,' he said, as though this was another disappointment. 'Well then, you're free to go. You should be off your crutches by Saturday. You've been very, very lucky indeed.'

Stella escaped, feeling oddly as though she'd let him down.

Dr Graves waved her into her office. A travel kettle boiled in the corner. 'Tea?' Dr Graves offered.

Stella accepted.

Dr Graves made it to Stella's specifications and handed her a mug with the words 'PROZAC: Fluoxetine Hydrochloride' emblazoned across it, the 'o' in Prozac was represented by a cartoon sun.

'What did Dr Youseff have to say?' Dr Graves asked.

Stella told her the good news.

Dr Graves smiled. 'That's great,' she said. 'Now, how's it going with Gina?'

Stella struggled to find a place to start. 'Up and down,' she finally said.

'How's the carer working out? Did they send Grazja?'

Stella sat up. 'Yes, Grazja. She's brilliant. She doesn't let Gina get to her at all and she works so hard.'

Stella relayed the events of the last couple of days to Dr Graves, including yesterday's new Bing drama. 'Grazja was fantastic last night. She even managed to get Gina watching 'Meet Me in St Louis' to calm her down. She doesn't react to Gina the way I do.'

'She hasn't got an emotional link with Gina,' Dr Graves said. 'It's easier for her to deal with. Besides, Grazja's dealt with much worse situations.'

'You know Grazja?' Stella asked.

Dr Graves shrugged, shifting slightly in her chair. 'The agency has sent her a couple of times. She's good at keeping her head with difficult patients.'

'That she is,' Stella said. 'I can only thank you for finding her. She was a trained nurse back home, you know?'

Dr Graves nodded. 'Yes.'

Stella considered. 'I wonder why she isn't a nurse here.'

Dr Graves. 'She probably qualified before 2004 when the EU rules changed. Post- 2004 qualified EU nurses can work here, although only if they're registered.'

'That's a shame,' Stella said. 'I wonder why she came to Britain?'

Dr Graves shrugged. 'Perhaps she's able to earn more here as a carer than as a nurse back home.' She changed the subject. 'So, if Dr Youssef's right you should be back on your feet in a day or two. You won't need the Mapton Mercedes.'

'Mapton Mercedes?' Stella said.

'You haven't heard that?' Dr Graves laughed again. 'That's what the locals call mobility scooters. There's so many around here.'

'Mapton Mercedes, 'Stella repeated. 'I like that.'

#

Giddy with the knowledge that Bing's bite hadn't inflicted permanent damage, Stella hopped on her Mapton Mercedes and headed to Rick's diner.

Rick wasn't there. Angela greeted her curtly. 'He's gone to the cash and carry near Lawton,' she said. 'He won't be back for another hour or so.' She started to turn away.

'I'll have a coffee please,' Stella said.

Angela turned back. 'To take away,' she said, as though she was suggesting it not asking.

'Um, no,' Stella said, a little taken aback. 'I'll drink it at an outside table. I'll have a date and walnut cookie too, please' she added, nodding to the glass jars of cookies on the counter. She just managed to stop herself saying 'If that's okay?'

Angela gave a tight smile. She rang up the amount on the till, wordlessly taking Stella's note, and giving change. 'I'll bring it out in a minute,' she said.

A teenage boy appeared from the kitchen. 'Mum, I'm sure I've just seen Mrs Robertson's Dalmatian trying to get in the bin. I went out and called him but he ran off.'

Angela frowned. 'Prince? Oh, he's a stupid dog. He must've wandered off again. I'll call Denise.' She pulled a mobile from her pocket.

Stella went outside, choosing a chair facing the sea. There was still a chill breeze but the sun was burning off the cloud, promising a fine day. The temperature was already rising.

Stella pondered why someone like Angela would work in a cafe. She clearly didn't like people. But then that was the British way - how many restaurants, shops, and hotels had Stella experienced where the staff treated the customer as a pesky nuisance rather than a valued source of income? Too many. And yet she still felt like she was the one who ought to apologise.

Gina had never put up with nonsense like that. She went the other way, being outrageously rude and demanding. If she caught a hint of condescension or disregard she puffed up like a defensive toad.

Once, in Blackpool, a B&B landlady slammed a plate of full English down on the table so hard, the tinned tomatoes slopped over the side. Gina demanded she wipe it up and was handed a serviette to do it herself, so Gina knocked the entire plate on the floor.

But the best time by far was on a day trip to London they took when Stella was fifteen. Gina booked them on a Skills coach trip which included entrance to Madame Tussuad's 'to see the stars'. Apart from the staggering queue-time to get into the wax museum, Madame Tussuad's went smoothly enough. It was their trip to Harrods that ended in farce.

It started when they needed to find a toilet and Gina asked directions from a sales-assistant in the perfumery hall. The woman cast a contemptuous eye over the two of them, Gina with her blazing hair and vivacious clothes and Stella with her hand-painted Doc Martins, before simply pointing a perfectly manicured finger to a sign by the entrance listing the departments on that floor, along with an icon for toilets. They had already read the sign but it gave no indication of where the toilets actually were, merely that they existed, hence their decision to ask for directions. Before she had even finished her languid pointing, the woman turned away.

Gina swelled. Stella instinctively stepped away from her, expecting an explosion but none came. Gina maintained the swell but said nothing. She seemed frozen in a moment of rare indecision.

Stella wondered if the swankiness - the smell of wealth and privilege so beyond their reach - had cowed Gina. It was one thing to cause a scene in a Blackpool boarding house, quite another to cause one in Harrods.

Gina grabbed her by the wrist and dragged her away, muttering under her breath. They found the toilets, although it took some searching, and relieved themselves. Then Gina went to work. She fished a black bingo marker and two lipsticks out of her bag, one called Scarlett O 'Hara and the other Tangerine Passion. She handed Tangerine Passion to Stella. She scrawled 'snobbish bitch' on the outside of the stall door in huge lettering with the bingo marker. Then she started on the mirrors with Scarlett O 'Hara. 'You bitches in perfume are nothing but trumped up shop-girls' she wrote on a mirror.

The door to the toilets started to open. Gina sprang to it. 'Sorry,' she said to the two women trying to enter. 'Someone's been sick on the floor in here. You should use the ones on the next level.' The women backed away fearfully.

'Give me your book,' Gina demanded of Stella.

'What for?' Stella said.

'Just gi' it to me,' Gina snapped.

Stella rummaged in her bag, pulling out her dog-eared copy of 'One Flew Over the Cuckoo's Nest'. Gina grabbed it and flipped the pages until she figured she had the right thickness to wedge the door shut. She slid it under the door until it jammed.

'Right,' she said, 'Let's show these bleedin' snobs what we can do.'

They went a little crazy. Stella allowed herself to be

swept up. She'd felt the sting of the perfume-seller's condescension, the all too familiar humiliation of being considered inferior. She swiped Gina's marker and tattooed 'Capitalist Pigs' large on another stall door. Gina crowed.

Between them they covered the room in lipstick and marker pen. Finally, sweaty and exhilarated they stopped to admire their work.

Gina was delighted. Stella felt a little sick.

'C'mon,' Gina said. 'We've got one more thing to do before we go.'

They unjammed the door, Stella shoving the tattered book back into her bag, and headed back to the perfumery hall.

'Remember me?' she said to the sales-woman. 'You think you're so much better than me, don't you? Well, you're just a shop-girl, that's all you are. Don't matter what the shop is, job's the same.'

The woman tried to sneer but she looked scared.

Gina wielded a small bottle of perfume. 'Thought you might want to try some of my perfume,' Gina said, stepping forward aggressively. 'It's called Charlie.' She held up the bottle and pressed the nozzle, spraying the woman from head to foot. The sales-woman shrieked like the melting witch from The Wizard of Oz.

Stella spotted a security guard hurrying towards them. 'C'mon.' She tugged on Gina's sleeve. Gina saw him too and they ran. The guard chased them but they burst out of the store and kept on running until they were sure they'd lost him. Then they collapsed into hysterical laughter, hanging onto each other to keep upright.

'You never got your souvenir,' Stella choked out.

'Oh, I got one,' Gina said. She pulled a full tester bottle of Chanel No. 5 out of her bag. 'I swiped it on the way out.'

Almost twenty years later, gazing unseeingly at the ocean, Stella found herself laughing again. It was one of her few happy Gina memories.

A shadow fell over her. Angela had brought the coffee and cookie. 'See something funny?' she asked acidly.

Stella blushed. 'Oh, I was just remembering something,' she explained.

Angela walked away.

Stella watched her go. It was strange to think of Rick employing someone so unfriendly. Then Angela stopped to chat with a man at another table and her whole demeanour changed. Her shoulders relaxed. She laughed. Stella couldn't hear the conversation but the tone was light, bantering. Perhaps Angela was only unfriendly with strangers? Or with women?

Stella took a sip of her coffee. It was excellent as ever. She broke off some cookie and tasted it. Who cared if Angela was frosty? The food and drink were great and Rick would be back soon.

She closed her eyes, enjoying the sensation of the sun on her skin and the sound of the waves hitting the sand. Her whole body felt relaxed and she wondered how long it had been since she felt like this. Even before the fateful phone call she couldn't remember feeling so unfettered.

The harsh honk of a bike horn roused her. Sue had arrived with her flotilla of pensioners.

'Beautiful morning,' she called, drawing up on her

scooter. Scampi yipped, offering Stella her paw. She laughed and took it. Scampi gave her a quick lick on the knuckles, wagged her tail, and commenced an alert watch on the cookie.

'You can't have that, silly,' Sue teased her. 'Not without yer teeth.'

Bing would have lunged for it by now, Stella thought.

'I 'eard about Gina and the dog catcher,' Sue said.

Stella grinned. 'That's Gina,' she said. 'Armed with a handbag and dangerous.'

Sue guffawed. 'Still, I'da been the same if it was Scampi.' She leaned forward conspiratorially. 'I was hoping to see you. I've got a favour to ask. A big one.' She glanced over at her gang of marauders. They'd settled round various tables but Stella saw them all darting looks her way. Blue Rinse gave her a wave.

'Er, what is it?' Stella asked. Frank was peering at her over the rim of a mug. She caught his eyes and he looked away shiftily.

Sue took a deep breath 'Can we borrow your Rascal?'

'Sorry?' Stella said. 'What?'

'Your Rascal Vision. Your mobility scooter,' Sue explained.

'Why?' Stella demanded. She possessively reached out to touch the scooter.

Sue nudged her own scooter closer, placing poor Scampi within tantalising inches of the cookie. Her pink tongue quivered. Sue lowered her voice. 'Tomorrow night's the rumble,' she said. 'First full moon of the month we take on the Siltby Wanderers. Last three months they've thrashed us since Tom

Turner got his Drive Royale 4.'

'What does the rumble involve?' Stella asked, trying not to laugh.

'We race,' Sue said. 'Halfway between Mapton and Siltby along the darkest part of the prom.'

'I thought these things had a set speed limit?' Stella said.

Sue shrugged. 'They do. And we don't allow no souping. We banned George Wentworth for pimping his Prism. Tried to sneak it past us - added batteries to ramp up his voltage.'

'George!' Stella said. 'George doesn't have a scooter. He doesn't need one, does he?'

Sue snorted. 'Oh, he doesn't use it regular but he liked the idea of racing one well enough. He's a speed freak, George. He wontoo, but Siltby sniffed him out. Brought shame down on us. Since then we have two rules: you have to be a genuine scooter pooter and no souping.'

'Well, well, George,' Stella said, shaking her head in disbelief. 'A boy racer. Does Gina ever join in?'

Sue gave her a cynical look. 'Gina don't know about it,' she said. 'Can you imagine the trouble she'd cause?'

Stella could imagine it very well.

'We like a bit of friendly rivalry,' Sue said. 'Gina would make it a war.'

Stella nodded.

'So, what about it?' Sue prompted. 'Can we borrow the Rascal?'

Again Stella felt that surge of possessiveness. 'I can't,' she said. 'It's not mine, it's Gina's.'

Sue looked crestfallen. 'We'd take care of it. She'd

never know.'

Stella shook her head.

Sue's chin sank lower. Then she perked up. 'Well, what about this? We make you an honorary member of the Marauders and you come with us.' She started to get excited. 'You can race the Rascal!'

Her excitement was infectious. Stella almost bit. Then she recovered her senses. 'But I'm not a regular scooter pooter,' she pointed out. 'And I'm only going to be using the scooter for a couple more days.'

'Yeah, but you're a genuine scooter user,' Sue countered. 'You need it. You've been temporarily disabled. And, what more perfect way to celebrate the end of that than with a race. Let's see what the Rascal can really do before you give it up.'

Maybe it was the sea air that made Stella susceptible. Perhaps it was the chance to do something slightly naughty with Gina's property, or maybe the opportunity to see two gangs of pensioners 'rumble' on the promenade under a full moon was too good to pass up.

'Okay.'

'Yes!' Sue punched the air. She gave a thumbs up to the Marauders who cheered.

Rick emerged from the diner, greeting the Marauders as he threaded his way through the tables to Stella. He wore a blue short-sleeved shirt that matched his eyes. It was patterned with faded palm trees. It suited him, Stella thought, suddenly hot and flustered. She noticed the deep hollow at the base of his throat and a tuft of hair peeping over the v made by his collar. She knew how Scampi felt about the cookie and quickly dropped her eyes.

'Look at you,' Sue whistled loudly. 'I like the new look.'

Rick grinned easily. 'You've seen me in a shirt before, Sue.'

'Not in the day I haven't. Only for special dos,' Sue said. 'Have you finally worked up the courage to ask me out, Ricky?'

Everyone laughed. Angela appeared in the doorway of the diner and leaned against the jamb, watching.

'I don't think I'll ever have enough courage for that, Sue,' Rick said.

'Am I too much woman for you?' Sue countered.

Rick shook his head sadly. 'You are Sue, you are.'

Sue threw her head back, guffawing. Tears leaked out of her eyes. Her scooter shook and Scampi shook with it. She finally took her eyes off the cookie, yipping excitedly.

Recovering herself, Sue leaned towards Stella. 'Meet us tomorrow night, here, at ten.'

'Ten! That's very late,' Stella said. She was an early to bed early to rise sort of girl.

'It has to be dark,' Sue said. 'Otherwise the police would break it up.' She manoeuvred her scooter away from the table and gave the honk that signalled the gang to saddle up and ride.

Stella and Rick watched them go.

'So,' Rick said, cocking an eyebrow. 'What was that about?'

He cracked up when Stella told him. 'You've got to be kidding,' he said. 'You. You!'

Stella was almost insulted. 'Yes me,' she said. 'What's so funny about that?'

Rick stopped laughing. 'Think about what you're doing and ask me that again.'

Stella did think about it. 'Oh God,' she groaned, starting to laugh. 'What's happened to me?'

'Mapton,' Rick said. 'Mapton madness. And I guess you've got a bit more of Gina in than you than I thought.'

Stella closed her eyes and groaned again. She opened them to see Rick looking at her mouth. He looked away.

'So,' Stella cleared her dry throat. 'Angela said you wouldn't be back for another hour or more.'

Rick looked surprised. 'Nah. It doesn't take that long,' he said. 'How long have you been here?'

'About twenty minutes,' Stella said.

'Uh.' Rick raised his eyebrows. 'Ang musta got mixed up. I'm lucky I caught you then.'

Stella smiled. 'I was going to wait.' She blushed. 'It's a lovely morning to just take in the view.'

Rick nodded, following her gaze to the sea. 'Sure is.'

'Oh, I brought you something,' Stella said. 'If you like it I can frame it.' She slid the drawing of the crab out of a bag.

'Hey,' Rick said softly, taking the picture and examining it. 'Wow. This is great. Wow!' He looked at her admiringly. 'You're really, really talented.'

'It's how I make my living,' Stella said.

'Yeah, I mean… Oh God, did I sound patronising? 'Talented'. You don't need me to say that. You're a professional.' For the first time since she met him Rick looked flustered.

Stella laughed. 'No, I like hearing it,' she said.

'Artists are very needy. We never get tired of compliments. Would you like it?'

'Yeah!' Rick said. 'But you don't have to get it framed, I can do that.'

'No,' Stella shook her head. 'It's a present to say thank you for looking after Henry. I'll get it framed.' She put her hand out for the picture but Rick held onto it, gazing at the delicate drawing.

'Is this the crab you brought into the diner?'

'Yes,' Stella laughed. 'I knew I had to draw it. That's why I wanted a bag.'

Rick looked at her. Stella felt her head swim. 'I guess you're not such a crazy crab lady after all,' he said, smiling.

'Oh I am,' Stella promised him. 'Really, I am.'

Painting the Past

When Stella got home she found Gina and Grazja bickering through a game of Gin Rummy. Grazja had set up a folding card table at Gina's behest. It was just after twelve o' clock so Stella asked if they'd like her to make some lunch.

'It's my job,' Grazja dismissed her, barely looking up from her cards.

'I'm hungry,' Gina said.

'I make ham sandwiches after I whup your ass,' Grazja said. Her eyes had a manic glaze.

'I'll make them,' Stella said, shuffling into the kitchen on her crutches. She was relieved to see Gina occupied.

'Tomato on mine but no seeds,' Gina shouted.

Stella rolled her eyes. She propped her crutches against the wall and hobbled about the kitchen gathering ingredients. She noted the sliced bread was a half and half white/brown flour mix. Grazja's cunning attempt to trick Gina into healthier eating. It looked white so Grazja knew what she was doing. She spread the bread with Flora, laid on the ham and sliced the tomatoes, careful to scoop all the seed jelly out of Gina's. She shredded an iceberg lettuce, added a scrape of mayo to hers and assembled the final products. Tentatively, she tried her weight on her ankle and was pleased to feel it hold. Placing the plates on a tray she shuffled back into the lounge.

'Drinks?' she asked.

Neither answered for a moment. Gina slammed down her cards and rapped on the table. 'Gin Rummy,' she cried, triumphantly.

Grazja swore in Polish. 'One more,' she said.

'Do either of you want a drink?' Stella repeated.

Gina grinned. 'Tea,' she said.

'Water,' Grazja said, and began to expertly shuffle the cards.

The game was well under way when Stella returned with their drinks. They barely noticed her so she left their lunch on the coffee table and took her own out to the static.

For the first time in days she dug out her smartphone and plugged in the charger. Guiltily she picked up her messages and texts. A call from her agent regarding a new commission; two emails from Proclivity, the prestigious London gallery that sold her work; a couple of newsy chatty ones from friends; Facebook notifications on her artist page and numerous promotions. Most importantly was a volley of texts from her best friend, Lysandra, wanting to know how she was, when she was coming back, did she need any help, and why the hell wasn't she replying to her texts?

Stella winced. She'd texted Lysie early Monday morning to say she was going to pick up Gina and that she'd call and let her know how it went.

Lysie was the only person in Stella's life who knew about her difficult history with Gina. Somehow, Stella had managed to shed all the old friends from her teenage years, discarding them one by one until she had no links to the past. Even Lysie didn't know it all, only the bits and pieces Stella had revealed throughout the years, most deliberate but some unwittingly.

Lysie would be at work so Stella texted her. 'Am

fine. Will call u 2nite. Sorry - things a bit mad here. Tell u l8r. Hope u ok?'

She shot off emails to her agent and Proclivity explaining that she was dealing with a family emergency and that she would be back in touch on Monday.

Hitting send, Stella let out a sigh of relief. She wanted to concentrate on the here and now.

A lot of it was to do with Rick, she knew. He was making her giddy. The prospect of romance floated enticingly like a helium balloon. She could make a leap, grab on and be swept away. She could let it float out of reach. Or, if she was feeling mean and cowardly she could pull out a needle and pop it.

Stella was handy with a needle.

Restless, she realised she wanted to paint. Yesterday she'd drawn delicately with coloured pencils. Today she wanted the thick, sticky explosion of acrylic on canvas.

She eyed Gina's tubes of paint. She could buy more, replace what she took. Surely Gina wouldn't mind. Well, she would because she was Gina, but still… and besides, Gina couldn't get out to the static yet. Stella had plenty of time to replenish her stock.

She looked for a clean canvas and found some wedged into the space between the floor and the workbench shelf. Negative space, Stella smiled to herself, remembering an art teacher at university who was obsessed with the potential of the space between things.

Carefully, she removed Gina's chrysanthemum painting, propping it against a wall, blank side out and fixed her larger canvas into place. Her fingers itched to start. She gathered tubes, brushes, a palette and palette knife, and placed them carefully on the workbench. Next she filled a jam jar with water.

Usually she painted something she could see. An arrangement she'd planned, a model, a set of photos she'd taken. Or she worked from a brief - a story to illustrate, a magazine article. Today she simply stared at the blank canvas. It stared back. Her fingers twitched; the urge to paint was almost painful but her mind was as blank as the canvas.

Frustrated, Stella ground her teeth. At school she'd had an English teacher - the sort that wore social worker shoes and a beret - who would encourage them to 'just write' 'Don't think about it,' she'd say. 'Just do it. It doesn't matter what it is. I don't care if it's nonsense and you have to rip it up. It's just a way of getting the creative juices flowing.'

Stella had found her faintly ridiculous. Her friends laughed about her. If one of them took too long making a decision someone would inevitably mimic Mrs Timkin. 'Don't think about it. Just do it. Get those creative juices flowing.' They'd laugh hysterically at their scintillating wit. Stella suspected that Mrs Timkin had coined the slogan long before Nike.

Stella grabbed a tube and squeezed a blob of dazzling emerald onto the palette. She picked up a size 8 flat headed brush. 'Just do it,' she muttered and planted a bold, green stroke onto the virgin white.

Three hours later she was still doing it when Grazja knocked on the door. She came out of her trance to find her arm was tired and her buttocks numb from perching on the stool.

'Stella,' Grazja called. 'I bring you refreshments.'

'Come in,' Stella said, laying down her brush. She stretched before hobbling to the sink to wash her brushes and clean up.

'Stella!' Grazja cried. 'It so hot in here. You open windows.' Tutting, she set her tray down and began opening them herself.

Stella blinked. The heat hit her suddenly. The static was sweltering in the June sunshine, yet all the time she'd been painting it hadn't registered.

She was sticky and acrid with sweat. And thirsty. Parched in fact.

Grabbing a clean jam jar Stella filled it with water, gulping it down.

Grazja watched her. 'Gina say you like this rubbish,' she said, pointing to a can of Diet Coke on the tray 'She make me get this for you, but you no want it now?'

Stella wiped her mouth with the back of her hand. The can glistened with moisture droplets. It looked seductively cold. Stella picked it up and pressed it against her forehead and then rolled it down her neck and breastbone. Oh, it felt good. How had she not noticed how hot she was getting?

'Gina asked you to get me this?' Grazja's words finally penetrated.

Grazja nodded. 'We went for walk. We saw you painting from kitchen window and we no want to disturb. We ate ice cream on seafront. Gina not attack anyone. She saw Diet Coke and say you like it, so we got you some and put it in fridge. Been a good day for Gina. She behave herself.'

Stella tried to take all this in. She was still a little dazed. She popped the tab on the can and took a swig of artificially sweetened fizz. Grazja had supplied her with a plate of cheese, crackers and grapes. Stella almost teared up looking at them; she wasn't used to being nurtured.

'You are so good,' she said to Grazja. 'You don't have to look after me.'

Grazja shrugged. 'It my job.'

They both knew that wasn't true. Grazja's job was to look after Gina.

'Thank you,' Stella said. 'I didn't realise I was so hungry.' She picked up a cracker.

'You artists,' Grazja said. 'You are all same. Once you are in flow you forget everything else. My husband was same.'

It was the first time she had made any mention of family. Stella was intrigued. She was about to ask about him when Grazja moved to look at the painting. Stella instantly forgot about Grazja's husband, fighting an intense desire to block the painting from view. She wasn't even sure what she'd produced; the process had been a blur.

Instead, she joined Grazja in gazing at the image.

The picture showed two gardens divided by a fence, extending from adjoined, yet distinctly different house-fronts. One was a rose-bowered depiction of a fairytale cottage, the other the gingerbread house of Hansel and Gretel. These were barely sketched in with diluted paint, as were the figures in the gardens, one huge and looming over the fence, the second shrinking back in terror. What drew the eye was the vivid portrayal of the gardens. The cottage garden was just that - a quintessentially English cottage garden, bursting with joyful, harmonious colour, every inch singing with beauty. Where the cottage garden was a controlled riot of naturally exuberant colour, the opposing garden was gaudy. It jarred the eye. The scrubby flowers sprouting intermittently defied nature, vulgar in their artificiality. More disturbing yet, beneath a layer of emerald gravel the dark earth held bones - the skull and skeleton of a dog - but other bones too, unidentifiable and terrible.

It was unlike anything Stella had ever painted. Looking at it scared her.

Grazja nodded. 'It reminds me a little of Frida Kahlo,' she said. 'It not like the work you sell.'

Stella looked at her. 'You've seen my work?'

'Oh yes,' Grazja said. 'I look you up on my iPad. Your work very nice but this...'

Stella shrank.

'This,' Grazja nodded solemnly, 'is powerful. I think you must finish this, yes?'

Looking at it Stella wished she could disagree. She wished she hadn't started it at all but in the pit of her stomach she knew she would have to finish it. Those houses and gardens weren't realistic but she instantly recognised what she'd created. It was time to go back to Bobbin Street.

Bobbin Street

In the late spring of 1991 Stella was twelve. Her parents had died only three months earlier. When she was younger Stella imagined that living with Gina would be fun but it turned out that living with Gina wasn't fun at all. Stella didn't see how anything for the rest of her life could be fun again. The concept had died in the car crash that killed her mum and dad.

It came as a surprise, barbed with piercing guilt, when she registered the exact moment the feeling of pleasure re-surfaced. It was fleeting but definite. It stopped her moving forward; it confused her. The object that caused it was a tulip, hot pink with a streak of yellow. Stella stared at it. She widened her focus and realised the tulip wasn't alone. A suffusion of tulips filled her view. They were skirted by baby-blue forget-me-nots, mixed with the delicate nods of Bleeding Heart and the showy wax heads of dwarf azaleas. Not that Stella knew the names beyond 'tulip'. Beauty filled her senses and it proved too much. With a sob Stella turned away and sought the scrubby grass of Gina's garden.

The garden that caused this reaction belonged to a Mrs Jenkins, Gina's opposite neighbour.

Mrs Jenkins had green fingers. Her husband died in his early sixties, leaving her nothing but debts and memories. Her only real financial stroke of luck came when her late mother left her the house on Bobbin Street, and so she returned to her childhood home forty years after she'd left it. Her passion was gardening. The back yard and front patch were small but Mrs Jenkins was ingenious at utilising every bit of space, cramming the soil with plants of every kind, building window boxes and hanging baskets from hooks, layering upwards on potting benches, planting old chimney pots, chamber pots and teapots. Mrs Jenkins could turn almost any old thing into a vessel for planting, yet she had an impeccable eye and a knack for grouping items together in a way that seemed natural and pleasing.

She had no patience for lawns.

Some people on the street maintained tiny scraps of front-lawn edged by a neat border, with a few flowers – pansies or begonias perhaps – spaced regularly, surrounded by brown soil. These people did not believe in jostling.

Mrs Jenkins was all for jostling. Her flowers jostled. They intertwined, danced together, threw their leaves around each other, and swayed drunkenly. But they never fought.

Mrs Jenkins was too good a planner to allow her flowers to fight. She spent hours in the winter choosing her seeds, sketching her designs, finding the exact place for every plant. She knew who to pull out and who to put in, so that there were never gaps in her display or lulls in the season from early spring to late autumn.

She had no time for stragglers either. Mrs Jenkins plants did not straggle. They sprang up with vigour, stayed erect, paraded themselves shamelessly, and were cut down before they flopped.

It was Mrs Jenkins' garden that saved Stella from her grief.

The following day Stella looked again, once on her way to school, once on the way back. She did this for two weeks. Then one Saturday when Gina was still in bed - she was a night owl and not a morning person - Stella peered out of her bedroom window and saw Mrs Jenkins working in the garden. She was down on her hands and knees rooting around in the borders.

Stella pulled on her clothes. Two minutes later she stood at Mrs Jenkins' gate politely waiting to be noticed.

Mrs Jenkins was startled when she finally looked up. She'd been engrossed in weeding. She'd even been muttering while she did it and looked faintly embarrassed. Then she smiled and Stella felt it like a shaft of sunlight on a cold, cloudy day.

Gingerly Mrs Jenkins rose to her feet and walked to the gate. 'You must be Stella,' she said.

Stella nodded. She'd avoided meeting the eye of any neighbour for three months, so everyone had stopped trying to say hello. 'I like your garden,' she blurted.

'Thank you,' Mrs Jenkins said. Neither seemed able to think what to say for a moment until Mrs Jenkins said: 'What bit do you like best?'

Stella looked perplexed.

'I mean, do you have a favourite flower?' Mrs Jenkins explained. She gestured to the numerous blooms.

'The tulips,' Stella said. 'I love them.'

'Yes,' Mrs Jenkins nodded. 'I love tulips. But they die off so quickly.' The word 'die' hung between them. Mrs Jenkins looked mortified. Stella blinked back sudden tears. She hated those tears; they were ever-present these days.

'What are those?' she demanded, jabbing her finger

at a spectacular flowering shrub.

'Peonies,' Mrs Jenkins said. 'This one's called Karl Rosenfeld.'

'You name your flowers?'

Mrs Jenkins laughed. 'I don't,' she said. 'But all flower cultivars are given names. It's the name of the type, you see. You can grow all sorts of peonies in different colours and shapes. That one over there is called Sarah Bernhardt.'

'It doesn't look like a Sarah,' Stella said.

Mrs Jenkins' smile twinkled. 'What does it look like?'

Stella wrinkled her nose. 'An Olivia,' she decided. 'Sarah's too plain a name.'

'Ah, but Sarah Bernhardt was a famous actress,' Mrs Jenkins said. 'It was named after her.'

Stella was unimpressed. 'She should have changed her name to something more glamorous. Actresses can you know. Judy Garland was born Frances Ethel Gumm.'

'I see,' Mrs Jenkins nodded. 'Well, we'll change Sarah Bernhardt over there to Olivia if you like. What about a surname?'

'De Havilland,' Stella said instantly.

'You know your old film stars,' Mrs Jenkins said.

Stella nodded. 'I've watched a lot of films with Gina.'

'We'll re-christen the peony Olivia de Havilland,' Mrs Jenkins said. 'Come in, I'll show you some other flowers.'

'Ok,' Stella said.

Mrs Jenkins unlatched the gate.

It became a routine. Stella spent Saturday

mornings with Mrs Jenkins, weeding and planting, pruning and primping. The weather that May was fine. At ten they stopped for tea and biscuits, sitting companionably on the bench nestled against the wall of the house, admiring their work. Most of the time they sat in silence. When they did speak it was usually about the garden. On the fourth Saturday Stella reached out to touch the wisteria and noted that her mum would love it. She began to cry. Mrs Jenkins took hold of her hand and let her sob.

Stella had stopped crying in front of Gina, who veered dramatically between sobbing with her or getting irritable and telling her that life moves on. Mrs Jenkins simply squeezed her hand occasionally and produced a handkerchief to brook the bubbling of Stella's nose.

It was the first time since her parents' death that Stella felt cleansed by her tears.

Neither of them realised that Gina was jealously watching them from behind the nets of her bedroom window. She'd begun to rise early just so she could. It was a special kind of self-inflicted torture.

Still, on Saturday afternoons Stella and Gina continued to watch old matinees on BBC two. Although neither had felt like Eggs Yolka Polka since the car crash, the old ritual of watching the afternoon film comforted and united them.

In June, Stella started to take coloured pencils and a sketchbook when she visited. She produced small drawings of various flowers, proudly showing them to Mrs Jenkins.

'You've got an artistic eye,' Mrs Jenkins said, admiring a sketch of welsh poppies. 'You're very good.'

On the last Saturday of the month Mrs Jenkins presented Stella with a gift. 'For being such a help in the garden,' she announced, before handing Stella a beautifully wrapped box. Stella, careful not to rip the paper, unwrapped the present slowly, revealing a shoebox. She prized off the lid. Inside she found three paintbrushes lying on top of a hinged plastic paint box. Stella opened it and gasped at the gorgeous cakes of watercolour paint.

'Thank you!' she breathed. 'I love it.'

Shyly, Mrs Jenkins reached down the side of the bench and brought out an A5 sized pad of watercolour paper. 'You're so talented,' she said. 'I thought you might like to paint the garden.'

Stella took the pad like it was made of gold. 'I will,' she said, eyes shining. 'Can I start now?'

Mrs Jenkins laughed. 'I'll get you some water,' she said.

It took a couple of false starts before Stella found her way with the new medium but by lunchtime she was utterly engrossed, painting an arrangement of flowering baskets, planted boots and crowned chimney pots in Mrs Jenkins' back yard.

Mrs Jenkins brought her a cheese sandwich and orange squash. Stella was in her zone. She barely noticed the sandwich going down and took a sip out of the paint water jar instead of the squash glass.

With Stella at the back of her house Mrs Jenkins thought she should tell Gina where her granddaughter was. She hadn't talked to Gina, other than a passing 'hello' since the terrible night of Ivy's death, when Gina had turned her out of desperation. She'd heard the knock on her door and answered it to find Gina, normally so brash, trembling on her doorstep, ashen, her eyes wild and lost, brimming with tears. Since then, Gina had clearly wanted to forget it but Mrs Jenkins hadn't.

Bracing herself, she approached Gina's door with some trepidation. Fred Astaire had a reputation as an ankle-biter. The postman hated him. The moment she'd creaked the gate open he'd started yapping in the house. For an old dog his hearing was still sharp.

Mrs Jenkins heard Gina say something to him and the soft clunk of a door shutting within. She hoped that Fred Astaire was being safely locked away and was relieved when Gina opened the door and no small hornet of a dog shot out.

Gina gazed at her, face blank, the way you would greet a stranger at the door. It was unsettling.

'Ah, Gina,' Mrs Jenkins smiled quickly. 'I just wanted to let you know that Stella is at my house. She's painting a picture in the back yard. Just in case you were worried.'

Gina snapped. 'I know where she is.'

'Right,' Mrs Jenkins said. 'Well, just so long as you know.' She turned to go.

'Not being able to have your kids don't give you the right to steal mine,' Gina said to her back.

Mrs Jenkins froze and then forced herself to walk away. She crossed back to her house feeling Gina's eyes drilling into her. Gina couldn't have said anything crueller. Her barrenness was the great sadness of Mrs Jenkins' life.

That afternoon when Stella forgot about the matinee with Gina, Mrs Jenkins didn't remind her to go home like she normally did.

Stella finally returned home for her tea, clutching her picture and paints to her chest. At the table Gina slammed down a plate of corned beef hash topped with Smash. Stella hated corned beef and Smash and said so.

'Well you should've got yer new best friend to feed yer then,' Gina said. 'Seeing as it's not good enough here.' She grabbed the plate and dumped the hash into Fred Astaire's bowl before flouncing out and leaving Stella to get her own meal.

Yul Brynner's Head

Lysie answered on the third ring. 'You better have a good excuse for not calling sooner,' she said.

Stella started with a description of picking Gina up from the hospital, Henry yowling in the back of the car, and the nightmarish toilet break.

'Okay,' Lysie said, after she stopped laughing. 'Not bad, but not good enough. Carry on.'

'Gina's dog bit me on the ankle so hard I've had to use crutches and a mobility scooter all week.'

Lysie paused. 'You're making that up,' she said.

'I'm not. I had a tetanus shot and I saw a consultant this morning just to make sure he hadn't damaged my ligaments.'

'No!'

'Yes,' Stella crowed.

'Okay,' Lysie said. 'Del's just brought me a beer. I'm on the sofa. I'm settled in. I'm ready to hear the whole story. Leave nothing out.'

'All right,' Stella said. 'But I'm warning you, this could take a while.' She eased back into her chair, relaxing into the warmth of Lysie's familiar friendship.

'The dog's name is Bing Crosby,' she said. 'He's a Jack Russell and he's gone on the run...' Once she started to talk the whole ludicrous week came spilling out.

Lysie had questions. How old was Rick? What did he look like? Why were there so many mobility scooters in Mapton? Why did Stella suddenly know so much about mobility scooters?

And she needed clarifications. Was Stella sure that

Gina had deliberately wet the bed? Stella had really given her cat to a stranger? Stella hadn't lost her mind? This last was a reaction to news of the forthcoming rumble.

'I think I may have,' Stella laughed. 'Everything feels a little surreal in Mapton.'

'It sounds like a David Lynch film,' Lysie said.

'No, it's more like a Carry On film on steroids,' Stella said.

'So,' Lysie launched. 'Rick sounds nice.'

'Yeah, he is,' Stella replied lightly.

'Nice looking?'

'Okay,' Stella said. 'Rugged.'

'Rugged!' Lysie cried. 'A rugged American. A rugged American you trust with your pussy.'

'Nasty!' Stella guffawed. 'You're so crude.'

'Do I smell a romance?' Lysie demanded.

Stella fell silent.

'A holiday fling?' Lysie pushed hopefully.

'Maybe,' Stella said. 'I don't know yet. It's probably not a good idea.'

'That sounds like the Stella I know,' Lysie said. 'Cautiously over-thinking things. I'm relieved. I was beginning to think the real you had been abducted.'

'Ha ha.'

Lysie changed the subject. 'Grazja sounds amazing.'

'Oh God, yes,' Stella agreed. 'I wouldn't have survived the week without her.'

'So, you're getting on with Gina?'

'Better than I'd expected. Again, that's down to Grazja. It's like having a buffer between us. Today they were playing Gin Rummy. Gina gets really competitive and Grazja seemed as bad, so I left them to it. I expected it would all end in tears but later on I asked Grazja how they'd managed to finish up without a fight. She said: 'It easy. I cheat.' And I said, 'Gina hates losing. She always accuses the winner of cheating. How did you get away with it?' Grazja laughed. 'I cheat to lose. I play like I really, really want to win. I get upset. But really I let Gina win most times. She is happy. Life is quiet.'

Lysie laughed. They chatted about Talia, Lysie's daughter for a while and about Lysie's work and how all the stupid admin made teaching crap nowadays. Lysie was an art teacher; she and Stella met at art college and went onto get their teaching certificates together. She was a talented sculptress but like most artists never made enough money from her art to live on.

Del came to tell Lysie that the evening meal was ready and they hung up.

Stella knew how lucky she was to make money from her art and how rare that was. She had Mrs Jenkins to thank for encouraging her talent. Gina had taken little interest in her paintings.

She glanced at the canvas on the easel and felt a squirm of discomfort. Whatever had possessed her to paint like that? 'Possession' was the right word for it. It had almost felt like a fugue - three hours she could barely remember. Yet she itched to get back to it.

Sighing, she tamped down the impulse and the emotions the picture evoked. She had an evening of Gina ahead of her and she'd promised herself (and Grazja) she'd be nice.

#

Gina and Grazja were bickering over which film to choose from Gina's collection. It came down to a choice between Singin' in the Rain or The King and I.

'I never see King and I,' Grazja argued.

'Singin' in the Rain has a happy ending,' Gina countered.

'Gina! You spoil end of King and I for me. Now I know it not happy.'

Gina shrugged.

'Stella,' Grazja said. 'You choose. Which one?'

'I watched Singin' in the Rain at Christmas,' Stella said. 'It's great but I haven't seen The King and I in years. Let's watch that.'

Gina, puffing up to argue, seemed to think better of it. 'It's all the same to me,' she shrugged. 'I love em both.'

Grazja had made a bowl of popcorn and propped Gina's leg under a cushion on the coffee table so they all could squeeze on the sofa. Grazja popped the DVD in and the movie began.

Half way through they stopped for a toilet break, a rigmarole that involved heaving Gina in and out of her wheelchair, doing the same in the bathroom and then back onto the sofa.

Gina carped. 'Oh fo' God's sake, just give me a pan.'

Grazja held firm. 'No Gina,' she said. 'You use the bedpan in bed. It good to get you moving and doing normal things rest of time.'

'It's not bleedin' normal to go to the toilet in a wheelchair. And it hurts every time you haul me in and out.'

'Yeah, yeah,' Grazja said. 'It hurt a bit but that is

life. You get better.'

'You're like a bloody Nazi,' Gina said. 'I think you like hurting me.'

'Nazi's invade my country, Gina. I am insulted you say that about me.'

'We should've left Poland to the Nazis,' Gina said. 'It's cos of you lot we went to war.'

'Of course, Gina. I forget you know everything. Now lift up.' Grazja lifted Gina onto her chair and wheeled her to the bathroom.

Stella let out a breath. She didn't know how Grazja coped with Gina. She could hear them squabbling, even as Grazja helped support her on the toilet.

At the end of the film Grazja was misty-eyed. 'I think Yul Brynner was very handsome man.'

Stella agreed.

'Too bald,' Gina pronounced.

Stella laughed. 'How much baldness is acceptable then?'

Gina squinted at her. 'None,' she said. 'A man should have hair.'

'But Yul suits being bald,' Grazja said. 'It show off his good bone structure. No, he is very good-looking man.'

'Wasn't he part Russian?' Stella said.

'Ah,' Grazja nodded. 'East European cheekbones. That's why he so good-looking.'

Gina snorted. 'Bald and too short,' she said. 'Now Cary Grant, he was good-looking. And he was English.'

'Hmm, yes. Cary Grant not bad,' Grazja said. 'But not masculine. Not powerful like Yul.'

'Cary Grant was debonair,' Gina said. 'Like Fred

Astaire and Bing Crosby. I like em debonair.'

'What's this 'debonair'?' Grazja asked.

'Sophisticated,' Stella explained.

'It means they got class,' Gina added. 'They're gentlemen.'

'Yul Brynner not got class?'

'Bald men aren't classy,' Gina said. 'Not their fault, just the way it is.'

'Fred Astaire looked bald,' Stella said. 'His hair was so thin and slicked back. He's so bony he always looks like a dancing skeleton to me.'

Gina spluttered, eyes popping.

Grazja nodded. 'He great dancer but he moves like a woman - how do you say? Fem...'

'Effeminate,' Stella agreed.

Gina was apoplectic. 'How bloody dare you! He was the best bloody dancer the world's ever known. He wasn't a poofter.'

'No one said he was,' Stella said. 'I just think some of his movements were quite feminine. Like the way he wafted his hands.'

'Wash your mouth out with soap,' Gina said. 'Any woman would die to be spun round the floor by Fred. And he could lift Ginger up like she was a feather. He was strong.'

Stella shrugged. 'I don't doubt it,' she said. 'But I prefer Gene Kelly. He was just as good a dancer and he looked like a man. He even had muscles in his buttocks.'

'Male ballet dancers have big buttocks,' Grazja said.

'Ah! Now, they are all poofters,' Gina declared. 'And the way you can see their private parts is disgusting.'

'They are wearing a dance belt, Gina,' Grazja said. 'You not really seeing their privates.'

'Don't matter,' Gina said. 'It looks like you can. You don't know where to put your eyes.'

'So, Gina,' Grazja smiled. 'Tell me, was Stella's grandfather classy? How you say… debonair?'

Stella stiffened. An awkward silence interrupted the congenial mood.

Grazja immediately realised her mistake. She started to apologise when Gina said: 'I thought he was. I was young and stupid and I didn't know what men were like. He were a good dancer and a sharp dresser, I can tell you that. But once he'd taken the honey he didn't want the hive.'

Stella stared at her. She knew her mother was illegitimate but neither she nor Gina had ever spoken about Stella's grandfather. She held her breath waiting for more.

'Oh, Gina. That's terrible,' Grazja said. 'He left you with baby?'

Gina nodded. 'Oh aye,' she said. 'Then 'e married me best friend.'

'Maggie?' Stella asked, remembering their conversation of the previous day.

Gina's lips disappeared into a thin line. Her expression iced over. 'I don't like to talk about it,' she said. She turned to Grazja and asked, almost savagely: 'What about you Ms Polack? You got any tales o' heartbreak?'

Grazja hesitated. 'My husband die,' she said softly. 'That break my heart.'

'Oh,' said Gina, taken aback. 'Sorry.'

Grazja smiled. 'I like you, Gina. Don't like to talk about it.'

'It's for the best,' Gina said. 'No point dwelling on the past.'

Stella involuntarily glanced at the multitude of classic films on Gina's shelf. The Sound of Music was the most recent – nothing past nineteen sixty-six. Here was a woman who dwelt in the past.

'You wouldn't like the past, Gina' Grazja said. 'They say it is foreign country.'

'Yer what?' Gina said.

But Stella laughed and found herself wondering, not for the first time, how she'd been so lucky to find Grazja.

The Rumble Rumbled

Stella was surprised to see Rick astride his bike when she reached the cafe at ten on Friday night. The diner had closed for business hours ago. She was also delighted and more than a little fluttery in her stomach at the sight of him. She'd spent the day painting, so engrossed that she hadn't even popped along to the cafe for her morning coffee.

Rick was chatting to Sue when she pulled alongside on her Rascal. The Marauders fanned out along the promenade, buzzing excitedly.

'I didn't expect to see you,' Stella smiled at Rick.

'I wasn't going to miss this,' Rick said. 'No way.'

'Strictly speaking Rick shouldn't be here,' Sue said. 'Not being a member and on a bike. But I've wangled it so he can referee.'

'I'm completely impartial,' Rick said. 'So don't try to bribe me, Sue.'

'I was going to offer you my body, Rick,' Sue barked out.

'Tempting,' Rick said. 'But I'm a man of honour, Sue. You can't use your wily charms on me.'

'Mebbee not,' Sue gurgled dirtily. 'But I bet Stella can.'

Rick met Stella's eyes briefly. Even in the gathering gloom she saw the sizzle and felt it zap her.

Rick looked away, casually bending over his bike to check his brake wires. 'Are we ready?' he asked.

In answer Sue honked her horn and yelled. 'Time to rumble, Marauders. Let's go kick some Wanderer butt.' She rolled off, closely flanked by Frank.

The Marauders cheered, honked and parped,

moving out in formation behind them.

Stella tagged onto the back, while Rick peddled slowly beside her.

'I can't believe I'm doing this,' she laughed.

'Nope,' Rick agreed. 'Mapton's got to you all right.'

'So,' Stella said lightly. 'I've made it to Friday. I'm still holding you to the deal on Sunday.'

'The best meal you've ever tasted,' Rick nodded. 'Still, let's see if you get through tonight's ordeal first.'

Stella was silent. Didn't he want her to make it to Sunday? Was he hoping tonight would finish her? Maybe she'd misinterpreted his earlier look. Perhaps she was the only one sizzling?

'How's it going with Gina?' Rick asked, after a few minutes.

'Okay,' Stella said.

'Great,' Rick said. 'You must be relieved.'

'Yeah, I am,' Stella said. 'I could probably leave her with Grazja now and go home.'

'Really?'

'Probably.'

Stella was hoping for more than just 'really'.

'You didn't come by the diner today,' Rick said.

'I was painting,' Stella replied.

'Yeah? What?'

Stella didn't answer straightaway. She'd worked most of the day in the same frenzied trance-like state, only stopping for meals when Grazja reminded her to. This time, however, she'd made sure to swig water and ventilate the caravan. She didn't allow herself to think about her subject matter, simply letting her hand and eyes create. The imagery burst onto the canvas like weeds erupting from the soil after spells of rain and sun. The process felt ferocious. And freeing.

Gina was a monster, flaming hair snaking around her head, lips peeled back in a snarl, skin a sickly green reflecting from the unnatural hue of the glass chips covering the ground. Mrs Jenkins bore an uncanny resemblance to Glinda the good witch of the North, but a defeated, bedraggled version, withering under the malevolent glare of her neighbour's wrath. The roses around Mrs Jenkins' cottage wept. The roof of the witch's house was a Bird's Trifle, deliriously melting, sliding in gobbets down the walls. At an upstairs window a figure stared out - a girl wearing a lopsided conical princess hat, streamers hanging limply. The girl screamed, hands pressed to the glass.

Grazja, gazing at in the late afternoon, remarked. 'Hmm, do you think you have some issues with your grandmother?'

Stella looked at her. Grazja was smiling wryly.

'She can't see this,' Stella said.

Grazja gave one of her indeterminate shrugs. 'She knows you painting. She will ask what.'

Stella shook her head. 'She never has before,' she said. 'When I lived with her she never wanted to know, even though I drew all the time.'

'That was then,' Grazja said. 'She can't get up the steps but I would keep blinds drawn when you out.'

Stella agreed.

Rick, riding alongside her, waited for her answer.

'It's hard to explain,' she said. 'It's personal and not like anything else I've ever painted.'

'Sounds intriguing,' Rick said. 'I put your crab up in the diner today. It looks fantastic.'

'Really?' Stella couldn't help grinning. 'That was

nice of you.'

'Are you kidding? I've got a genuine Stella Distry hanging in my diner. I googled you. Your stuff's amazing. I had no idea.'

'Ah, Google,' Stella said. 'The people's spy. Grazja looked me up too. Maybe I should look you up?'

Rick missed a pedal and almost went over.

'Steady!' Stella cried, braking

'Damn promenade needs re-paving,' Rick growled. He found his rhythm and they pushed on. 'You know, folks tell me that bikes used to be banned along here, and then in 2000 they tore all the no-cycling signs down and stuck up new ones that said: Millennium Cycleway! Suddenly they had a new attraction at no extra cost.'

Stella laughed. 'Innovative,' she said.

'Yeah,' Rick agreed. 'Innovation the Mapton way - on the cheap.'

Stella noticed how dark it was. She fiddled with her controls until the headlights flicked on. Until now the promenade had been illuminated by streetlights but now that they were a mile along, halfway to Siltby, the lights had petered out. The beach was a black void beyond the seawall, the moon hidden behind a cloud. Lights twinkled from ships far out at sea.

Sue's voice floated back. 'Marauders halt!'

Ahead the headlamps of another battalion of motor scooters glittered.

'All right, game's on,' Rick whispered. 'You ready for this, slugger?'

Now they were here Stella didn't think she was at all ready for this, whatever 'this' involved.

'Stella, get up here,' Sue shouted.

'Good luck,' Rick said. She nudged her Rascal forward. The Marauders parted for her as she went.

Just as Stella reached Sue, the clouds parted and the scene was dramatically lit by moonlight. Sue eyeballed her opponent, scooters almost nose to nose. Stella took in the skull and crossbones emblazoned on the tiller panel of an aggressive looking scooter. The man riding it wore a black cap, bearing the same pirate symbol. He was pudgy, bearing enormous fleshy bags beneath his eyes - Stella judged him to be in his sixties - but the eyes sunk into the doughy face were sharp and alert. They gobbled up the sight of Stella's Rascal, barely touching on the rider until Sue introduced them.

'Stella, this is Pirate Tom. He's the captain of the Wanderers.'

'Hello,' Stella said.

Pirate Tom favoured her with a dismissive grunt, eyes returning to the Rascal. In college Stella had a large-breasted friend who got sick of men talking to her breasts rather than to her face. Stella suddenly knew how she felt. She felt a ridiculous desire to cover her scooter.

'This is highly irregular, Susan,' Tom said, eyes crawling along the Rascal's carapace. 'I'm only agreeing to it as a gesture of goodwill between our clubs.'

Sue snorted. 'Get off yo' bleedin' high horse, Tom. You want to race a Rascal. Admit it.'

Tom twinkled. 'Who bloody wouldn't?' he snickered. He tore his eyes away from the Rascal. 'Right, what's the booty?'

'Mildred's baked a Victoria sponge, a lemon meringue pie and two dozen cherry scones,' Sue replied. 'What's yours?'

'A large roast chicken, barbecued spare ribs, pigs in blankets. Bob's thrown in three packets of Scotch eggs, but the date's up tomorrow, so you'd need to eat 'em quickish. Not that you'll be winning 'em,' he added. 'Even with the Rascal.'

Sue scoffed. 'Dream on pirate boy. Right, let's sort out the order.'

Sue pulled a clipboard out of her basket, disturbing Scampi, nestled beneath a blanket. Scampi popped her head out to take in the surroundings. Her tiny nose began to fibrillate, thrusting towards Pirate Tom.

He laughed. 'She can smell the chicken,' he said. 'It's in my rear basket.' He patted her with his meaty hand. 'Sorry, Scampi. You're gonna be disappointed again.'

Scampi seemed to accept this, snuggling back down into her blanket.

Stella listened, bemused, as Sue and Tom decided the order of play. The races were run in heats, four riders at a time. Points were awarded to the club who won each race. The points given increased as the heats gave way to quarters, semi-final and then final. This added an extra frisson as the trailing team still had a chance to win if they weren't too far behind in points.

Pirate Tom returned to his crew and Sue to hers.

'I put you in the second race,' Sue said to Stella. 'So you can watch the first one and see how it goes. There're a few things to remember. Getting off the start-line as fast as you can's most important. If you can do that move into the middle where the ride's smoother. Outside and you're liable to get stuck in the sand piled up; inside and you can be bumped against the wall.'

Stella nodded. She was surprised by how nervous she felt. What if she completely ballsed up? The Marauders were depending on her based entirely on the reputation of the Rascal. Why had she insisted she ride it? She could have agreed to let Sue borrow it.

'Maybe you should ride the Rascal,' she said to Sue.

Sue gave her a stern look. 'Too late,' she said. 'Tom would never agree now. Besides, I love Betty.'

'Who's Betty?' Stella asked.

'My scooter!' Sue said. 'I'd feel a bit unfaithful.' She patted her handlebars. 'And where would Scampi go?' She eyeballed Stella. 'You're Gina Pontin's granddaughter,' Sue scolded. 'She's a cow but she's not a coward. Remember who you are!'

'Right,' Stella said. 'I'm Gina Pontin's granddaughter.' She repeated this like a mantra. 'I'm Gina Pontin's granddaughter. I'm a cow not a coward.'

She caught Rick's eye. He was laughing at her so she stuck her tongue out at him.

It took a few minutes to get the scooters in line for the first race. The start and finish had been marked out in chalk, torches placed at each end so if the moon went in again the lines could still be seen.

Stella found herself parked next to Mildred, she of the blue hair and baking prowess.

'You play for food,' Stella said to her.

'Yes,' Mildred nodded. 'The victors have a celebration meal tomorrow. If we win and the weather's good we're going to have a picnic.'

'That's nice,' Stella said.

'It is,' Mildred nodded. 'As long as Sue doesn't get drunk. Last time we won she broke out the Spumanti and ended up driving into the sea. Well, she didn't actually get to the sea. She got stuck in the sand and had to be dug out, but she was trying for the sea.'

Stella was too nervous to laugh. Not that Mildred was laughing either.

A whistle blew and the first race began.

'C'mon, Alf,' Mildred called, her wavering voice lost among the cheering and general hullabaloo.

Stella watched the race, two riders from The Marauders, two from The Wanderers jostling for lead position. An elderly woman nudged ahead, veered dangerously in front of Alf, causing the onlookers to gasp, cheer or boo, and took the coveted middle ground. A scooter on the outside banked into the grass-tufted sand on the side of the cycleway, and stuck, buzzing angrily like a wasp caught in a honey-trap.'

'Ooh, Carole's down,' Mildred said. She raised her voice. 'Bump her, Alf!'

Alf, who Stella later discovered was Mildred's third husband, obeyed and rammed into the back of the elderly demon-driver in front of him. The Wanderers booed.

'Foul!' someone shouted. But Alf's transgression had little effect on the scooter in front. The woman was tiny, her frail frame crouched low over her handlebars, but her eyes were blazing.

'Drive that buggy home, Dorothy,' Pirate Tom yelled. Dorothy did, raising her arms as she crossed the chalk line. Her scooter began to veer alarmingly but she grabbed the tiller and wrestled it back under control.

Alf followed a close second, swearing profusely.

Rick ran down the track to help push Carole out of her tussle with the tussock.

The other Wanderer came third.

'Right,' Sue drew up. 'Remember, foot to the pedal, and get off the line quick as you can, then all the way on eight.' She escorted Stella along the prom to the start line.

Stella had a moment's problem reversing into position. Flustered she heard titters from The Wanderers. Finally in line, she tried to focus on the task ahead. Rick caught her eye, giving a wink and reassuring nod. Stella sucked in a deep breath, set her speed control to the 'hare' symbol (she'd always driven on tortoise mode) and prepared to race.

The whistle blew and Stella rocketed forward on full thrust, doing zero to eight in two seconds, leaving her competitors trailing like snails. Her hair whipped behind her, mostly because of the blustery wind rather than speed, but after days of moving at a crawl, on and off the scooter, Stella felt like she was flying. She let out an enormous whoop and swung into the middle of the cycleway, not even looking to see who she might hit. She charged down the course, as demonically possessed as Dorothy had previously been.

All too soon it was over. Stella crossed the finish line to wild cheers from The Marauders, slamming on her brakes to avoid careening into them.

Rick cycled up. 'Oh my God, you're the new

Senna! You showed no mercy.' He bent over, laughing.

Elated, Stella laughed with him. 'Again!' she cried. 'I wanna go again.'

Sue zoomed up. 'You will,' she said. 'After a couple more heats. You gotta win to race Tom. I bet he's cacking himself. He hardly ever loses.' She shook her head admiringly. 'That Rascal's a beauty.' Her expression grew serious. 'Look, it won't be so easy on the next one. We knew as long as you didn't bottle it you'd win this one. Dick there's so fat it's like towing an elephant, and the Parker twins never manage more than 6mph, and that's between 'em.'

Stella glanced anxiously at Dick, clearly within earshot. He nodded in agreement with Sue. 'I broke my record. Topped 28 stone on my scales this morning but Spirit still carried me.' Wheezing, as though he'd actually run the race, he gave Spirit a loving pat.

The Parker twins were slumped glumly over their handlebars some distance away. Indistinguishable, they looked to be about eighty.

'I've never seen really old identical twins,' Stella said.

'Oh, they're not identical,' Sue corrected her. 'The one on the right's Gladys and the one on the left's Bill. They're those other type of twins.'

'Di-zygotic,' Stella said.

'Gesundheit,' Sue replied, roaring at her own joke.

Stella spotted Rick had moved to the seawall. He pulled a thermos out of his backpack.

'You got coffee?' she said, reaching him.

'Uhuh,' he said, pouring hot liquid into a plastic

cup.

'Any for me?'

'No way, José ' he said. 'You're high as a kite as it is.'

'Who knew mobility racing could be such an adrenaline kick?' Stella said.

'Not me,' Rick said. 'Now I've seen it with my own eyes I gotta get myself one.'

'Mapton's the place to do that,' Stella said.

'Yep. Five whole scooter stores in one small seaside town and two more in Siltby. We are the nation's scooter capital. It's something to be proud of.'

'I'm beginning to see that,' Stella said.

Pirate Tom won the next quarter and Sue the one after that.

They were into the last two semis.

Sue rolled up, flushed with the exhilaration of her win. 'Right, it's me against you,' she said to Stella.

'Just the two of us?' Stella asked. 'Shouldn't it be a Marauder against a Wanderer?'

'Nah, this way you end up with one of each for the final,' Sue said. 'Now much as I want to see that Rascal take Tom down, I'm not gonna throw this race for yer, so be prepared. Yer first race was piss-easy but this ain't gonna be. Comprehend?'

Stella thought she did.

They scooted back to the start line and manoeuvred into place.

Stella grinned over at Sue but Sue was hunched over her steering column, jaw set within her double chins. She was ready.

The whistle blew and this time Stella was taken by surprise as Sue lurched ahead. Angry at herself Stella hit the throttle and charged off the line, the Rascal's powerful motor roaring. She surged up to eight and soon she was almost nose-to-nose with Sue. Sue nudged to her left, grazing the Rascal. Stella instinctively veered away, losing important ground. Angry, she righted herself and powered forward, only to discover Sue had wandered into her 'lane'. Swearing, Stella moved out, determined to overtake her on the inside but Sue narrowed the gap so that Stella was forced into the sandy side.

Furious, Stella swung her scooter to the right, bumping Sue outright. The Rascal was heavier. Stella could hear Sue's engine whining as she forced the smaller scooter aside. The Rascal's pneumatic tyres ate up the sand and grass, barely registering the terrain. The finish line was approaching fast. Stella leaned forward and willed the Rascal on. They were fused, human and machine, with one purpose. To win.

Sue's scooter squealed - a high pitch sound like a toddler's tantrum. The night air stank of burning wire and hot metal.

Stella's Rascal moved past it like a cheetah. Sue nipped at her heels but it was too late; the Rascal took the race.

The scooter pooters were rapturous but Stella hardly heard them. She slammed on her brakes and turned to find Sue.

'What the hell were you doing?' she shouted.

Sue motioned for her to drive to a quieter spot. Stella followed her. Sue switched off her engine. 'Gotta let Betty cool off,' she said. 'Worried her motor's gonna burn out.' She was panting.

'You bumped me!' Stella said.

Sue nodded. 'Yeah,' she said. 'Sorry about that but yer did good. To be honest I wasn't sure you had it in you but bleedin' hell you do!'

Stella snorted. 'So it was a test?'

'Nah,' Sue said. 'It was training. Pirate Tom plays rough. He hates to lose and he'll do anything to stop you. That's why he usually wins. Most of us don't like to mess up our rides but Tom don't mind. He sees all them scratches and bumps as battle scars. Thinks it makes him look tough.'

'But don't you have rules?' Stella demanded.

Sue sniffed. 'Pirate Tom's got influence around here. Besides, it's more fun this way.' She gave Stella a devilish grin. 'Tell me you didn't find that fun?'

Stella couldn't help but grin back. She made a gap between her thumb and forefinger. 'Maybe just a bit.'

'Thatta girl. Now get over there. Tom's about to race his semi. You need to watch his tactics.'

Stella rode back to watch the semi. It was between Tom and Dorothy, the demon pensioner of the first race. But there were no tactics to speak of. Tom won easily - so easily that it was clear Dorothy had thrown the race.

Pirate Tom escorted Stella to the start line. He used the time to psyche her out. 'You're playing against the big boys now,' Tom said. 'Sure you can handle it?'

'I just see one old boy,' Stella retorted.

Tom sucked through his teeth. He chortled. 'Fighting talk. I like a cat with claws. But let me tell you this. My machine's a Drive Royale 4. Fast as the wind and as mean as they get - a real bruiser. She eats other scooters for supper.'

'Uhuh,' Stella said. 'I suppose it's got a name?'

'Black Bertha,' Tom said. 'After me mother.'

'Oh,' said Stella. 'Was she fast too?'

They reached the start line. Pirate Tom shot her a vindictive look. 'I'll make you regret that,' he snarled.

Turning in tight circles, they reversed into place. A pirate flag fluttered from the Royale's rear basket. Stella caught an unmistakable whiff of roast chicken.

She gritted her teeth and prepared to race dirty. This time she was positioned on the right, closest to the sea wall.

The whistle blew and both scooters lunged forward. The Royale matched the Rascal in speed and grace and they rode neck and neck until Tom slammed the Royale hard against the Rascal, knocking it towards the seawall. Stella struggled to regain control. Instead of using the chance to move ahead, Tom moved into the space Stella had vacated and slammed her again, this time into the wall. The Rascal scraped against concrete, sparks flying but Stella kept it running. It shrieked a protest but Stella turned the rudder towards Tom and slowly began to force him away. The Royale was fast because it was lighter than the Rascal. It began to succumb to its superior weight and engine capacity despite Tom's struggle to keep it under control.

Stella experienced a rush of power. She was about to ram Tom off course when she saw the oddest thing. A small dog was sprinting along the seawall, keeping pace with her.

The cheers of the crowd turned to gasps, although she was barely aware of this.

The dog looked at her. A spark of recognition

jumped between them.

Bing Crosby!

He snarled and launched off the wall towards her. Stella ducked as he sailed right over her and landed on Pirate Tom.

Tom screamed, hitting the emergency brake and jolted to a stop. Stella did the same. Then she saw the other dogs, surrounding them in a pack.

Bing scrambled over Tom's chest and shoulder into the basket on the rear of the scooter and dived in. He emerged shaking a heavy package, flung it out of the basket and plunged back in, reappearing a nanosecond later with another package. This he repeated twice more. His pack retrieved the meaty prizes in their jaws. Bing sprang to the ground barking orders. Then they were off, racing into the night.

For a moment there was stunned silence.

'I've been robbed,' Tom roared. Everyone began shouting at once, scooters bumping into each other. The noise and commotion blocked the sound of a much larger engine approaching from the Siltby end of the beach. Headlights dazzled them, freezing the gangs into place.

Sue yelled. 'It's the fuzz!' Pandemonium broke out as people started to panic.

Stella leapt into action, gunning the Rascal forward, leaving Pirate Tom dazed in her wake. Rick joined her on his bike, peddling hard. Sue was ahead of them parping her horn for The Marauders to follow. The Marauders collected themselves with surprising efficiency, falling into line behind her.

They fled the scene, not stopping all the way back

to Mapton. No sirens chased them.

When they reached Mapton, the gang mysteriously split up, melting away into the night, leaving Rick and Stella alone. They'd got the giggles. Rick clutched his stomach he was laughing so hard. Stella was on the verge of hysteria. When they had themselves briefly under control, Rick said. 'Do you want to come back to mine for a nightcap?'

Stella wiped tears from her eyes. 'Oh, God, yes,' she wheezed. 'I need a stiff drink.'

It took ten minutes longer to reach Rick's house than it should have. One of them would start to giggle again, setting off the other and they had to stop for a minute of tear-inducing hysterics before regaining enough control to go another few yards before it happened again.

Finally they reached the house, Rick leading Stella around the back so he could lock his bike in the garage. Stella parked the Rascal there too and they stumbled into the house still giggling. Henry greeted them rapturously, snaking round their legs.

'Henry!' Stella picked him up. 'I've missed you.' Henry purred and rubbed his damp nose on her neck. It was rare that he allowed himself to be held. After a moment he began to wriggle and she let him go.

'He looks so happy and healthy,' she said. 'You've been taking good care of him.'

'He's easy. Feed him, stroke him, let him go poop in his litter tray.'

'You haven't let him outside?'

'Of course not, but except for the kitchen he's pretty much got the run of the house.'

'It's a big house,' Stella said.

'I think he's enjoying the space.'

Poor Henry, Stella thought. All he had with her was a small loft with a great view. She felt a stab of guilt.

'Go into the garden room,' Rick said. 'I'll get us a drink. D'you drink whisky?'

'Malt. Not bourbon - too sweet,' Stella said.

'Ah, a woman after my own heart,' Rick said. 'Single malt it is.' He disappeared into another room - not the kitchen - and Stella got a glimpse of a pool table before the door swung shut.

'He's got a games room!' she whispered to Henry. Henry was unimpressed. He led her into the garden room. Rick had left the lamps on so it glowed softly. Stella noted the lack of curtains or blinds. Night pressed against the glass and she felt exposed, but she reminded herself that it was only garden outside and the room wasn't overlooked. She assessed the seating - two chairs and a large, comfortable-looking sofa. She chose the sofa. Henry chose her lap. She caressed his ears.

'I saw your friend Bing Crosby tonight,' she whispered. 'He's gone feral.'

Henry dug his claws into her jeans.

'Ow.'

Rick returned bearing a bottle and two tumblers.

He chose the sofa too. 'I broke out the good stuff,' he said. 'Glenfiddich eighteen year reserve. Tonight's entertainment demanded it.'

Stella laughed. He poured and they chinked glasses.

'To the rumble to end all rumbles,' Stella said, drinking.

'To wild dogs and pensioner gangs,' Rick added.

'To escaping the fuzz,' Stella sang, 'and the fangs of Bing Crosby.' They drained their glasses and their eyes locked and held for a loaded moment. Henry took that moment to move from Stella to Rick's lap, almost knocking Rick's glass out of his hand.

'Oh, hey,' Rick said. 'Watch it big guy.'

He waggled the bottle at Stella. She nodded and he poured them another shot.

'Was that really the police?' Stella asked. 'I didn't get a look at them.'

Rick shrugged. 'Maybe. There's been some vandalism to the beach huts lately. Sometimes they patrol the beach. God, I wish I could've seen their faces.'

'I can't believe Bing,' Stella said. 'I thought he was going for me, but he had it planned, didn't he?'

'Oh yeah, that was organised. That was the Great Chicken Robbery. I mean he took Pirate Tom down.' Rick began laughing again. 'God, it was amazing. Did you see Denise Robertson's Dalmatian? I thought he was too stupid to train but Bing's done it.'

'It's terrible really,' Stella spluttered, wiping away tears. 'It's my fault. If I hadn't brought Henry with me none of this would have happened.'

'Well, I say amen for Henry.' Rick drained his glass. He set it down and gazed at her. 'Stella Distry, queen of the mobility scooter, I would like to kiss you if I may?'

Stella tingled. She set her own glass down. 'You may,' she said.

Rick leaned in and their lips met and parted. The kiss started light and then deepened. A flame of desire licked through Stella. They pressed together.

Rick yelped as Henry, squashed, sank his claws into his thigh. Rick and Stella sprang apart. Henry leapt off Rick's lap and stalked away, wriggling under a chair where he could stare at them balefully.

Rick grinned at Stella. 'Shall we go somewhere more private?'

Stella nodded, breathless. The kiss had gone to her head like the whisky.

Rick stood and held out his hand. Stella took it. 'How far do you want to take this?' Rick whispered. 'Lounge or bedroom?'

'Bedroom.'

Rick pulled back to look at her. 'Sure?' he said. 'Not the adrenaline or the whisky talking?'

'Maybe, but I don't care. I know I like you.'

'I like you too.' He pulled her in and kissed her again.

'Where's your bedroom?' Stella breathed, feeling giddily brave.

'In a turret,' Rick murmured.

'How very phallic.'

He led her there. They kissed and fumbled and groped their way up the stairs.

In the bedroom Rick took her face in his hands and kissed her silly. They stumbled towards the bed. Stella took a double take. Henry was lying on it.

'How did he get past us?'

'I don't know about you but I've been distracted,' Rick said. He grabbed Henry and unceremoniously dumped him on the stairs.

'Your cat is kinky.'

'So am I,' Stella said.

Rick shut the door in Henry's face.

The Morning After

Stella woke to an empty bed. Well, almost empty. Henry had wandered in and was purring beside her left ear. She shifted, body heavy with post coital satisfaction, and then winced. Ooh. There was a certain soreness between her legs just to remind her how long it had been since she'd previously had sex. Too, too long.

She took in the room. The turret was octagonal, with two high arched windows. Sunlight streamed in, indicating she was in an eastern facing tower. She had no recollection of which direction they'd taken through the house.

Stella panicked. What she'd done hit her. She'd had sex with Rick. More than once, maybe a few times; after a while the night had blurred into one intoxicating super-lay.

Super lay! She sniggered. She'd have to tell Lysie. Then she panicked again. Where was Rick? Did he regret it? Had he just used her? Was she supposed to crawl out of the house unseen, conquered, and vanquished, the way she had at seventeen after losing her virginity to Oliver Gates.

Not that it was *that* long since she'd had sex. There had been others. Relationships. But she'd never been so naive again - especially after Gina had found out.

Well, if that's how it was with Rick she was damned well taking her cat.

Stella scrambled out of bed, jolting Henry out of his dreamy state. He meowed indignantly as she found her knickers and slid them on, followed by her jeans. She looked round for her bra and saw Rick leaning against the doorjamb with a tray in his hand. He looked both amused and aroused.

Stella felt impossibly stupid with her jeans on and her breasts jiggling.

'I like the look,' Rick said. 'It's kinda like Woodstock all over again. But what's the hurry. I brought breakfast.'

Stella spotted her bra crumpled in a corner and snagged it. She tried to put it on with as much dignity as she could manage.

'I thought you'd left,' she said, off-handedly retrieving her T-shirt from under the bed.

Rick put the tray down on the bedside table - there was only one bedside table and it was on his side - and took her hands.

'Hey. Sit down.'

They sat on the edge of the bed.

'It's early. I didn't want to wake you up before I had to. I got to open up the diner - Saturday's a busy day - but I wanted us to have breakfast together before I left. You can come with me if you want?'

Stella shook her head. She looked at him, embarrassed. 'Sorry. I've never done this before. I mean...' She rolled her eyes. 'Obviously I've had sex before...'

'Obviously,' Rick grinned.

'But, it's always been in a relationship. Last night... I don't know what came over me.'

Rick's smile got wider. 'Me neither. But I liked it.' He sobered up. 'Look, we've only known each other a few days, it's true. But I know I like you - a lot - and I want to get to know you better. And, yeah, I know it's stupid because you live in London and I live here, but

I still want it. And it might surprise you to know Stella Distry that I'm not a casual sex type of guy either.'

'You had condoms in your bedside drawer,' Stella pointed out.

'Uhuh. Good job I did. Were you prepared?'

'There's one in my bag,' Stella admitted. 'I think it's still in date.'

Rick chuckled. 'Mine were. I bought them yesterday.'

Stella gasped. 'You planned this?' She didn't know whether to be pleased or horrified.

'Nope. I thought if it was going to happen it would be Sunday or maybe next week. But, hell, I'm glad I got them. There's something about a woman on a mobility scooter makes me horny.'

Stella bumped him. 'You planned to seduce me on Sunday?'

'I planned to wine and dine you and see if I liked you as much as I thought I did. It didn't hurt to be prepared for something more.'

Stella nodded. 'I still get that meal, right?'

'A deal's a deal. You wanna come to the diner with me? I gotta get going soon.'

Stella shook her head. 'I better get home before Gina realises I stopped out.'

'You're a grown woman.'

Stella sighed. 'Yes, but I can't face the intercourse lecture.'

'Tell her it was great.'

Laughing, they fell back on the bed and forgot about breakfast.

#

Gina had noticed.

She'd insisted that Grazja get her up and dressed despite the early hour. She was waiting on the sofa when Stella crept in, intending to head out to the caravan and pretend she'd been there all night.

Grazja was cleaning the bathroom with the radio cranked up and the door shut.

Stella knew she was busted as soon as she saw Gina's face. Lysie would say she had the face of a bulldog chewing a wasp.

Stella plastered on a smile. 'You're up early.'

'I haven't slept a wink,' Gina snarled. 'No thanks to you. I've been outta me head wi' worry. You stay out all night - not a call, nothing - and then you prance in here smelling of booze and sex like a cheap tart.'

Stella blushed. 'I'm an adult Gina. I don't need permission from you for anything. Not one single bloody thing. If I wanted to have sex with an entire football team I could.'

'Wash your filthy mouth out! I didn't raise you to be a floozy.'

'You didn't raise me, Gina. You took me in and you fed me but that was it.'

Gina gasped. 'You're an ungrateful little cow. You always have been. I suppose it was that Yank you been with?'

'As a matter of fact it was,' Stella said.

Gina snorted. 'He's got a reputation all o'er town. You're just another notch on his bedpost my gal. You'll see.'

Stella was furious. 'You are such a bitch, Gina.' The words flew out.

Gina turned purple. 'Don't you dare speak to me

like that. After all I've done for you.' She was apoplectic.

Stella hated herself but somehow, with the words out there, she couldn't stop. 'What have you ever done for me, Gina? Other than humiliate and shame me?'

'Shame you?' Gina yelled. '*Shame* you?'

'Yes, shame me. What about the time you came to my sixth form and shouted at Oliver Gates. Publicly. Let everyone know what I'd done.'

Gina spluttered. 'That boy used you,' she said. 'He tricked you into intercourse and then he dumped you. He deserved what he got from me. Do you think I'd let him treat my granddaughter that way. He coulda got you pregnant.'

'He didn't trick me, Gina. I wanted to lose my virginity. I wanted to do it.'

'You were head over heels in love wi' him,' Gina said. 'He knew it and he let you think he felt the same. That boy broke your heart. I know he did.'

Hot tears ran down Stella's cheeks. 'You only knew about it because you read my diary. My private diary. You found where I hid it and then you did the worst thing possible.'

'I did it for you!'

'How on earth can you possibly believe that's true? How did it help me, Gina? How did publicly attacking Oliver Gates help? How did screaming in the school grounds about intercourse and taking my virginity make it better? Not only was I heartbroken, not only did I feel used and stupid, I became a public laughing stock. It was like the Femfresh saga all over again but ten thousand times worse. And that wasn't even the pinnacle of what you did to me, Gina and you know it.'

'Oh, so we're back here,' Gina hissed. 'Always back to this - your sainted Mrs Jenkins and what the terrible monster, Gina, did to her.'

Stella jerked at the word 'monster'. 'You know about the painting?' she asked slowly. 'Did Grazja show you?'

Gina blinked at the sudden change of direction.

'Painting?'

'Wait here.' Stella ran through the kitchen and out to the caravan. She returned bearing the large canvas and turned its face to Gina.

The Emerald Garden

The emerald garden came about in the summer of 1992. Mrs Jenkins' garden was again in full bloom. During the long winter months Stella helped Mrs Jenkins plan a new layout, sketching designs for her with coloured pencils. Except for that one afternoon when she had missed the BBC2 matinee, Stella had been careful to spend Saturday afternoons with Gina. She'd understood the message contained in the corned beef hash.

Still, that didn't stop her visiting Mrs Jenkins. When they weren't gardening - doing it or planning it - Stella liked to sit at Mrs Jenkins' kitchen table and paint.

She was touchy and moody with Gina and all sweetness with Mrs Jenkins. Gina responded to her adolescent foulness with her usual sensitivity.

'Just cos you got a couple of fried eggs on yer chest don't make you a grown up.' Or 'I never let yer mum dress like a tart at your age, so take that skirt off, and put on summat decent.' And 'Why don't you ask Mrs Jenkins. *She* knows everything.'

Stella was over at Mrs Jenkins' the morning Gina started to rip up the weeds and patchy lawn in her front garden. She looked over to see her grandmother, red-faced and wheezing, while Fred Astaire sniffed around her feet. Stella went over. 'What are you doing?'

'We're having a new garden,' Gina puffed, straightening. She wore a turquoise 1940s' style turban. 'Seeing as you like them so much.'

'Really?' Stella forgot to be sulky. She liked this

idea. Their scrubby, weedy frontage embarrassed her. 'Do you want some help?'

Gina smiled. 'I wouldn't mind,' she said. 'It's hot work.'

'What are we going to do with it?' Stella asked, bending to yank up some weeds.

Gina glanced over to where Mrs Jenkins was peeping over a display of lupins. She smiled smugly. 'You'll see,' she said. 'I'm having some things delivered this afternoon, so I got to get it ready.' She turned her back on Mrs Jenkins and returned to her annihilation of the lawn.

By midday they'd cleared the area. Sweaty and dirty, Stella considered the heap of refuse they'd created in one corner. 'What will we do with this?'

'Dave Smeld'll take it away,' Gina said. 'He's bringing the other stuff, so 'e can put this lot in his van.'

'Dave Smeld,' Stella repeated. She didn't like Dave Smeld. He had a glide in one eye and gave her the creeps.

'Yeah. He's done me a good deal,' Gina said. 'You should go inside when he comes. I don't want you wearing them shorts around him. I've seen him letching at you.'

'Ugh!'

'Ugh is right,' Gina said. 'Better get used to it. That's men for you.'

Stella watched from upstairs when Dave Smeld came round. Unable to drive his van up the pedestrianized street, he delivered his load by wheelbarrow, making numerous journeys back and forwards. Stella, expecting to see vegetation - new turf and plants - was bewildered by a different sort of greenery pouring out of the wheelbarrow. Load upon load of green glass chips, glinting in the summer sun.

It did look like treasure.

And then came the plants, or rather flowers. Buckets and buckets of plastic carnations.

'Got a job lot from a funeral parlour,' Dave called to Gina.

'They're beautiful,' Gina said.

'Only thing missing from 'em is the scent,' Dave said. 'Otherwise yer can't tell the difference between them and real. And these don't need no watering, neither.'

Stella was horrified. After Dave left she rushed out.

'What are you doing?' she shrieked. 'This isn't a real garden.'

'O' course it is. Now grab a spade and we'll start spreading the chips.'

'A garden has soil and plants and grass, Gina. Not glass chippings. And look at those plastic flowers. Ugh.'

Gina looked at the carnations. 'What are yer on about? They're beautiful. Look at all the different colours.'

'They're awful. They look cheap.'

'They don't! They look real as can be. And the beauty is yer don't have to water them, or deadhead them or anything. They take care of themselves.'

'But the whole point of a garden is to look after it,' Stella protested.

Gina looked at her like she was mad. 'Have you gone out? Who wants to grub around in the dirt? I got better things to do.'

Stella glanced over to Mrs Jenkins' garden.

'Oh,' Gina hissed, turning red. 'So that's it. Yer think it's not good enough for Mrs Perfect Pants over there. Well let me tell you, miss, I still work for my living. I work to keep a roof over our heads and food in your mouth. I don't have the luxury, like some people, to have relatives leave me a house and be able to retire. I ain't had a husband paying me way all these years. Mrs Jenkins has all the time in the world to waste on her garden, and the money to do it. She ain't got anyone to support and clothe, like I do. So, if I want a lovely garden it's got to be easy to look after. Unless, of course you want to do it and pay for all the plants and whatnot? Maybe get yourself a job too?'

Stella glared mutinously at the ground.

'Yeah, thought not,' Gina said. 'So stop your mardin' and get on wi' it.'

By late afternoon, Gina's garden had attracted a small crowd of local kids who milled in the street, licking dripping ice-lollies, casting covetous glances at the glass chips. They'd given up trying to reach through the railings and grabbing the emeralds because Fred Astaire patrolled the border, nipping at small, eager fingers.

In their eyes the garden, sparkling in the sunlight, sprouting candy-coloured flowers, was magical. The little girls particularly liked it and brought their dolls along to admire the view.

Gina spiked the plastic carnation stalks directly into the soil beneath the emerald chips, so they stood proud and erect, and lined the pathway to the front door with a parallel parade of pink and white carnations.

When she deemed it finished she fetched a couple of deck chairs from the back shed and placed them on the glass gravel, facing the street.

Stella had disappeared inside some time ago, supposedly to use the toilet. She had failed to re-emerge.

'Stella,' Gina called. 'It's finished. Come have some squash outside. It's beautiful.'

Stella hovered in the doorway, squinting out. She had changed into a long skirt.

'Sit here,' Gina nodded to the deck chair next to hers.

'I'm not sitting out in front of the whole street,' Stella said.

'You sit on Mrs Jenkins' bench,' Gina snapped. 'What's the difference?'

Stella gave her the 'how can you be so stupid look?' she'd recently perfected.

'It looks amazing,' another voice said before Gina could respond to Stella.

Fred Astaire yipped, this time a welcoming sound, and trotted over to the fence. Dave Smeld had returned. He leaned over and patted Fred. Fred hated kids but he loved Dave Smeld.

Stella rolled her eyes. Idiot dog.

'I love it, Dave,' Gina said. 'It's just as I imagined.'

'You know what would look nice,' Dave said. 'A wishing well.'

Gina's eyes lit. 'You know, you could be right. Could you get me one?'

'I'll see what I can do.'

'Would you like a glass o' squash Dave, or lemonade?' Gina asked, unusually hospitable.

'Lemonade,' Dave said, taking it as an invitation to unlatch the gate and enter. He settled himself into the second deck chair and flapped his T-shirt. 'It's 'otter than Torremolinos.'

'Stella, get Dave a lemonade.'

Mumbling, Stella melted back into the house. By the time she returned, which was considerably longer than was polite, two other neighbours had turned out to admire Gina's work.

'Put Fred in the house, would yer?' Gina said. 'He'll get overexcited.'

Stella coaxed Fred into the kitchen with dog biscuits then shut him in.

A little crowd had gathered on the street - more neighbours coming to investigate - and Gina was up, chatting to them as they gawped at her creation.

'There's a good girl,' Dave said as Stella handed him his drink 'You're growin' up quick.'

Stella, who had begun to fill out in the chest area, shuddered and moved away.

Mrs Cookson shouted over to Dave. 'Can yer get me some of this green glass?'

'I can try. It weren't easy getting it for Gina.'

'I love it.'

'Yeah, looks great.' Dave lifted his glass to the garden. 'I was just saying, a wishing well'd look grand.'

'Ay, now you're talkin', duck.'

Vera Dunston commented to Gina. 'Don't them flowers look real.'

Gina swelled. 'I know. But just think, no watering.'

Vera nodded. 'I prefer artificial flowers in my house. I just gi' em a quick hoover when I do my cleaning.'

Stan Dunston, Vera's husband, grew vegetables in their front garden, all neatly trained in rows and trenches. In the winter he covered the ground with tarpaulin to keep the weeds and the local cats away. He gazed in dismay at Gina's work but wisely kept his mouth shut. His neighbour and pub-mate, George Tomlin, shook his head in disgust. He grew roses, spraying them obsessively to keep them black spot and aphid free.

'After seeing this I need a pint,' he murmured to Stan.

Stan nodded. 'Meet you down The Lion in ten minutes.'

George touched the side of his nose and walked away.

Mrs Jenkins had tentatively joined the gathering from behind the safety of her garden gate. Mrs Cookson turned to her. 'Gina's giving you a bit a competition,' she cackled loudly. 'What do you think of that?'

Mrs Jenkins smiled wanly. 'Very nice.'

'I'm gonna get some of that green gravel,' Mrs Cookson said. 'I think it's lovely. Easier than grass.'

Mrs Jenkins nodded. She met Gina's eyes for a moment and saw the challenge there. Inside her house the phone began to ring. She looked grateful for a reason to leave. 'That'll be my sister,' she said.

'Jean?' Mrs Cookson called after her. 'She hasn't been down this way in years. Say 'hello' for me.' She turned back to Gina. 'Jean always was a stuck up cow. Yer remember how she used to refuse to fetch her poor grandma a bottle of stout from The Lion? Said it were 'common'.'

Gina snickered.

Mrs Cookson cocked an eyebrow at Mrs Jenkins' house. 'She's not much better...' She was going to say more but Bill Topliss interrupted her.

'Gina,' he said in his know-it-all voice. 'Please tell me you've put a liner underneath that gravel.'

'How's that any of your business?' Gina bristled.

Bill ignored her, shouting over the top of her head to Dave. 'Dave, has Gina put a liner under this gravel?'

'Ah,' Dave waved him off. 'She don't need one.'

Bill goggled. 'Don't need one! Are yer off yer head? She's gonna have weeds springing up in no time.'

Dave waved him away and turned his back.

'Seriously, Gina. Dave should've tode yer. It's gonna be a scrubland in two weeks.'

Gina bared her teeth at him. 'Ger off wi' yer,' she said. 'You're just trying to wind me up. Anyway, a few weeds won't matter. Stella'll pull em up. She loves gardening. Helps Margaret Jenkins all the time.'

Gina looked around for Stella. She wasn't in the throng. Maybe she was in the house again, sulking as usual. Then Gina spotted her. Stella was coolly watching proceedings, sipping a drink from the comfort of Mrs Jenkins' bench.

#

The transformation of Gina's garden galvanised Bobbin Street. Bill Topliss dug up his own lawn and hired a compacter to flatten and level the area. He kept the neighbours fully updated on every stage and made sure they all knew the quality of the liner membrane he laid to keep the weeds at bay. His design was more elegant than Gina's. He used 'Golden Corn' gravel for the most part, only using green glass chippings to create an illusionary pond ringed with sandstone rocks. He completed the look with a resin heron dipping into the pond.

Soon garden fever spread along the street. Within a month Bobbin Street had metamorphosed; grassy or gravelled, leafy or stark, organic or plastic. There were those who went for the entirely artificial: Gina, Mrs Cookson, Bill Topliss. And those who loved plant-life: Mrs Jenkins, Stan Dunston, George Tomlin. Then, of course, were those in between, who chose the convenience of gravel or slabs mixed with the convenience of potted plants and shrubs.

George Tomlin branched out from roses into dahlias. His friend, Stan, took the radical step of interspersing his neat vegetable rows with marigolds and sunflowers.

Everybody on the street wrought some sort of change on their front garden, whether large or small. Only Mrs Jenkins seemed untouched but as her garden was in a constant state of flux it went unnoticed.

Something insidious had taken root in Bobbin Street's psyche. Whereas the residents had for the most part rubbed along before, a division had appeared, not obvious at first, but subtle. Those who chose the gravelled or slabbing route secretly resented their green-fingered neighbours and vice versa.

It was Mrs Cookson who first gave poisonous voice to the divide.

'Acts like the lady of the estate' she whispered to Janice Topliss. 'All them plants must cost a fortune.'

They were peering at Mrs Jenkins' garden. 'She comes home with more every day,' Mrs Topliss said. 'It's never enough.'

'It's showing off, that's what it is. We remember what Margaret Jenkins was like when she were young, don't we?'

Janice Topliss didn't, but she nodded anyway.

'She were all right then. A laugh. It was her sister, Jean, that was hoity-toity - never went to the club, never wanted to go dancin' at The Palais. Now Margaret's the same. Don't play bingo, won't do the Pools. All she does is spend money on the bloody garden. Knows most of us don't have the money to burn.'

'I seen her staring at Gina's front,' Janice said. 'Saw her the other day peeping out from behind her curtains.'

'Don't like the competition,' Mrs Cookson said. 'Not the queen bee anymore. 'specially since Dave got Gina that wishing well.'

'Why don't you like Mrs Jenkins, nana?' asked little Ellie Cookson, as she tried to reach through Gina's railings to swipe a couple of green jewels.

Mrs Cookson exchanged a knowing look with Janice Topliss. 'Oh, we like her fine, love. It's her that don't like us.'

'Why?'

'I dunno, love. She thinks she's better than us.'

'Why?'

'You ask too many questions, Ellie. Gi' over.'

There were other rumblings. 'If I hear one more word from Bill about his 'Golden Corn' gravel,' George Tomlin was heard to growl, 'I'm gonna buy a lion and use his garden for its litter tray.'

The first stone cast wasn't a stone but a transparent sandwich bag of dog poo hung on Mrs Jenkins' gate. Two days later Gina's railing was liberally stuffed with litter.

Then George woke the next morning to find a mass decapitation of his yellow roses. Only the yellow ones. The following dawn Bill Topliss discovered his gravel had been seeded with the cigarette butts from a pub's worth of ashtrays.

Accusations flew, tempers flared. George and Bill nearly came to blows. But there was no proof of who had done what, only suspicions.

Things settled for a week, bad feelings simmering but contained. Then came another outbreak. This time Mrs Jenkins' garden had the contents of a neighbour's bin scattered over it - Gina's bin.

Trembling, Mrs Jenkins' knocked on Gina's door. Stella answered it, smiling when she saw Mrs Jenkins. She soon lost the smile. 'Would you get your grandmother, please?'

Gina came to the door.

Mrs Jenkins pointed to the bin she'd dragged with her. 'This is yours?'

Gina crossed her arms and leaned on the doorframe. 'It's got my number on,' she said. 'What about it?'

'The contents have been thrown all over my garden,' Mrs Jenkins said.

Gina straightened. 'So? You think it was me? You've got some bloody cheek to accuse me.'

'Well who else would do it?'

'How should I know?'

Mrs Jenkins glared. 'I think we both know who hates me enough.'

'You're right, I do hate you, but I'm not bleedin' stupid. If I was gonna do that I'd use someone else's bin.'

'Gina!' Stella gasped. She looked apologetically at Mrs Jenkins. 'I'll help you pick it up.'

'You will not,' Gina said. 'You've got school.'

'I've got time,' Stella said.

'You'll get your uniform dirty.'

'Mrs Jenkins keeps an apron I wear for painting. I'll wear that.' Stella squeezed past.

Gina slammed the door after her.

A week passed. Gina, leaving for work, immediately knew something was wrong but it took a moment to register exactly what. Rage hit her. All her artificial carnations were gone. Stolen.

She marched up the path to Mrs Jenkins' door and leaned against the bell until Mrs Jenkins stumbled downstairs in her dressing gown and opened the door.

'Give them back you thieving bitch,' she screamed.

Mrs Jenkins shrank back. 'What?'

'My flowers. I know you took them. Give them back or I swear I'll tear up every plant in this garden.'

'I don't know what you're talking about!'

Gina turned to the nearest flowers - a display of dew-fresh Cosmos - and began ripping them out of the border.

Mrs Jenkins shrieked and pushed Gina away. Gina leaned round her and grabbed a few more heads, viciously yanking. Neighbours, hearing the hullabaloo began appearing.

Mrs Jenkins slapped Gina hard on the cheek.

Gina clutched her enemy by the hair and clawed her face. They grappled, stumbling wildly through the foliage, crushing delicate stems and cherished plants, grunting and shrieking until Stan Dunston and Dave Smeld pulled them apart. Mrs Jenkins fell backwards onto her bottom and sat weeping among the carnage.

Gina struggled against Dave. 'You've stolen everything from me,' she spat at Mrs Jenkins. 'But not anymore. You keep away from Stella.' She allowed herself to be led away by Dave, past Mrs Cookson's gleaming eyes and a gathering of other neighbours.

It took Stan a few more minutes to get Mrs Jenkins to her feet; she was crying too hard. 'Go back inside,' he snapped at the gawpers. 'Show's over.'

#

Stella heard about it first from the local kids. They were waiting for her as she turned onto the street. They couldn't wait to tell her how Gina had gone off 'er 'ead and punched old lady Jenkins' lights out.

She was mortified.

To her relief Gina was out – she'd gone to work and shouldn't be back for another hour at least, so Stella scurried across to Mrs Jenkins, aware that net curtains would be twitching all along the street.

Mrs Jenkins answered the door looking tired and wary. She turned pale at the sight of Stella.

'I'm sorry,' Stella whispered. 'I'm so, so sorry. Please, can I come in?'

Mrs Jenkins peered over Stella's shoulder at Gina's terrace.

'She's not in. She won't be home from work for a while. Please.'

Mrs Jenkins nodded and opened the door cautiously. 'You can't stay long,' she said.

Grateful, Stella darted in. Mrs Jenkins didn't offer her some squash like she normally did. Instead she perched nervously on the edge of a chair. Her eyes kept sliding to an envelope on the table.

'What happened?' Stella asked.

Mrs Jenkins shook her head as though clearing it. 'What. Oh. Gina thought I'd stolen her flowers. The plastic ones in her garden. She went mad. She started to tear up my Cosmos. It was my fault.'

'Your fault?' Stella fiddled with her fingers, bending them back and forth - an anxious habit.

Mrs Jenkins stared at Stella's hands. 'Um, yes. I slapped her you see. I lost my temper over the Cosmos. I started the fight.'

Stella found it hard to imagine Mrs Jenkins slapping anyone. She bent her left index finger entirely back, a nervous habit she did when she was anxious.

'You're double jointed?' Mrs Jenkins asked.

Stella was startled. She hadn't even realised she was doing it. She looked down at her finger. 'Yes, sorry. It makes some people feel sick.'

'My husband was double-jointed,' Mrs Jenkins said. She appeared transfixed. Stella let her hands fall into her lap.

Mrs Jenkins looked up. She smiled tentatively. 'I think it might be best if you don't come over for a while, Stella.'

Stella felt like she'd been punched. 'Why?' she said. 'Gina'll get over it. She's always falling out with people.'

'I don't think so this time. And I'm not sure I can 'get over it' either. Besides, Gina will see it as you taking sides. You should spend more time with her.'

'I spend loads of time with her!'

'Not as much as you should,' Mrs Jenkins insisted. 'She's jealous, you see.'

'That's ridiculous,' Stella protested.

'No, I don't think it is. Let's just let things cool off for a couple of months.' Mrs Jenkins rose. 'Thank you so much for all your help, Stella.'

Stella stumbled back over to her own home, hurt and confused.

That night she took it out on Gina.

'She stole my flowers,' Gina defended herself.

'Of course she didn't. Why would she?'

'Because she hated them,' Gina said. She adopted a mock posh accent. 'They offended her sensibilities. Besides, she was paying me back for the bin.'

'So you did do that?'

'Oh, fo' Christ-sakes, no. But she thought I did. Why are you on her side? You should be on mine.' Gina sulked. 'Anyway, I don't want you seeing her no more.'

'You don't have to worry about that,' Stella retorted. 'She told me not to come back.' Her eyes filled with hateful tears. 'So congratulations, Gina. You've managed to take away the only person on this whole street I care about.' She stomped upstairs, triumphant to have finally got the last word.

Behind her Gina blinked back her own tears.

#

As predicted by Bill Topliss, the weeds and grass began to grow through Gina's gravel. The water in the wishing well turned stagnant. Gnats began to breed in it. The high hopes of early summer blew away with the dandelion seeds as Gina lost all interest in her garden. She seemed to actually encourage Fred Astaire to poop in it. By the end of September, Stella was calling it the Emerald Shitty and the neighbours who'd supported Gina's project chuntered about her lowering the tone of the street. Not that anyone dared say that to her face. Always considered volatile, since the fight Gina's reputation as a loose cannon rocketed. Children ran away when they saw her coming and even Mrs Cookson, not easily intimidated, gave her a wide birth. Gina radiated aggression, as though by tearing her away from the fight, Dave Smeld had temporarily tamped down a volcano. One that was still ready to blow.

Stella and Gina barely spoke through autumn and winter; Stella spent as much time with her school-friends as she could, including Saturday afternoons. Gina bought a new television and a video player for her bedroom, withdrawing into a fantasy world of old-style Hollywood glamour.

The most significant change on the street didn't become apparent until the spring came round again.

It hadn't gone entirely unnoticed that after the fight Mrs Jenkins had let her garden go over, just the slightest bit. The Bobbin Street folk weren't surprised. Mrs Jenkins had been humiliated. Why would she want to spend time in full view of Gina's house?

As Gina's garden declined, sympathy for Mrs Jenkins increased, even among the anti-naturals. So, in November, later than usual, people were pleased to note that she was once again out in her front garden planting bulbs for the spring. Good for her. How terrible it must be to look out and see Gina's mess every day.

It was a surprise then in February when Mrs Jenkins snowdrops only showed two or three heads before disappearing completely. Where was her white, frothy mass? March and April and May lacked crocuses, daffodils, aconites, tulips. Very little sprang up in Mrs Jenkins' garden, in fact, because she had not spent November planting bulbs. She had been tearing them out.

Rumours grew about the state of Mrs Jenkins' mental health. She was seen only rarely and looked thin and unkempt when she did go out. Vera Dunston took her some early potatoes from Stan's veg patch but couldn't get past the door to see inside the house. Mrs Jenkins accepted the potatoes with a faint smile before gently shutting the door in Vera's face.

Just look what Gina had done to her. 'And they used to be such great friends when they was girls,' Mrs Cookson remembered.

It was July when it happened. A wet, dreary, unseasonably cold weekend. Mrs Jenkins staggered out of her house at six in the morning. She knew exactly what the tightness in her chest meant, the light-headedness, the pain running down her left arm. She had stopped taking her heart medicine months ago. She only wanted enough time to make it across the street.

She just managed to get through Gina's gate when she collapsed. She crawled the rest of the way - not to the door - but further into the weedy gravel. With the very last of her strength she rolled on her back,

smothered herself in emerald glass chips, and died.
It was Stella who found her.

Gina Hits Eject

Gina stared at the painting. Her face crumpled. 'Get out,' she cried. 'I don't want you here. Get your things and go home.' She began to weep so bitterly that it frightened Stella.

'I'm sorry,' she said. She cast the painting aside and went to Gina. 'I'm sorry,' she repeated, touching her shoulder.

'Get out!' Gina screamed, the sound so primal that it brought Grazja running.

'What is it?' she said.

'Make her leave,' Gina wept. 'Make her leave, please. I can't stand it no more.'

Stella had never seen Gina so distressed. Angry - often - harrowed, no.

Grazja bustled Stella out of the room. 'What you do to her?' she demanded.

'I showed her the painting. I was angry…'

Grazja tutted. 'You stupid, eh? I told you to be nice to her.' She looked disgusted. 'You must go - stay with boyfriend. Don't go to London. Don't run away. We sort this out but best if you not here today. I calm her down.' She clicked her tongue. 'Go pack a bag. I unlock back gate so you can go out that way, not through house.' She shot Stella another disgusted look.

Ashamed, Stella did as she was told, grabbing clothes and toiletries from the static. She grabbed her car keys and flexed her ankle. She could drive.

Grazja let her out of the gate. 'I text you later, yes?'

Stella nodded.

'Someone else not look pleased.' Grazja pointed.

Stella followed her direction to see George standing by the Rascal Vision she'd parked by the gate. He was scowling.

Grazja pushed her out and locked the gate behind her. Stella approached George. She saw what he was scowling at. Last night and this morning, loved up and dreamy, she'd failed to notice the terrible state of the Rascal. Angry scars ran along its flank, where Pirate Tom had forced her against the sea wall. The paintwork was ruined.

'How did this happen?' George asked, shaking his head.

Um, I had an accident,' Stella said.

'These things don't tip over,' George looked puzzled.

'It didn't tip over,' Stella said. 'I ran into a wall.'

Desperate to be off she walked to her car, dumping her stuff on the back seat. She turned back to George. 'Of course they tip over. That's what happened to Gina.'

George reddened. 'I've left the cooker on,' he mumbled and strode away.

Stella couldn't think. Her hands trembled on the steering wheel. How could she have shown that painting to Gina? She'd felt so self-righteous and now... she felt awful and sick to her stomach.

Suddenly Gina was the injured party and Stella the monster.

Biting back her own tears she started the car.

#

Rick smiled when he saw her. He looked surprised and then worried. 'Hey you,' he said quietly. 'Didn't expect to see you so soon.' He took in her pale face.

'You okay?'

Stella shook her head. 'I've been thrown out. Had a massive row with Gina. The shit's really hit the fan.'

'No,' Rick groaned. 'Really? Because of me?'

'No. Because of me and something stupid I did. I hate to ask... I don't want to smother you but can I stay at yours tonight?'

'Of course. I was hoping you would.'

'Thanks. I'm upset. I might not be up for...' Blushing she mouthed the word 'sex'.

He grinned, mouthing the word silently back. "Sex' is not a requisite.'

'I've got my stuff in my car,' she said. 'I'm parked on the central car park.'

'You want my keys?' Rick offered. 'You can let yourself in. Take a nap. Make a fuss of Henry.'

'It would feel weird... I don't want to intrude.'

Rick rolled his eyes. 'That's so British,' he said, guiding her outside by the elbow. He leaned into her ear. 'You'll have sex with me but you won't take a nap on my sofa?'

'Shhh,' Stella said. She caught Angela's hostile glare. 'People will hear.'

Rick took the keys out of his jeans pocket and held them out with a flourish. 'So what? I haven't done anything I'm ashamed of. Have you?'

'Nooo, but...'

He walked her to the sea wall. 'Honey, when you left this morning you were glowing. Now you look like hell.'

'Thanks!'

'I don't mean it like that. You walked in here looking like you're barely holding it together. You want sanctuary, you got it, but this,' he gestured to the diner, 'ain't it. Come noon on a hot Saturday like this it's gonna be jumping. Me 'n' Ang and the two Saturday kids will be run off our feet. I'm glad you came to me. I'm sure as hell glad you didn't run back to London. Knowing you got Henry to cuddle, a fridge full of food and a quiet place to be will help me out. So …' He dangled the keys.

'Okay,' Stella said, taking them. She couldn't deny the attraction of a place to hide for the day. Impulsively she stretched up to give him a quick kiss on the lips

Frank, enjoying an early coffee after last night's miscreant behaviour, caught her eye. He already had his phone out.

Rick raised his eyebrows. 'Well you've blown our cover now,' he said. He leaned down and gave her a longer, gentle kiss. 'I'll see you later.'

#

Ensconced on the sofa in Rick's garden room, with the venetian blinds three quarters closed, Stella lay on her back, staring at the ceiling. Henry purred on her stomach, oblivious to the nausea Stella felt. She supposed this morning had been inevitable. Proximity to Gina always brought it back. She'd successfully kept Gina at a distance for years and with her the memories of Bobbin Street and that fateful Saturday morning, when at fourteen she'd opened the front door to find Mrs Jenkins dead.

The entire street blamed Gina. So did Stella. She refused to speak to her grandmother for a whole two months. Hate mail popped through the letterbox, never stamped because it originated locally and never signed. Those who'd spitefully gossiped about Mrs Jenkins when she was alive now declared her a saint and Gina the Devil.

Stella, on the other hand, was accepted into the community. Everyone knew she'd helped Mrs Jenkins in her garden, had seen them together down on their knees in the borders or Stella sketching on the garden bench.

'Gina was jealous,' Mrs Cookson declared. 'Spiteful cat. And her only grandchild just orphaned too.'

Stella ate one or two nights every week at one or another neighbour's house. She became the pet project for a few months, until interest petered out and life on the street moved on.

Gina said nothing about any of it. She walked with her head up. Whatever she felt or thought she kept to herself.

Eventually a kind of normality was re-established in the Pontin household - or as close to it as Gina was likely to get - and they began to speak again. A fragile truce existed. Stella worked hard to get to art college - her means of escape - while Gina provided food and board and the occasional horrendous humiliation (like the Oliver Gates incident). Happier moments existed too, such as the trip to London and the infamous Harrods graffiti.

But Mrs Jenkins haunted them. She was a restless ghost; one they never had the means to exorcise, only to ignore. She loomed at the end of every fight, so they learnt, for the most part, not to fight, only to squabble like irritable children.

Stella gained a prestigious place at the Royal Academy of Art to study Fine Art. There she met

Lysie, who fitted into middle class student life as awkwardly as Stella.

Stella never returned to Bobbin Street, other than for a couple of days at Christmas. In the holidays she worked; bar work, temping, cleaning - anything honest that paid. She shared a tiny flat in Clapton with Lysie and they took their teaching certificates together. She was too busy to visit, she told Gina. She was teaching and trying to build a career as an artist at the same time. She would come when she could.

By twenty-nine she was lucky enough to achieve what most artists never do - a full-time, self-employed career doing what she loved. She had an agent, a growing reputation in illustration, exhibitions where her work sold out and a studio flat. After two failed significant relationships she rescued Henry from an animal shelter. When she had to she spoke to Gina on the phone. The last four Christmases she'd told Gina she was too snowed under with commissions to join her.

She'd managed to be away on holiday when Gina had moved to Mapton.

Stella shivered. She'd justified it easily. Gina's very Gina-ness made it excusable. Now she understood; she hadn't just been avoiding Gina. She'd been afraid to face up to Mrs Jenkins' ghost and the bitter hatred it stirred in her towards her grandmother.

The ghost had caught up with her at last. It had taken possession as she painted. It was crying out to be heard.

She recalled her screams when she'd found Mrs Jenkins. The coldness of her skin as she tried to wake her, the staring eyes... She'd woken the entire street.

Gina had reached her first. 'Oh my God!' She'd run for the phone.

For the first time Stella felt anger towards Mrs Jenkins. She cut it off guiltily. Mrs Jenkins must have been coming for help. It was a terrible accident. She was having a heart attack. But by burying herself in the glass gravel the message was clear.

The heart attack was brought on by Gina's actions. It was her fault.

Other images rushed back. Snippets of conversation. There was a woman - tall, severely elegant. She came to clean out Mrs Jenkins' house. Her sister? Yes, her sister. What was her name? Mrs Cookson had told Stella about it over tea one night. Even Mrs Cookson had taken care of her! What did she say?

'That woman?' Mrs Cookson replied to Stella's question. 'That's Jean, Mrs Jenkins' sister. She came to sort out the house. A bit uppity if you ask me. Always was, even as a youngster. Her father had been a businessman of some sort and when it failed he moved the family onto Bobbin Street. They spoke a bit hoity-toity and Jean thought she was above us, but her sister, Maggie - that were Mrs Jenkins - was a bit younger and a bit of a tear-away. Her and Gina were great mates. Yer couldn't split 'em apart as kids.'

Stella shot upright, causing Henry to leap off her stomach with a yowl. She tried to remember what else Mrs Cookson had said, but it was too long ago. Was she even remembering this part correctly?

Maggie. Margaret Jenkins. Maggie Bone?

Her heart fluttered rapidly. Maggie Bone - the best friend who stole Gina's fiancé had been Mrs Jenkins?

Oh no. No.

Yet it made sense. Finally it made some sense. Gina hadn't simply been jealous of Stella's relationship with Mrs Jenkins; she had already hated her and with good reason.

Stella grabbed her iPad. She searched Nottingham Evening Post obituaries and discovered she could pay for past copies on ancestry.co.uk. She typed in Margaret Jenkins, née Bone, died 1994, and was rewarded with an obituary from the time. It mentioned the sister as the only surviving kin. Her name was Mrs Jean Simmons.

Stella smiled wryly. Her life seemed to be littered with the names of old film stars.

She used 192.com to search for a Mrs Jean Simmons in the Nottinghamshire area. It scared her just how easy it is to gain information from the internet. For a small fee to oil the wheels you have access to the electoral role, family records, telephone numbers and addresses. Perfect for private detectives and stalkers.

Sure that she had the correct Mrs Simmons, Stella took a deep breath then keyed the numbers into her phone. She almost hung up twice while it was ringing. A man answered.

'Hello?'

'Hello? May I speak to Mrs Simmons, please?'

A pause. 'Who should I say is calling?'

'Stella Distry. Er, she may not know my name. I knew her sister, Margaret.'

'Hold on.'

Stella heard his muffled footsteps, indistinct voices. Someone picked up the phone.

'Hello?' A woman's voice. Wary.

'Oh, Hello. Mrs Simmons?'

'Yes.'

'I'm sorry to bother you. You won't remember me but I knew your sister, Margaret Jenkins, when I was young. My name's Stella Distry…'

'Gina Pontin's granddaughter,' Mrs Simmons said.

'Oh! Er, yes. That's right.'

'Margaret told me about you,' Mrs Simmons said. 'You found her, didn't you?'

'Yes. I'm afraid so.'

'It must have been terrible for you.'

Stella was surprised. 'Yes. Yes, it was. Mrs Simmons, I know it was a long time ago now but I have some things I'd like to know - like to ask you. Would I be able to come over, tomorrow maybe?'

Mrs Simmons was silent. 'Just a moment,' she said. 'I'll have a word with my husband.'

Stella sweated as she waited. Again the muffled sound of voices.

Mrs Simmons returned. 'That will be fine,' she said. 'How about eleven tomorrow morning?'

'Really? That's great. Thank you.'

'I'll give you directions,' Mrs Simmons said.

'It's okay, I've got the address. I'll use my sat nav.'

Mrs Simmons sighed. 'The internet, I suppose?'

Stella had the decency to blush. 'Yes. Sorry. I really wanted to find you.'

'And if I hadn't wanted to be found?'

'Well,' Stella said apologetically. 'That's why I rang first. I wouldn't have pushed.'

'We'll see you tomorrow then,' Mrs Simmons let it drop. 'At eleven. Call me if your sat nav gets you lost.'

'Thanks,' Stella said. 'See you tomorrow. Bye.'

'Good bye.'

Stella ended the call with shaking hands. She saw the text message symbol on her phone display. It was from Grazja. 'G mad still. U stay away and then she miss u soon. U come home now she shoot u. Ha! U still in Mapton like I tell u?'

'Yes. At Rix. Thanx. Xxx'

Fatigue took over. Stella reached for the throw strewn on the back of the sofa and curled under it; she fell into an exhausted sleep. Henry, deeming it safe, re-joined her on the sofa, nestling into the warmth of her belly. It was how Rick found them hours later.

'Hey,' he said as she woke. 'You really zonked out. You must've needed it.'

Stella was relieved to find she hadn't drooled in her sleep. She sat up.

'I fed Henry,' Rick said. 'He was curled up with you when I got home. What about you, you eaten anything today?'

Stella shook her head. 'I wasn't hungry,' she said. 'I felt too sick.'

'And now?'

As Stella considered her belly rumbled.

'I guess that's the answer,' he said. 'I bagged up a couple of burgers and fries from the diner. I can't be bothered to cook after doing it all day.'

The food was lukewarm but really good. Rick added cold beers and they ate it at the kitchen counter.

'Great burgers,' Stella said.

'Good beef,' Rick said. 'One hundred percent, ground it myself. No horsemeat in these babies.'

They finished with chocolate cake.

'Ooh, even better,' Stella groaned, licking the last bit of icing off her fork.

'Can't take the credit,' Rick said. 'This is Ang's speciality.'

'Really? She's good.'

'She is.'

'She seems to hate me,' Stella said.

Rick started. 'What, Ang? You must've misread her. She's a bit shy at first, that's all.'

Stella didn't think so but she kept quiet. She had her own thoughts about why Ang didn't like her but she wasn't ready to voice them to Rick. Not this early in their relationship.

'I brought something to cheer you up,' Rick said. 'It made me laugh so hard that Ang ordered me outside.' He handed her a newspaper. It was the Lawton Post, East Lincolnshire's local paper. The headline screamed: **Mad Dogs and Pensioners Menace Mapton Seafront.**

Stella clapped a hand to her mouth. She scanned the article.

At 11.30pm on Friday night, police broke up an illegal 'rumble' between two gangs of pensioners racing mobility scooters on the promenade between Mapton and Siltby. Rumours of monthly races in a number of seaside towns have been rife but this is the first time police have caught them red-handed. More shocking is that the leader of one gang - The Siltby Wanderers - is Tom Turner, recently elected deputy mayor of Mapton & Siltby District Council.

'Pirate Tom's the deputy mayor!' Stella squealed.

Rick nodded. 'Keep reading. It gets better.'

Police questioned Deputy Mayor Turner, who revealed the name of the rival gang as The Mapton Marauders and their leader as Ms Susan Mulligan, of Paradise Crescent, Mapton. The Leader spoke to Deputy Mayor Turner upon his release from the police station. He said: 'This is ridiculous. We presented no danger to anyone and simply like to meet up occasionally and have some fun on our scooters. We choose to race late at night in order not to endanger any pedestrians. What is far more dangerous is the pack of feral dogs that attacked us last night. It was a terrifying ordeal. I wouldn't be surprised if they are rabid. What are the police doing about that?'

In reply Sergeant Chris Bramble said: 'The promenade between Mapton and Siltby is intended for cyclists and pedestrians. Mobility scooter users are required to keep to the legal maximum for pavements, which is 4mph and most do. However the scooter gangs are racing up to (and possibly beyond) 8mph and riding two or three abreast. We consider this a serious risk to the public and to themselves. This time we have only cautioned those involved but future infringers will face charges.' He then went onto say: 'We are taking the issue of the dog attack very seriously indeed. This is the third incident reported this week. We do know the identity of one of the dogs - a Jack Russell - and believe two of the others to be dogs that have been reported missing in the last few days. The dogs did not hurt anyone yesterday, but seemed to be attracted by the smell of cooked meats kept in Mr Turner's scooter basket. They also seemed to be very well organised. This leads us to believe that

someone is training them. We ask that anyone with any information comes forward.'

Sergeant Bramble also advised the public to be vigilant when eating outside, especially with meat-based foods.

Stella gaped at Rick. 'Should I go on the run?'

'If you can make it over the border to Norfolk you should be safe.'

They cracked up.

'You should've heard Sue today,' Rick gasped for air. 'She was hopping mad. Called Tom a snitch, a grass and a fink all in one breath. She had a visit from the police first thing this morning.' He saw Stella's concern. 'Don't worry; it was just a verbal caution. They're not coming after you or any of the other Marauders. Sue's lovin' it really. She likes to see herself as a rebel. By the end of the week she'll have bigged up this story until she's the Queen of the Bandidos. It'll make her year.'

Stella sobered. 'It's getting serious with Bing. He's got a pack.'

'Yeah,' Rick agreed. 'But no one was bitten. They were after the food.'

'I'm responsible,' Stella said. 'It was me that locked Bing out in the garden. I didn't know he'd tunnel out.'

'How could you? And he'd just savaged your ankle. In fact it's really his fault you joined a criminal gang. If he hadn't gone for your ankle you'd never have ridden the scooter.'

'That's true!'

'He's a criminal mastermind.'

Bing Beds Down

Last Night's wildly successful hunt consolidated the pack and Bing's alpha position within it. His diminutive size was outstripped by his ferocity and his own firm belief that he was much, much bigger than he actually was. He'd led the hunt, dazzling his pack-mates with the boldness of the enterprise and the way he'd leapt upon his prey - the machine on wheels - with precision, tearing from its rump a juicy selection of meaty packages.

Of course it was luck, really, that Bing's pack happened to be nearby as the rumble took place. After Bing's near miss with the 'catching man' he understood that town, while rich for picking, was no place to den. It was too risky. Having assembled his pack, he sought out a suitable place for a den. He and Mitch found it halfway between Mapton and Siltby, in a dried-up drainage tunnel covered by overgrown brambles. Being crepuscular animals the pack dozed, played, and groomed around the den during the day, mostly venturing out at around dawn and dusk to scavenge.

The quickest way to reach the bins of Mapton was to head straight along the seafront. Too busy during the day, only the occasional zealous jogger might take to the beach at the crack of dawn, and as dusk came late in June by the time of full dark it was rare to encounter people along the unlit part of the promenade. Even bored teenagers preferred to huddle in shelters or work the arcades in town.

However last night the darkest strip blazed with light from the sort of machines common in Mapton.

Even Gina drove one, although he'd always refused to ride it with her.

He'd paused, his pack stopping behind him. Mitch joined him. They conferred. Best to circle around and use the beach rather than the hard path, Bing concluded. He was about to lead them off again when he and Mitch simultaneously caught a scent. A very faint scent but a very good one.

Roast chicken.

Bing snapped at Tammie and Prince to stay while he and Mitch cautiously crawled towards the light and commotion. The smell grew stronger. It made them salivate. And it wasn't just chicken but other good savoury smells too.

Bing's nose quivered. He couldn't pinpoint the location exactly, but he could tell it came from the herd of machines.

He and Mitch returned to the others. Tonight, Bing told them, they wouldn't scavenge. Tonight they would hunt.

The pack could hardly contain their excitement, especially Prince, who was easily excitable. Bing had to nip him twice to stop him blundering off towards the herd.

We work as a team, he told them. We must separate the prey from the herd. We must be cunning.

And they had been.

The booty was a bounty of meaty goodness, plenty for all. The pack had worked perfectly as one, taking their cues from Bing. Even Prince did well.

Fleeing with the meat packages in their jaws, they'd triumphantly returned to the den. Later, after the feast, a fox, drawn by the smell of scraps, tried to dart in and snatch a ripped packet. They'd chased it joyously across the farmers' fields beyond the scrubland and caravan parks, howling at the full moon. It got away; after all, they weren't hunting-hounds trained to run. Exhausted yet exhilarated, they slunk back to their tunnel where they slept safely through the following day, blissfully unaware of the rumpus they'd caused.

Friends and Enemies

Stella watched Mapton slide past as Rick manoeuvred his jeep through the main street, past the arcades and cheap fast food, The Rock Stop and tacky gift shops. It was early Sunday morning so most shops were shut but some were beginning to open up. She peered up at the stuccoed side of a peeling pink building sporting a cerise sign: Flamingo City.

'Are there any flamingos?' Stella asked.

'No flamingos and it's not a city.'

'What is it?'

'Sort of a complex. A couple of cafes, a bar - always empty - and kiddies' play centre. My personal favourite is Witchywicca World.'

Stella raised an eyebrow. 'Witchywicca World?'

'Yeah, you know - for all your white witchcraft needs. Crystals, tarot packs, fairy figurines, dragons...'

'Dream catchers, incense and patchouli oil?' Stella finished for him.

'Hey,' Rick said. 'You love that stuff too? You know, I really think this relationship is gonna work.'

Stella snorted. 'Even Gina thinks that kind of thing is rammel.'

'Don't diss the magic! And what the hell is rammel anyway?'

Stella laughed. 'God, I haven't used that word in years. It's a Nottingham term for rubbish. Stuff that's useless and ugly.' They'd stopped at a red light. Stella glanced in a shop window 'Fancy Goods and Gifts'. 'Stuff like that,' she pointed out to Rick.

He leaned forward to peer past her. 'What! A tits

mug! Who wouldn't want a nice pair of ceramic tits to cheer him up in the morning?'

Stella rolled her eyes. 'Rammel,' she stated firmly.

'Snob.' Rick grinned.

She smiled back. He reached over to push a curl off her face. 'But cute.'

They left Mapton for the flat farmland of East Lincolnshire. The further they drove the more anxious Stella felt. She was grateful to Rick for coming with her, more grateful that he hadn't taken offence when she told him her plan. After all, this was the day he'd promised to make the best meal she'd ever eaten and she'd blown it to go chasing after the past.

She glanced over at Rick, at the set of his jaw, the light stubble on it and the line of his strong, tanned forearms. His hands were relaxed on the wheel, masculine but finely shaped. She flushed hot, remembering where they'd touched her last night. He looked over at her and smiled, making her a little dizzy.

Crazy. Her life had gone crazy. She had gone crazy. One week back in Gina's orbit had flipped her ordered existence upside down and yet it wasn't a bad thing. Perhaps it was what she needed.

One week ago she would've sneered at the idea. A major bust up with Gina? Probing the wounds of the past? Hot sex with an American diner owner she hardly knew, who chose to live in a faded, dusty has-been holiday resort that clung to the edge of 'The Land That Time Forgot'?

This was what she needed? Really?

Really.

'Thanks for listening last night,' she said. 'I didn't

mean to dump it all on you.'

'I'm glad you told me,' Rick replied. 'I get it now - your feelings about Gina.'

She'd told him all of it.

'Not exactly what's meant by 'pillow talk,' she said sheepishly.

'I think it is,' Rick said. 'If you can't be honest after sex when can you be?'

Stella was silent, thinking. She wasn't sure she'd ever been that intimate with anyone before, either physically or emotionally. The thought scared her.

'You were going to tell me how you ended up in Mapton.' Stella changed the subject.

'As part of the dinner deal,' Rick said. 'That ain't happened yet. I'm still gonna make you the best meal you ever ate.'

'What? And you won't tell me your story until then?'

'Nope. They kinda go together.'

'Mysterious,' said Stella.

'Not really,' Rick laughed. 'Don't go imagining anything terrible. Let's just get this done today - you got plenty of stuff to be thinking about without listening to me.'

'I need something to distract me from thinking!'

'Okay. I'll tell you about the town I grew up in and how I started cooking.'

He was a good storyteller. His mid-west accent and easily rhythmic anecdotes made her laugh and relax. For a time she forgot the reason for the journey and the nauseating memory of yesterday's row and just listened, occasionally asking a question or teasing out more detail.

Her anxiety came back once the signs for Nottingham began to appear. Mrs Simmons' village was southeast of Nottingham in the Vale of Belvoir so they wouldn't be going as far as the city, thank God.

The village was well-to-do, manicured gardens and chocolate-box cottages rolled past, but it had grown since the seventies and branched off into neat, modern estates, equally maintained but less picturesque, though their back windows looked out over rolling countryside.

Mrs Simmons lived in one of these houses. Even in her nervous state Stella noted the 'weed and feed' immaculateness of the front lawn, edged by filled borders. The flowers were beautiful but lacked the ebullient joyousness that had infused Mrs Jenkins' patch.

Rick parked at the kerb. He gave Stella's knee a reassuring squeeze before they stepped out.

Mrs Simmons opened the door as they reached it. She was tall, with grey hair swept elegantly into a bun.

'Stella?'

Stella nodded, offering her hand. 'Mrs Simmons?'

Mrs Simmons shook with her. 'Jean, please,' she said. She turned to Rick enquiringly.

Stella realised she hadn't given a thought to how she'd introduce him. 'Oh, this is my friend, Rick. I hope you don't mind him coming?'

'Not at all,' Jean said. She accepted his hand.

'Nice to meet you,' Rick said.

'Come in, please.'

They followed her into a clean, carpeted hallway. A vase of irises stood elegantly on a small table.

'Would you mind taking off your shoes?' Jean asked. 'We've just had the lounge re-carpeted.'

Stella and Rick slipped off their shoes and padded after her.

The lounge was tasteful with a large patio door looking out onto the back garden. Nothing jolted the eye. Nothing much caught it either. Mr Simmons - Jeff - was waiting in there. He was the same height as his wife. His eyes were vivid blue and kind. He asked them if they'd like tea, coffee, or something cold. Stella went for tea, Rick for coffee. Jeff left them to make small talk with his wife before returning with a laden tray.

'Jeff made the cake,' Jean told them. 'Would you like some?'

It was a particularly good-looking Victoria sponge. They both said yes.

'This is great,' Rick said.

Jeff swelled. 'Started baking when I retired. The Great British Bake Off inspired me to start. Now I'm addicted.'

'It's not doing my waistline any good.' Jean smiled at her husband.

Again they made polite conversation until Jeff said, rather abruptly. 'Do you like gardens, Rick?'

'Um, sure,' Rick said.

'C'mon, I'll show you ours,' Jeff said rising.

'Okay.'

It was clearly a ruse to leave the women alone. Rick shot an enquiring look at Stella; she gave him a small nod.

When they had gone, Jean said. 'I thought we could discuss this alone.'

Stella agreed. 'Thank you for agreeing to see me. It's very good of you.'

Jean waved off her gratitude. 'I'm glad you found me. I should've talked to you years ago.'

Stella was puzzled. 'Why? You didn't know me.'

'I knew of you. I saw you once, a pale, unhappy little thing you looked. But I was too bitter at the time to think of you. I should have. A girl who had lost her parents having to discover my sister like that.' She sounded angry.

'I'm sure she didn't mean to do it.' Stella had a powerful urge to defend Mrs Jenkins. 'Maybe she was coming for help.'

Jean gave her an appraising look. 'She had a telephone. She could've rung 999.'

'Perhaps she just panicked.'

Jean bobbed her head slowly. 'Perhaps.' She sounded unconvinced. 'Tell me, Stella, why did you want to talk me?'

Stella hesitated. Haltingly she told Jean about her relationship with Gina; recent events had brought them together, triggering the old feelings she'd repressed - guilt about Mrs Jenkins and her bone-deep anger at Gina - and how, secretly Stella had always believed it was her friendship with Mrs Jenkins that had caused Gina's hatred of her, a jealousy that kicked off the Bobbin Street War, a fight between the two women which eventually culminated in Mrs Jenkins' death.

'And then this week,' she said. 'Gina mentioned a best friend, Maggie Bone and how she'd stolen Gina's fiancé after he'd got her pregnant.' She stumbled over the words, almost incoherently. 'And then yesterday I remembered Mrs Cookson telling me... and I remembered you and I thought...' She began to sniffle.

Jean fetched a box of tissues and put one in her hand. 'You poor thing,' she said. 'What a tangled web Margaret and Gina spun themselves. And you, at fourteen, thinking my sister's death was your fault. Of course at that age you think the sun and moon revolve around you and you have the power to knock them out of orbit.'

She patted Stella's back awkwardly.

'You were right to come,' she said. 'I've never been a fan of Gina's but I think I need to set you straight on some things.'

Stella peered at her through swollen eyes. 'I'm sorry,' she said. 'I've made a fool of myself.'

'Nonsense,' Jean said briskly. 'Wait here. I'll be back in a moment.'

Stella used the time to wipe her face and collect herself. She hated soppy displays of emotion. What was happening to her?

Jean returned, bearing an old photo album pristinely kept. She settled next to Stella on the sofa and opened it. Lifting the gauzy tissue paper protecting each page, she pointed to a photograph of two girls, about ten, holding ice-cream cones, arms twined round each other's waist. Their grins were wide and cheeky, eyes bright with youth and mischief.

'Margaret and Gina,' Jean said. 'My father took the picture on a day trip to Skegness.'

Stella leaned over to get a better look. Margaret's face had the delicate bones she recalled but none of

Mrs Jenkins reserve. Her smile crackled. But it was Gina that took her breath away. Her fresh unmade-up face tilted towards the camera; apple cheeked and snub-nosed, dark plaits hanging down each shoulder, she radiated happiness. And she was pretty.

Stella couldn't associate this Gina with the one she knew, whose mouth was so often drawn in a bitter line.

'From the moment we moved to Bobbin Street they were inseparable,' Jean said. 'Gina didn't live on Bobbin Street then, but around the corner. She spent so much time at our house she might as well have lived there. Her father was a drinker - always out of work - so I think she preferred our house.

'Still my mother didn't much like her - she thought she was a bad influence on Margaret - but my dad liked her. He found her funny and what dad said went in our house. He didn't think it mattered that they occasionally skipped school to go to the pictures or hang about in town. Girls weren't expected to have careers, so what did an education matter?

'I didn't have much to do with Margaret and Gina. I'd gone to grammar school after taking my eleven-plus. I was a couple of years older and had a different set of friends. Both of them went to Secondary Modern and couldn't wait to leave school. I had to fight my dad to stay on and do my A levels. I was the only girl on Bobbin Street to go to grammar school. It didn't make me popular, I can tell you.'

She flipped a page and pointed to a photo of a gangly looking girl in school uniform squinting shyly at the camera. 'First day,' she said, sounding wistful. She paused examining the photo, then turned another few pages, and continued brusquely.

'Anyway, enough about me. Look, here's Margaret and Gina at fifteen. They're just about to go off to their first jobs together at Holmes and Baxter.'

Five years on and the girls had blossomed into fashionable young women. Both wore powder and lipstick, their hair set into fifties fashion. The radiance remained; the expression of hope on their faces and the cockiness of their smiles bore the hallmarks of youthful over-confidence.

Jean smiled ruefully. 'Mum hoped they'd drift apart after leaving school. She was dismayed when they found a job together. They were even stationed next to each other - at least for the first week, until the foreman split them apart for gossiping too much.

'I could never understand why they didn't get sick of each other. They walked to work together, lunched, walked home, and then went out in the evening. Even when they dated, half the time it was on double dates. And could they talk. Yapping and giggling, whispering behind their hands. I know Gina referred to me as Miss Primknickers. They were inseparable.'

'I can't imagine Gina being that close to anyone,' Stella said.

'It wasn't natural,' Jean said.

Stella looked at her sharply. 'You mean they were lesbians?'

Jean startled. 'Good gracious, no. It would have been simpler if they were. No, I mean they were too close. Girls of that age often have intense friendships. When I was young it was common for girls to hold hands - nobody thought a thing about it - but Margaret and Gina didn't have other friends. Or didn't seem to. They were utterly wrapped up in each other.

'I think one of the reasons my father liked Gina was because she brought Margaret out of herself. As a child she'd been quiet but Gina, outspoken and bold, rubbed off on her. I don't know why. And Gina found someone who genuinely liked her.

'Going to a school where I knew no-one forced me to make new friends. It's part of growing up and learning how to socialise. Margaret and Gina met in primary school and that was it. I mean, they spoke to other girls but I don't recall Margaret having a single other friend and the same goes for Gina. They'd found what they needed.

'I got the impression that before Margaret, Gina had been a bit of a bully. As I said her father was a drunk and the family dirt-poor. Gina's dresses were always dirty and before secondary modern she sometimes smelled of wee so I suspect she got teased at school and her reaction was to beat the other kids up. It certainly stopped the teasing but it made her unpopular.'

Stella felt a pang for Gina. She thought of the Femfresh wipes and Gina's obsession with personal hygiene.

Jean looked at her. 'I'm telling you this so that you understand what happened later,' she said.

'I know. I'm grateful.'

'So you can guess what happened next?'

'A man came between them?'

Jean nodded. 'Indeed. Carl Jenkins.'

'My grandfather?'

'It appears so.' Jean studied her. 'At least his name

was on your mother's birth certificate.'

'How do you know that?'

'That comes later,' Jean said. 'Although I haven't got much more to tell you. I managed to persuade my father to let me go to teaching college and I was living away by then, so I didn't see the friendship break up, only heard about it from my mother, and she was delighted to be rid of Gina's influence. I half suspect that she had a hand in it. She adored Carl. Well into old age she'd flutter her lashes at him despite his potbelly and thinning hair. But as a young man he was a handsome devil and on the up. He joined Holmes and Baxter as an apprentice millwright but soon became the youngest foreman to work there. It was obvious he was bound for management. Margaret was mad about him. At eighteen, her letters were full of him even before they started courting. She wrote when Carl noticed her new dress or Carl said the German's had developed a new machine that would ruin the British lace industry or Carl held open the door to the cafeteria. I noticed it because previously she'd just twittered on about the latest escapades she'd had with Gina. She still did, but a new person had crept in. I was glad. I thought it about time. Oh, they'd both always had crushes on boys and talked incessantly of them, but never seriously. Mostly they were mad about movie stars, especially Gina.'

'She still is,' Stella commented.

Jean harrumphed. 'Well. Gina stepped out with Carl first. One night Margaret arrived home sobbing, stormed straight up to her room, and threw herself on the bed. At first she wouldn't tell mum what had happened but mum wormed it out of her. She and Gina had gone dancing at The Palais as usual. Margaret hoped to see Carl there and she had - they'd even danced together - but he also danced with Gina. Now it wasn't unusual then to dance with more than one partner, so Margaret had been a bit miffed but not too upset. At the end of the night Margaret went to fetch their coats but when she got outside she found Gina and Carl clinched in a kiss. She flung Gina's coat in a puddle, stamped on it and ran home. She was furious that Gina would do that to her. Gina knew how Margaret felt about Carl.'

'So that was the end of the friendship?' Stella asked.

'Not completely. Gina begged Margaret's forgiveness. I think Margaret suddenly realised she only had one friend - Gina - and couldn't afford to lose her. Not yet. They limped on for a while, but Gina continued to see Carl.'

'Really?'

'Yes, really. Margaret claimed she was fine about it. It had been a silly crush, that was all and Gina was welcome to him. But she started to go out without Gina; sometimes on dates and other times on work outings. Bear in mind they had done everything together since they were girls. Then Margaret attended a Christmas club social with mum and dad. Carl had gone with his parents and they were all seated at the same table. Carl impressed mum and dad and charmed Margaret – not that she needed much charming. That was a pump that was already primed. All the parents were pleased when Margaret and Carl started to court.'

'But wasn't he engaged to Gina?' Stella exclaimed.

'As far as I know he never was engaged to Gina,' Jean said. 'If he was it wasn't public knowledge. She didn't have a ring. Carl Jenkins would never have married the likes of Gina Pontin. She had a reputation among the boys for being a good time but not the sort of girl you'd marry.'

Stella felt outraged. 'That's horrible,' she said.

Jean took pity on her. 'Yes. It is. But it's also the way of the world. Or at least it was then.'

'But wasn't Margaret tainted by her friendship with Gina?' Stella said, almost savagely.

Jean shrugged. 'I don't think Margaret ever went … quite so far as Gina.'

'You mean she slept around?'

Jean smiled. 'This was the late fifties,' she said. 'Not many girls "slept around". Some just allowed more leeway than others. Besides, Margaret had been pulling away from Gina for some time. By the time she married Carl she'd dropped Gina completely.'

Stella frowned. 'I can't imagine Mrs Jenkins doing that.'

Jean sighed. 'I loved my sister but she only ever seemed to be able to fully love one person at a time, whether a friend or husband; she hadn't much room for others, even family. Once she had Carl, she didn't need Gina. But also, more than that, Gina snapped the bond between them when she kissed Carl outside The Palais. I'll never know why she did that.'

'Did Margaret know Gina was pregnant? Did Carl?'

'Ah,' Jean sighed softly. 'But she wasn't.'

Stella started to protest, but Jean held her hand up.

'At least she wasn't when Carl and Margaret married.'

'I don't understand.' Stella frowned.

'Gina didn't even get an invite to the wedding,' Jean said. 'Margaret and Carl moved to West Bridgford - it was affordable then, not the astronomical house prices of today. Margaret wanted children. We all assumed she'd be pregnant within the first couple of years but nothing happened.

'It happened for Gina though. Eighteen months after Margaret married Carl, Gina moved into Bobbin Street as a single mother with a newborn. It was a scandal in the street. Mother was outraged.

'But Gina's a survivor. She made herself a life on Bobbin Street and brought up Ivy on her own and she never revealed the identity of the father, although there was plenty of speculation as to who he was.

'Meanwhile, Margaret stopped working when Carl made management but she still didn't get pregnant. I know it pained her. When I had my boys she avoided them until they were older. It hurt my feelings but I understand now. How awful to see everyone around you bouncing babes on their knees when that's all you want and can't have. People ask too, you know. 'Do you have children? Do you want children? Why don't you have children?' Women are the cruellest - always those with children, of course, as though a woman who doesn't have them is incomplete and a failure. I suppose it used to be worse - it's more common nowadays for a woman to choose not to have them. But of course, Margaret didn't make that choice. Life made it for her and never let her forget it.

'Yet she and Carl seemed reasonably happy. They

put their energies into material things - a nice house and new cars, holidays abroad, dining out. Margaret created a magnificent garden - that's where she channelled her nurturing instincts - while Carl went through numerous expensive hobbies. He never seemed to pick cheap ones and would obsessively throw time and money into something or other - Go-Karting, golf, scuba diving, etcetera - before losing interest and moving onto another. He took early retirement at fifty and then died unexpectedly from a stroke ten years later. That's when Margaret discovered he'd secretly re-mortgaged the house and left her with debts.'

'Ouch,' said Stella.

'Ouch indeed,' Jean agreed. 'It could have been worse, though. Not long before, our mother had passed away and left the house on Bobbin Street to Margaret and myself. My father had bought it off the council in the big 80s sell-off. We'd intended to sell it and split the profit between us but when Margaret found herself in dire straits it seemed more sensible for her to move into it.'

'Even with Gina across the road?' Stella asked

'I think Margaret actually hoped they might be friends again.'

Stella snorted derisively.

'Well,' Jean said. 'Stranger things have happened. You know the night Gina got the call to say your mother had died it was Margaret she went to?'

'No!'

Jean nodded. 'Maybe they would have become friends again, too, if not for you. Still, we'll never know.

'So,' Jean drew a deep breath. 'We come to the nuts and bolts of the matter, or at least my perception of it based on what little Margaret told me.'

Stella drew up straighter, ready.

'On the day of the fight between Gina and Margaret - yes, Margaret mentioned it but Mrs Cookson saw fit to really fill me in when I came to sort out the house - Gina posted an envelope through Margaret's door. This was after the fight; it didn't cause it. The envelope contained a copy of a birth certificate - your mother's. Both parents had signed it. Gina and Carl. Margaret swore it was his signature - not a forgery. Lord knows how Gina persuaded him to do it - a married man with a wife putting his name to a legal document that proved his infidelity. Yet he did.

'It destroyed my sister. She was quite hysterical when she phoned me. I came over to comfort her. I wanted to take her home with me but she refused and I had to get back because I was due to teach an evening class. I phoned her again later. She said you'd been round and she'd told you she couldn't see you for a while. She said she could see Carl in you, now that she was looking for it; couldn't believe she hadn't seen it before, and that you were double jointed, just like him.'

Stella remembered Mrs Jenkins staring at her double-jointed finger. 'It must have been terrible,' Stella said. 'To find her husband had fathered a child when she had none of her own.'

'Yes. Terrible. And he'd had it with Gina.'

They sat in silence contemplating this.

'So Carl and Gina were still seeing each other after

the wedding,' Stella stated.

'Perhaps. Or maybe it was a fling or a one-night stand. Only Gina knows that. Either way your mother was the result of it.'

'Poor Mrs Jenkins,' Stella said.

'Um,' Jean said. 'Well, Gina got her revenge but then so did Margaret.'

'What do you mean?'

Jean shifted in her seat. 'You think that Gina caused my sister to become depressed - possibly to start 'losing her marbles' - don't you?'

'I suppose so, yes,' Stella admitted. 'The whole street thought that. The way she stopped gardening and hardly came outdoors, and then when she did she looked so thin and ill. Of course I didn't know about my mother then, but after Gina's stupid garden divided the street and finally the fight... well everyone felt sorry for Mrs Jenkins and hated Gina.'

'I know they did,' Jean said. 'Because my sister told me. Perhaps she really did 'lose her marbles' but not in the way everyone thought. Everything she did - running down her garden, losing weight and letting her appearance go - she did deliberately. She'd ring me up and tell me how the neighbours were shunning Gina, how concerned they were about her, how she planted a hint in Mrs Cookson's gossipy mind that she was too afraid of Gina to go out.

'I begged her to stop; to sell the house and move nearer to me; to let the whole sorry state of affairs go. She wouldn't listen. She was obsessed with punishing Gina, slowly and carefully. After she died I discovered she'd stopped taking her heart medicine - oh, yes, she had a condition. She continued to collect the prescription but hadn't touched the pills, just left them piling up in a drawer for almost a year. She knew that eventually her heart would fail and when it did I think she managed to get herself over to Gina's garden to die. It was her way of taking revenge.'

Stella felt ill. 'That's crazy,' she whispered.

'It's sick,' Jean nodded. 'But I believe it's true. I never much liked Gina but I don't think you should blame everything on her. It takes two to tango and right up to Margaret's death they were, in some twisted way, tied together.'

In the Wee Hours

Stella arrived back in Mapton as confused as she left it.

She and Rick had managed to get into a squabble at lunchtime. It was completely unexpected and afterwards they both felt embarrassed, trying to pretend during the journey home that it hadn't happened.

'Drop me off here,' Stella said. 'I'll walk to Gina's. It'll be better if she doesn't see you.'

She reached for the door handle.

'Hey,' he said, catching her arm. 'Are we good?'

She turned back to him. 'Yeah. Of course.'

He held her with his eyes. 'I'm sorry,' he said. 'I was stupid to get cranky. I must be tired.'

Stella smiled weakly. 'We didn't get much sleep last night...'

He grinned back. 'Nor the night before.'

They relaxed slightly. 'Call me or come round if you need to,' Rick said.

Stella shook her head. 'I want to stay at Gina's if she'll let me.'

'I know... but if you need to.'

'Thank you,' Stella said. She kissed him lightly. 'Thank you so much for everything.'

'No problem. See you tomorrow?'

Stella nodded.

'Okay. Good luck.' He leaned over and planted a serious smacker on her lips. Stella responded by grabbing the back of his head to hold the kiss.

'Better?' she asked when they broke apart.

'Better,' he said.

Stella waved him off before turning resolutely towards the park and Gina's house.

The holiday season was heating up with the weather but this late on a Sunday afternoon, with the schools not yet broken up, the day trippers were packing up their cars to go home and the park was almost deserted but for one couple boating on the lake and a bored teenager waiting for them to row to the dock so he could close up. He laconically blew a whistle to signal their time was up and Stella automatically glanced towards them. A gigantic man, enormous in girth and stature, was struggling to row the tiny boat. He'd opted to sit on the stern bench and stretch for the oars rather than sit in the middle. His tiny girlfriend perched at the bow end. The problem, Stella saw immediately, was the man was trying to row forwards rather than backwards. At the same time his great weight was dropping his end of the boat too low whilst the bow end was lifting right out of the water, making his girlfriend look like a figurehead on the prow of a ship.

Another time Stella might have stayed to watch but she was focused on the task ahead - talking to Gina - and hurried past the teenage boat boy, barely noting the sweet waft of marijuana curling from his spliff.

Automatically treading between the geese droppings she made her way towards the railings where the inflatable slide was deflating into a yellow puddle of dirty plastic.

Gazing at Gina's bungalow, she stopped, clutching

the railing, took a deep breath and moved forward again before her courage ran out. When Gina was really angry - and she *was* really, really angry - her fury could last for days.

She decided to knock on the door rather than use her key; it felt right.

Grazja answered, peering at her warily. 'Oh, it's you,' she exhaled. 'I thought it was police again.'

'The police?' Stella asked, alarmed.

Grazja nodded. 'Yes. They come round earlier. Think Gina train Bing to attack and steal.'

'That's crazy!'

'Yes. Crazy. Gina tell them so - not politely. Maybe now not best time for you to see her.'

'I have to,' Stella said. 'I need to talk to her - to apologise.'

Grazja sighed. She stepped aside to let Stella in. 'I be in my room,' she said. 'I come if I hear sounds of murder.'

Stella could hear the TV on in the lounge. Bracing herself, she tentatively reached for the handle and quietly pushed the door open, sticking her head through first. Gina was dozing while some filler programme wittered on the screen. Stella entered and bent over Gina, placing her hand on Gina's shoulder.

'Gina,' she said softly. 'Gina. It's Stella.'

Gina eyes fluttered open. For a moment she looked confused then rage swept her features. 'Get out. I told you to go home. You're not bloody welcome here.'

'Gina,' Stella tried. 'I'm sorry. I really am. We need to talk…'

'You've got some bleedin' cheek,' Gina interrupted. 'You've had years when you could've talked to me.

Did yer? No, Miss Toffee-nose of London town. Didn't want nothing to do wi' me. Always too busy to see yer ode Gran. Well you weren't too busy were you? I thought it was because you were too good for me but since I seen that painting I know it's cos you hate me.'

'I don't,' Stella protested. 'Well, perhaps I did, a little bit. But I don't anymore. Listen Gina, I went to see Jean Simmons - you know Jean Bone, Mrs Jenkins' sister...'

Gina went rigid. Her face turned to marble. 'You did what?' she hissed.

'I went to see Mrs Jenkins' sister,' Stella repeated. 'I know what happened, Gina. Jean told me it all. I understand now.'

Expressions scudded like stormy clouds across Gina's face. If this was in a movie and Gina really a malignant witch, a howling wind would rise.

Gina erupted. 'How fucking dare you?' she screamed. 'How fucking dare you think you have the right to pry into my life.'

Stella had never heard Gina use the F word despite her proclivity for colourful language. Gina abhorred it.

'But,' Stella began. Then a mug smashed against her arm. 'Ow!' Half a packet of Polo mints bounced off her head. 'Stop it,' she yelled, flailing backwards. 'Gina. Stop it.'

But Gina had gone berserk.

She grabbed a small vase of flowers Grazja had placed on the coffee table and hurled it at the wall. It smashed, water flying with flowers and glass across the lounge.

'Get out,' Gina shrieked. 'I never want to see you again.'

Grazja ran in. She grabbed Stella and pushed her into the kitchen, slamming the door in her face.

Stella stood stunned, hearing Grazja try to calm Gina down. Something else broke. Gina yelled. 'Get her out of my house.' Grazja spoke too low for Stella to hear.

Eventually Grazja calmed Gina. Stella heard her helping Gina into her wheelchair and the sounds of them moving into the bedroom.

Stella sat down at the kitchen table, head in her hands. She was shaking. Why did everything with Gina have to be so bloody dramatic?

Half an hour later Grazja reappeared. 'That went well,' she snapped.

'Sorry,' Stella said in a small voice.

'Oh,' Grazja deflated. 'Not your fault maybe. Long time coming, yes?'

'Yes.'

'Could have handled it better.'

'Yes.'

'You should go. I promise Gina I kick you out.'

Stella refused. 'I'm staying,' she said. 'We need to deal with this. I've avoided it for too long and so has she.'

Grazja sighed. 'You stubborn as each other. You stay in caravan not house.'

'Fine,' Stella said. 'I was planning to do that anyway.'

'But,' Grazja held up one finger. 'If Gina get like that again you must go. I don't want to deal with this.'

'Okay,' Stella agreed.

'I get your bag out of lounge,' Grazja said. 'Gina had medicine. Hope to make her sleep for while.' She looked back as she left the kitchen. 'I charge you extra for emotional trauma.'

As usual Stella couldn't tell if she was joking.

#

Stella stayed in the static for the rest of the afternoon and evening. Around ten she crawled into bed, falling into a fitful, dream-riddled sleep. She awoke, groggily, some hours later to a tapping on the caravan door. Stumbling to the door she unlocked it to find Grazja in her night robe.

'What is it?' Stella asked, coming fully awake. 'Is Gina ill?'

'Not ill, crying,' Grazja said. 'For about an hour now. I went in, try to talk to her but she won't stop. Not usual Gina tears - not childish tantrum and hysterics. Just crying - like her heart is breaking.'

'I'll come,' Stella said. She shoved her feet into her sandals and followed Grazja back to the house.

Gina was lying on her side in bed, facing the wall, her body racked by sobs.

'Gina,' Stella said softly. 'Tell me what's wrong.'

Gina gave no sign that she heard her, just went on weeping.

Stella sat on the bed and stroked her grandmother's shoulder. 'I really am sorry,' she whispered.

Gina continued to cry. Not attention-grabbing wails but the sort of desperate sound that only grief can wring out.

Finally, despairing, Stella lay down on the bed and spooned herself around Gina's back, making soothing noises and stroking Gina's hair, simply letting her cry herself out. It took some time but gradually Gina's sobs began to lessen. In the semi-darkness, Stella felt Gina grope for her hand and gave it to her, clasping it warmly. When Gina's crying had subsided to sniffling, Gina whispered: 'Tell me what you know.'

Stella told her, softening some of it, leaving odd bits out but sharing most of what Jean Simmons had told her. When she got to the final year - the year Mrs Jenkins purposely ran her health and house down to gain revenge (according to Jean's theory) , Gina began to tremble, so Stella held her tighter.

'She were my best friend,' Gina explained a little later. They'd sat up and Gina had blown her nose. 'Until Maggie I don't think anyone had a kind word for me.'

Stella nodded. She prodded gently. 'Why did you kiss Carl? Didn't you know how Maggie felt about him?'

'I knew. That were the trouble. We'd both had crushes and dated before but neither of us took it seriously. But Maggie, I could tell she were gone on Carl. I was afraid, I think. Afraid that this would be the man who took Maggie away from me. She weren't just the best friend I had she were the only one. I knew Carl had the eye for me and I quite fancied him. I thought if I got in there first Maggie would be mad at me for a bit but we'd get over it and she'd forget about him. But I didn't reckon on how angry Maggie'd be at me and for how long. She didn't show it straightaway, not to me face, but she started to cut me out o' things, going out with other friends and stuff. The other thing was I didn't expect to fall for

Carl. I liked him well enough - he were fun - but before I knew it I'd fallen for him. He were a great kisser, good-looking and made me laugh. In fact he laughed me right out of me knickers. Despite what folks thought I was a virgin until Carl. He said the only thing could make him love me more was intercourse. So I did. I felt guilty about Maggie and sad I was losing her but at least I had Carl. He told me we'd get married in a couple of years. Then he broke up with me and it turned out it was Maggie he was going to marry. So I lost both of em. It broke me heart and on top o' it I felt like they were all laughing at me.'

'Who were?' Stella asked.

'Maggie, Carl, everyone I knew. Carl must've let it be known I was easy because the local boys took to making me the kind of offers they'd want to protect their sisters from.

'I didn't get an invite to the wedding. Maggie cut me out of her life as neatly as you chop an eye out of a potato. She moved to West Bridgford, quit her job and I never saw her after that. But Carl still worked at Holmes and Baxter. I hated him by then but I wanted to get me own back and moreover I wanted something fo' me sen - a baby. I didn't care that it weren't done in them days, though things were changing. I thought if I could a have a baby I'd always have someone who loved me. Summat of me own.

'It weren't hard. Carl was a randy bugger. You know the type - charming, good looking; everyone thought the sun shone out of his arse. He hadn't even been married a year but he were keen to meet me secretly around the back of the cafeteria block. I only had to do it a few times, thank God, before I got pregnant.'

'How did you get him to sign the birth certificate?' Stella asked.

'Blackmail,' Gina said bluntly. 'When he were doing his business I'd swipe things off him - little things, like his comb outta his pocket, a photo of Maggie outta his wallet. Stuff like that. I got a little collection. Once I knew I was pregnant I told him how it was going to be. I'd go to Maggie and show her all the things I had and tell her everything. I'd go to the boss and tell him too. You might think he wouldn't care - men protect their own - but Mr Grall was a Methodist - teetotaller, kept a bible in his office - and he didn't put up wi' stuff like that. Carl panicked. Of course he wanted me to have an abortion back street like. But I stuck to me guns and won. Carl signed the certificate and paid me a small allowance every month. It weren't much but it helped, especially in those first years before I could go back to work. All I had to do were keep my mouth shut.'

Stella absorbed this. 'He died in debt,' she said. 'That's why Mrs Jenkins - Maggie - had to move back to Bobbin Street.'

Gina snorted. 'That weren't my fault. I only ever wanted enough for childcare - what do they call it now? Maintenance. Anyway, nowadays girls have babies on purpose to get all they can from the government. You should see 'em - four or five kids by different fathers, all different colours.'

Stella headed off the rant. 'It must have been hard when Maggie moved back?'

Gina sniffled. 'It weren't so bad as you might think.

She hardly seemed like the same person. Ivy had flown the coop but I had you to visit me. I'd bought my house in the big council sell-off and paid off the mortgage. Me and Maggie mostly avoided each other or just nodded hello. Only Mrs Cookson remembered we used to be friends. She lost interest when it became clear we weren't going to fall out again.

'Sometimes, I'd look across the street and see Maggie's lights on and think, wouldn't it be nice to just pop over there. We could have a cuppa and talk. Laugh about how stupid we were as youngsters and become friends again. Then I'd remember how she'd treated me and feel bitter. Or I'd think about Ivy and how Carl was her father. It was impossible. The funny thing was that most of the time I felt sorry for her. She seemed old. Older than me. She'd had to live with Carl for Lord knows how many years. I won't be the only woman he cheated with, believe me. Maybe he was paying off a stack load of women. Maybe that's why he died in debt.'

'Jean said you went to Maggie when mum and dad died,' Stella prompted gently.

Gina snuffled again, nodding. 'She was the first person I thought to go to.'

'But you didn't become friends after that?'

'I think she wanted to,' Gina said. 'But I couldn't. It weren't just a matter of Carl. I didn't want to need her again. And then I had you…'

'And I went to her,' Stella said.

They sat in silence for a while. Stella took Gina's hand.

'It was the tulips,' she explained.

'What?'

'Mrs Jenkins' tulips. When mum and dad died I couldn't feel anything but grief. Then one day I saw the tulips and felt a bit of pleasure. Not much. But some. I started to look at her garden after that and one day she invited me in. It felt like an escape. You were grieving too although I didn't consider that. I was twelve. You only think about yourself at that age. Mrs Jenkins' garden was a sanctuary. A place to forget.' It was Stella's turn to start crying.

Gina passed her the tissue box and squeezed her hand. 'Look at us. We're a right pair o' waterworks,' she laughed. Then sobered. 'I was so bleedin' jealous,' she admitted. 'I wanted to be the one you came to. But I was no good at stuff like that. Never was, never will be. And to think that it was *her* - Maggie - you went to. I wanted it to be just you and me against the world.'

'Like it was with Maggie when you were young?' Stella said.

Gina was quiet. Then she bobbed her head in acquiescence.

'I don't think it really ever works like that,' Stella said softly. 'I don't think one person can carry that much weight. It has to be spread around a bit between a few people; even when one of them is the main one, you still need others.'

'I don't like sharing,' Gina said, a touch petulantly.

'I know,' Stella sighed. She impulsively kissed her grandmother's crazy red hair. 'I know.'

Soon after Grazja knocked on the door.

'Come in,' Stella answered.

'You want tea?' Grazja asked, peering into the gloom. Dawn was just creeping round the edges of the curtain.

'Yes please, duck,' Gina said.

Grazja hustled off to the kitchen. Even at this hour she exuded efficient energy.

'Gina?'

Something in Stella's tone made Gina stiffen. 'What?'

'If you had an accident on the Rascal why didn't it have a scratch on it? Aren't they almost impossible to tip over?'

'I wasn't on the Rascal,' Gina said slowly. 'I was on me ode scooter.'

'But George brought back your Rascal,' Stella pointed out.

Gina pursed her lips.

'Did you organise your accident, Gina?'

Gina sucked in her lips, as though trying to stop whatever truth was trapped behind them from bursting out.

'But you really hurt yourself,' Stella said. 'You could've killed yourself.'

Finally Gina burst. 'Well, it were the only way I could think of to get yer to visit,' she blubbed. 'E'en if I killed me sen yer still would have come for the funeral, wouldn't yer?'

Stella stared at her aghast. It was awful. It was terrible. It was funny. She started to giggle, clapping a hand to her mouth in an attempt to stop.

Gina poked her. 'Oh, that's nice,' she said, starting to laugh too.

Grazja returned to find them almost hysterical. She tutted. 'They say English no show emotions. If only that were true, eh?'

The three of them sat on the bed with mugs of tea, munching biscuits.

'Gina,' Stella began again.

'What now?'

'Your Rascal has some scratches on it. I took it racing.'

For a moment Gina looked like she was going to swell into a Gina rage. Instead she nodded. 'Fair enough.'

A sudden thought struck Stella. 'Did you ever find out who did all that nasty stuff on Bobbin Street? You know – tear up your flowers, tip rubbish over gardens, that sort of thing?'

Gina cocked her head. 'Not for sure,' she said. 'But I had me suspicions. I think it were the Timmins boy from around the corner. He got sent to juvie in his teens for starting a fire in a warehouse. He liked to stir up trouble even as a kid. I saw him shove a banger through the Topliss letterbox once. Tried it with me the next time but got himself a nasty surprise.'

'Why? What did you do?'

Gina smiled smugly. 'Let's just say it involved a mousetrap and an electric shock and leave it at that.'

Dog Days

How the authorities failed to catch such a rag-taggle gang of bandits would eventually morph into legend in East Lincolnshire but during the summer of Bing's reign, tensions climbed like mercury in a thermometer.

The local press were torn between covering the story and pressure from the council to play it down. It was the first dry hot summer in a few years and the season was shaping up to be a good one. Mapton needed the income. The last few seasons had been brutal. Finally their luck had changed; the weather and the recession meant that people were holidaying in Britain instead of flying abroad. The only thing that could mar it would be a dog attack.

'It's like Jaws.' Stan Martin banged his fist on the table at the council meeting. 'And we can't afford to close the beaches.'

Tom Turner, aka Pirate Tom, added. 'It's worse. Jaws was only in the bloody water. These dogs can get everywhere. I tell you, when they attacked I feared for my life. They need rounding up and shooting.'

Martha Seaton, the current major, rolled her eyes. 'Don't be so melodramatic, Tom. The dogs were after your chicken - God knows what induced you to stick it in your basket…' She held up her hand to stop him interrupting. 'And I don't think I need to remind you that getting caught scooter racing is nothing to be proud of.'

Surly, but chastened, Tom subsided.

'The police and the wardens are working flat out to catch them,' Martha said. 'And so far only the Jack

Russell has bitten anyone - Gina Pontin's granddaughter - and only after she brought a cat into the house. I don't think we need to panic yet.'

What Martha hadn't calculated, other than the ineptitude of the authorities, was Bing's ambition. By the time his escapades came to an end he'd made two key recruits to the gang, formed a successful street-theatre group, and caused a stampede.

Surprise Surprise

Rick didn't hear from Stella all day. It made him twitchy. Twice he messed up the orders and once spilled a pot of coffee over the counter. Ang hovered around him, watchful for the next mishap. She'd been moody for the past few days, veering between attentively sweet or brittle and snappy.

Sometimes he wished he'd never slept with her.

It had been loneliness on both their parts; she had recently separated from her husband and he had been struggling to fit into Mapton during his first year. They'd gone on a few dates and had awkward sex, once. Then Ang's husband had reappeared, begging Ang to take him back. She'd been in such a state. She didn't really want to but her little boy missed his daddy so much, and her husband, Des, was so persuasive, that Ang said yes.

Secretly Rick had been a little relieved. He'd known his heart wasn't ready for a relationship - hell, not just his heart but his head too - and especially one that came with a child attached. Ang hadn't told him she had a kid, not at first. If she'd thought it would scare him away she'd been right. After what had happened in London he couldn't trust himself with something as fragile and precious as a child.

And that had been that. A few months later Ang asked him a favour. She needed some extra income - Des was a builder but work was sporadic - and could she do some shifts at the diner? It so happened that his business was growing and he welcomed another pair of hands. There was no tension, no sexual chemistry that he could detect; he and Ang worked well together. Within a year he'd made her deputy manager and relied on her to run the diner when he wasn't there.

It was a good system.

Then Stella Distry turned up and Ang got a little weird. He pretended to Stella he hadn't noticed that Ang was 'off' with her. But he had, because she'd been a little 'off' with him too.

Unfair, he thought. Ang had made her choice to return to Des. It wasn't his fault she wasn't happy. And God knows, despite how he'd lived for the past couple of years, he wasn't a monk. He was entitled to see women - to fall in love.

To fall in love. The phrase made him shudder.

He was falling in love. And it was scaring the bejesus out of him.

During a mid-afternoon lull he ducked out to draw breath. Sitting on the steps overlooking the beach he pulled out his phone and checked it again. Nothing.

Pathetic, he berated himself. Absolutely fucking pathetic. And it had hardly been a fight. Just a stupid tiff over something neither of them could prove.

Stella had been wired from her talk to Jean Simmons. Her mouth ran like a motor during lunch. He didn't mind, he liked to listen and he liked to watch her mouth while she talked. She had pretty lips.

Stella told him about Mrs Jenkins, who turned out to have been Maggie Bone - Gina's best friend - and how she'd purposely and relentlessly driven herself into the grave just to gain revenge. It was a damned confusing story but one Rick did his best to follow.

Stella's sympathies had taken a dramatic swing towards Gina which was a good thing. That was one huge wound that needed to heal. But Rick felt sorry for Mrs Jenkins too.

'Sounds like she was seriously depressed,' he commented.

Stella disagreed. 'That's what she wanted us all to think. And that Gina was to blame. But all along it was about revenge.'

'Yeah, but what she did, that doesn't sound like the actions of a mentally well person,' Rick argued.

'She wasn't depressed,' Stella insisted. 'She was angry.'

'Anger's a symptom of depression,' Rick countered.

Stella gave him an incredulous look. 'I'm not going to give her that excuse. Weren't you listening?'

'Mental illness is not an excuse,' he snapped. 'Why are people so ignorant?'

Stella gaped. 'I'm sorry you consider me to be one of those 'people',' she said icily.

Rick had been immediately chagrined. And embarrassed. 'Oh God,' he said. 'I'm sorry. Wow. I don't know why I said that. It's a bugbear of mine.'

He tried to make light of it, and so had she but it wasn't until they reached Mapton and said goodbye with that final kiss that she'd really thawed out.

Now it was three-thirty the following day and still no call. Was it because she and Gina were still going at it? Or had they kissed and made up and soon Stella would be on her merry way back to London, the weight off her shoulders, and her sexual battery re-charged courtesy of a casual fling?

Or was she brooding over his words, and concluding, correctly, that this was man who knew first-hand about mental illness?

He'd planned to tell her some of it as part of the 'best meal she'd ever tasted' deal - afterwards, when they were fed and happy. Not everything but as much as he could deal with. If she ran after that, so be it… except that wasn't the truth. There was no 'so be it', not in terms of his emotions. There would be 'so broken-hearted' and 'why am I such an asshole?'

Of course she'd be going home anyway. It was inevitable. So why had he started this affair?

His phone vibrated in his pocket. He grabbed it eagerly. 'Hello?'

It wasn't Stella. Rick's shoulders stiffened as he listened, blood draining from his face. 'How did you find me?' he asked quietly, pressing his fingers to his forehead.

#

The Pontin household seemed suspended in a state of dreamy bliss. It was unusually quiet. After the wee hours of unburdening and the constant drama of the past week, all three residents slept through most of the day, Stella in the caravan, Gina and Grazja in their respective beds.

At three-thirty, the same time Rick was receiving his call, Gina woke desperate for the loo.

'Grazja,' she yelled. 'I need to pee.'

Having become accustomed to Grazja's alacrity she was astonished when Grazja didn't immediately appear.

'Grazja,' she bellowed. 'I'm going to wet me sen.'

She heard the sound of stumbling, followed by the spare room door opening. Grazja came in wearing a dressing gown, with a face still rumpled with sleep.

'I can't believe you're still bloody asleep,' Gina crowed. 'What am I paying you for?'

'You're not,' Grazja grumbled, helping to hoist Gina into her chair. 'Stella is.'

'About that,' Gina said, then promptly forgot it. 'Oh, it's coming, Grazja. Hurry up. I can't hold on.'

Grazja got Gina to the toilet in record speed.

'I've got used to having a servant,' Gina said, knickers puddled around her ankles. 'I never thought I'd say that.'

Grazja used her big toe to hook the knickers, sliding them up to Gina's knee for Gina to grab one-handed. She regarded Gina out of slitted eyes. 'I am not servant,' she said. 'I am paid carer.'

'Same thing,' Gina taunted.

'Not same thing,' Grazja replied. 'Servant comes from word 'servile' to mean 'under' in lower position. I not lower than you, Gina. You not my master.'

'You cleaned up my pee,' Gina pointed out. 'That's pretty low.'

'Mother clean up baby's poop, not make baby superior.'

'I'm not a baby!' Gina protested.

'Hmm. I see you are in good mood today, Gina. You happy, eh? You make up with Stella.'

'Where is she?'

'Don't know. Out maybe. Or still asleep. I go check after I shower and dress.'

Stella emerged from the caravan just as Grazja re-appeared.

251

'What time is it?' Stella grumbled.

'After four,' Grazja said.

'What? I've slept all day?'

'We all did. Up most of the night, yes? Do us all good.'

'Is Gina awake?'

Grazja rolled her eyes. 'Yes. Unfortunately. She chippy today.'

'Chipper,' Stella corrected.

'Whatever,' Grazja said, making them both laugh.

They decided to celebrate the newfound equilibrium in the house by going out for fish and chips. Stella pushed Gina's wheelchair while Grazja walked alongside, keeping a wary eye on Stella's ankle to see if she was limping.

'I take over when you get tired,' she fussed. 'You just tell me.'

'Oh, gi' over,' Gina said. 'She's all right, aren't you, Stella?'

'Fine,' Stella said.

There'd been a tricky moment when Gina had asked Stella to uncover the Rascal and show her the damage to its side. Stella complied, bracing herself. Gina winced. 'Bloody hell,' she exclaimed. 'What were you doing?'

'Racing,' Stella said in small voice.

Gina eyed her brightly. 'You were one of them the other night? The ones in the news, Pirate Tom and such-like?'

Stella nodded.

'Bleedin' Nora! Did you win?'

'I was in the final two. Me and Pirate Tom. I might've won but… that was when Bing attacked.'

Gina gave a strangled laugh. 'Oh aye, the police think I'm behind that one. Think I'm some kind of criminal mastermind.'

'I heard,' Stella said.

'Tell me about the 'rumble',' Gina demanded. 'Tell me everything. Do yer think yer would've beaten Tom Turner? He needs takin' down a peg or two, smug bastard. Thinks Siltby's better than Mapton.'

'I could have taken him,' Stella said. 'Though he plays dirty.'

'Tell me.'

So Stella entertained Gina and Grazja with blow-by-blow recall of the rumble. When she described Bing's successful highway robbery, Gina laughed till tears trickled from the corners of her eyes. 'He's like Dick Turpin. Or no, Robin Hood, with his band of merry dogs. I wish I'd seen it. Tom Turner must have been shiten himsen.'

Grazja tutted. 'The way you say things so lovely.'

'You can talk.'

They reached The Mermaid, Mapton's best chippy, choosing to eat inside. Stella parked Gina at the end of a table. 'You'll have to stay in the wheelchair,' she said. 'The seats don't pull-out.' They were the moulded plastic chairs that fixed to the table, designed to wipe clean and deter malingerers. The menu was wipeable too.

'I'll have the fish 'n' chip special,' Gina said.

Stella picked up the menu and read the special. 'Haddock/Cod and chips, mushy peas, bread and butter + pot of tea/mineral.' She laughed. 'Who says 'mineral' anymore?'

'What is 'mineral'?' Grazja asked. 'Water?'

'Pop,' Gina said. 'Coke, lemonade and stuff. Fizzy.'

'You don't hear it much,' Stella said. 'But Mapton's stuck in the past.'

'It's not,' Gina said. 'We get wi fi and everything.'

Just then Cyndi Lauper blasted out of the speaker. 'Girls Just Wanna Have Fun.'

'See,' said Stella. 'The music's always from the eighties.'

'That's Golden Coast Radio,' Gina explained. 'Maptonites won't listen to Radio Lincolnshire since they had a phone-in inviting comments on Mapton as a holiday destination.'

'Were the comments bad?' Stella asked, trying not to laugh.

'Bleedin' snobs,' Gina spat. 'Said it were past it's sell by date 'n' scruffy. Called the locals inbreds. Well, that's not true for a start. Half of us are from away - moved here for a better life. Like me. Some cheeky bugger said it was the ugliest seaside town he'd ever seen in his life. Look out there,' Gina waved at the window. 'Tell me if that's ugly.'

The Mermaid's view was of the bank of peeling, shuttered beach huts that Stella had glimpsed as she drove into Mapton on the first day. She remembered commenting that Seaview Road had no actual view of the sea.

She exchanged a glance with Grazja.

'Why are the red and yellow huts on the main part of the beach kept up but those aren't,' she asked Gina.

'The others belong to the council,' Gina explained. 'Most of these are private.'

'They're a mess,' Stella said.

'One of them's mine,' Gina bridled.

'Yours?' Stella gasped. 'Gina, how can you keep affording these things? The Rascal's an expensive scooter, the caravan's customised, and now you have a beach hut. How?'

Gina's mouth tightened. 'That's none of your business.'

Stella stared at her exasperated.

'Tell her,' Grazja said.

'You know?' Stella swung on her.

Grazja nodded. 'Tell her, Gina. Nothing to be ashamed of. In fact you should be proud.'

Gina clenched her jaw defiantly and then exhaled. 'You see that picture over there?' She pointed to a large, generic scene of a beach. The sort of pleasant painting found in dentist surgeries, or hotels and offices. Nice. Unchallenging. Well done. Inoffensive.

'That's mine,' Gina said. 'I painted that.'

Stella laughed uncertainly. 'I can see it's an off the rack print, Gina.'

'I don't mean I painted the exact one on the wall. It's a copy. I painted the original and sold it to an agency. They use it for cards, prints… Ikea bought the rights. I've done it with a lot of paintings. I don't sell the original; I sell the image for reproduction. That's where I get my money.'

Stella was stunned. She looked back and forth between the print and Gina.

'Um, it doesn't seem your style,' she offered weakly.

'Oh, it's not. Too bloody boring. But that's what sells. I got the idea in Dr Graves' office. All those bland waiting room pictures. I thought 'I can do that.''

'Isn't it fantastic?' Grazja chirped.

'Fantastic,' Stella repeated weakly.

Gina rolled her eyes. 'Told yer she wouldn't like it,' she said to Grazja. 'Doesn't want her old gran beating her at her own game.'

'Gina!' Grazja reprimanded. 'S'not a competiton.'

A teenage girl rolled up to take their order. Gina ordered three fish and chip specials.

'All with tea?' the girl asked.

'A diet coke for me,' Stella said. She still looked dazed.

'And bring red sauce,' Gina shouted after the girl. 'And make sure it's not all vinegar.'

#

Stella surreptitiously checked her phone a few times while they were out. No message or missed calls from Rick. He was probably giving her a bit of space to work things out with Gina. Still, maybe she should pop along to the diner to just say hello; let him know she was okay.

She was already missing him. God, it had only been a day, and she'd been asleep for most of that.

She would tell him about Gina's latest revelation which she could hardly process herself. Gina a successful commercial artist? Rick would love it. But did she?

They finished their fish supper - Gina magnanimously paying. A mermaid clock, her tail a pendulum swishing back and forth, told Stella it was just after five. Rick would be closing up but she might just catch him.

'I'm just going to pop along to the diner for a few minutes.'

Gina grimaced. 'Is that it then? Time's up. Had enough of us and back to the boyfriend now?'

'Just for a few minutes,' Stella said. 'Then we can go home, watch a film together, do whatever you want.'

'I suppose I should be grateful?'

'Go ahead,' Grazja said. 'We catch you up and walk along seafront before home.'

Stella was out of her chair and off like a child released from the dinner table. She heard Gina grumbling behind her and Grazja's chiding. Half way to Rick's her ankle started to throb, slowing her down. If only she was on her Rascal.

Ang was wiping down the outside tables before folding and storing them inside the diner. Stella approached warily.

'Hi, is Rick around?'

Ang gave her the usual stony look. 'No.'

'Oh, have I just missed him?'

Ang straightened. 'He left a couple of hours ago.'

'Oh, okay.' Stella turned to go.

'I see you're on your feet again,' Ang said.

Stella paused, surprised to be engaged in conversation. 'Yes, luckily it wasn't serious.'

'I bet you've been spending a lot of time on your back.' The insult was clear.

Stella narrowed her eyes. 'Meaning?'

Ang shrugged and went back to scrubbing the table.

Stella considered challenging her but decided against it. She'd had enough drama. Besides, she could always set Gina on her later.

She started back along the promenade, tugging her phone from her pocket. She called Rick and was disappointed when it went to answer phone. Was he avoiding her? Why did he leave work early?

Gina and Grazja met her coming the other way.

'You see him?' Grazja asked.

'No. He's gone.'

'Of course he has,' Gina said. 'He's had what he wants. That's what they do after intercourse. Scarper.'

'He's left work, Gina,' Stella growled. 'Gone home. Not done a runner.'

Gina sniffed. 'We'll see.'

'Let's do circuit,' Grazja said. 'Along front and back through park.'

Stella agreed, despite her sore ankle. It seemed easier. They passed Ang again and Stella gave her a sarcastically cheery wave.

'I don't like her,' Gina said loudly.

'Why not?' Stella asked.

'Her hair. She pulls it back so tight she looks like it's stretching her skin.'

'Maybe her skin goes slack if she lets it down,' Stella sniggered.

'Yeah,' Gina cackled. 'Like a temporary face-lift. Her poor husband.'

Grazja tutted. 'You too are bitchy. Cannot dislike someone because of their hair.'

'You can,' Gina and Stella said together. They broke into catty laughter. It felt good to Stella. Mean but good.

'Oh, you two so alike,' Grazja said, leaning down to pat Gina's head. 'Nasty girls.'

They watched 'An Affair to Remember' when they got home, sniffling through half of it and outright blubbing at the end.

Gina grabbed Stella's hand. 'The first time I saw that it was with Maggie at the Empire. We were thirteen. Thought it were the most romantic thing we could imagine.'

Stella squeezed her hand.

Grazja said: 'You like Deborah Kerr, Gina, in your wheelchair.'

'Yer cheeky bogger, I'm not crippled. I'm on the mend.'

'You right.' Grazja gazed at her seriously. 'We need to get you walking again. Your ankle is only sprained. Need to get back on it this week.'

Gina looked suddenly fearful. 'I'm not ready yet!' she protested. 'And me ribs are still killing. Not to mention this.' She bobbed her head towards her plastered arm.

'Not saying you ready to run marathon, Gina,' Grazja said. 'Just time to get you standing and taking small steps. Inside house at first. No need to panic. No one abandoning you.'

'I'm not panicking,' Gina lied.

'You stay at least another week, Stella?' Grazja asked.

'Um, yes. I suppose. I need to sort some things out with my agent though.'

'You afford me for another week?' Grazja asked bluntly. 'I can go if you want but Gina need physio and I still don't trust two of you not to kill each other.'

'No!' Stella and Gina shouted.

'Ahem,' Stella cleared her throat. 'I mean, yes, I want you to stay.'

Gina nodded vigorously. 'About the money,' she said to Stella. 'I should pay. After all Grazja's my carer.'

'Okay,' Stella agreed. 'Or we can go halves.'

Grazja fixed Gina with a stern look. 'You pay still not make me your servant, Gina.'

Gina just grinned.

Rick's Past Pops in

Gina and Grazja stayed up late playing cards; after all, they'd spent much of the day asleep.

Stella feigned tiredness after a couple of games ('Can't take losing,' Gina sniggered) and retired to the caravan. She checked her phone for the umpteenth time. A text from Lysie, a missed cold-call but no Rick. Now she was beginning to feel paranoid. Perhaps he'd had enough of her tribulations. Maybe he'd had time to think it over and regretted the weekend.

Maybe Gina was right.

She swatted the thought away. It had been up to her to contact him. That's how they'd left it. He could have lost the charger for his phone or just not seen her missed call-status. It was only one measly day. It shouldn't bother her at all. She often spent days without speaking to anyone. Enjoyed it in fact. How could she miss Rick this much only hours after she'd last seen him?

Over twenty-four hours, her heart whispered. Thirty hours.

'Right,' she decided, pulling on her trainers. Then she pulled them off again, unpeeled her jeans, changed into fresh underwear, and applied a lick of mascara. Jeans and trainers back on, she sneaked out of the caravan, ducking under the lounge window, and crept crab-like to the back gate. Through the open window Gina hooted raucously over a winning hand, drowning out the gate's squeaky hinge.

Stella was free. Of course creeping out was not the most mature course of action but it did provide a wonderful frisson. Mostly though, despite a huge (she couldn't quite get her head around it) breakthrough in her relationship with Gina, she wasn't willing to face Gina's scathing tongue-lashing were Stella to announce she was going out late at night to meet a man - hopefully for intercourse - who hadn't even had the decency to call her.

She felt slightly nervous being out in the dark alone and briefly toyed with taking her car before deciding against it. The engine might alert Gina and Grazja, or even George. And if they happened to look out at some point and see it was gone, they'd know she was too.

Mapton was quiet. The fair shut at eleven, and while there would be bars and pubs open in the centre, the park and surrounding back streets were empty.

Stella hurried past the boating lake. An occasional goose hissed at her, but most of the wildfowl were huddled on the island, except for one unfortunate duck hanging limply from a fox's jaws. Both Stella and the fox froze, eyeing each other. Then the fox turned and trotted away, disappearing into the darkness with his dinner. He was the only living soul she saw.

Rick's lights were still on. Stella was about to unlatch the gate when she noticed the unfamiliar car in the drive. A sleek, sporty BMW. The front door opened and a woman walked out, dark, slick-backed hair and elegantly tall. She pointed a fob at the car, popped the boot, leaned in, and retrieved a small-wheeled suitcase which she carried into the house. The front door shut.

Stella stood at the gate, mind whirling. A woman was staying the night at Rick's. A beautiful woman. A woman with a suitcase which suggested it was a planned visit. Rick hadn't answered her calls. He didn't want her to know. Rick had another woman.

Of course there could be another explanation. That woman could be his sister. Wasn't it always the case in films? Hero/heroine mistakes love-interest's sibling for love-rival. Jealousy ensues. Misassumption leads to hilarious actions. All comes good in the end.

Again the sneaky thought: Gina was right. This time Stella didn't slap it away, she let it slither right in. What did she know about Rick? Really? She'd known him for a week. He was novel, with a gorgeous accent. He had sexy eyes and hips. He ran the only joint in Mapton to make decent coffee. He knew she was vulnerable; knew what brought her to Mapton; knew she was only passing through. What a great opportunity for a lay. For 'intercourse'. He had no reason to be faithful. Why, they barely knew each other?

Stella was lost in her bitter thoughts when a hand fell on her shoulder. She shrieked and leapt away.

'Hey, it's just me,' Rick said. 'Why are you standing here?'

It took her a moment to understand that he'd approached her from the street. He hadn't come out of the house, he was going to it.

'There's a woman in your house,' Stella said bluntly.

Even under the dim streetlights Stella saw him blanch.

'You spoke to her?' he demanded.

'No. I saw her take in her suitcase. Clearly she's staying the night.' Her voice was ice.

'Yeah. She is. In the spare room.'

'Right,' Stella sneered. 'I suppose you're going to tell me she's your sister?'

'No,' Rick said. 'She's my ex-wife.'

The air was sucker-punched right out of Stella.

'Look,' Rick sighed, taking her arm. 'I haven't seen Justine for five years. I didn't know she was coming. Didn't even think she could find me. I've been walking around for the last hour trying to sort out my head. I was gonna call you first thing in the morning because there's stuff I need to tell you.'

Fear slid into Stella's gut.

'You're getting back together with her?'

Rick laughed bitterly. 'No,' he said. 'Look, let's go sit on the seawall and talk.'

Stella nodded uncertainly. 'All right.'

'You going to be warm enough?' Rick asked, looking at her tee shirt.

'I'll be okay.'

They walked in silence until Rick said. 'You and Gina sort things out?'

'Yeah. Mostly.'

'Good.'

The wind was chill by the seawall. Stella shivered as they sat down.

'Okay if I put my arm around you?' Rick offered. 'Warm you up.'

Stella wrapped her arms around herself. 'Maybe in a bit,' she said.

Rick lowered his arm, shifting away slightly.

'You know how I was going to tell you my story

after the meal I never got to cook you?'

'Yes.'

'Well, I'm gonna tell it now, but this will be a more truthful version.'

'You were going to lie to me?'

'No. But I would have left out some of the details. I didn't want to put you off.'

'And now you want to put me off?' Stella asked miserably.

Rick grinned at her pathetic tone. 'No,' he said. 'Now I want to be honest because you matter to me. I want you to have the full facts so you can choose.' He became serious. 'If I put you off that will hurt like hell but at least we'll both know where we stand.'

All sorts of terrible ideas were racing through Stella's mind. Was he a criminal, a killer, a bigamist? What was so terrible about his past?

'You remember when you asked me if I was on the run because you couldn't see why else someone like me would choose to live in Mapton?'

Uh oh! 'Yes,' Stella squeaked.

'Well, I'm not a criminal.' He paused. 'Ah, I can see you're relieved to know that.'

Stella blushed.

'But in a way you were close to the truth. I was on the run and when I got to Mapton I saw a place I could be lost in. Who'd come looking here? This town…' He looked inland. 'Hidden on the edge of the mid-east coast, struggling to survive, dusty, provincial, eclipsed by Skegness and Cleethorpes. It reminds me of an old scab clinging to a knee. One day it could just drop off the edge and who'd notice beyond a few folk riding their mobility scooters?'

'I thought you loved Mapton?'

'I do,' Rick said. 'Now. But back then I just recognised the last place on earth my past might look for me.'

'You're building this up very dramatically,' Stella said.

Rick looked surprised. He smiled. 'I guess I am. You'll be disappointed. Anyway, I'll get to the beginning.' He took a breath. 'Once upon a time I was the head chef of my own Michelin three star restaurant.'

'Three stars' Stella exclaimed. 'Wow!'

'Wow, yes. Three Michelin stars is the holy grail of cookery. And I achieved it. Not bad for a small town boy from Iowa. My mom cooked at the Truck Stop Diner. Nothing fancy, but she had a natural palate for combining ingredients. Her pies were famous amongst the trucking community. Me and my sister ate there most days. My father died in a mill accident when I was five, so my mom's cooking brought in our only income. I started cooking when I was nine, helping with the baking first. By the time I was twelve I was flipping burgers and hustling fries like a pro. I started checking out cookery books from the library and experimented at home. By fifteen I was attending school, working the diner, and holding down two other jobs. My mom wouldn't accept a dime. It all went towards college and occasionally on fancy ingredients for some concoction I was working on. I took correspondence courses in cookery. My friends dropped away. Partly because I had no time for them and partly because they didn't know what to make of me.

It was one thing to work as a short order cook but to want to become a chef in some fancy-pants restaurant serving sissy French food was as good as saying you were gay and where I grew up homosexuals were going to Hell.

But I was determined I'd make it out of that town. So was my mom. Anyway, to cut it short, I won a scholarship to study at the L'Acadamie de Cuisine in Washingon DC.

I left Iowa just three weeks short of my eighteenth birthday.'

'Washington must've been a big change,' Stella said.

'Oh God, yes. The biggest city I'd seen was Des Moines but Washington… The capitol for Chrissake. It was a rush. I mean the energy - not as tangibly electric as New York, but still… Cookery school was incredible. Suddenly I was surrounded by people who could not only pronounce all the dishes I'd only read about but actually cook them. It was competitive too. It was the first time I'd encountered that level of naked ambition. As part of the course you had to work in a restaurant. I started as a kitchen assistant at La Jolie. The first day I went home and cried. I'd never been yelled at so much in my life.'

'Like Gordon Ramsay,' Stella said.

Rick snorted. 'Ramsay's all show for the cameras. Real kitchens are far more brutal. But I went back, took the flak, and worked hard. I progressed quickly. By the time I left I was Sous Chef - you know, second in command to the big cheferooni - and screaming at my underlings like the best of them. Or worst. Depends on your perspective.'

'I can't imagine you yelling at anyone,' Stella said.

Rick gave her a pained look. 'Trust me. I did. You've only met the new and improved me.'

Stella met his gaze. 'Go on.'

'I did well - more than well - I shone. Top of my class, building a reputation as a star in the making. My boss, Antoine Rieve, was a great chef - a bastard on a personal level - but I learnt an enormous amount from watching him. I can't say he mentored me, exactly. He was too competitive for that. But we respected each other and made La Jolie into the place to eat in and be seen at. After graduation I stayed at La Jolie for another two years. One night, when Antoine was off, Andre Soltner came in...' Rick paused for Stella's reaction.

She looked at him blankly.

'Andre Soltner, chef and owner of Lutece in New York?' Rick prompted.

Stella shook her head. 'Never heard of them.'

Rick nearly fell off the wall. 'Lutece was one of the most famous French restaurants in the world!'

'Sorry,' Stella offered.

'Philistine. Anyway, Andre Soltner eating your food is every aspiring chef's dream. In fact, forget the aspiring. He ate mine. On Antoine's nights off I did my signature dish. And Andre Soltner ate it.'

'How many times can you say Andre Soltner?' Stella mused.

'Never enough,' Rick said. 'Andre Soltner. He ate my food and he loved it, so much so that he offered me a job.'

'At Lutece?'

'Nah. He'd sold it by then. It was never the same

after that. No, he was starting a new restaurant in the south of France. Did I want to study under him as his sous chef? Did I? God, I nearly exploded.'

'Well, none of this sounds bad,' Stella said.

'Not yet. Although there were signs. I drank too much. Found it hard to sleep. Couldn't switch off. Life was high-pressured - in an haute cuisine kitchen it's all ups and downs. I flew to France and began my apprenticeship. God, I learnt so much. It remains the most exciting part of my life. Have you ever seen the food markets in the Mediterranean? When Howard Carter opened Tutankhamun's tomb he must have felt the way I did seeing my first French market. And believe me, being a chef I'd seen beautiful markets before. Soltner took me around himself.'

'Now I'm getting more and more worried about how you ended up here,' Stella said.

Rick's laugh was strained. 'Maybe I'm stalling,' he said. 'To cut a long story short, I met Justine in France. She's English but was working over there as a buyer for Harrods food…'

'Another high flyer,' Stella interrupted.

'Oh, yes. We were both ambitious. I guess it's one of the things that brought us together. Justine has a great palate, knows a lot about wine, but has a degree in business and is a wiz at understanding finance. We fell in love with each other, for sure, but looking back I think we fell harder for the idea of what we could achieve together. It was Justine who suggested we take the leap and create our own restaurant in London. She said with her business talent and my incredible cuisine we couldn't lose. Soltner gave us his blessing, even attending the opening. We called the restaurant Francais de L'Americaine.'

'Wait!' Stella hopped off the wall. 'Oh my God. I ate there once.'

'You did?' Rick looked incredulous.

Stella laughed at his expression. 'Yes. It was after my first big sale. The guy who bought it asked me to dinner. He picked me up in his Porsche and took me to Francais de L'Americaine.'

'Hard to get reservations,' Rick commented. 'What was his name?'

Stella waved dismissively. 'I can't even remember. He turned out to be a bit of a prick, but the food. The food was sublime...'

Rick smiled.

'Except the first course,' Stella added. 'That was some fancy fishy thing.' She wrinkled her nose. 'It still had eyes. And legs.'

'I repeat, philistine.'

'But, wow! The rest was divine. I haven't eaten anything that amazing since.'

'You never went back?'

Stella tilted her chin. 'I felt out of my depth. Elizabeth Hurley was there. I'm sure I spotted De Niro as we were leaving. I felt like a right scruff. An imposter.' She paused, considering. 'Honestly? It brought out the Gina in me, all that expensive taste. I wanted to graffiti the Ladies. God, I can't believe that was your restaurant.'

'It was,' Rick said soberly. 'Mine and Justine's. We were married by then and shared equal ownership. It was Justine that ran the business, her genius for marketing, design, networking and so on that garnered initial interest. My cooking that gained a reputation. And then it became the place to be. Half the customers hardly touched their food. They weren't there for food. They were there to show they had made it to the top of the tree.'

'So,' Rick sighed. 'We finally get to it. I was at the top of the tree too. I've made it sound like it was easy. That it all magically fell into place but it didn't. It was hard, hard graft, twenty-four seven. It's a true cliché to say that professional kitchens are like pressure cookers. The noise, the heat in a small space shared by highly driven, competitive perfectionists. And I mean perfectionists. That is the definition of Michelin star cooking. Pretty good won't do. Fine won't cut it. Only absolute perfection on a plate can go out, time and time and time again. Every single cog in that kitchen must work to that standard, from the dishwashers to the assistant cutting vegetables, to the saucier, pastry chef, sous chef to the servers. And above them all the chef is God. A mini dictator. In that kitchen the chef has absolute power; that's why most chefs are monsters at work. That and because if one person under that chef slips up - overcooks a scallop, under-seasons a sauce, serves a messy plate - the customer doesn't know and won't care which individual caused the problem. It is the chef's name on their lips and it's that name they'll repeat to their friends or write up in a column.

'The chef is surrounded by people yet at the same time always on his own. At least that was how it felt to me. As our popularity rose, so did the pressure to constantly perform. Justine was negotiating for a TV series with the BBC. She was in her element. We didn't spend much time together out of the restaurant, working late nights and long days. In the final year I'd begun to have chest pains. I put it down to heartburn and too much wine. I'd drink myself into sleep every night. It was the only way I could drop off. Out of work - in bed, in my car - I could still hear the roar and rattle of the kitchen, could still hear the constant questions bombarding me.

'The first panic attack hit me in the shower. I thought I was about to die. Afterwards, I didn't tell Justine. The second came a week later, when I was checking over fish in Billingsgate Market at about five in the morning. Gerald, my supplier, was with me. I couldn't breathe, had palpitations, and had to sit down. Gerald thought it was a panic attack. He told me to go see a doctor. I said I thought I might be starting with flu and stopped using Gerald because I was so goddamn embarrassed.

'Again, I didn't tell Justine.

'I convinced myself that it was a matter of willpower. I was feeling crap all of the time, like my skin was lead-lined. I often felt furious. I was like a powder keg in the kitchen. My staff tiptoed around me. I knew it but I couldn't help myself - the slightest irritation sent me into a fury. Nothing they did was right.

'That's when Justine finally noticed. Things had started to slide.

'I kept sneaking into the toilet to cry. And I hated myself for being weak. I forced myself to work even harder, even longer, determined to show myself I could.

'Of course it began to tell in the food. I didn't enjoy the taste of anything. I mean anything. It was my terrible secret. I made mistakes and tried to hide them with a dash of this or a soupcon of that.

'Then one day I saw my sous chef, Jeff, tip a plate of my food in the bin. I demanded to know what the hell he was doing. Clearly he'd had enough. He was ready to get fired. Keeping his back to me he said: 'I don't know what your problem is, chef, but lately everything you cook tastes like shit.'

The entire kitchen froze.

Without hesitation, with no thought at all beyond pure rage, I picked up a cleaver and hurled it at him. At his back. He moved, miraculously, at the last second and the cleaver sailed just over his shoulder and hit the wall.'

Stella looked at him. He held her gaze. 'I could have killed him,' he said quietly. 'I nearly did. And I'd intended to. That was the end for me. I walked out and never went back. In fact, I walked for miles. I heard my name whispered by passers-by and believed I still held the cleaver in my hand. I didn't and people weren't whispering my name. What I was having was a psychotic episode - I don't mean psychotic because I threw that knife - but in the clinical sense, I was having a complete mental breakdown. After hours of walking I found myself in front of The Maudsley. Lucky eh? A hospital for the mentally ill. I admitted myself. After that it's a bit of a blur.'

He smiled weakly. 'So, now you know. When folks say: 'Oh that Rick, he's such a crazy guy, they don't know the half of it.'

Stella was trying to process this idea of a different Rick. 'What did Justine do?'

'Oh,' Rick shrugged. 'The hospital let her know where I was. She came to see me a few times while I was there, although I barely remember. I collapsed into myself. Shut down.'

'How long was that?'

'Weeks,' Rick said. 'When I came out I needed a quiet place to be, so Justine arranged for me to stay in a cottage of a friend. It was a holiday home they had in Suffolk, near Southwold.'

'Did she go with you?'

'No. She had Francais L'Americaine to run. She promoted Jeff in my absence to head chef, partly to keep him from charging me for assault or intention to murder, or whatever it might've come under.'

'Would he have done that? Surely it was obvious you were ill - especially after you were admitted?'

Rick shrugged again. 'I'm not sure anyone really knew about that. Justine kept it all very quiet. It didn't even get into the papers. She called my mom to let her know. She told the staff I'd taken a vacation due to exhaustion. Close enough but nowhere near the real truth.'

'But they'd seen you flip out.'

Rick grimaced. 'Yeah. But the awful thing I realised later - when I'd got my perspective back - was that my behaviour wasn't that much more extreme than was expected. The cleaver - yeah it was bad - but not that much worse than kitchen staff experience all of the time. Don't get me wrong, not all top chefs behave that way but plenty do. Like I said, it's a high-pressure environment. It's amazing how unacceptable behaviour quickly becomes the new norm. I wasn't living an 'ordinary life' and I lost touch, especially with myself.'

'And you're in touch with yourself now?' Stella asked.

Rick grinned ruefully. 'For the most part, yes, I think I am. I'm... content.'

'How did you end up in Mapton? Why not stay in Southwold? I went with Lysie a couple of years ago and we loved it. Well, I did. Lysie thought it was a bit too la de da.'

Rick cocked a questioning eyebrow.

Stella said. 'She said it was so middle class it made her want to vomit, actually.'

Rick laughed. 'Can't say the same of Mapton.'

'I'll have to tell Lysie. But, sorry, Southwold? Gorgeous town, lovely pier, beautiful beach. Why didn't you stay there?'

'Too pretty,' Rick said.

'No!'

'Seriously. It was the beginning of the bunting phase. Southwold bought into chintzy bunting big-time. Chintzy teashops with mis-matched cups and Farrow and Ball paint.'

'Oh,' Stella said.

Rick bumped her with his shoulder. 'I'm guessing you being a girly, arty type go in for all that.'

'Maybe,' Stella said defensively.

'Secret Cath Kidston hoarder?'

'Not telling.'

'I'm gonna take that for a yes,' Rick said. 'That's okay. But I'm a red-blooded guy. I don't do twee.' He shifted. 'Still, Southwold was the perfect place to recover. I took long, long walks along the beach and did a lot of thinking while I was there. I knew I would never go back to Francais L'Americaine. Knew I didn't want to be Michelin star chef anymore. I wasn't sure what I did want, only what I didn't.

'I expected Justine to be mad as hell. But she was surprisingly understanding. Said she'd hoped I'd go back but that she respected my decision. Jeff had done a good job in my absence so she would make him permanent chef. He'd be delighted. She asked me what I'd do next and I admitted I didn't know. Justine wished me well with whatever it turned out to be. She explained her life was with the restaurant (and I later found out with Jeff; they'd begun an affair months before) and calmly suggested we divorce and that she buy me out. I quickly agreed.

'So that was it,' he said, looking at Stella. 'That was my marriage and my career over. What a great guy, eh? Now you know. God, you must think I'm a jerk.'

Stella put her hand on his arm. 'Not a jerk,' she said.

'No? What about a mental case?'

'I don't know? Do you think you are?'

'Not now,' Rick said. 'I've been fine for a long time. I was on anti-depressants for a year after hospital but not since. It was the pressure… I thought I was cut out for that kind of life. I wasn't. I don't want to be.'

'I couldn't live like that,' Stella said. 'I'd crack up too.' She rose to stand in front of him. 'I'm still cold.'

He wrapped his arms around her and she hugged him back, hard.

'Better?' he mumbled into her neck. She nodded.

'You?'

'Relieved,' Rick whispered 'Relieved you don't hate me. I feel so ashamed.'

She hugged him harder. 'I'm glad you told me.' She snuggled into his chest and sniffed him.

'Did you just sniff me?'

'I like it,' she murmured. 'You smell right.'

'So do you,' he said and snuffled against her neck.

Laughing Stella pulled back. She smiled into his eyes. 'You *still* haven't told me why Mapton?'

Running with Wolves

Sam 'Wolf' Hodson had recently made a purchase that he assumed would come third on the list of his most treasured possessions, the first being his custom kit Harley and the second his tattoos, which covered his arms, chest and back entirely. And neck. And one placed where only the eyes of a lucky lady might see it.

Unfortunately for Sam, he couldn't ride his Harley due to terrible haemorrhoids; only he, his doctor, and the pharmacist knew this. Everyone else believed he'd lost his licence because of speeding. It was a rumour he started himself.

Wolf ran one of Mapton's two tattoo parlours. His had once been a greengrocer's but demand in Mapton for fresh produce was low and the desire for tattoos high, especially among the holidaymakers.

Wolf mostly stood up to do his tattoos. He wore a kerchief on his bald head and a leather waistcoat that his arms stuck out of like enormous inked ham hocks. He'd perfected the American Hell's Angel look, though his voice let him down with a nasal whine and a Lincolnshire accent. Still his recent purchase completed his bad boy look; a two-year-old Siberian husky that resembled a wolf as closely as any dog could.

He named him Killer.

Killer was a bargain at £200. A husky pup could set you back between four to six hundred. His owner was moving to a static caravan park outside Northcotes; he said Killer was too big for the downsize but that he was a great guard dog and he'd be sad to see him go.

He'd had the dog tethered in his garden when Wolf arrived. Called the damn dog Mumbo. What sort of name was that for a guard dog? Wolf assumed the dog was tethered so he wouldn't attack but he noted that Mumbo greeted him with a wag of his tail and a lick. 'Oh,' the seller said. 'That's because you're with me. We shook hands, see. He smells me on you so he knows you're a friend. If I weren't with you he'd have gone for your throat.'

Wolf had come to realise that the man was a liar who'd sized him up accurately and sold him what he wanted to believe. In actuality the dog suited his original name much more than Killer.

Killer was a friendly dog. He particularly liked children and would offer his belly for a scratch with hardly an introduction. He habitually appeared to be smiling, with his tongue lolling out and a sparkle in his mismatched eyes. Worse, Wolf discovered, with some belated reading at the library, that huskies were far more likely to invite a burglar in for a cup of coffee than see him off with a bite on the ass. Good natured, but independent, they were difficult to train and were renowned for being escape artists, hence the tether. They were also very intelligent.

Perhaps most disappointing to Wolf was the lack of bond between him and the dog. Killer was as pleased to see Wolf as anyone else, delighted to share food and shelter, ecstatic at walk times but something was missing.

Wolf had expected Killer to know he was his dog. He'd imagined a mystical link between man and beast, as though they spirit-walked together. (Wolf was drawn to Native American mysticism. He'd bought a dream catcher from Witchywicca World to hang over his bed.) Killer seemed as oblivious to the spiritual side of his nature as he was to his new master.

And he had already escaped twice. The first time he amiably wandered back on his own, and the second time Wolf found him on the beach playing fetch with some kids.

The third time it happened - late Monday night - Wolf was asleep, completely unaware that Killer, roaming around the house, had found a small window of escape in the downstairs loo. Literally a small window; Killer stood on the toilet to reach it, precariously balancing his back paws on the lid (which, fortunately for him, Wolf had left down) and his front paws on the window sill. It was a very tight squeeze getting through the tiny space. For a moment it looked as though Killer might be stuck but he wriggled and panted his way out, finally thudding to the drive below. He peed against the wall to mark his way back but he never did return.

On the way to the beach - which he loved - he met a group of dogs led by a small but dominant Jack Russell. Just like that, Killer discovered the bond he hadn't even known he was missing. He had found his pack.

#

Monday night was a busy one for Bing. He'd led his pack silently along the beach, out of reach of the light cast by bulbs strung along the main section of the prom. It was late and quiet but there were still a few people about, including the female he'd bitten at Gina's. He caught a waft of her as they trotted past the sea wall. He was briefly tempted to do a nip and run but it would mean veering off route and besides, he had his pack to think of now. No point taking unnecessary risks. Further on they ran into the husky. Potential foe became friend, and after a few minutes of tussling, and sniffing and snarling, a new order was established and the pack ran on.

Their destination was the circus.

Tiller's Big Top rose out of a field on the outskirts of town. There for the summer season, Mitch reported that it was a rich place for pickings. Circus goers were clumsy creatures, shambling in and out of the show with ice creams, popcorn, and hot dogs clutched haphazardly in greasy fingers. They regularly dropped food. Then, after the Big Top went dark, the performers cooked, and if the weather was fine, barbecued outside. A very clever dog might well be able to slink away with a few links of sausages or a juicy steak.

But caution was needed. The circus had no big animals - the law had stopped all that - but they did have dogs, personal pets and a working miniature poodle act.

It was with one of those poodles that Bing Crosby fell in love.

Her name was Curly Sue.

Only a season ago Curly Sue would not have been remotely open to Bing's advances. A season ago she had been the star of the dog act, alpha female to three fawning males. The audience adored her. But this season her owner had brought in another female, younger and prettier, top knot as fluffy and white as a powder puff, nose and eyes bright as obsidian. The fickle males swooned. Worse, her beloved owner, Max Dawson, master of the poodle act, demoted Curly Sue to simply teaching the new bitch tricks behind the scenes.

He didn't even want her to perform anymore. True, she was fractionally slower than she had once been, and her joints clicked when she jumped through the hoops but she still had it.

It was just too humiliating to bear.

Curly Sue had been with Max so long that he trusted her. She was allowed to freely wander round the encampment, sticking her nose into one caravan or another. She was greeted warmly by most of the performers, but they knew better than to feed her. Max wouldn't stand for that.

Sue was sniffing around in the deep shadow of the Big Top when the Jack Russell approached her. She shied back, snarling. He crawled on his belly, showing submission. She allowed him to approach and worship her. He did so nicely. After a while he signalled to his pack and they emerged out of the night, a motley crew of varying shapes and sizes, so different to the uniformity of her miniature poodle troop. She eyed them warily. The Jack Russell snapped out orders and they came to greet her cordially. It was clear he was the alpha male, despite his size.

Curly Sue was impressed. She did a back flip to show her appreciation. It stunned the other dogs. They crowded around her. It was so good to be appreciated again, she ran through her repertoire. The pack went crazy, forgetting to be quiet.

Caravan doors opened. Voices called and the camp

dogs barked. Footsteps approached.

'Curly Sue?' Max called. 'Here girl.'

The pack began to melt away into the night. The Jack Russell stayed, body poised for flight. He yipped, calling to her.

Curly Sue was torn. Conditioned to obey Max, she turned towards his voice.

'Curly Sue!' He was closer now.

The Jack Russell began to back away, time running out as torchlight sought them. He called again, begging her to come with him.

Curly Sue caught the scent of Max and almost ran to him. Then her nostrils flared. She caught another smell, the one of the new bitch who had taken her place. She smelled of Curly Sue's shampoo, the one Max had always used exclusively on her. He had washed the usurper with her special shampoo.

Enraged, Curly Sue made the split second decision that would change her life and fled the circus, Bing Crosby racing at her side. The pack closed in around them and they ran as one. Curly Sue had never felt such exhilaration; even the fire hoop paled before the joy of this wild break for freedom.

Bing led them back to the den, triumphant. He had his female by his side and his pack was complete. His dreams that night were sweet.

Ex Marks the Spot

Stella sneaked Rick into the static for the night. She refused to stay at his with Justine there and was equally adamant that she wasn't prepared for him to either.

'Don't you trust me?' he asked.

'I trust you,' Stella replied. 'I don't trust Justine.'

'You don't know her.'

'Exactly.'

He didn't protest. After his big confession and a whole night and day apart they were desperate to get their mitts on each other.

'Make the most of this,' Rick mumbled as they thrashed around trying to tear their clothes off in the tiny confines of the static's bedroom. 'They say the initial sexual chemistry doesn't last.'

'How long?'

'About two months to a year.'

'I'll take it.'

Rick crept out around five-thirty in the morning, just enough time to go home and change before opening up for breakfast at the diner. The irony was that his early bird customers were often the other cafe owners along the front - those from further along on the main part of the beach - who opened at eight or nine - and appreciated a stack of American pancakes and strong coffee before firing up their grills and slapping on the bacon and sausage. Rick closed up before they did, so it all worked out.

Stella breakfasted with Gina and Grazja.

'Do you want to see the beach hut?' Gina asked, around a mouthful of toast. 'I ain't had it long. Not had a chance to do owt wi' it.'

'Yeah. I'd love to,' Stella said.

'You can wheel me up there,' Gina said.

'Okay. I need to do some emails first. Sort things out with my agent, see what commissions I've got, stuff like that.'

'That good,' Grazja added. 'Gina need to start physio this morning. Got to get you off your bum, Gina. You get fat.'

'Cheeky bogger.'

'You need to get on feet. Get circulation going.'

'Gina?' Stella pondered. 'When did you start using a mobility scooter? You used to walk everywhere.'

'Oh, I only use it for distances,' Gina replied. 'Not like most of the lazy boggers around here.'

'But did you need it in the first place?'

Gina looked defensive. 'I'm a pensioner aren't I? Been wearing my feet out all me life. I'm entitled to a bit of comfort now and then. Don't have a car, do I? Not like you? All that petrol and fumes 'n' stuff, warming up the planet.'

'That means she not need one,' Grazja said to Stella.

Stella agreed. 'But it's a way of life round here,' she said. 'You never know who really needs them or not.'

'Yes, Grazja nodded. 'I notice this. And lots of fat people too.'

'I'm not,' Gina protested.

'Not yet,' Grazja said. 'C'mon. Let's get you started.' She wheeled Gina away from the table.

'Bloody bossy boots.'

'Are you trained in physio?' Stella asked, following them.

'Yeah, I do course in it,' Grazja waved her off. 'You go do your work.'

At ten-thirty, Stella suggested she go along to Rick's to pick up some sandwiches. They could take them to the beach hut and have a picnic up there.

Gina, red and panting from the exertion of shuffling across the lounge, snapped. 'You just want to see your bloody boyfriend.' She winced as she collapsed into her wheelchair. 'Ow, me ribs.'

'That enough for today, Gina. You've done very well.'

'Patronising cow.'

Grazja smiled affectionately. 'That sounds nice, Stella. You go get some. We meet you at the hut in a while.'

'I want Stella to take me.'

Grazja began to retort but Stella stopped her.

'Okay,' Stella said to Gina. 'Do you want to go now, or have a rest first? You look done in.'

Gina's ruffled feathers settled. 'Now,' she said. 'While the sun's shining.'

'I like to see it too?' Grazja said. 'I bring some sandwiches up at lunchtime?'

'Great,' Stella said.

'Ham, not cheese,' Gina added. 'And not so much salad. I'm not a rabbit yer know?'

'You'd be nicer if you were,' Grazja said.

#

'Phew, it's hot,' Gina said.

Stella just grunted as she pushed Gina up the ramp that led to the west promenade and the run-down huts. She was out of breath by the top.

'Blimey, you're unfit,' Gina observed.

Once she'd caught her breath Stella said. 'Which one's yours?'

'Down the other end,' Gina pointed. 'The one with the brown doors.'

'Why are they all such dark colours?' Stella asked, wheeling past peeling huts painted in navy, burgundy, brown, and black. A turquoise one stood out in the middle, but all the others favoured dingy shades.

'Dunno,' Gina answered. 'Apparently this part of the beach used to be popular and all these huts were used, but nowadays hardly anyone uses them. They're all privately owned, see. They don't get much attention except for a couple of weeks a year when the owner comes or they hire them out to someone else. I'm planning to do mine up.'

'Oh yes?' Stella perked up.

'Yeah, nice bright colours,' Gina said. 'Liven it up a bit.' She jingled the keys in her hands. 'Here it is. You'll have to undo the padlocks. The bottom one's really stiff.'

Stella regarded the hut. The pagoda style roof was made from corrugated iron trimmed with a wooden fascia. The huts were built from breezeblocks, weathered a dark greenish grey. The doors and shutters had been glossed in the most unappealing brown.

'What shade would you call that?' Stella mused.

'Shite brown,' Gina said.

'We finally agree on something,' Stella laughed. She caught Gina's eye and they grinned at each other.

There were three padlocks, top, bottom, and centre. Gina was right about the bottom one. It was as stubborn as Gina herself but finally gave way with a grinding resignation.

The hinges creaked as Stella pulled the doors wide to reveal a surprisingly spacious rectangular room with a sink and a gas hob. A couple of decrepit deck chairs leaned against a wall.

'Hob doesn't work,' Gina said. 'No gas connection nowadays. But water should. There's a little loft too, for storing things in.'

Stella ventured in, peering warily at the ceiling, half-expecting a fat spider to drop onto her face. None did, though cobwebs indicated the presence of the eight-legged monsters. She spotted the small loft hatch.

'It's like the Tardis,' she said. 'Bigger inside than it looks.'

'And sturdy,' Gina pointed out. 'These huts were built after the war outta what was available, not like the flimsy wooden ones along the way.'

'That explains the corrugated iron,' Stella said. 'And the concrete.' She surveyed it all critically. 'This could be really nice with some work.' Stepping outside she reclosed the doors and stood next to Gina's chair. 'What were you thinking colour-wise?'

'Not sure,' Gina said. 'I'd like some pictures too - maybe a mermaid.'

'Yes! That would be lovely.' Stella fished around in her bag, drawing out a small sketchpad and half-size coloured pencils. 'Let's try some designs. I could do with somewhere to sit.'

'Try one of them deckchairs,' Gina said. 'They came with the hut.'

Stella dragged one out. It was a sturdy, old-fashioned wooden one. She checked it for spiders - two indignantly scurried away - and grimaced as she brushed off the cobwebs. It took a few minutes of struggling to set it up. Gina jeered at her and the pointlessness of a university education. 'Oh fo' God's sake. It's the other way round. No, it goes over that one!'

When it was finally in place, Stella inspected the green and blue striped canvas warily for fraying before gingerly lowering herself onto the seat. The chair held. Stella let out a breath. She'd half-expected it to collapse and Gina with it in gales of laughter.

They looked a little peculiar, facing the hut rather than the sea. Stella dug out her Kindle, ripped a few sheets of paper from her pad, and handed the rest of the pad to Gina.

'I suppose you've got the kitchen sink in there as well,' Gina said, indicating Stella's large bag.

'I like to be prepared,' Stella replied. She propped her sheets on the back of her Kindle and began to sketch the hut. Gina watched her for a couple of minutes then began to do the same.

It was possibly the most peaceful time they'd ever spent together, except for the occasional squabble over a pencil and Gina's complaint that there weren't enough shades. They each completed a few sketches between them, comparing colour schemes and images, choosing their favourite elements out of each design, reworking and collaborating, absolutely absorbed in the project.

It came as a surprise when Grazja arrived with a picnic at half past twelve. Time had flowed away.

She oohed and aahed over the sketches, snapped

out the folding seat she'd brought with her and produced drinks and Tupperware boxes of sandwiches out of a cool box. Stella turned Gina to face the sea, along with her deckchair and the three of them sat outside the hut admiring the view.

Mapton's beach really was a good one, Stella decided, watching the families and dog-walkers on the sand. It would be busier on the central beach. She realised she preferred it here.

The sun was hot. Grazja produced sunscreen and floppy hats for each of them.

'Told yer it's great having a servant,' Gina said, popping the tab on her lemonade.

'I clear out your bank account this morning,' Grazja replied. 'I hope you don't mind.'

'Ha ha,' Gina said.

Stella heard a familiar honk and saw Sue sallying towards them, Scampi alert in the basket of the scooter.

'Yoo-hoo,' Sue called. 'Look at you all taking the sun.' She drew up alongside them. 'Hello Gina. You on the mend then?'

Gina grunted.

'Hear your dog's still on the run,' Sue said. 'Two more went missing last night. Big husky and one of the circus dogs. One of them performing poodles. I bet it was Bing. He's gathering himself quite a gang.'

'Really?' Stella jumped in, seeing Gina about to launch. 'You can't know it's Bing. Dogs wander off all the time.'

'Nah,' Sue said. 'They don't. Scampi wouldn't, would yer Scamp?'

Scampi licked her face.

'Little rat'd get eaten,' Gina sneered.

Sue bridled. 'Now there's no need fo' that. I'm only making conversation.' She turned pointedly away from Gina, nudging her scooter closer to Stella. 'I'm not one to stir,' she said in a stage whisper. 'I'm just telling you as a friend, but did you know Rick's ex is in town?'

Stella avoided looking at Gina. 'Yes, he told me.'

Sue looked slightly crestfallen. 'Oh. Good. That's good. I feel better. I was worried for yer. She's at the diner right now, sipping on her coffee like she owns the place. Looks like a model. Not that it matters, I'm sure. Ricky's sweet on you, that's plain. Still,' she paused. 'According to Ang she's been hanging round all morning, just watching and trying to get Rick's attention.'

Despite the lurch in her stomach, Stella kept a smile on her face.

'Anyway,' Sue continued. 'Perhaps you ought to pop along there. It's plain Rick likes you but them city women, once they get their claws in… Rick's a catch I wouldn't let get away. That's all I'll say.' She motioned zipping her lips. Scampi barked once. Sue nodded. 'Scampi agrees.'

'She's already told yer she knows about it,' Gina piped up. 'Stella don't need you telling her what to do.'

Sue drew back, offended. 'I wasn't talking to you, Gina Pontin, so mind your own business.' She backed up the scooter, preparing to be on her way. 'I had a man once,' she said ominously to Stella. 'Didn't fight hard enough and let him get away. Enough said.' She put the scooter into drive, powering dramatically away.

Gina snorted her derision, but as soon as Sue was out of earshot she said: 'Right let's go.'

'Where?' Grazja asked.

'To Rick's diner,' Gina said.

'Whoa,' Stella sprang up. 'No way.'

'But we've got to stop this woman.'

Stella pulled a face. 'Why? You don't like me seeing Rick.'

Gina stared at her as if she was stupid. 'Yeah? So what? I'm not letting some posh cow take what's yours, whatever that is. So c'mon, let's go. You want to don't you?'

Stella did but not with Gina. 'I'll go,' she said. She pointed at Gina. 'You stay here.'

Gina pouted. 'I can scare her out of town.'

'Yes,' Stella said. 'And you'll scare Rick away while you do it. Anyway,' she took a breath. 'I know about Justine already. Rick's explained it all. She wants him to go back into the restaurant business with her but he's already said no. She's just hanging around trying to change his mind but she won't. I'm not threatened at all.'

'Then you're bloody stupid,' Gina said. 'Haven't I taught you nothin' about men? They're not to be trusted. You go along there and let him know you're watching. Ain't that right, Grazja?'

'I don't know,' Grazja said. 'He might think Stella not trust him.'

'Of course she don't trust him,' Gina said.

Stella chewed on her thumbnail. 'I need a coffee,' she declared. 'I'll just pop along and get a coffee. There's nothing wrong with that.'

'That's right,' Gina said. 'You run along and get your coffee. Stay, have a piece of cake. Take your time. Me 'n' Grazja'll come along in a bit.'

'You won't,' Stella said. She looked at Grazja.

'We won't,' Grazja agreed. Gina glared at her. 'Unless Gina walk all the way.'

'Oh all right,' Gina grumped. 'But I'll want details.'

'I just want a coffee,' Stella said.

Gina and Grazja laughed.

'Here,' Gina said, reaching into her handbag to pull out an orange lipstick. 'Yer need a bit o' lippy.'

Stella wrinkled her nose. 'I don't wear it.'

'Well if she looks like a model you should.'

'Thanks!'

'Just trying to help.'

#

Stella hurried along the promenade, the green-eyed monster of jealousy nipping at her heels. Why hadn't Justine packed up and gone by now? Surely Rick had told her to go. He vowed he wasn't interested in her proposal to return to Francais L'Americaine, which was in decline. Justine promised it would be different - three days a week in the kitchen, a consultant the rest of the time. She would run everything else. All Rick would need to think about was cooking and planning menus. If he trained up her under-chef to his standard he could leave after a year. She'd pay him handsomely and as an employee he wouldn't feel the enormous pressure he had as owner.

Rick had said no. Definitely not interested.

So why was Justine still here?

Stella easily spotted Justine as she reached the diner. She was sitting outside, talking on her phone.

She stood out like a hawk among pigeons, her sleek dark hair perfectly cut, gym toned arms slim and lightly tanned, black silk top expensive and beautifully tailored. Around her locals and holidaymakers displayed the imperfect flesh of people who lived on processed sugar and fat and fried their skin in fake tan and cleavage crinkling sun worship.

Stella couldn't see her eyes; Justine wore sunglasses, no doubt designer - the real deal, not the cheap imitations sold in Mapton, with names like G&D or Kalvin Clein.

Ang came out with plates of food for another table. Justine called her over, put her hand over her phone, and asked for something. Ang glowered but nodded. She caught Stella's eye as she swung past and she almost seemed to freeze. Her face registered something - the simultaneous presence of Rick's ex and Rick's current paramour, Stella guessed - and her mouth twisted into a sneering smile. She disappeared into the diner.

Stella hesitated, suddenly unsure. Rick appeared, expression anxious.

'Hi,' he said. 'Ang told me you were here. Sorry, we're busy - lunch crowd - not much time.'

Stella looked over at Justine, who had snapped her phone shut and was watching them. 'Justine's still here?' she said quietly.

Rick flushed. 'Yeah. Sorry. She insists on hanging around. But that's Justine. Very persistent.' He glanced towards Justine as he spoke and she waved them over. 'I'll introduce you.'

Stella braced herself. Justine stood as they approached. She was tall and slender in a way that made Stella, no shorty herself, feel stout and stumpy.

Justine took off her shades. Her smile was disarmingly warm. 'You must be Stella,' she said. 'I am so excited to meet you. I bought one of your originals last year - Girl in Blossom. I can't believe I'm actually getting to meet you in person. Justine Hamilton- Blake.' She offered a manicured hand

It was the last thing Stella had expected. She blinked. 'Oh. Thank you. That's so nice to hear. I sometimes wonder where my pictures end up.'

'I have an eye for art investments,' Justine said. 'Your worth has gone up even since I bought it.'

'Ah,' Stella said.

'You can't believe how amazed I was when Richard mentioned he was seeing you!' Justine said. 'Please, will you join me for coffee or some lunch?'

Richard? Stella glanced at Rick. Of course. Richard Blake, famous chef of Francais L'Americaine. Everything he'd told her last night sharpened into focus and became a reality.

Mark, Angela's son, appeared at Rick's side. 'Mum says she needs you,' he told him. 'We're getting behind on the orders.'

Rick clearly didn't want to leave Stella and Justine alone together, but Ang needed him. The diner was full. He gave Stella an apologetic, almost desperate look. 'Sorry,' he said.

Justine waved him off. 'Duty calls. We'll be just fine, won't we Stella?'

'I'll send you out some coffee,' Rick said to Stella. 'Need something to eat?'

Stella shook her head. 'No thanks. Coffee's good.' Impulsively she gave him a quick kiss, marking him like a cat spraying its territory. Justine knew it too and simply smiled benignly.

Rick gave Stella's arm a squeeze and left.

Justine placed her sunglasses on the table. Her eyes were blue, stunning with her dark hair. She pulled out a chair for Stella and resumed her own.

'So,' Justine said. 'Richard told me you're visiting your sick grandmother?'

'That's right.' Stella inwardly smiled at the image of Gina as sick and frail.

'How very Little Red Riding Hood,' Justine said and laughed. 'Did you bring a basket?'

Stella ignored her joke. 'Rick told me about your proposition – you want him to go back to Francais L'Americaine.'

'Did he?' Justine raised an eyebrow. 'He said no. I assume he told you that too.'

'Yes. He's happy here,' Stella said. 'After, you know... what happened.'

Justine looked genuinely surprised. She re-appraised Stella. 'I had the impression you haven't known each other that long. Richard must be serious about you. He's always been a very private person you know. To share that...' She gave a low whistle and leaned forward conspiratorially. 'It was terrible, truly awful. I partly blame myself; I didn't really understand the pressure he was under, didn't read the signs...'

'Then why would you want to put him through that again?' Stella asked quietly.

Justine shook her head. 'Oh I wouldn't ever! It would be so different this time. He wouldn't be a co-owner, wouldn't have any of that responsibility. He'd only have to be in three days if he wanted to. His genius lies in cooking and creating. I'd give him the chance to do that again but cushion him from the pressure.'

'In a Michelin star kitchen! It's all pressure.'

'Ah,' Justine sighed. 'But we've lost our stars. Jeff was a great chef but not a brilliant one. He's not Richard Blake, that's for sure.'

'Was?' Stella asked.

'We had a parting of the ways last year,' Justine said. 'I've got a hot new talent in - real potential but raw. That's why I need Richard. He could train Sam into a fantastic chef and Sam could take the load off him. They'd be a dynamite combination. I'm sure of it.'

Mark arrived with a tray. Black coffee for Stella and a burger for Justine.

The burger surprised Stella; she didn't think Justine seemed the type.

'If you don't mind me asking' Justine said, picking up the burger. 'Do you see this thing with Richard as a summer fling or a long-term relationship?'

'I do mind you asking,' Stella said.

Justine smiled, undeterred. 'It's just that Richard said you're based in London. Well, if you're having a fling down here, fine. Great. But if it's long term how will that work - you down south and Richard up here? Long-term relationships rarely work out. But if Richard accepts my offer…' She let it hang while she took a bite of burger.

Stella followed the thought through. Rick would be in London. They'd be able to see each other. Of course the idea had already occurred to her. It gave her a strange little tingle.

'Rick has a life here,' Stella said. 'He has the diner. He's happy. This has to be about what's best for him not our relationship.'

Justine chewed. 'This is good,' she said, waggling the burger. 'I knew it would be. You know, I walked round Mapton this morning. It's quite possibly the ugliest resort I've ever seen. It's definitely one of the poorest.'

'It's not that bad,' Stella said defensively, momentarily forgetting her own condemnation of Mapton. 'It has its charms.'

'I particularly found the sugar tits and cocks charming at the Rock Shop,' Justine observed, 'or the B&B that had advertised a pint with breakfast.'

'Only The Edward does that,' Stella protested. 'Nowhere else.'

'Is it specially aimed at alcoholics?' Justine asked sweetly.

Stella floundered. It was all so true. Like she'd asked Rick last night: why choose a place like Mapton?

After Southwold Rick had bought a camper van and began a meandering odyssey around the British Isles. He headed west first, then up, around the tip of Scotland (or as close as he could get) and down the east side of the country. He saw the good and the bad, the beautiful and the bleak, the average and the extraordinary. He didn't plan where to go, just let the road take him, mind still healing and building scar tissue as he went. One day he was driving through the flat, open farmland of East Lincolnshire, fields of golden wheat bordered by dykes along the narrow roads, when a great feeling of peace filled him. He kept that tranquillity as he drove into Mapton, the odd little town on the edge of the land, and decided to stay a few days. By the end of the week he knew he would stay. Mapton and its prim little sister, Siltby, were spiritually and culturally as far from a cosmopolitan life as one could get. No one who might want to find Michelin star chef Richard Blake would look in Mapton and there was nothing here to remind him who he'd been. Ambition, cordon bleu, and high culture were not concepts on Mapton's radar.

'Look,' Justine said, turning serious. 'I'm sure Mapton is lovely in its own way but is it really the place for a talent like Richard? I can see why he came here; it's the antithesis, the antidote, the anti-full stop to his life in London. He was scared and he wanted to crawl into a hole. This is the hole. But for how long? He's well now. He looks great...' She smiled coyly. 'Hey, I'm a woman, as well as an ex. I can still look, can't I?'

No, Stella thought. No looking and definitely no touching. The grim line of her mouth must have made her thoughts clear.

Justine laughed. She held up her hands. 'Relax. I'm joking. We're history on the romance front. I'm not interested in getting back together and neither's Richard. But I need his talent and I don't want to see him waste it.' She pointed to the half-eaten burger. 'Take this for example. I checked out the other cafes and I can guarantee their burgers won't taste like this. They'll be half-unidentifiable meat, half cereal fodder, come in freezer bags of a hundred, and work out about thirty pence a burger, meaning that even at

Mapton prices the cafe owner will turn a profit.

'This, on the other hand, is pure beef, onion, and seasoning, homemade for sure. If it wasn't Richard's place I wouldn't have ordered it. It cost a little bit more than the burgers along the way but not by much. Not enough for Richard to be making a profit. I know him. He's interested in the food, not the money. I doubt this place really pays its way.'

Stella disagreed. 'But it's busy,' she said.

Rick appeared, hustling plates of food to a table nearby. He flashed her a quick, anxious smile.

Justine watched his retreating back. Stella was convinced she was checking out his bum. She knew *she* always did.

'There's an empty table over there,' Justine pointed out. 'At lunchtime. They're run off their feet because they prepare it all fresh. It's not fast food. I'll bet if you took a stroll along to the main strip of cafes you'd find it swarming. And how busy is it the rest of the time?'

Stella thought about all the times she'd been able to have a leisurely chat with Rick because the diner was quiet, but wasn't about to admit it.

'You just want me to talk Rick into taking up your offer,' she said. 'But like I said, it's got to be about what Rick wants. If he's happy here then that's all that counts.'

Justine sighed. 'Okay,' she said. 'I'm glad Richard has someone like you. It's a relief, actually. I care about him and I can't see him continuing to be happy here. He's got too much to offer. If you were staying perhaps I wouldn't be so worried. Are you thinking of moving to Mapton?'

'No!'

'Thought not,' Justine said. 'You've got too much talent.' She stood up. 'Well, I've given it my best shot. Time to say goodbye to Richard. I've got a dinner meeting tonight.' She offered her hand again. Stella rose to take it. 'It really was great to meet you in person,' Justine continued. 'I am such a fan of your work.'

'Thank you. It was nice to meet you too,' Stella said.

She watched Justine walk into the diner and speak to Rick. They embraced, Justine planting a kiss on each cheek. Justine whispered some last words in his ear and Stella saw Rick's eyes find her. She turned away, embarrassed to be caught staring.

Justine re-emerged, whipping her shades on against the glare of the sun. 'Mind the waitress,' she murmured to Stella as a parting shot. 'She's got a thing for Richard.'

Startled, Stella looked for Ang and found her at the counter, hand hovering over the cash till. She was watching Justine leave.

Of course she does, Stella realised. Doh! How naive of me. No wonder Ang's so rude. It's jealousy, pure and simple. Being married isn't proof against a serious crush.

She examined Ang closely with new eyes. Just how serious a crush was it, she wondered.

Bright Lights

When Stella got back to the beach hut she found it locked up. She checked her phone and saw the text from Grazja. 'G need nap. C u @ home'.

Gina was asleep on the sofa but roused as Stella came in. 'Did you give 'er what for?' she called.

'She's gone,' Stella said, sidestepping the question.

'Because you tode 'er to?'

'Nooo,' Stella. 'It wasn't like that.'

'Oh, you're too soft. I'd a taken her down.'

'You don't have to approach everything like it's a fight, Gina.'

Grazja came in from the garden where she'd been hanging up washing. 'You back. Come on. We want to hear all.'

Stella rolled her eyes. 'It's like the inquisition.' Still, she gave them an edited version of Rick's story – minus the psychotic breakdown.

'So, Rick is top chef,' Grazja declared. 'This is impressive, yes Gina?'

Gina grimaced. 'I don't go in for fancy food.' She put on a posh voice and stuck out her little finger. 'Oh, I'll have a robin's egg on a nest of far quaaaaaaa and caviaaaaaaaar.'

'I no idea what you saying,' Grazja said.

'Neither does she,' Stella laughed. 'Anyway, Rick retired from all that. He hated the pressure. He wanted a quieter life.'

'But this Justine, she want him to be chef again?'

'Her restaurant isn't doing so well.'

Gina scoffed. 'There're plenty of chefs out there. She wants him back, you mark my words.'

'She pointed out that if Rick took the job he'd be closer to where I live.'

Gina looked as though she was about to retort but clamped her mouth shut.

'That what you want, Stella?' Grazja asked. 'You could carry on relationship if he moved to London.'

'I don't know,' Stella said. 'We've only just started but...' They watched her intently. 'It feels so right when we're together.'

'Ha!' Grazja leapt up. 'It is love.'

Gina sneered. 'It's lust,' she said. 'And we all know what that leads to...'

'Intercourse,' Stella and Grazja shouted together, starting to giggle.

'No. Well, yes.' Gina waved her hands in frustration. 'Heartbreak. It always ends with heartbreak.'

'Oh, pah,' Grazja dismissed her. 'You old cynic.'

Stella looked at Gina and saw the genuine fear in her grandmother's face. Perching next to her she said. 'It is scary, but I think Rick's worth the risk.'

Gina wrinkled her nose like she could smell something bad. 'If you say so. I've lived in Mapton for five years and this is the first I've heard of an ex-wife, and most folk who live here year round know all about everyone else. What else don't we know about Rick, eh? Think about that before you give away your heart.'

Stella jumped up, stung. 'Thanks, Gina. As supportive as ever. Let's forget it. I want to get started on the beach hut. I'll start by cleaning it out and sanding down those doors. Is there a hardware shop in town?'

'Sanderson's on Canary Road. It's on the outskirts,' Gina replied, a little taken back by Stella's abrupt change. 'We'll meet yer up at the hut, should we?'

'Do whatever you want,' Stella said crisply. She grabbed her bag, swiped the beach hut keys off the coffee table, and headed out.

'It's my bloody hut,' Gina called after her. She caught Grazja's disapproving eye. 'What?'

Grazja shook her head and tutted.

#

Stella attacked the beach hut doors with sugar soap, a wire brush, and sandpaper. She wanted to do, not think, so threw herself into the task. It was hard, grimy work, perfect for her mood. Gina and Grazja didn't show up for a couple of hours, which suited her too. When they did, Gina came bearing gifts; coffee and Danish pastries in a brown paper deli bag. Stella recognised it immediately.

'You got this at Rick's?'

'Yes,' Grazja said. 'We went for a walk, popped in, got you some coffee. Your favourite, yes?'

'Let me wash my hands,' Stella said.

She re-emerged, wiping her hands on kitchen towel. Grazja set up the deckchairs. Once they were seated, Gina handed them the coffees.

'My bum almost on floor in this,' Grazja said, as the old canvas sagged.

Frowning, Stella asked. 'Did you see Rick?'

'He was there,' Gina nodded. 'I said hello.'

'He very nice,' Grazja added. 'Handsome. Sexy bum.'

'Dirty bogger,' Gina reprimanded her.

'I can't help what my eyes see.'

Stella wasn't letting them distract her. 'You didn't just 'pop in' did you? You went there on purpose. What did you say to him, Gina?'

Gina feigned hurt. 'You don't have to say it like that. I was just being friendly.'

'She was,' Grazja stuck up for her. 'She was very good girl.'

'I'm not five,' Gina told her. She focused on Stella. 'You like him so much I thought I should make the effort to get to know him better.' She bristled under Stella's glare. 'Being your grandmother.'

'What did you talk about?'

'Small talk. The weather. Whether it would be a good summer - schools break up soon and then the season really starts - that sort of thing. Oh, and I invited him out with us.'

'You did what? Why? When?'

'Tomorrow night,' Gina said, popping a piece of danish in her mouth. 'It's karaoke at the Diving Bell. I've heard Rick sing karaoke a couple of times. He's pretty good. Thought he'd enjoy it if we all went together.'

Stella was furious. 'I hate karaoke. And I don't like the idea of us all going out together. Anyway, aren't you banned from doing karaoke?'

'Only from The Paradise,' Gina said. 'Who told you?'

'I overheard it the first day I was here.' Stella thought it best not to mention names. 'I don't know them,' she lied.

'Vicious gossips,' Gina spat.

'Why you banned?' Grazja asked.

'Heckling,' Stella said.

Gina pulled an outraged face. 'I wasn't heckling. Pam Stimpson's just got no sense of humour. It was friendly ribbing was all. She sounded just like her cat when I threw it in the lake.'

'You threw her cat in lake?' Grazja said. 'No wonder she not find you funny.'

'Oh, that was after,' Gina dismissed her. She gazed intently at Stella. 'Aw, c'mon ducky. It'll be fun. I promise I won't embarrass yer; I just want to get to know Rick better. If you like him I'll make sure I do too.'

Stella regarded her disbelievingly. Her mobile rang, giving her a moment of grace. She flicked it open. It was Rick. Setting her coffee down, she clambered out of the deck chair. 'I'm just going to take this,' she said, moving towards the beach. Once out of earshot she took the call.

'Hey,' Rick said warmly. 'You okay?'

Stella gazed at the sea. 'Yes. No. Maybe. Has Justine definitely gone?'

'You saw her go,' Rick said. 'She didn't come back, thank God. I think she finally got the message.'

'Okay. Good.'

'Er, I did get another unexpected visitor,' Rick said.

Stella closed her eyes. 'Gina?'

'She told you.'

'We're at the beach hut now. Don't worry, she can't hear me.'

'Beach hut?'

'Tell you later. So …'

'So, she shanghaied me into going out tomorrow night. I never imagined Gina could launch a charm offensive. She kinda blind-sided me.'

Stella laughed. 'I've never seen it either. Is this a new Gina?'

'Maybe so,' Rick said. 'So, how about it? You, me, Gina, and her Polish side-kick, what's her name?'

'Grazja.'

'That's it. Grazja. She looks like a tough cookie in a nice sort of way.'

'She can handle Gina,' Stella said. 'She checked out your bum.'

'Verdict?'

'Sexy.'

'Now I'm blushing. So what d'you say?'

'Okay,' Stella sighed. 'But don't blame me for whatever happens. You remember the Dr Pepper ads?'

'"What's the worst that can happen?" I getcha. Still, it's good that Gina seems to accept me.'

'Hmm,' Stella said.

'Ominous.'

'Experience.'

'Right. Well, I'll bear that in mind. How about you and me have this evening together? No exes, no Gina, no harrowing confessionals. You haven't seen Mapton at night yet, have you? Not the main strip?'

'Is it spectacular?' Stella laughed.

'Las Vegas, baby. I'll take you to the fair and then we'll hit the slots.'

'Wow. You know how to show a girl a good time,' Stella said, feeling her feet leave the sand just at the sound of his voice. 'Eight okay?'

'Great. I'll call for you. See you then.'

Stella said goodbye. She felt so much lighter. She was ready to tackle that Danish pastry.

#

Rick found Stella waiting outside Gina's front door.

'Let's go,' she said. 'I can't take anymore.'

Rick caught the bass of music inside accompanied by voices raised in raucous song. He raised his eyebrows.

'They're practising for tomorrow,' Stella explained. 'Grazja picked up an old copy of the Grease soundtrack in town. They've been playing Summer Nights over and over since six-thirty.'

The image tickled Rick. He laughed, offering Stella his hand. 'C'mon. Let's make a break for it.' She grabbed on and they ran like children, only stumbling to a stop once they reached the promenade panting for breath.

'I'm not as fit as I used to be,' Rick puffed.

'Oh, I don't know,' Stella replied, wrapping her arms around him. 'I've been impressed by your stamina.'

Rick smiled against her hair, breathing in the scent of her shampoo and Stella-ness. He ducked his head to find her lips and they kissed, deep and long, Rick clasping Stella hard against him. He felt the blessed relief of being able to kiss her without the weight of his past a secret between them. Stella murmured her pleasure.

A familiar honk broke them apart.

'Get a room,' Sue shouted, trundling past. Her gang whistled and parped as they followed her, cackling at the public display.

Rick grinned at Stella.

'That's settled their minds,' Stella said. 'Sue was all in a flurry about Justine.'

'This town…' Rick shook his head.

They walked past the closed diner, heading towards the main part of the beachfront, where the fair was set back behind the promenade. In July it was still light at this time of the evening but later Mapton's sparse illuminations would switch on. Rick preferred it in mid-August, when the holiday season was in full swing, and the nights drew in sooner. The dusk seemed a magical time then.

The fair was small and as ramshackle as the rest of Mapton's attractions. There was a waltzer, dodgem cars, The Paratrooper, a bouncy castle and inflatable slide, a penny arcade and some sedate rides for little ones, as well as a Hook a Duck and a small funhouse. More impressive was the ghost train.

Still, it all struck Rick as pitiful. Damn Justine, he thought; I'm seeing it through her eyes. He blinked to clear his vision. 'Behold, the grand fair,' he said, sweeping a hand towards the rides.

Stella laughed, taking in the scene. 'Very Mapton,' she said. 'Are any of these rides safe, do you think?'

'Sure,' Rick said. 'Or they were in 1982.'

'Well,' Stella declared. 'I'm ready to live dangerously. What should we go on first?'

'How about The Paratrooper?'

Stella eyed the rickety umbrella ride with a certain amount of trepidation. 'Okay.'

According to the handwritten signs posted around the fair, all rides were a pound after seven pm. Rick dropped a couple of coins into the operator's palm, a youth who had the usual dead-eyed disinterested look of a teenage ride operator. He waited for a few more customers to board before hitting the start button. Pumping music blasted as they began to move. It was Ricky Martin's Living La Vida Loca.

'Ricky Martin!' Stella said. 'Hey, that's the late nineties. What's going on?'

'Mapton's moving forward,' Rick shouted back. The arms of the ride started to lift them higher and faster as it spun. 'We're about to hit the millennium.'

Compared to the more modern rides, The Paratrooper was gentle, but it was exciting enough for Stella, who clung onto Rick as though she feared for her life. She giggled her way through, her laughter infectious. Rick enjoyed the way she held onto him; the warmth of her thigh pressed closed to his, and her small hand gripping his arm, eased the disquiet that Justine's offer had stirred up. He determined to take her on the ghost train next. There was nothing like a spooky ride to give you an excuse to put your arm around your best girl.

They staggered giddily off The Paratrooper in the direction of the ghost train.

It was a fine looking attraction, stylishly black, grey and red, hand painted and hung about with skulls and shrunken heads. It lacked the lurid airbrushed horrors of most ghost trains, having the look of a ride that was loved and bespoke. It was operated by a monk. At least a man wearing a monk's robe and hood, the cowl so deep that only the man's eyes glittered from its depths.

'Brother Frank,' Rick nodded solemnly to the monk.

'Rick,' Brother Frank nodded back. 'Do you dare face your sins in the dark?'

'I do,' Rick said. 'And so does my good lady

friend.'

'So be it,' Frank said, sonorously. He lifted the bar of the first car and motioned them in. Stella scurried past him. Rick settled himself in next to her and drew her close. 'It's all right,' he said. 'I'll protect you.'

Stella looked genuinely scared. 'He's creepy,' she whispered, as Brother Frank attended to a family behind them. She jumped as he noiselessly reappeared to slap the safety bar into place.

'If you are sinless you have nothing to fear,' he said, and started their car rolling.

Stella gripped Rick's free hand. He squeezed back. He felt a bit mean because he knew what was coming next. At the same time he relished it.

True to form Brother Frank crept behind the car, grabbing Stella's shoulder just as they slid through the doors into the dark. Stella screamed, almost leaping out of her seat. Chuckling, Rick drew her closer as the fake cobwebs tickled their faces and the first fright lit up to the sound of a ghost train's classic wail. It was a tiny ride but cleverly structured. Even Rick shrieked as they crashed out of pitch-black darkness into a mirrored door that reflected their distorted, weirdly lit faces back at them.

Brother Frank leapt out, roaring, as they emerged, giving Stella a final, squeal-inducing shock.

'Well done,' Brother Frank said, as he lifted their bar. 'You are pure as the driven snow. The truly sinful remain locked within the ghost train forever. You may have seen them.' He hurried to meet his next victims as they emerged to his roar.

Rick helped Stella out of the car. She seemed genuinely shaken. 'That was really scary,' she said.

'It wasn't,' Rick said. 'You don't mean it.' He hoped she didn't. He felt guilty.

'I do,' Stella said, looking pale.

'Aw,' Rick tried to make light of it. 'But the props were cheesy. The clown, a skeleton, an axe-maniac. The scariest thing was the mirrored doors when we saw ourselves.'

'I only saw that,' Stella said. 'The rest of the time I kept my eyes shut. Brother Frank freaked me out! Especially when he grabbed me.'

'Poor baby,' Rick said, hugging her. 'I'm sorry. But you know Frank comes into my diner for breakfast Saturday mornings. He's a fairly regular kind of guy.'

'Does he wear his robe?'

'No,' Rick laughed. 'Rumour is he used to be a high-flying stockbroker or something like that. He's owned the ghost train for the last ten years at least. There's a guy who loves his job.'

'Stockbroker?' Stella's interest was piqued. 'And like you he ended up in Mapton. Haven't you wanted to ask him about it?'

'No,' Rick said. 'Mapton's the place you come to forget your past.'

'Hmm,' Stella considered. 'I wonder if he has a Justine out there somewhere, waiting to bring it all back to him.'

Rick shuddered. 'Hey,' he said, trying to keep his voice light. 'This is our night, remember. Let's keep the exes out of it.'

'How many exes do you have?' Stella asked.

'I meant ex-everything,' Rick said. 'Including grandmas, wives, lovers of yours and dark secrets.'

Stella relaxed. 'Okay,' she said. 'I fancy the dodgem

cars. But I warn you, I'm a demon on them.'

She wasn't joking. She slammed him so many times he thought he might have whiplash, but they were laughing so hard it was worth it.

They exited the fair next to Flamingo City, but the only place open in the complex was an empty bar called Carp. Stella was disappointed to find Witchywicca World closed for the evening.

'Witches have too much going on at night,' Rick said. 'They can't be expected to run the shop too. You'll have to come back in the day.'

After a swift half in the bar of a 'family entertainment centre' called Chubby Sam's they entered the world of the main street arcades, with names such as The Oasis and Strike it Rich. Rick insisted the best for prizes on the two pence slotties was The Midas Touch Casino but first he wanted to take her to the oldest arcade in Mapton, The Penny Arcade. Clearly on its last legs, it occupied a corner lot, a third of the size of the others. They passed an old pinball machine, The Vibrator (which you stood onto be shaken about like a washing machine on spin), one-armed bandits, and penny coin pushers.

Rick led Stella right to the back to his favourite machine. It was called 'Death of a Miser' and was an automated diorama enclosed in a glass case. Sometime in the past few years the coin slot had been modified to take ten pence pieces.

'It's 19th century,' Rick said.

'Wow,' Stella said, peering through the glass. The diorama depicted a Victorian bedchamber, sparsely furnished with a single bed, bedside table, and small cabinet. The bedroom door was positioned on the right hand side of the back wall. The miser lay on the bed in his nightcap and white gown.

Rick fed ten pence into the coin slot. The diorama reluctantly creaked to life. The cabinet inched open and a small imp popped out, withdrawing again as the cabinet door closed. The miser sat up in bed, as slowly as an arthritic old man. The bedroom door opened, ushering in a jerky skeleton. He too withdrew as the door closed. Finally, the cupboard door of the bedside table juddered downwards, revealing another demonic imp. The miser sank back with his final Hell-bound expiring breath as the bedside cupboard closed. All was still.

'That's amazing!' Stella gasped. 'I can't believe it still works.'

'I know,' Rick said, pleased by her reaction. 'I doubt there are many left in working order. I've asked CJ - the guy who owns this place to sell it to me if he closes down or retires. CJ junior wants to upgrade it all.'

'What?' Stella gasped. 'Why? Surely it's unique.'

'Yeah,' Rick said. 'But look around you? There's hardly anyone here. It'll be busier next week with the schools out and more holidaymakers, but you'll see when we go into the other arcades. They'll be full. Especially since The Midas Touch opened. The others have had to up their game to keep up.'

'Then we won't go to The Midas Touch,' Stella declared.

Rick, grinning at her loyalty, shook his head. 'I promised you the whole Mapton experience,' he said as he guided her out of the Penny Arcade.

A sudden, discomforting thought struck him: In

the same way public taste had moved on from the Penny Arcade was he perhaps ready to move on from Mapton?

#

Stella, reaching out for Rick in the early hours of the morning, found an empty space. Henry, curled up by her feet, was none too pleased when she roused herself. Descending the turret she caught the delicious aroma of baking and headed for the kitchen.

The kitchen island was covered by neatly arranged ingredients. Whatever he was making looked complicated to Stella.

Rick was crouching to draw a tart tin out of the oven. He almost dropped the tin when he saw her but managed to get it safely to the heat-resistant mat.

'God, you made me jump. I didn't hear you. Sorry, did I wake you up?'

'It's okay,' Stella said blearily. 'What are you doing?'

'Making breakfast,' Rick said.

'But breakfast isn't for hours,' Stella pointed out.

Rick looked sheepish. 'I know. I couldn't sleep.'

'Are you thinking about Justine?' She tried to keep the note of jealousy out of her voice.

Rick winced. 'Not like that - not about Justine herself…'

'I didn't mean it like that either,' Stella said, half-truthfully. 'I mean about her offer. Are you thinking about that?' She perched on a stool, facing him over the island worktop.

Rick was silent for a moment as he removed the baking parchment and ceramic beans from the pastry case. He picked up a small bowl of egg yolk and brushed the case with it, then popped the tin back in the oven and set the timer for five minutes.

He pulled a large Pyrex jug towards him and started to crack eggs into it.

Stella waited. He was thinking.

'Justine's proposal is crazy,' he said finally. 'I know that. Whatever she says, the pressure would be as high - or nearly.' He added egg yolks to the three eggs he'd already cracked, crème fraiche, milk, and a sprinkle of chopped herbs that Stella didn't recognise and started to beat the mixture.

'But?' Stella prompted because she'd heard it in his voice.

He beat vigorously for a minute. 'You remember when I said you needed to wear different lenses to see the beauty in Mapton?' He looked at her. Stella nodded. 'Well, it's like Justine has come along and ripped one of those lenses off. I cover one eye and I still see the Mapton I love, I see my life in it and I'm happy. Then I cover the other eye and I see Mapton the way Justine sees it - or the way you see it - the butt ugly end of nowhere. The last resort for losers.'

It was Stella's turn to wince. She had called Mapton 'butt-ugly' hadn't she? Did she still see it that way? Was Sue a loser because she lived on disability benefits and motored around on a mobility scooter? Was Gina? Or Brother Frank? Two weeks ago she would have answered 'yes'. Probably not out loud but she would have thought it. And had she thought that of Rick on some level?

Rick echoed her. 'And when I see out of that lens - the butt-ugly one - I see myself as one of those losers, hiding out, too afraid to reach my potential.'

Stella reached for him. 'You are not a loser. Never.' And she knew that whatever she might have secretly considered two weeks ago she no longer believed. 'You succeeded at the highest level in what you set out to do, irrespective of what happened after. And you made a decision to simplify and downsize your life. God, that's what everyone in London dreams of. You have a lovely diner, an amazing house and get to walk by the sea every day. How does that make you a loser?'

Rick smiled. 'Sounds better when you put it like that.'

The timer beeped and Rick went to the oven. He took out the pastry case, dabbed it again with the last of the egg yolk, and returned the pastry to the oven, resetting the timer for ten minutes.

He seasoned the custard mixture and set it aside, reaching into the fridge for bacon.

Stella watched, fascinated as he chopped the streaky rashers into ragged bits. 'This is a complicated breakfast,' she commented.

'Nah, it's just a quiche,' Rick said. 'A bit of cooking therapy. This isn't fancy food, not what I used to create.'

'Do you miss it?'

Rick rinsed his hands, heated oil in a pan, and began to sauté the bacon. It smelled delicious.

'Sometimes I miss the creative intensity of the kitchen and a team working on separate elements to make an astonishing whole, but then I remember the cost of that pressure. But I still cook once a week for a friend of mine who lives in Lawton. Jill.'

'Oh, a woman,' Stella said, trying to sound casual.

She failed.

Rick grinned. 'You got no competition there. Jill is a sixty five year old lesbian.'

'Oh,' Stella couldn't help grinning back foolishly. 'Is that allowed in these parts?'

'Only if you're a local and don't wear it on a tee shirt. Lawton's the big town around here, further inland. Really nice. Doesn't allow big chain supermarkets. Lots of small shops. Anyway, Jill owns a deli - 'Delicious' - that's the name not a comment on the food, although it is. I discovered it the first year I moved here. Jill ran it with her partner, Jessica. Then Jess died three years ago. Jill was devastated and, like I thought it would somehow help ease her grief, I started to make meals and drive them over to her. We're good friends now. She's getting by and I cook either in her kitchen or mine on Wednesday evenings. She supplies the ingredients.'

He tipped a chopping board of diced onions and red leafy bits - 'Chicory,' he told Stella - into the pan of bacon and continued sautéing.

'Has Jill found someone else?' Stella asked.

'No. Jess was the love of her life. And she jokes that older single lesbians are rarer than honest politicians. There are far more widowers knocking around Lawton wanting a woman to darn their socks for them. Jill's actually had a couple of proposals from men. One assumed Jess was just her business partner and the other knew she was gay but didn't care. Said he wasn't interested in sex, just companionship and a meal on the table every night.'

'Was he a good friend already?'

'Nope. Hardly knew her. Just marched into the

shop one day and presented his idea like a business plan.'

'What did Jill say?'

'She sold him some nice cheese and told him to go away.'

Stella laughed.

'Talking of cheese,' Rick said, pointing to bowl of grated cheese on the counter. 'A fine mature cheddar and top notch Gruyere from Jill's deli.'

'You see,' Stella said. 'Even in Mapton you can still reach a good deli. It's not the backend of nowhere. You've got friends and a life.'

Rick tipped the bacon, chicory, and onions into a sieve to drain off the juice before dumping them into another bowl. He seemed to be considering her words. Pouring a bit more oil in to the pan, he turned up the heat and stir-fried some mushrooms.

'I know,' he said. 'You're right. But Justine's visit has made me look at my life more closely. I don't actually have many real friends here - Jill, and Bob Morton - he lives in Siltby. The rest are just people I know and occasionally hang out with. And that's fine. It's suited me till now.'

'And no girlfriends?' Stella asked.

Rick pulled his mouth down. 'A few dates here and there. Nothing serious. I didn't want it. Wasn't ready.'

The words hung between them.

Rick removed the mushrooms from the heat, drained off the juice, and added them to the bacon mixture. He threw a handful of rocket leaves to wilt in the cooling pan and pulled a hand blender out from under the island. Adding the rocket to the custard mix he tipped in the grated cheese and whizzed them all up.

The oven timer beeped again. Rick took the pastry case out and turned the oven down. He spooned the bacon mixture into the bottom of the case and then poured the custard over it. Then he popped the tin back in the oven.

'How long?' Stella said. After all the great smells she was ravenous.

'Fifty mins to an hour,' Rick said.

Stella groaned. 'I'm huuuuungry.'

'And then it'll take an hour to cool.'

Stella thumped her forehead on the island top, making Rick laugh. 'Let me clean up and then you can have a piece of toast to tide you over. Or you can go back to bed. It's four o' clock in the morning, you know.'

'Toast first' Stella said. 'You've set me on.' She watched him stack the dishwasher and wipe down the worktop. He worked with quick efficiency.

'You can clean my kitchen anytime,' Stella said.

Rick looked at her sharply. 'The kitchen at Gina's or your real home?' He came round the island.

Stella tipped her head back to look up at him. 'My home,' she said quietly.

He laced his fingers through hers. 'I wasn't ready for a relationship before,' he said. 'I am with you.'

She searched his eyes and saw the same mix of tenderness and fear she felt in her own. 'Me too.'

'It scares me that I've only got you for a bit of time. Soon you'll go back to your real life and forget about me.'

'I won't,' Stella said. 'Now I'm on the mend with

Gina I'll be up all the times for weekends and holidays. You can come down to me.'

'But it's a factor,' Rick said. 'You know that. Justine's offer. You being down there's a definite incentive.'

'It can't be,' Stella countered. 'I won't let it. If for even a second you're seriously considering returning to Francais L'Americaine it has to be because you want it. It has to be right for you irrespective of us. Justine's already played that mind game with me and I told her the same thing.' She put her hand to his cheek. 'I want what's best for you.'

Rick's eyes darkened, intense on hers. 'I think that's the definition of love,' he whispered.

Stella's legs turned to jelly; she was glad to be sitting on the stool. 'Yes,' she whispered back. 'I think it is.'

#

They hadn't made it up to the bedroom. Passion drove them as far the rug in the garden room. They were dozing in a warm post-coital sprawl when the oven timer beeped again. The quiche was baked.

Wearing nothing but oven mitts Rick drew it out of the oven. The house phone rang.

'Who's that?' Stella demanded, stumbling into the kitchen, wrapped in a throw. 'It's five o' clock in the morning.' Her hair stuck up in wild ringlets.

'It'll be my mom,' Rick said, reaching for the phone. 'She swears she can never work out the time difference between here and the States, but I think she rings early because she knows I'll be in.'

'You can't talk to her naked,' Stella hissed, as though his mother could hear them.

'She can't see me,' Rick said.

'But we've had sex.' She almost mouthed it.

Rick mimicked her. 'She doesn't know that. Should I tell her?'

'No!' Stella squealed. She flung the throw at him and headed out of the kitchen, towards the stairs, giving him the joy of a little bum waggle as she went.

She heard him stifle his laugh as he picked up. 'Hi Mom.'

Stella took a shower, pulled on Rick's bathrobe and went for a wander round the house. Henry joined her, snaking around her ankles. She petted him, noticing how sleek and healthy he looked. And happy. If a cat could look happy. She felt a pang of guilt. Although still a house cat, Henry had space to roam in Rick's house, unlike the confined conditions of her studio loft. How would he cope going back there?

She decided to check out the other turrets.

'Hope we don't find anything kinky,' she said to Henry, who was following her. 'Or the heads of his previous girlfriends.'

She didn't. What she found was a spare room, tainted by the lingering trace of Justine's perfume. The western turret had a rotten stair-tread that creaked so ominously she retreated.

It was the light in the northern tower she fell in love with. Even with the dawn just spreading from the east the artist in her saw the potential light. It was a small space really - Rick's bedroom was pretty cramped - but she couldn't help seeing it as a studio. Bare, white-walled, and unfurnished it was easy to fill the room with her imagination.

'Where are you?' Rick called, breaking her vision.

'In the north turret,' she shouted back.

A few moments later Rick found her.

'You finished with your mum already?'

Rick looked glum. 'Know how Justine got my number?'

'No.'

'My mom gave it to her. She and Justine never got along that well but seems they're in cahoots about this. Mom says it's time to 'get back on the horse'; she didn't work her ass off to get me into college so I could run a diner. Says I've had all the time I need to get better and then some.'

'Ouch,' Stella said. 'What did you say?'

Rick sighed. 'Told her I was old enough to make my own decisions.'

'Bet she didn't like that.'

'Nope. But she'll get over it. Probably try again tomorrow. Damn Justine.' He shook off his irritation like water off a dog's coat and smiled at Stella. 'Quiche for breakfast?'

'Finally,' Stella said, taking his arm. She gave the turret room one last wistful look as they left.

Two Weeks Grace

The next fortnight was a happy time for Stella. She painted the beach hut under Gina's supervision, with only a few minor skirmishes between them. They named the hut Ethel Mermaid, after the Hollywood singer Ethel Merman. It was a toss-up between that and Esther Williams, the 1940's swimming star, but Ethel won, name emblazoned on a plaque over the doors.

Children were drawn to the vivid hut, enchanted by the brightly depicted sea creatures and merfolk. (A mermaid on the right side, a merman on the left.) Dog walkers paused to admire the view and chat. Scooter pooters tooted their appreciation as they went past.

Gina, sunning herself outside the hut, basked in the attention while Stella sketched beside her, or until Grazja forced her to walk with the aid of a crutch. Near the end of the row of huts a public toilet and a boarded up cafe became a target for her to reach. Grazja or Stella walked to the left of her, while George Wentworth flanked her right side. Gina snapped at his hovering concern but he steadfastly hung around, taking whatever abuse she threw at him.

'It's your fault,' Gina snarled at Grazja. 'You should never've invited him to the karaoke.'

Grazja shrugged unconcernedly. 'He is lonely. I was being neighbourly. Besides, he did you big favour didn't he? He helped you get Stella here.'

'Just because he pushed me down some steps and called an ambulance don't mean I owe him. I paid him for that.'

Stella's tongue, about to lick her ice cream, froze

motionless. She stared at Gina. 'Is that how you did it? You got George to push you down the steps?'

Gina glared back. 'Yeah. So? Then he let me ode scooter run over the side, called the ambulance, and skedaddled on my Rascal. It was a perfect plan.'

'I can't believe he did it. He could've killed you.'

'Oh don't be so bloody dramatic. I had something he desperately wanted so he couldn't refuse.'

'What?'

'Never you mind,' Gina said, clamming up.

Stella exchanged a look with Grazja.

'Oh Gina, no. Not that,' Stella said, trying not to laugh.

'Not what?'

'Intercourse,' Stella whispered.

Gina's cheeks flamed and her red hair seemed to stand on end from its grey roots. 'I'm not a bleedin' whore,' she shouted, causing a passer-by to do a double take.

Stella and Grazja collapsed into giggles, laughing until their sides hurt.

'Yer're a couple of cheeky boggers,' Gina said. 'Now mind yer own business.'

George was so impressed by the beach hut that he asked Stella and Gina to do-over his hut. That he owned one four doors along was a surprise. Gina seemed quite put out by it. 'Aren't you a dark one?'

'I haven't used it since my wife died,' he said. 'Never had the heart to sell it because she loved it so much. I've maintained it, but that's about all. Seems silly now. If I did it up I could sell it or hire it out to a family. Let someone else get the pleasure out of it we used to.'

'Doesn't your daughter use it with her kids?' Stella asked.

'They prefer the other end of the beach when they come. Got the fair and donkey rides and all that.' He brightened. 'Reckon, if the beach hut looked like yours they might want to come down this end more.'

He said he didn't have much to pay Stella but if she gave him a quote he'd let her know. She dismissed the suggestion. If George would buy the paint, she'd do the work for free. It was a pleasure. He could sit down with Gina and discuss a design; she'd like to do one a little different to theirs. Oh, and they still had some paint left over so he didn't need to buy a lot.

The second hut attracted even more attention with its yellow background peppered with ice creams and ice-lollies in delicious candy colours, and its trim painted bubble-gum pink. Stella had to gently detach a small child whose tongue was pressed firmly against a lolly. Fortunately the paint was dry by then and no harm was done to child or hut.

A contingency of Siltby Wanderers, led by Pirate Tom, came to inspect them. Siltby beach huts were locally famous for their pretty pastels, so word of Gina Pontin's infringement on Siltby territory (decoratively if not physically) soon reached their ears.

Tom drew up on his Drive Royale, holding his hand up to halt his gang in front of Gina's beach hut. Gina, snoozing in her wheelchair, felt the shadow on her face and squinted at him. Stella was decoupaging a small table inside the hut, along with two chairs she'd picked up at a car boot held on Sunday morning. Seeing Pirate Tom, she wiped her hands on a cloth, pulled out her phone and fired off a quick text to Sue. 'Wanderers @ hut!?'

'Hello Pirate Tom,' she said, stepping out of the hut.

'Stella,' Tom said. 'Er, no need for pirate here. That's my gang name.'

'But your gang's with you,' Stella pointed out.

'No, no,' Tom said. 'We're the Siltby Seafront Committee.'

Gina snorted. 'The Nosy Parker Committee more like. You heard about our beach huts, Tom Turner?'

'Lots of people are talking about them, Gina. How are you by the way?'

'Ger on wi' it,' Gina said. 'So what's your verdict?'

Tom gazed past her at the hut. His committee studied it too.

'Very colourful,' Tom said, finally.

'Is that it?'

'It's bright,' he offered. He turned to his followers. 'More Mapton than Siltby?'

There were murmurs of assent and vigorous nods.

'What does that mean?' Stella asked, but before Tom could reply a harsh honking cut through the afternoon heat. Sue had arrived and she'd brought the cavalry.

She parked her scooter nose to nose with Tom's Royale. Scampi's nose quivered as she poked her head out of her basket, tiny tongue lolling.

'Afternoon Tom,' Sue said. 'I see you've brought your gang. You know the agreement. No more 'n' four together on either side of the border except on rumble nights. I count seven o' yer.'

Tom rolled his eyes. 'This isn't the gang. We're the Seafront Committee.'

'For Siltby,' Gina added. 'Not Mapton.'

Sue gave her a stern look. 'It's all right, Gina. I've got this one.' She levelled her gaze at Tom. 'You may very well be in the Siltby Seafront Committee, I don't doubt it. But every one of you,' she looked at Tom's followers individually, 'is also a Siltby Wanderer.'

'That's right,' Mildred of the blue hair echoed. 'And you dobbed us in.'

Sue raised her hand to cut her off. 'True, Mildred. But not the issue here.'

'There is no issue here,' Pirate Tom said, exasperated. 'As chairman of the Seafront Committee I brought some committee members to admire Stella's handiwork on the beach huts.'

'And what do you think?' Sue asked.

Stella said. 'They think they're more Mapton than Siltby.'

'And what's that supposed to mean?' Sue demanded.

Tom showed his palms appealingly. 'Only that because of the choice of strong colours and the cartoons...'

'Cartoons!' Gina bristled.

'Pictures,' Tom amended. 'They're more suited to the sort of holiday maker Mapton attracts.'

Just then a woman walked past wearing a Day-Glo pair of cargo pants that did everything to show her pasty muffin tops. She completed the look with a lime green bikini top and a slew of tattoos.

Tom turned to his followers with a knowing smile. 'Siltby holiday makers are more discerning.'

With huge effort Gina clambered to her feet. 'Do you know who this is?' she roared, pointing at Stella. 'Only an internationally famed artist. And here you are talking about being discernin'. My hut is an original Stella Distry, Tom Turner, and so is George Wentworth's hut. Just one of them would sell for more than your whole house is worth.'

Tom sniggered, but Stella saw the uncertainty in his eye when he looked at her.

'It's true,' Sue told him. 'I looked her up on the internet. Have you got the internet, Tom?'

'Of course I've got the bloody internet,' Tom said irritably.

'Then you should go home and look it up,' Sue said. 'Now get your sorry sen back to Siltby or I'll invoke the forfeit, Tom. I swear I will. No matter how you argue it you've broken the agreed rules. 'And,' she leaned forward threateningly, bosom spreading over the handlebars like an amorphous creature out to get him. 'You did dob us in.'

Tom knew he had been bested. Eyes blazing he barked an order. 'Back to Siltby.' His committee silently reversed and turned towards home.

As Tom was backing up, he snapped at Gina. 'Your dog's still on the loose, Gina. He's a terror to the neighbourhood.'

'Don't get your sausage out in public and you'll be all right,' Gina mocked him.

'It was a roast chicken,' Tom said tersely. 'Better hope someone doesn't mistake him for a fox one night and shoot him.'

'Gerrof wi yer,' Gina shouted to his retreating back. 'And good riddance.'

#

Bing was undoubtedly still on the loose. Dan Joules, the dog warden, knew it better than anyone. Catching Bing had become his obsession.

It annoyed Dan that people thought of dog wardens as the bad guys, jobsworths waiting to pounce on innocent canines, lock them up and put them down.

It was far from the truth. Dan's favourite part of the job was watching the jubilant reunion between lost pet and owner, or seeing a stray or abandoned dog re-homed.

Occasionally he assisted the police in capturing a dangerous dog or an abused one. The threat in those situations often came more from the owner than the animal.

Still, Gina Pontin's attack with a handbag had been a first for him. She was lucky he'd decided not to press charges. In the end he had taken the police advice that only a fool (not quite their words) would take on Gina Pontin but he got the impression it was the police who didn't want the trouble; they'd even stopped considering Gina might be masterminding the crime ring. He couldn't actually believe, despite his admiration for canine abilities, that one dog could train a pack to perform tricks so he could steal from an audience. But that was precisely what had happened that afternoon in Siltby.

Until recently Dan had been part of a small team; he and two other dog wardens had shared the duties between them. Council cut backs meant that when Bill had retired they didn't replace him. Then restructuring led to the unpleasant situation of having to re-apply and compete for his own job against his colleague, Jackie. That he 'won' didn't make him feel better or stop him missing her. So, his workload tripled. In an area where more people had dogs than not and an influx of holidaymakers brought their own pets with them, Dan was overworked to the point of exhaustion. Add to that the spate of dogs reported missing from home - Denise Robertson's dalmatian, the Ferguson's miniature collie, Wolf Hodson's husky - and Dan was at breaking point. The one person who hadn't reported her dog as missing was Gina Pontin.

Then at the start of the week the circus dog-act trainer reported his poodle as stolen. He refused to consider the possibility that she had wandered off of her own volition.

At three o' clock Dan got an excited call from a Siltby local babbling about performing dogs and thievery on the beachfront.

By the time Dan reached Siltby the dogs had disappeared but the place was astir. According to witnesses four dogs had arrived in a troop - a white poodle, a husky, a miniature collie and a dalmatian. They started to perform tricks on the beach, jumping over each other, somersaulting and walking on their back legs. The dalmatian was the funniest as he hadn't mastered any of the tricks. People gathered round to watch, throwing them snacks, and responding to cute begging with more food.

More and more folk came to watch until there was quite a crowd gathered on the sand and sea-steps. They left picnic bags and lunch boxes unattended behind them as they clapped and cheered the performance. It took a while before anyone noticed two other dogs quietly snatching the contents of the picnics and stockpiling it.

When one man turned to reach for a sausage-roll only to find it gripped between the jaws of a Jack Russell terrier, the game was up. His outraged yell alerted the performers to make a swift run for it. They darted round the crowd, up the steps and joined their comrades in crime. Each grappled its jaws around as much of the stockpiled food as it could and raced away, all taking different directions so it was impossible to tell where the pack was really heading.

Dan was furious. He'd never hated an animal in his life, not even one of the vicious bull terriers he'd encountered. They were the result of human mistreatment.

But today he hated Bing Crosby, especially after his boss rang him and gave him a tongue-lashing. Word of the pack's latest escapades had spread at the hare speed of a mobility scooter to Mapton. If it got into the Lawton Post, Mapton and Siltby would be laughing stocks. The scooter rumble had been enough of a debacle for one year. And what if some child had been bitten? What then?

Dan had tersely pointed out that as he was doing the job of three people it hardly seemed fair to blame him when his under-resourced department of one couldn't keep up.

His boss chuntered a bit more before finally conceding the point. 'Fine,' he said. 'I'll temporarily reallocate someone to aid you.'

That night Dan dreamt about chasing Bing. In his sleep he twitched and snarled like a dreaming dog.

#

The sunny weather continued into the following week. Stella and Gina passed their days playing house in the beach hut, or sitting outside it and sketching. Stella carried Gina's easel down to the hut, lowering it so Gina could use it. With only one arm to balance a pad on her knee while she drew, Gina was growing fractious. The easel wasn't ideal either. It was difficult to get the wheelchair close enough.

George came up with a solution. He disappeared into his garage for two days. Gina pretended not to notice his absence but by the second day she was fretting.

'The idiot's probably had a heart attack,' she said. 'Best go and check on 'im, Grazja.'

Grazja came back. 'He's fine. Is doing man things.'

'What sort of man things?' Gina demanded.

'Oh, I don't know. He got tools and screws and bits of metal. I not ask him. He seem too busy.'

George knocked on the door that evening, baring a mysteriously shaped parcel wrapped in a blanket. Stella let him in.

'George is here,' she announced, leading him into the lounge.

Gina, propped up on the sofa, watching TV, gave him the evil eye. 'I thought you was too busy for us.'

'Where's your wheelchair?' George asked.

'In me bedroom,' Gina replied. 'Why? And what's that you got there?'

'Would you get the wheelchair?' George asked Stella.

Stella shot Gina a 'what's this all about' look and went to fetch it.

The doorbell chimed 'God save the Queen' again.

This time it was Rick. 'I'm just getting the wheelchair for George,' Stella said. 'He's up to something.'

Rick, curious, followed her to the lounge.

Grazja, hearing voices, emerged from her room, hair in a towel.

'Right,' George said. 'Let's see if this works.' He unfolded the blanket and drew out a jointed metal arm, clamp on one end and flat tray on the other.

'What the bleedin' hell's that rammel?' Gina asked.

'This,' George explained slowly, carefully screwing the clamp onto the frame of the wheelchair. 'Is a retractable table for you to sketch on. Or read on. Or rest a drink on.'

He demonstrated how it could be moved in or out and how to lock it into place with little levers on the joints.

Gina stared at it, stunned.

'Man, that is genius,' Rick said, inspecting it. 'You made this?'

George nodded, blushing.

'C'mon,' Stella said to Gina. 'Try it.'

She and Grazja helped Gina to her feet so she could hobble to the wheelchair. George swung the arm aside so she could get seated and then locked it back into place.

It was in exactly the right position for Gina to use.

Stella fetched a sketchbook and slid it onto the table-tray.

'Oh, I forgot,' George said, rootling in his trouser pocket. He drew out two bulldog clips. 'These should hold your pad in place.'

Gina hadn't said a word. Stella saw the teardrops shimmering in her grandmother's eyes and impulsively dropped a kiss on Gina's forehead.

Gina drew in a shuddering breath and said. 'Oh gerrof wi' yer. Yer acting like it's my bleedin' birthday.' She wiped her eyes and laughed uproariously.

#

'Well,' Rick said, as he drew the front door closed behind them. 'George Wentworth. A man of hidden talents.'

'Nothing George does surprises me after last week's karaoke' Stella said, linking her arm through his. 'That was a revelation.'

Rick nodded absently.

Stella squeezed his arm. The only blight during the last two weeks had been Rick's occasional lapses into introspection. Justine's proposal gnawed at him.

'Have you made any decisions?' she asked.

'Nah,' Rick said. 'I wish I could forget it. I try to but the idea keeps pushing back in. What bothers me most is the way I see Mapton. Mentioning the karaoke reminded me. Usually I enjoy it. I get a buzz outta seeing folk I know get up to sing a tipsy tune. Makes me feel warm and fuzzy and part of the crowd.'

'I thought you did enjoy it,' Stella said. They'd reached the promenade and begun to walk along the seafront, watching the sun sink into the sea. 'I loved your song.'

Rick had sung a mellifluous cover of 'Gentle on my Mind' which earned him a hearty round of applause and the attention of more than one woman in the pub.

'I did and I didn't,' Rick said. 'It was great being out with you and fun to be with Gina and Grazja. What a double act! And George. God, my heart bled for the guy... but... you remember what I said, that Justine had ripped one of my lenses off?'

'The special Mapton lenses,' Stella nodded.

'Yeah, the special lenses. Well, Karaoke night my other lens dropped out. I saw the Diving Helmet as it really is. A badly lit pub with a dingy back room where drunks slur sentimental songs under a single cracked disco ball. Most of them are the same people singing the same songs week after week.

'It made me feel sad. Despairing. I thought: is this what my life is? Is this what I want it to be? Yet at the same time I had my arm round you.' He bumped his forehead gently to hers. 'My best girl. I had your crazy grandma and friends around me. That felt right, you know?'

Stella did know. She'd felt it too. 'So, confusing night,' she said.

'Confusing weeks,' Rick answered. 'The only thing I'm not confused about is the way I feel about you.' He stopped to wrap his arms around her.

Stella pressed her ear against his steady heartbeat and breathed him in. 'Me too,' she whispered.

'But you're leaving, sooner or later.'

'Ah,' she said, pulling back to look at him. 'About that...'

'Uh oh.'

'My agent called me today. She's getting anxious; I've got a commission she needs to negotiate. The gallery's getting antsy because I haven't shown them anything for the new exhibition in the autumn. And my fridge must be about to explode. I didn't have time to clear it out before I left.'

Rick looked horrified. 'That was almost a month

ago!'

'I know,' Stella admitted, embarrassed. 'I know.'

'You won't be able to get in the door for the mould,' Rick said. 'It'll try to grab you.'

Stella agreed. 'Gina would say I'm a filthy bogger.'

'What about your post?' Rick asked. 'Won't that be piling up?'

'I have a box,' Stella said. 'Once my neighbour got back from holiday I asked her to pick it up. She has a key.'

'So,' Rick said. 'When are you going?'

'Tuesday morning,' Stella said. She rushed on. 'But I'm coming back. It's only for a few days to sort things out. I need to make sure Gina can take care of herself before I go home for good.'

'She's got Grazja,' Rick pointed out. 'Any other reason you might want to come back?'

Stella looked him innocently. She pretended to rack her brains. 'Can't think of one,' she said. 'Can you?'

Rick laughed. 'Oh, you're hard-hearted like your grandma. She completely ignored George after he sang to her.'

'She was embarrassed' Stella said. 'He stared at her the whole way through. The entire pub knew who he was singing to.'

'His choice of song could've been better,' Rick said. 'You Spin Me Round's not Gina's style.'

'I know. He should've gone for an old classic, the stuff Gina likes.'

'Still,' Rick said. 'It accurately expressed how he feels about her.'

'What? *All I know is that to me/You look like you're lots of fun/Open up your lovin' arms/Watch out, here I come.'*

'Hmm, I was thinking more about the being spun round part. She makes him feel giddy.'

'That's not what Gina heard. She heard 'intercourse'. It took all of mine and Grazja's persuasion to stop her clocking him one in the bar.'

'She can't be too adverse to the idea. She's let him hang around since.'

'The way a dog lets a flea hang around.'

'George pulled it out of the bag tonight, though. Gina was really touched.' Rick smiled. 'She didn't even insult him.'

'I'm sure she has by now,' Stella replied. 'I couldn't figure George out at first but Sue told me his late wife was obnoxious. A real fire-breather. So either he's a masochist or he's so sweet he only sees the good in people.'

'Fifty Shades of Gina,' Rick said. 'By George Wentworth.'

'Or How to Train your Dragon,' Stella laughed.

'C'mon,' Rick said, tugging her hand. 'Let's go back to my place.'

'I thought we were going for a walk.'

'I've only got you till Monday. I need to make the most of you.'

'It's only going to be for a few days,' Stella protested, but she let him change their direction.

Paradise Lost

On Monday Gina was as fractious as a tantrumy two-year old. Grazja had escaped to do the food shop and even George had slipped away, leaving Stella to take the brunt. Stella was, after all, the reason for Gina's foul-mood, although Gina had yet to admit it. Instead she was petulant, complaining of boredom yet refusing every suggestion Stella made.

'Let's go up to the beach-hut.'

'No. Done it every day. It's boring.'

'What about a walk? Or we potter round the shops?'

'Too hot and too crowded. Don't want to go in the wheelchair. Sick o' it.'

She wiped a finger along the coffee table and stared at the infinitesimal specks of dust on her fingertip.

'The house is filthy,' she snapped. 'Dunno what I'm paying Grazja for.'

Stella held her tongue.

'I'll do it me bleedin' self,' Gina said. 'Get me a duster.'

So Gina hobbled around the lounge, ineffectually flicking a duster over her knick-knacks until she finally knocked a ceramic Betty Boop off a shelf. It smashed on a plant pot, taking a chunk of the pot with it. Gina screaming her rage, collapsed onto the sofa in tears.

Stella ran in from the kitchen. 'What happened?'

'What do you care?' Gina sobbed.

Stella took in the broken shards of Betty Boop. 'Accidentally' breaking things was a long established way of Gina expressing anger.

'Gina,' Stella said, trying, unsuccessfully to take her grandmother's hand. 'I'm only going for a few days. I'm coming back.'

'I broke Betty,' Gina cried, as though Betty was her most treasured possession. She'd bought her on a whim last week, when Stella had wheeled her into town. Any number of the gift shops sold Betties.

'I'll buy you another,' Stella said. 'When I come back.'

'You won't come back,' Gina sniffed. 'Once you get to London you'll forget all about me.'

Here we are, Stella thought. Now we get to it.

'Of course I'm coming back,' Stella said. 'I won't leave until your cast comes off and your ribs heal.'

'I got Grazja for that,' Gina said. 'Ain't that why you got 'er? So you wouldn't have to stay.'

'I had a bad ankle, remember. I couldn't look after you.'

'You didn't send Grazja away once you got better, did you?'

'Did you want me to?'

They both knew the answer to that. Gina sulked. 'That's not the point,' she said.

'What is the point?' Stella asked.

Gina stuck out her bottom lip. 'Even if yer do come back after a few days, what about after that? When yer go home proper? Will it be another five year again before I see yer?'

'Of course not,' Stella said. 'Things are different between us now. Aren't they?'

Gina conceded gracelessly. 'S'ppose so.'

'I want to visit you,' Stella said. 'You're my family.

Besides Rick's here too.'

Gina harrumphed. 'Oh, he'll be in London soon enough.'

'What do you mean?'

'I were talkin' to him last night in Chish n Fips when you'd gone up to pay the bill. Said he was thinking of just goin' to check it out. That fancy restaurant he used to own.'

This was news to Stella. He hadn't said a word about it to her last night.

Gina read her expression. 'Oh, so he ain't tode you. Din't know I weren't supposed to mention it.'

It was Stella's turn to read her. 'I doubt that.'

Gina reddened. 'Well, what did he expect? I'm loyal to you not him. I like 'im well enough but he's a man - one month back in London and he'll be diddling Justine. He won't be able to help himself.'

Stella glared at her.

'What? I'm just saying is all. Now if you moved here he'd stay in Mapton, I'm sure.'

Stella gritted her teeth against the old, familiar resentment of Gina's meddling. And it needled her that Rick had been talking to Gina; he was playing right into her manipulative games. 'So, you're saying there's no competition for me in Mapton? If I moved here I could keep Rick, whereas if we were both in London I'd have no chance against Justine?'

'Well, she looks like a model, don't she?' Gina said. 'You're pretty enough duck, but you're no oil-painting.'

Stella blew up. After she'd tried all morning to be nice. 'God, Gina! You'll say anything to have your own way, even if it hurts me. This isn't about me and

Rick, it's about you wanting me to stay here and be with you forever. Haven't you learnt anything this summer? Isn't that what happened with Maggie? You tried to manipulate it so she'd always be your friend and look how that ended?'

Gina flinched as though Stella had struck her. 'That's not fair.'

'It is. It's completely fair,' Stella said. 'You can't always have things the way you want them, Gina. No-one can.' She stood.

'Where are you going?'

'Out,' Stella said.

'But I'm on me own,' Gina panicked. 'Grazja's out.'

'If you're able to do dusting,' Stella retorted, 'you're fine to look after yourself for a bit. And if you're sick of being alone you should try being a bit nicer.' Fuming, she stormed out, slamming both the lounge and front doors behind her.

Grim-mouthed she set her feet in the direction of Rick's diner. If what Gina claimed was true she wanted to know about it.

He'd be closing up the diner soon. She should just catch him. And if that bitch Ang gave her one more dirty look she'd have it out with her too. That was another thing; the way Rick had brushed off her questions about Ang with: 'I love that you're jealous, but there's no need. Nothing's going on with Ang. She's just a bit moody.'

Since Justine had tipped her off (a humiliation in itself; something she hadn't mentioned to Rick) Stella had kept her eye on Ang. Not because she didn't trust Rick, who seemed genuinely oblivious to Ang's feelings as he went about his work, but because now

Stella was looking for it, she could see how Ang felt about him. Her eyes sought him out when she thought no one was watching. When he bussed tables and stopped to chat with customers, Ang lurked in the diner watching, or came to the door.

She'd observed this on Thursday morning when she, Gina, Sue, and Grazja had sat outside the diner, enjoying the sun. Since the schools had broken up the summer season was in full swing. The diner was bustling, Stella noted, smugly counting it as a point against Justine's business predictions. Rick, Ang, and Ang's son Mark, were kept busy, yet Stella saw how Ang still managed to watch Rick, almost as though it was a habit so deeply ingrained she didn't even realise she was doing it.

Once, Ang, perhaps sensing Stella's eyes on her, swung to meet her gaze. It was as though a visor slammed her face shut, expression unreadable. Rick said something to her as he headed back into the diner, jerking his chin in the direction of another table. Ang nodded and disappeared inside.

'Who's Ang married to?' Stella had casually asked Sue.

Sue and Gina appeared to have developed a tolerance for each other. Gina went so far as to feed Scampi a bit of tea-softened biscuit. She shot Stella a curious glance.

'Des Jones,' Sue informed her. 'Waste o' space if you ask me.'

Gina nodded. 'You saw 'im at the Diving Helmet,' she told Stella. 'He was the MC.'

'Really?' Stella recalled a skinny man with thinning gelled hair, sporting a shiny grey nylon suit. He'd had a line in cheesy banter and in between the punters' songs he belted out a few of his own with classic 'pub-singer' intonation. Mostly Elvis. To Stella, he'd been part of the night's delightfully sleazy enchantment.

'Why's he a waste of space?'

Sue stirred her hot chocolate. She tipped some into a saucer and popped it on the ground next to her chair. Scampi was out of her basket like a bullet from a gun and began to lap it up.

It was the first time Stella had seen the whole of Scampi.

Grazja tutted. 'You two feeding her sugar is not good for dog.'

'Ah, she's got no teeth anyway,' Sue said.

'Chocolate very bad,' Grazja muttered. 'Bromide is bad for dogs.'

'Who made you the sugar police?' Gina demanded.

'I just saying.' Grazja said. 'Dog dies, not my fault. I warn you.'

'She has it every day,' Sue laughed. 'Not done her no harm so far.'

Grazja flipped open her magazine in answer.

'So, why's Des a waste of space?' Stella tried again.

'Oh, he's one of them dreamers,' Sue said. 'Does a bit o' that, bit o' this. Always got a plan to make it big. If he does make any money he blows it in some daft 'get rich quick' scheme. I dunno how Ang puts up wi' him. They separated a few years back. That was the first year Rick was here, I think. Before he started the diner. But Mark - he were only about ten - he were devastated. Loved his dad. Blamed Ang. She were right upset about it, so she ended up getting back wi' him.'

'She never seems happy,' Stella commented.

'She's a miserable cow,' Gina said.

'She's all right,' Sue said. 'Used to laugh and chat a lot more. But I'd be a miserable cow married to that twat. He's got an eye for the ladies, too. Ricky's a good lad. Gave her a job when she needed it - can't rely on Des for it - and made her his deputy. Pays her fair so she can raise Mark. Des is the sort of dad who'll give him a fancy present now and then - an X-box, or whatever - but no consistency. Now Mark's almost sixteen I reckon Ang will give Des the old heave-ho. Although if Rick does decide to chase after you to London, Stella, she'll be outta job. Thinkin' about it Ang hasn't seemed like herself since Rick's ex came to visit. Bet she's worried she'll have no job if Rick sells the diner.'

Stella found none of this reassuring. Without seeming to realise it Sue had almost presented Rick, Ang, and Mark, as a family unit.

Spoiling for a fight after Gina's tantrum, Stella marched towards the diner. The tables had been neatly stacked inside but the door was still open. Squeezing past the furniture, Stella headed toward the kitchen, but stopped when she heard heated voices behind the kitchen door.

'No Rick,' Ang said. 'It's the busy season. It's not fair.'

'For God sakes Ang, we've been through this. It's only for one day. I told you Marie's agreed to come in and help.'

'I hate that woman,' Ang hissed. 'She gets all the orders wrong. She's useless. You can't go and that's final.'

'Whoa,' Rick raised his voice. 'Did you tell me I can't go? Are you the boss now?'

'Maybe I should be,' Ang retorted. 'I wouldn't be letting my dick make the decisions for me.'

Stella held her breath, listening to the sudden terrible silence.

'And what the hell does that mean?' Rick finally asked.

Ang took up his challenge, voice defiant. 'Only that you'd never consider taking a day off to run to an interview with your ex-wife if you weren't screwing Stella.'

'What?' Rick sounded furious and astounded.

'How humiliating,' Ang taunted. 'Begging your ex for a job so you can be near the Perfect Artist. It's pathetic.'

'I am not 'begging' anyone for a job,' Rick growled. 'I have a meeting with Justine to consider her offer. It has nothing to do with Stella, and don't you dare insult her again.'

Stella froze. So Rick had organised a meeting with Justine and he hadn't even told her about it.

Ang made a sound of disgust. 'It has everything to do with Stella. You've been a complete idiot since she arrived. It's like watching a dog around a bitch in heat. You haven't made a single good decision lately. You've been mixing orders up, forgetting to buy stock. I've had to work doubly hard just to keep things going.'

Rick laughed coldly. 'Well, that's love for you Ang. That's what this is about. You're jealous of Stella. But face it, Ang, it was never there between us. And it's never going to be.'

Stella heard footsteps approach and then Ang squealed with rage. Something smashed into the door, making her jump.

'Ang!'

'You were happy enough to sleep with me,' Ang screamed. 'Bet you haven't told her that.'

The handle moved but Stella was rooted to the spot. Rick and Ang had slept together.

'Oh for fuck's sake,' Rick yanked the door open, but he was looking back at Ang. 'It was lousy sex. For both of us. Why would I tell her?' He turned and Stella met his eyes dead on.

His face turned white as he read her face. 'Oh shit, Stel...' he said, reaching for her but she'd already found her legs. She turned blindly, shunting past the stacked chairs to stumble to the open door. Hearing him behind her she lurched for one of the chairs and flung it behind her. Rick grunted as it hit him.

Then she was out of the door and running.

At the Bottom of a Glass

Stella arrived back at the same time as Grazja, who was just unlocking the front door. Grazja took in Stella's hitching breath and tear-stained cheeks.

'What's happened?' She grabbed Stella's arm to steady her.

Stella barged past her to the back gate. 'Rick slept with Ang,' she blurted, and then slammed the gate shut and bolted it, leaving Grazja on the other side.

Inside the static she hauled her suitcase out and began to ransack the drawers and wardrobe. It didn't take long to pack; she'd brought few clothes with her.

Grazja came in without knocking. 'You not go right now,' she said. 'You're too upset.'

'Oh, I'm going,' Stella said, slamming her case shut.

'What about Gina?'

'Gina's been a bitch all day,' Stella said. 'I can't face her 'told you so, men are all bastards' speech.'

'You sure about Rick?' Grazja changed tack. 'Who told you, eh? Probably a lie.'

'He told me,' Stella said. 'Although he didn't know I was listening.'

'Oh.' Grazja frowned. 'I not understand.'

'Neither do I,' Stella snarled. 'Neither do fucking I.' She swept the studio, grabbing bits and pieces and stuffing them into her carrier.

Her phone rang for the umpteenth time. Rick. She turned it off and buried it in her handbag. She slung it over her shoulder, grabbed the carrier and handbag, and headed out, Grazja trailing her.

Gina was leaning on her crutch outside the kitchen

door, expression anxious. 'Ducky, what happened?'

Grazja replied. 'Rick have sex with Ang.'

Gina's face darkened. 'I knew it! That bastard.'

Stella rolled her eyes. 'Save it, Gina. I'm not staying round to listen to this.'

Gina registered her suitcase. 'You can't leave.'

'I can. I am. It's just a day early, that's all.'

'You'll be back in a few days though?' Gina pressed. 'Won't you? You said you would.'

'I don't know,' Stella said. 'I don't know anything anymore.'

'But,' Gina began, working herself up. 'You…'

She was interrupted by Rick's voice. 'Stella?' he called. The gate latch rattled. 'C'mon Stella, it's not what you think. Talk to me.'

Gina answered. 'Bugger off, Rick. She don't want to talk to you.' Beet-red, she hobbled over to the gate and yelled. 'You're all the same. Can't keep your trousers buttoned.'

Rick ignored her. 'Stella, I know you're there. C'mon, open up.'

Stella, mouth mutinously set, looked at Grazja. 'Open the gate and let Gina loose on him. I'll go through the front door.'

'No,' Grazja said. 'You need to talk to him.'

It was too late. Gina managed to wrestle the bolt open one-handed and launched a tirade of insults at Rick.

Stella hurried through the bungalow and out of the front door to her car. She threw her bags on the passenger seat and jammed the key in the ignition. Rick saw her. He turned away from Gina.

'Stella, wait.' He started towards the car when Gina

whacked him behind the kneecaps with her crutch. Rick staggered and fell onto his hands and knees.

Stella felt a flash of concern but steeled herself when she saw him rise. She revved the engine and shot into the lane. In the rear view mirror she glimpsed a tableau: Gina mouth wide, shouting something after her, Rick with his hand up in a stop gesture and Grazja watching it all with her hands on her hips. Just before she turned the bend she saw George walk across the street to join them.

Unaware of the tears rolling down her cheeks, Stella took Seaview Road out of Mapton, passing the huts to her left and the houses with no sea view to the right.

She was just past Lincoln when she abruptly swerved into a layby and skidded to a halt.

Henry. Oh God. She had forgotten her cat.

#

Stella's flat stank, and that was before she opened the fridge. She had emptied Henry's litter tray before she'd left but had forgotten about the bin.

Stella groaned as she lifted the slimy leaking bag into a second liner and tied it tight. She opened the fridge. Things seemed to be breathing so she slammed it shut to gather courage before trying again. Wearing Marigolds she dumped the offending items into another bin liner and swabbed out the fridge with sudsy water. She carried both bags down the communal stairs and out to the bins. On her way back, Christine, her neighbour, peeped out of her ground floor flat. Seeing Stella she opened the door wider.

'Thought you'd done a runner,' she said in welcome. Leaving the door ajar she disappeared. Stella waited. Christine returned with a stack of post and a couple of Amazon packages.

'Thanks so much,' Stella said, taking the post.

'Nice to see you back,' Christine said.

'Thanks,' Stella repeated. They stood awkwardly for a moment. Stella could hear the TV.

Christine cocked her head. 'End of the ads,' she said. 'Better get back.'

Stella nodded. 'Well, thanks again.'

Christine shut the door, leaving Stella to trudge up the stairs.

Christine was a good neighbour, Stella reminded herself. Willing to do a favour but kept to herself otherwise. Quiet after eleven. Not a busybody and didn't want to grab Stella for a gossip every time she walked past her door. Everything Stella liked in a neighbour.

It felt odd after the constant presence of Gina and Grazja to be alone in her own space. She opened a window to let in the noise of traffic and London nightlife. It still felt too quiet.

The flat missed Henry. It felt empty without him. Stella cursed herself. What sort of person abandoned their pet? A horrible one.

She turned on her phone. The screen blinked with message alerts and missed calls. Stella ignored them and thumbed in a text. 'Don't want 2 tlk. Promise 2 look after Henry until I fetch him.'

The response was almost immediate. 'Of course I will. I love Henry. Need to talk. Please.'

No sooner had she read the message than the

phone started to ring. She scrambled to turn it off, and then stuffed it under a cushion. Feeling lost, she wandered over to the studio-side of the flat to study the canvas she'd left half-done on her easel. Under the electric light the picture looked flat. Gazing at the perfectly rendered images Stella thought it looked dead, the way the idealised proportions of a shop mannequin can only mimic the spark of life in a human body. The painting was a tightly controlled re-imagining of reality. It didn't allow for messy complications. Stella resisted breaking it, retreating to her bedroom instead.

She hadn't eaten since lunchtime, but despite her stomach's rumblings she wasn't hungry. Impulsively she reached for the landline phone on her bedside table and dialled Lysie's number.

Lysie answered warily. She had a strict rule that anyone who phoned her at home after nine was rude. Stella remembered it was after ten.

'Lysie, I'm sorry, I didn't realise it was so late.'

'Stell? Where are you?'

'Home,' Stella said. 'In my flat.' Her voice cracked as she said it.

'Are you okay?' Lysie sounded anxious.

'Nooooo,' Stella moaned.

'Okay,' Lysie said, taking charge. 'You are coming over to mine. Del's out so I can't come to you, but Talia's in bed, so we'll have the house to ourselves. Can you do that?'

'Yes,' Stella said gratefully. 'Thank you.'

'Bring your toothbrush. I'll open a bottle and you can crash on the sofa.'

'Won't Del mind?'

'Nah. He sees you as a pity case anyway.'

'Thanks,' Stella laughed. 'I'm on my way.'

Lysie opened her door before Stella knocked, welcoming her into a warm hug. Stella followed her in to her Camden flat. A three bedroom flat in Camden would have been out of Lysie and Del's budget in the current market, but Lysie had grown up in the flat when all the families in the 1950s block were ordinary working people. Her mum and dad had retired to a tiny bungalow in Southend, selling the flat for a knockdown price to Lysie. She sculpted in one bedroom, so there was no spare room and any guest slept on the sofa bed in the lounge, except her mum and dad, who took Talia's bed when they stayed.

Often Lysie's home looked a little haphazard and messy to Stella, with piles of magazines and books on the floor, as well as Talia's toys scattered everywhere. Tonight it looked wonderful - like a home should look, Stella thought. Lived in and vibrant.

Lysie led her to the sofa and handed her a glass of red wine. 'Chocolate or cheese straws?' Lysie asked.

'Both,' Stella said, suddenly feeling ravenously hungry.

'Where's Del gone?'

'Oh, he's out with some old friends from uni. I don't expect him to stagger in till one or two. School hols, remember.' She smiled. 'So, c'mon. Let's hear it. Two days ago you were fizzing with joy. What's gone wrong?'

Stella told her. It took a while, with digressions and questions, stops for wine-swigging and cheesy chocolate munching.

Lysie twirled a few long cornrow braids around her finger as she considered. 'At least he said sex with Ang was lousy,' she offered.

Stella laughed bitterly.

Lysie leaned forward. 'You need to talk to him, Stel. All you heard was the end of a row. They've known each other ages. This could have happened years ago. Or even the day before you arrived. How could Rick know he'd meet you?'

'It doesn't matter,' Stella said vehemently. 'He lied to me. Even when I asked about him and Ang - it was so obvious the way she felt about him - he acted like I was imagining things. And he didn't tell me he was going to meet Justine next week. He's obviously a liar by nature.' She pounded her fist on the sofa. 'I feel so stupid.'

'You don't know that he wasn't going to tell you about the meeting. He might have told you tonight. Or maybe he wanted to come to London and surprise you. He knew you were coming home didn't he?'

'Why are you defending him?' Stella demanded. 'You don't even know him.'

Lysie sighed. 'No, I don't,' she said. 'You might be right. He could be a complete bastard. He might have flings with holidaymakers every season. Every two or three weeks for all I know.' She smirked at Stella's horrified expression. 'But I'll tell you this, Stel. I have never heard you sound as happy as you have the last few weeks.'

'That's not true, I'm happy,' Stella said. 'I'm a happy person.' She forced a rictus grin.

'Right,' Lysie said. 'And I'm married to Brad Pitt.'

'Del's much nicer than Brad Pitt. Brad's getting a

bit hamsterish around the jowls.'

'You're right. And I'm better looking than Angelina so we're the perfect couple,' Lysie agreed. 'I'm not saying you're a miserable cow.'

'Thanks.'

'But you often seem unhappy, Stella. You've got a really successful career, enough money, a cute cat …'

Stella groaned. 'Oh, no, not the 'you can't be happy if you haven't got a man', please Lysie.'

'Insulting! You know me better than that. I'd much rather see you alone than with the wrong person. I just mean that in all the years I've known you, whether you've been single or in a relationship, you've seemed lonely.'

'Ouch!'

'I've always put it down to your parents dying. And your relationship with Gina. And that's another thing. A really big thing. You've mentioned Gina a lot - not in the way you used to but with affection. God, Stel, that's huge. What did you tell Rick about Gina?'

'Everything,' Stella admitted.

'More than you've ever told me? Or anyone else?'

'Yes,' Stella whispered.

'I'll try not to be offended,' Lysie said, topping up their glasses. 'I'm only your best friend.'

'Sorry.'

'Again, huge. And did he run away? No. He helped you didn't he? He drove you to Nottingham. That's a lot to do just for sex with you.' She waved her arms expansively as the wine took hold.

Stella pointed to herself 'Not for this body.' They giggled.

'And, and…' Lysie continued excitedly. 'You

handed him your most precious possession.'

'I wasn't a virgin,' Stella said.

'No,' Lysie choked. 'Henry. You gave him Henry.'

'I didn't give him Henry,' Stella protested.

'You did. You told me. You're so possessive with Henry.'

'Am not.'

'You get jealous when he sits on my lap. He's *your* cat. And you hand him to a man you've only just met.'

'I was desperate. Bing was going to eat him.'

'You knew,' Lysie waggled her index finger in Stella's face. 'It was instant. Love at first sight. You gave Henry to Rick because you trusted him. It was intuition.'

'Well, I was wrong about that,' Stella said. 'So bollocks.'

'You weren't wrong.'

'He lied to me.'

'No, he omitted to tell the full truth to someone he was scared of losing. Haven't you ever done that?'

'No,' Stella said primly.

'Well good for you Miss Perfect Pants.' Lysie set her glass down. She went over to the lounge door and stood listening for a moment, checking her daughter was still asleep. Satisfied, she closed the lounge door and returned to the sofa. Tucking her feet up under her, she said quietly. 'I'm going to tell you something and you might not like me for it.'

'Don't tell me then,' Stella said. Lysie quelled her with a look.

'You remember that life model in the evening class you ran? Years ago.'

'Gorgeous Stu,' Stella said. 'We all fancied him.'

'Yes. But I slept with him.'

Stella processed this. Her eyes widened. 'But you were with Del?'

'Yes,' Lysie said.

Stella was truly shocked. 'Does he know?'

'Yes,' Lysie confessed. 'He found out. And he was devastated. I hated myself and thought I might lose him. All of that. And he got his own back by sleeping with someone else. It was messy and horrible but ultimately it made us stronger. We had to talk it out over and over. It wasn't easy.'

'That's the thing,' Stella eagerly grabbed her statement. 'You told each other. You didn't lie.'

Lysie looked at her as though she was crazy. 'I would have,' she said. 'If Del hadn't found out, I don't know if I would have ever told him. As soon as I'd done it I knew what a mistake I'd made. But you're not getting my point, Stella. It was *you* I couldn't tell.'

Stella felt it like a slap. 'Why? I don't understand.'

'I wanted to tell you. You're my best friend and I needed someone to talk to but I was scared you'd think less of me.'

'Am I that horrible?' Stella asked appalled.

Lysie grabbed her hand. 'Of course not! But you have very high standards. You adored Del and me. I didn't want to disappoint you. I didn't want to risk losing you, Stella. I was ashamed.'

'I always saw you as the perfect couple,' Stella said. She felt dazed. 'I always wanted what you had.'

'Exactly,' Lysie agreed. 'But there's no such thing as a perfect couple because there's no such thing as a perfect person.' She tried to make Stella smile, nudging her. 'Not even you.'

Stella couldn't smile. She felt sick. 'I'm sorry if I made you scared to tell me.'

'You didn't *make* me,' Lysie said. 'All I'm pointing out is that we all have weaknesses. It might be that Rick is actually a twat but it sounds more likely that he was scared to tell you because he didn't want to lose you. Or hurt you. Or hadn't got around to telling you yet. I know it's not been long but do you love him?'

'Yes,' Stella said. Relief and fear washed over her simultaneously.

'Are you running away?'

'Yes,' Stella admitted in a small voice. 'But not just from Rick.'

'What is it then? Gina?'

'Gina. And Mapton.'

'Mapton?'

'You know how Del is a bit ugly?' Stella said.

Lysie looked affronted. 'I can say that. You can't. But yes, what's your point?'

'Logically you see he's a bit ugly but to you he's beautiful,' Stella pressed.

'Again, enough with the ugly. And again, your point?'

'I feel like that about Mapton,' Stella said glumly. 'There's a French term 'jolie laide' for a person whose unattractive features make them attractive. You know, like Gerard Depardieu. Mapton's like that.'

Lysie, draining her glass, flopped back on the cushions and stuck her feet on Stella's lap. 'So tell me about Mapton.'

Forward Motion

Early Tuesday morning, while Stella was sleeping off the effects of too much wine on Lysie's sofa, a number of Mapton residents were awake.

Rick whipped up a soufflé that collapsed a second after it came out of the oven. Disgusted, he dumped it in the bin. He hadn't made a flat soufflé since he was sixteen.

'Look what's she's done to me,' he said to Henry.

Henry looked at him enigmatically.

Rick automatically reached into his jeans pocket for his phone. Maybe Stella had relented and sent him a message overnight. She hadn't.

He cleaned the kitchen, fed Henry an extra-large portion of Whiskas. 'Easy pal,' he warned as Henry chowed down. 'I won't be back till late, so make it last.'

He forced himself to shave and change into smart clothes, resisting the temptation to cancel and slob about all day wallowing in his misery. He was determined to make this meeting at Française L'Americaine. God knows, he needed something to distract him from Stella.

He winced as he settled into his car seat. The back of his knees were bruised from Gina's crutch attack, while his grazed kneecaps and palms still stung. But not as much as the humiliation had.

Wow, what a day that had been. He'd destroyed his relationship with Stella, lost his friend and deputy manager - he doubted Ang would be in today - and been attacked by a crazed pensioner.

Before he left Mapton he stopped at the diner with

the makeshift sign he'd written and fixed it to the inside of the door. Checking his phone again - nothing - he was startled when a troop of dogs filed past in single file. He recognised Bing Crosby leading them. Bing saw him behind the glass door and seemed to grin roguishly. Mesmerised, Rick watched them trot past; Mapton's most wanted. On automatic he slid his phone in his jacket pocket but was so distracted he didn't notice it slip out and hit the mat instead. After Prince had passed, dawdling a little behind the others as his nose hoovered the ground, Rick locked up and climbed back into his Honda.

'Mapton.' He shook his head wonderingly as he left town.

#

At six-thirty Ang arrived at the diner. The sign dismayed her: 'Sorry. Diner closed today due to unforeseen circumstances.' Her heart sank. She'd spent a long night in guilt-ridden introspection and had made some difficult decisions. She needed to make things right with Rick before she acted on the others.

Rallying, Ang unlocked the diner and tore down the sign. She wasn't going to let Rick lose business because of their fight. She would open up today, no matter how busy. Her foot nudged something on the mat, she looked down, expecting post, or perhaps a note from Rick, and saw a phone. Bending to pick it up, she recognised the patch of melted plastic on the bottom left corner where Rick had left his phone next to a hot pan.

He must have dropped it. Perhaps he'd be back for it, she thought hopefully, and they'd get a chance to talk. Popping it into her bag she went to fire up the kitchen for the early morning crowd.

#

Gina had slept restlessly too. Grazja, always the early riser, was surprised to hear Gina shuffling around at seven.

'Gina, you okay?' she called through the bedroom door.

'Would you do me a favour?' Gina called back.

Grazja entered the bedroom to find Gina standing in front of the wardrobe door in her nightie. 'Can you reach the top shelf and get that shoe box down?' Gina asked.

Grazja dragged over the chair from Gina's dresser to stand on and stretched for the box. She blew the dust off the top, making them both cough.

'What's in it?' She climbed down and set the box on the bed.

'Old photos and stuff,' Gina said.

'Oh, can I look through?'

'No,' Gina snapped.

'Okay,' Grazja shrugged and put the chair back in place. As she closed the door behind her Gina said. 'Grazja?'

'Yes?'

'Thanks, duck.'

Grazja paused. 'You're welcome,' she replied softly. The door clicked shut.

Gina slid the box to the top of the bed and then awkwardly clambered back in. With the pillows propped up behind her, she slid off the thick rubber bands that held the lid on and opened the box.

Despite what Grazja might have imagined, this

was not a box of sentimental memories, but a box of painful ones. It had started life as a container for the blackmail of Carl, to provide for his illegitimate daughter. And of course to punish him.

Gina plucked out the plastic comb she'd once pickpocketed during a tryst behind the factory skips. It still held a few strands of Carl's dark hair. She touched the silken strands, remembering the feel of his hair and the smell of his Brylcreem. She imagined it lingered faintly in the bedroom. Here was a monogrammed cuff link. A hanky. The keys he'd thought he'd lost. At one time, at her bitterest, she used to fantasise about using those keys to enter Carl and Maggie's home. The ideas she had. Leave her underwear in their bed and see how Carl would explain that. Or slash all Maggie's fine clothes, throw ink on her perfect carpets, scrawl Carl's dirty secrets on their lounge walls.

She never did any of them, not, Gina admitted to herself, because she wasn't capable, but because she hadn't wanted to lose her power over him in one vengeful spasm of madness. She'd preferred to hold onto and eke that secret power out over his lifetime. And over Maggie's, even if Maggie hadn't known it for years and years. Gina had known.

Next she took out the photo of Maggie she'd stolen from Carl's wallet. Even in that photo, taken in the early months of their marriage, Maggie's face was closed to Gina. Gina dug deeper in the box to find an older photo, this one showing her and Maggie as girls, arms clasped around each other, laughing with the confident optimism of the very young. It was a twin of the image that Mrs Simmons had shown to Stella.

Gina's eyes filled. She tapped a fist against her heart. What a bloody mess she'd made.

When she'd packed up the Bobbin Street house, Gina had added other bad memories to the box. She laughed as she scooped out some emerald glass chips from the bottom. How she'd come to hate that front garden. She blamed it for her failed relationship with Stella.

There were other things in the box; ridiculous mementos of grievances and slights, perceived or real.

Gina wondered what had made her hang onto such a collection of poisonous bad will. She didn't think she'd ever tell Stella about this.

The sound of a large vehicle rumbling along the street broke into her thoughts. Men shouted, banging and crashing at this ungodly hour. The bin men.

The bin men!

'Grazja,' she yelled, scrambling gracelessly out of bed, ignoring the shooting pain in her ribs. 'Grazja.'

Grazja rushed in. 'What is it. You hurt?'

'The bins,' Gina panted, shoving the shoebox at Grazja. 'Make sure this goes in the bin lorry.'

'What? No,' Grazja said. 'Your photos.'

'No, no. It's rubbish. Horrible. I don't want it no more. Now Grazja. Now. Please?'

Grazja hesitated.

'Please,' Gina begged. 'Please, Grazja.'

Grazja met her eyes, made her decision, and scurried away. Gina heard the front door open. She shuffled into the hall, following Grazja.

Hanging onto the front doorjamb to keep steady, Gina watched Grazja run down the road in her slippers, as the bin-lorry began to drive away.

'Wait,' Grazja cried. 'Wait.'

The driver saw her in his wing mirror and stopped the truck.

Out of earshot now, Gina saw Grazja waving the box as a bin man approached her. They appeared to have brief, lively discussion before he took the box off her and threw it in the truck's gaping maw. He and Grazja watched the jaws of the waste processor crush it.

Gina slumped with relief. She felt lighter. George had come out to watch - another bloody early riser, Gina thought. She raised her hand and he came over to join her.

'What was that about?' he asked.

'Just good riddance to bad rubbish,' Gina said. She straightened, giving him a good look over as though she'd never met him before. 'Would you like to take me out for the day, George? I could do with a day out.'

George beamed. 'I'd be delighted,' he said.

'Good.'

Grazja came up to them. 'I hope you did right thing.'

'I did,' Gina assured her. 'George's gonna take me out for the day. What d'yer think of that?'

It was Grazja's turn to beam. 'I think that very good,' she said. 'I can finally get some peace and quiet.'

'Yer cheeky bogger.'

#

Stella spent the morning taking Talia to the park and onto Camden Lock. She was giving Lysie and Del the luxury of a school holiday lie in. Talia had been delighted to wake up to find her Auntie Stella on the sofa. Stella's hangover had been less delighted to have an eight year old bouncing on her but she bore it with good grace.

After Mapton, Camden seemed unbearably crowded, full of hipsters, musos, creatives and the constant swirl of gaping tourists. Usually exhilarated by it, today Stella found it exhausting. She'd never quite fitted into the Camden scene; despite her success, her art was never edgy or hip. After a roasted veg and hummus pitta from a stall in Camden Lock, Stella dropped Talia back at Lysie's and took the tube back to her flat in Barnsbury for a quick shower and change, before heading out again for a meeting with her agent.

She'd let Lysie's words percolate at the back of her mind all morning. At least ten times, she'd checked her phone. Rick seemed to have given up trying to contact her.

It scared her. What if he'd decided not to bother with her? Ironic that, after she'd spent yesterday punishing him with silence, she'd given him the space to change his mind. No doubt Gina whacking him might have been a factor. God knows what she'd left him to face alone after she'd driven away. She pictured Gina wielding her crutch. She couldn't help grinning. Whatever else Gina might do, she would always be Stella's greatest defender. Stella suddenly felt a warm rush towards her grandmother.

On impulse Stella sent Rick a text. 'Calmer. Got meeting with agent now. Talk l8r?'

She checked for a reply numerous times on her journey to Lincoln Fields, even on the tube, before she remembered how stupid that was. Rick wasn't answering. He was probably too busy in the diner, Stella reassured herself. Or had he come to London to meet with Justine? She found that thought unsettling.

Susan Cadman, her agent, was cool and elegant, her grey hair cut into a precise, asymmetrical bob. She was the sort of woman who could wear a wrap and make it look effortlessly chic.

'Well,' she said, greeting Stella with an air-kiss to each cheek. 'The prodigal child returns.'

They discussed and agreed on the commission for a wealthy, influential client that Susan was extremely excited about and Stella less so. Commissions could be tricky, driven by another person' specifications and expectations. Still, it was a lot of money which would give her more freedom to experiment on her own projects. Saying so, Stella produced her iPad to show Susan a snap of the painting she'd done of Gina and Mrs Jenkins. Susan bent over it for a long time.

She looked sharply at Stella, assessing her. 'It's very different for you,' she said.

'You hate it?'

'No,' Susan. 'I rather like it. It's disturbing and full of rage, but still has classic Stella Distry traits - the detail in the flowers, for example. But it's very loose - freer than your usual work.' She examined it again. 'You know this isn't what the commission will want, don't you?'

'Yes,' Stella said. 'I know. But after that, I want to experiment more. Stretch myself.'

Susan nodded slowly. 'There's something different about you,' she appraised Stella. 'You look... happier. Going away must've done you good.'

Stella smiled. 'It has.' She felt the truth of it seep into her bones.

Susan tapped the iPad. 'I'll look forward to seeing this work in the flesh so to speak.'

Stella laughed. 'That might be difficult. I think my grandmother might have destroyed it. Even if she hasn't I'd never sell it.'

Susan raised her eyebrow. 'I'm not going to even ask,' she said.

Rick still hadn't replied by five o' clock. Stella screwed up her courage and called him. It went straight to answer phone. She disconnected without leaving a message.

She thought about looking up the number for the diner but didn't want to risk Ang answering. She wasn't prepared to deal with her yet.

Briefly, she toyed with the idea of going to Française L'Americaine; just casually turn up as though she was just in the neighbourhood. Oh, Rick, I didn't know you'd be here. I was hungry, thought I'd pop in. Oh, hello Justine.

She dismissed the idea as too pathetic. She didn't want to appear desperate. Anyway, Rick was still the offending party. He should be chasing her.

She went home instead to clean the flat. At six she ordered a pizza, and looked around her. This was home. Why didn't it feel like it?

Angrily seizing her phone she speed-dialled Rick again, ignoring the thud of her heart and trembling hands.

This time when the phone connected a voice answered, but not Rick's. A woman.

'Oh, sorry,' Stella stuttered. 'I thought this was

Rick's number.'

'It is,' the woman said. 'Hi Stella. This is Angela.'

Bing's Big Bang

As Stella drove back into Mapton she felt an overwhelming sense of coming home. She didn't fight it, even though The Paradise on her right was still missing an enormous plastic 'a' from its hideous facade. It was like a wart on your lover's body. You accepted it, although it would repulse you on anyone else.

Gina knew she was coming. They'd spoken last night on the phone. Stella, bracing herself for histrionics, was almost disappointed when they didn't come, and had instead found herself listening to Gina prattle about her day out with George.

Then, just before they said goodbye, Gina said. 'I'm glad you're coming back, duckie.'

Stella replied. 'I think I might be coming home, Gina, not just back.'

She thought she heard a sniffle. Gina said. 'Don't think you'll be living with me, yer bogger.'

Indicating a right turn onto Fisherman's Lane, Stella waited for a mobility scooter to cross the road. It was decorated with a multi-spectral array of pennants, fluttering in the light sea breeze. She didn't recognise the man riding it - not one of the Marauders - but she admired his choice of crossing place, on a bend near a junction. The speed at which he chose to drive could only be described as a death crawl.

There were five cars lined up behind Stella by the

time he reached the other side and one idiot was honking. She swore the scooter sped up the moment it hit the pavement. She was back in Mapton all right.

Grinning, she made the turn onto Gina's road. Excitement fizzed in her belly like pop, carbonated with a tinge of fear. She hadn't told Rick she was coming. This was too important to say over the phone. But what if he didn't want to hear it? What if he'd made up his mind to move to London and work with Justine? What if he wasn't even back from London? She'd feel like a fool.

But her gut told her otherwise and Stella had decided, for once in her life, to follow her gut. And her cat.

Stella pulled up outside Gina's. She almost expected a fanfare but the street was quiet. She let herself in, calling, 'Hello, it's me.' Grazja appeared from the lounge, smiling. She gave Stella a quick hug.

'Good girl. Gina tell me you come back.'

Stella followed her into the lounge. 'Where's Gina?'

Grazja resumed her seat. 'She at beach hut with George. She said to tell you.'

'Okay,' Stella nodded. She noticed the A4 pad of lined paper and pen on the pouffe next to Grazja's chair, as well as a print-out.

'What are you doing?'

Grazja looked almost guilty. 'Don't tell Gina,' she said. 'I apply for another job.'

Stella sat down. 'Why?' She suddenly felt stricken.

Grazja cocked her head. 'Gina's cast will be off in a couple of weeks. She almost better. Then I move on.'

'Oh,' Stella said. Grazja had become such a key

part of their life it was difficult to imagine it without her. 'Of course. I thought the agency gives you the job. I didn't know you have to apply.'

'It does,' Grazja said. 'But this is not agency job,' she said, tapping the pad. 'This is permanent position.'

'Doing what?'

Grazja smiled. 'This,' she said, sweeping her hand at the room. 'What I have been doing with Gina and you.'

'Isn't that what you usually do?'

'Sort of,' Grazja said. 'But this has been different. This the first time I live in with client, and usually I care for disabled people, or ill people, but Gina - and you - you were broken. Do you understand what I mean?'

Stella thought she did, although it hurt her pride to admit it. She nodded slowly. 'Yes, I think I do.'

'But you not now - Gina still crazy but not broken. I not saying I mend you but me being here to look after things, it helped, yes?'

'Yes. Oh yes,' Stella agreed. 'You've been amazing, Grazja.'

'Yes,' Grazja agreed. 'And I have enjoyed it. Gina was so lonely. Not surprising because Gina makes enemies like bunnies make babies.' She laughed. 'But she not so lonely now.' She tapped her pad again. 'This position, a friend sent it to me. It's for live-in carer and companion for elderly lady. My friend says lady is rich, but spoilt and awful. Her family hate her and everyone they hire to look after her quits. It sounds perfect for me.'

Stella agreed. 'You're like the Mary Poppins of

mad, bad, old women. I can give you the perfect reference if you need it.'

'Thank you. Don't tell Gina I apply. You know how jealous she gets. I'll be here anyway till her cast comes off and if I don't get this job I take another with the agency.'

'Okay,' Stella said. 'But I'll be really sad to see you go. I don't suppose the job is nearby.'

'It's in Edinburgh.'

Stella sighed. 'We'll keep in touch,' she said, rising.

'Are you going to beach hut?'

'I'm going to the diner first,' Stella said, feeling the renewed trembling in her stomach.

Grazja smiled delightedly. 'I hope it good news. You forgive him?'

'Yeah. Ang explained it to me.'

'Ang! Sour-face woman? Rick not sleep with her? She made it up?'

'He did, but it was a long time ago and only once.'

'So, Ang tell you this? Why? I thought she in love with Rick?'

'She says she thought she was but she's realised she's just really unhappy in her marriage, not actually in love with Rick. Anyway, he's not in love with her.'

'Oh,' Grazja raspberried her contempt. 'Anyone can see that. He in love with you. So, you and this Ang are BFF now?'

Stella laughed. 'Hardly,' she said.

'So, you already talked to Rick and he knows you coming?' Grazja pursued.

Stella looked at her feet. 'No,' she said. 'I wanted to surprise him.'

'You not already told him? Not texted him? Not

put him out of his misery? He been waiting two days.'

Stella felt small. 'No.'

Grazja humphed. 'You still punish him for not telling you? Ha! Just like your grandmother.'

Stella had to admit it was true. She'd kept her phone off because she wanted to tell him in person, but hadn't a little bit of her enjoyed knowing she was making him suffer? Well, he should've just told her the bloody truth in the first place.

Now, she was aching to see him and set things right. If she could.

#

Rick, taking a morning break while Ang manned the diner, felt as miserable as the old man in the Death of a Miser. Yesterday had been hard. First, he'd lost his phone. He was on the Lincoln to London train when he realised it was gone. Panic had hit him; losing his smartphone was like losing a chunk of his brain. And it was his link to Stella, even if she had been ignoring his messages. How had people previously survived without mobiles? It seemed unbelievable to remember life before smartphones and Bluetooth connection. He felt unplugged from life itself.

At least the train wasn't late, so he didn't have to worry about how to get a message to Justine.

He took the tube from King's Cross to Mayfair. On a summer's day the air in the underground was stifling and stale, and the carriage stank of sweat. At Green Park it was a relief to emerge, blinking, into bright sunshine. Still, even in this beautiful part of the city Rick found the noise and swarms of people overwhelming. It was exhilarating to be caught in the surging life of a capital city but scary too. He had forgotten just what it felt like. He hadn't even made a day trip to London in all the years since his breakdown.

Justine had changed the classical interior of Francais L'Americaine to a modern, minimalist style in shades of grey, glass, and chrome. The air conditioning sucked the heat out of his skin the moment he stepped through the door. Shivering, he spotted Justine sitting with a young man in chef's duds, their heads leaning close as they pored over a paper on the table. They looked up as he approached and Justine broke into a wide smile. Rick was struck how right she looked in this context, the perfection of her sartorial taste, the sharpness of her cheekbones, her understated makeup offset by the dramatic slash of burgundy lipstick over whitened teeth.

'Welcome back,' she said, rising to hug him. 'It's been too long.'

She introduced the chef as Sam Dyson and said they were just going over the menus. Did he want to have a look? He did, so they spent half an hour discussing them. Rick made occasional suggestions, asking Sam about his suppliers, who he'd trained under and so forth. Sam had all the arrogance of a young, up-coming chef, veering between boastfulness and defensive rudeness, trying to impress with his culinary innovation. Various staff arrived and the restaurant cranked up for lunch service. At the threshold to the kitchen Rick felt his stomach tighten. He gripped the swing-door momentarily, ignoring Justine's questioning look, took a breath, and went in.

The kitchen looked the same, laid out to his original strict specifications. It buzzed with activity.

Sam strode in and started to fire off orders and staff jumped to attention. It looked like an efficiently working kitchen. The menu was interesting, so why was the restaurant failing?

The answer came with lunch. Justine led him to a table tucked away in the corner.

'What's with all the grey?' Rick asked. 'It's too cold in here. It used to be warmer.'

'Grey's bang on trend,' Justine said. 'Although I'm toying with some pops of colour. The decor was out of date.'

Rick held his tongue. He gave his order to the waiter but declined the wine list.

He'd ordered Sam's signature dish, described as a fusion of classic French and contemporary Middle Eastern. The presentation was immaculate, the taste was good, very good, but not Michelin star. His chef's brain fired up, immediately beginning to sift and sort the taste and textures, the balance of seasonings, timings of cooking; all the minutiae that would transform this from a fine dish to an exceptional one.

Justine leaned forward, watching him, eyes bright. 'See,' she said. 'You're doing it already. I recognise your expression. You know what's wrong and you know how to fix it.'

For a moment Rick was caught up in the adrenaline rush. He considered barging back into the kitchen, donning his whites and showing Sam how to really do it. The spectre of himself as he used to be - running the kitchen like a dictator, losing perspective, treating staff like shit, manically chasing the dream until it consumed him – rose up to haunt him. He met Justine's eyes and saw her need as well as the truth.

'You don't want me to 'mentor' Sam,' he said. 'You want to fire him and have me back full-time.'

'Can't you feel it?' she asked. 'The rush, the excitement. Tell me you don't know how to fix this dish? Tell me you're not itching to go in that kitchen and show them how it's done?'

She still knew how he thought. But Rick shook his head. 'I know how to fix it. I know I'd do it better, but there is any number of talented chefs who could do that. Why don't you hire them?'

Justine snorted. 'Don't you think I've tried? Sam's the latest in a line of them. They all want to be flashy. They all want to be on TV. But they don't have what you do Richard, raw, innate talent.'

'So Francais L'Americaine is going downhill and I'm your last ditch attempt to haul it back up?'

'Last ditch? Are you insane?'

Rick cocked an ironic eyebrow.

'Sorry,' Justine said. 'Bad choice of word. But don't you see - you're not last ditch. It's more like I'm shooting for the moon. You're the moon and I'm the girl who used to have you.' She laid a hand over his. 'You can't blame me for trying again.'

Rick softened. 'Justine. We built something amazing. It was incredible. But we can't go back and re-build it.'

'Why not?' Justine said. 'Why are you wasting your talent, Richard? Just look at what's on offer. You can just walk in and take it.'

'I don't want it,' Rick said quietly. Relief washed over him. It was true.

Justine sat back, defeated. 'Stella will be disappointed,' she said peevishly. 'I got the impression she'd like a man with a future.'

Rick stood up. 'I've got a future,' he said. 'It's just not here. Goodbye Justine.'

He hadn't lingered in London, having no desire for sightseeing, but an accident on the line meant a train delay of two hours. By the time he rolled wearily into his drive it was mid-evening. Ang was sitting on the doorstep waiting for him.

Jeez, he thought. The good times keep rolling.

But he was in for a surprise; Ang had come to apologise, plus she'd found his phone. Praise be!

Henry had not taken Rick's advice to space out his food over the day. His resentful meows seemed to indicate he'd eaten everything in his bowl at first light and had assumed he'd been abandoned since it was well past his usual teatime.

Despite his exhaustion, Rick invited Ang in for a cup of tea. As well as her profuse apologies she said she wanted to explain her behaviour. Oh, and she was leaving Des. To be honest he was barely taking it all in until she confessed to answering a call from Stella on his phone. That snapped him awake. It took Ang a considerable amount of time to assuage his alarm. So Stella had finally rung only be answered by Ang. God, the knowledge made him groan. But no, according to Ang it was all okay. She had explained everything to Stella (including why she had his phone). The way Ang talked it sounded as though she and Stella were friends. Women could be weird that way. Listening to women over the years he'd always been struck by their capacity to make and break friendships on the flip of a coin. Best friends became deadly enemies and enemies became bosom buddies, or so it seemed to him.

When it came time for Ang to leave (not soon enough for Rick) they gave each other a tentative hug, saying 'See you tomorrow' with the relief of knowing they were okay.

So in that way things were good. Yet Stella still wasn't answering her phone, despite a text that said: 'Calmer. Got meeting with agent now. Talk l8r' But that was sent frigging yesterday and he was still waiting.

As well as feeling miserable, Rick was beginning to feel angry. Well, screw her, he thought, turning to go back in the diner to help Ang with the lunch orders.

He just missed seeing the little troop of dogs trotting purposefully along the beach.

#

Dan Joules got the call from Charmaine Terry; the performing dogs were back and this time they'd hit Mapton on the main beachfront, not far from the donkey rides. Charmaine said the presence of the dogs, and the crowd forming to watch, were spooking her donkeys and what was he going to do about it? Dan didn't have much time for the Terry family, who'd owned a donkey ride business for years. He felt the donkeys were poorly treated and he hated the way the Terry's used sticks to prod them when they slowed. He'd complained to his superiors many times but the council maintained that the annual licence inspections were always in order, and that it was in the nature of donkeys to look dejected and mistreated even when the opposite was true. It greatly frustrated Dan, but this morning his focus wasn't on the donkeys; it was on the dogs. One dog in particular, the elusive Bing Crosby.

Adrenaline pumped through him as he reached for his bite-proof gloves and dogcatcher pole.

'We're on,' he snapped out to his newly assembled team of three. 'They're on the central Mapton beach. Saddle up.'

Sarah and Justin, on loan from Boston and Grimsby respectively, leapt into action, grabbing their equipment and following him out. They took one van while he drove the other.

#

It would be fair to say that Bing had become hooked on the highs created by a criminal life. A repeat performance of the Siltby heist was risky but the pickings would be rich and the adrenaline factor high. He knew the best place was the central beach, near to the part of the promenade where the lights flashed and noise roared out of the gigantic flying machine. It was on the busiest part of the beachfront that people sat on the steps to cram their faces with food.

The pack had been delirious following the Siltby heist. They had reunited at the den for a celebratory feast. Prince ate so much he was sick for the whole of the following day but it hadn't dampened his spirits or his appetite. Curly Sue was so impressed with the success of Bing's plan that they'd coupled in spasmodic frenzy, but got stuck together for a further fifteen minutes after that so Curly Sue hadn't been so amenable since, snapping if Bing tried it on. Perhaps, a success today might put her in an amorous mood.

Bing scratched his fleabites. The plan was the same. Curly Sue, Killer, Prince, and Tammy would perform tricks to distract the crowd while Bing and Mitch stole their food.

It had worked so perfectly last time. Why wouldn't it today?

#

'Right,' Dan said to Sarah and Justin. 'We have to do this carefully. If reports from last time are correct, it's likely the pack leader, Bing, will be behind the crowd on the prom not on the beach. It's vital we get him. Without him the rest of the pack won't know what to do. I'll go after Bing and you stay on the beach to round up the others. Don't bother with the dalmatian. He's stupid. He'll be easy to pick up later. Go for the husky and the poodle first, but if you can't, grab any of them.'

'Are we going to clear people out?' Sarah asked. 'What if the dogs get aggressive?'

'The moment we start making a commotion the dogs will know and be off. Bing's clever. You can't underestimate him. We'll have to take the risk. To my knowledge Bing's the only one with a history of biting.'

They were clearly in time. The crowd gathered on the beach and steps indicated the show was in full swing. Children laughed and shrieked. Holiday makers and cafe-workers gathered together, enchanted by the impromptu canine performers cavorting on the beach. Sarah and Justin pushed quietly through fleshy, sun-mottled upper arms, brushed past beer bellies, slid around mobility scooters, and made their way down the steps to the beach, keeping their catching poles as inconspicuous as possible.

Dan watched the audience from behind, noting the

picnic bags abandoned and food trays forgotten in the commotion. He waited in the shadow of a public doorway, waiting for Bing to appear.

He did. Emerging from the narrow alley between two cafes, Bing darted towards the bags.

Dan's pulse picked up. Bing had his head buried deep in a cool bag. It was the ideal moment to spring.

Dan leapt forward and in a beautiful arcing motion, elegant as a spin-bowler, he swept the pole into position to slip the hoop over Bing's emerging head. He had him, he just needed to tighten the noose...

That was when the mongrel came hurling out of the alley and sprang at him, hitting him in the chest, snarling. Dan staggered back, letting go of the pole. His cry of shock caused people to turn. Bing started yapping the alarm, noose still over his head. The mongrel scrambled away as Dan threw himself forward to grab the end of the pole but Bing was too fast. He raced down the steps to the beach, the pole trailing like a tail. Dan sprinted after him. All was commotion. People shouted, some laughed while others booed. A small girl burst into tears.

Sarah hooked her pole over Killer's neck, while Justine managed to catch Curly Sue. Prince ran around in circles barking. Tammy fled in the direction of Siltby. Mitch chased after Dan, snapping at his heels, but Bing took a more draconian course of action.

Bing charged the donkeys. The donkeys, already unnerved by the antics of dogs on a part of the beach banned to dog-walkers in high season, panicked. Bing raced between their legs, nipping at their fetlocks, whipping them into a frenzy. As a herd they bolted.

Bing drove them (or so witnesses later swore) towards the ramp up to the promenade.

Dan saw them charging towards him and just managed to dive out of the way. People started to scream and scatter as the donkeys stampeded up the ramp, Bing snapping at their heels.

#

Rick stood outside the empty diner, trying to make sense of the noise and commotion erupting on the central beach. One by one his customers had left to see what the fuss was about. Ang and Mark had gone too, leaving Rick to hold the fort, although without customers there wasn't much fort to hold. He could hear donkeys braying and barking dogs among the cacophony of shrieking people. What the hell was going on? He considered locking up the diner to go see for himself, when a prickle on the back of his neck made him turn in the opposite direction.

He recognised her walk immediately, the way she swung her arms like a child and the nimbus of curls lifted by the breeze.

Stella. All his anger at her disappeared and he found himself grinning like an idiot. He wasn't aware of anything else, only her smile.

As she drew near he saw her eyes widen, her expression changing to horror. 'Rick, she yelled, suddenly charging towards him like a small American quarterback.

#

Stella's attention was so fixed on Rick that she didn't even notice the furore further down the beach. When his face lit up with a joyous grin her heart swelled and her own smile burst forth like sunshine out of clouds. She floated euphorically towards him.

The romantic moment was broken by a sudden stampede of donkeys storming along the promenade, heading directly for Rick. The sight was so ludicrous that for a second Stella couldn't react.

'Rick,' she screamed, and began to run towards him, lowering her head like a charging bull.

She slammed into him square on, knocking him out of the way just before the donkeys hit. They barely missed being trampled to death by inches. They tumbled onto the concrete, tangled together, while the clatter of hooves and brays of panicking donkeys roared past, followed by Bing Crosby trailing a long pole behind him like a banner.

The lead donkey swung towards the diner, followed blindly by his herd, and smashed through the open doors. Bing, shot right past them, carrying on along the promenade.

Inside the diner pandemonium ruled.

Rick grabbed Stella's hand and dragged her to her feet. 'C'mon, over the sea wall,' he shouted. He practically threw her over and then vaulted over himself. They hunched behind the barricade, listening to the sound of destruction from the diner.

People were running down the beach towards them, others along the promenade.

Rick stuck his head above the wall to see Dan Joules sprint past; the dog warden barely spared a glance at the diner being kicked apart by donkeys. Charmaine Terry arrived to scream abuse at her donkeys. Tinkerbell was the first out. She gave Charmaine a kick that sent her sprawling. The other donkeys emerged, congregating on the prom. Once they were all out their leader, Donkey Kong, took them home at a brisk trot, bells jingling as though it was the end of a normal day on the beach.

Everyone watched them go, except Charmaine who lay groaning on the ground.

Stella looked at Rick, stricken. 'Your diner,' she said.

Rick wrapped his arms around her. 'It can be fixed." His laugh was edged with hysteria. 'I must be insured for donkey stampedes. Thank God there was no one in it.' He kissed her nose. 'Hey, thanks for saving my life. And for coming back.'

Stella gazed at him seriously. 'About coming back,' she said. 'I want it to be here, in Mapton. I want to live here with you. I want to paint in your north turret. I don't want to live in London anymore. Do you?'

Rick's smile was glorious. 'No,' he said. 'Henry told me it was a bad idea and I agree with him.'

'Henry's so wise,' Stella said.

'He's our kid,' Rick said. He kissed her.

After that the diner blew up.

#

Gina and George were blissfully unaware of the goings on half a mile away. Gina was painting on her modified wheelchair table and George tutted at the shocking stories in the Daily Mail before completing the crossword. They sat outside the hut basking in the hottest summer for many a year.

A wild yapping made them look up. Gina gasped, seeing Bing Crosby hurtling towards her, that awful man's dogcatcher looped round his neck.

'Bing. Bingo,' she said, clapping her hands to call

him. Bing skidded to a stop at her feet. His flanks heaved as he panted. Flecks of foam flew from his mouth.

'He's rabid,' George yelped, alarmed.

'He's not. He's frightened,' Gina said. 'Come here Bing. Come to Mummy. Let me get this nasty thing off yer.'

Bing allowed Gina to loosen the noose and ease it over his head.

'Quick, into the hut,' Gina commanded Bing, pointing. He did as she said, diving under a beach blanket at the back. 'George, move that chair a bit to block the view and hide this pole round the back.

'Should I close the doors?'

'Best not. It'll look suspicious.'

Minutes later Gina and George had resumed their activities when Dan Joules arrived. He looked as rabid as Bing, sweat pouring off him, face beet-red and eyes crazy. It took a moment for him to catch enough breath to speak.

'Where is he?' he demanded.

'Who?' Gina asked. 'Are you all right, Mr Joules? You look done in?'

'You know who I mean,' Dan gasped. 'Bing. He ran this way, I know it.'

He looked past them into the beach hut.

'My Bing,' Gina said. 'I've not seen 'im fo' weeks, not since you last tried to catch 'im. What's he done now, the little scamp?'

'Have you seen him?' Dan addressed George.

'No, sir,' George said, looking guilty as hell.

'He's in the hut, isn't he?' Dan took steps to go around them.

Gina grabbed her crutch, jabbing it towards him. 'That's private property,' she said. 'Bog off.'

George stood up and blocked the doorway, or as much of it he could with his slight frame.

'This is council business,' Dan growled. He evaded Gina's crutch and moved to push past George.

'Oy,' Gina began, trying to rise. But her objection was cut short by an enormous boom that seemed to shake the ground. Shocked, they all swung in the direction of the blast to see a plume of flame shoot into the air somewhere near the central beach.

'Oh my God.' Dan forgot about Bing and raced off in the direction of the explosion.

Gina and George stared at each other, dazed and disbelieving.

Inside the hut Bing whined, the thunder still ringing in his sensitive ears.

Odds and Endings

It was staggering that no one was killed or seriously injured.

Although it was impossible to determine the exact cause of the blast, other than it was a gas explosion, it seemed most likely that in the chaos of the donkeys' invasion, a gas ring had been knocked on, probably more than one. A spark from a faulty electrical connection, or perhaps a tea towel catching light after being kicked onto the hotplate (the only thing Rick thought was left on) was enough to blow the kitchen to the sky.

Fortunately the explosion was mostly contained at the back of the diner, cushioning those outside the front from the worst of the force. Still, there were injuries. Glass and debris flew, causing minor lacerations. One woman spent the rest of her life hiding under her table during firework season, so badly did the explosion affect her nerves.

The explosion, coupled with the donkey stampede, caught the attention of the national press. When the story of the mobility scooter rumble and the bandit dogs was added to the mix, Channel 5 arrived, proposing to make a programme called Britain's Maddest Seaside Town. When it came out the following year it would make minor celebrities of Sue and Scampi, which went some way to consoling Sue, who wasn't so much upset at losing her daily coffee spot, but rather that she'd missed all the excitement on the day it blew up.

The assumption was that Rick would rebuild the diner in the same spot. Instead he decided to sell his lot and re-open in the boarded-up cafe at the end of the Seaview Road huts. At first Stella doubted the wisdom of this - their end of the beach had fewer visitors - but Rick insisted that the space was a better size for the diner and that he had a feeling Stella and Gina's hut painting had kicked off regeneration on the east beach. Certainly, this seemed to be true. Over the summer many of the huts were transformed. Gina's hut initiated a style of bright, cheery images that Siltby sniffed at. Even Gina was outraged, however, when Dean Benson painted a mermaid who was more suited to page three than a family beach. She called him a 'dirty bogger' and enjoyed a dispute for some weeks, until he finally conceded and added a bikini top. Gina wasn't much mollified as he made the bikini strain against the mermaid's erect nipples. Stella said they had to admire his skill with a brush. It appeared Mapton had a lot of hidden talent.

Rick decided to call the new diner 'The Last Resort'. Refurbishment began on it in September. With Stella's encouragement he was also discussing a new business idea with his friend Jill. They were excited by the possibility of opening up a gourmet pop-up restaurant, one night a week in Jill's Lawton deli.

Stella and Rick cleared out her studio-flat in London, spending a few nights there, meeting up with Lysie and Del, eating out in great restaurants (with the exception of Francais L'Americaine) and visiting galleries.

One fine, blue-skied October day, they let Henry out into the garden. Since kittenhood Henry had been a house-cat, his closest contact with the outside world came from hours watching through the window. Stella and Rick walked with him, protective as parents of their baby's first steps. Henry tentatively sniffed his way around the shrubbery. After fifteen minutes he went back inside and that was it. He was content with the spaciousness of his new abode, particularly liking to spend hours in Stella's north turret studio while she painted. All was well in Henry's world and thus in Stella's.

Gina set Bing Crosby free. She'd smuggled him in the blanket to her bungalow, aware that she was tracked by Bing's mongrel pal.

She'd fed them each a steak as a goodbye meal and after dark she persuaded Bing and the mongrel into George's car. They'd driven them out into the country to let them loose.

'Live free, Bing,' Gina cried. 'Don't let the bastards ever catch you.'

Bing and Mitch trotted away across the fields, the dark enclosing them as Gina sobbed. George slid his arm around her.

That was the last time Bing was seen in Mapton or the surrounding area, but it wasn't the end for Dan Joules. He scoured the internet for reports of stray dogs and finally, in November, he came across a snippet of local news from Derbyshire about a pack of feral dogs worrying sheep. Glimpses had been seen of a Jack Russell in the vicinity.

Dan handed in his notice and packed his bags. His colleagues thought him mad. Obsessed, they said. Like that Captain Ahab in Moby Dick. Undeterred Dan set off in his sturdy walking boots; all he needed for survival he carried on his back. His one ambition was to find that dog.

Grazja left the day after Gina's cast came off. She'd been offered the job with the irascible old woman in Edinburgh and had accepted it. Both Stella and Gina were tearful. Gina, emotionally dysfunctional, expressed her sadness by being huffy and rude. Grazja wouldn't have had it any other way. She hugged Gina despite the prickles.

'Oof, mind me ribs,' Gina griped. 'Call yourself a carer.'

'Stay in touch,' Stella said, squeezing Grazja's wiry frame. 'You're part of this family.'

'Huh,' Grazja snorted. 'What a family. You got my number. I come visit.' She turned to George. 'You take care of Gina, eh?'

'We're not a couple,' Gina said.

Grazja rolled her eyes. She slid into her car - a decade-old Clio - and gave them a cheery wave. Rolling down the window, she shouted. 'This for you, Gina,' and punched the button on the car's stereo. Ethel Merman's mighty lungs filled the close with 'You're the Top'. Grazja drove away laughing.

Gina's floodgate opened. She spent the day sniffling and moping.

The next morning, a sleepy Sunday, Stella and Rick walked around to Gina's following a leisurely breakfast. The smell of summer's end was in the air, faint but discernible even though the season was still in full swing. Mapton was waking up slowly, holidaymakers emerging from B&Bs to test the air, full English breakfasts still heavy in their stomachs.

'I just want to check she's all right,' Stella said, for the umpteenth time. 'She doesn't deal with partings well.'

The bungalow was quiet, curtains still drawn, so Stella let herself in. 'She's usually up by now.' She frowned at Rick. 'It's gone half-ten.'

'She's probably just having a lie in,' Rick said. 'Don't startle her.'

He followed Stella into the hall.

'Gina?' Stella called softly. 'It's me, Stella.'

There was no reply. Casting an anxious look at Rick, Stella quietly opened the bedroom door. She gasped, covering her mouth with her hand. Rick stepped quickly to her side and peered into the room, fearing the worst.

Spooned up together, fast asleep were Gina and George. Even with the curtains closed he could see the clothes scattered around the bed.

Stella looked at him over her hand, eyes dancing with mirth.

They backed out, shutting the door behind them and tiptoed out of the house. Out on the road they quivered with suppressed giggles.

'Looks like George finally got that intercourse,' Rick said.

Stella's laugh pealed joyously around the close. 'C'mon,' she said, grasping his hand. 'Let's go before we wake them.' Laughing, they ran together towards Mapton's beach.

Review Request

Thank you for reading Mapton on Sea. If you enjoyed this book (or even if you didn't) please visit the site where you purchased it and write a brief review. Your feedback is important to me and will help other readers decide whether to read the book too.

If you'd like to get notifications of new releases and special offers on my books, please join my email list by going to my website: sammaxfieldbooks.com

About the Author

Sam Maxfield is an author who writes about the funny things people do and say. She thinks fiction should be able to make you laugh and cry - sometimes at the same time.

Before writing the comic Mapton-on-Sea series, Sam taught English literature for many years. If teaching in FE doesn't make you see the funny side of life, little will. The novel Mapton on Sea (originally published as The Last Resort) was longlisted for the Best Women's Fiction prize and led to Sam's life being taken over by the slightly insane fictional characters of Mapton. Since then she has published three Mapton novels and two Mapton short stories. There is another Mapton novel currently on the way and a number of stories brewing.

In between Mapton stories Sam writes other novels, including ones for children.

Printed in Great Britain
by Amazon